MINDMAGE

BLACKWING PIRATES SERIES, BOOK 2

CONNIE SUTTLE

Print ISBN: 1-63478-004-3
Print ISBN-13: 978-1-63478-004-9
eBook ISBN: 1-63478-003-2
eBook ISBN-13: 978-1-63478-003-5

Published by:
SubtleDemon Publishing, LLC
PO Box 95696
Oklahoma City, OK 73143

Cover art by Renee Barratt @ The Cover Counts

To Walter, Joe, Larry, Lee, Dianne, Sarah and Mark.
Thank you.

ACKNOWLEDGMENTS

As always, this book is the result of collaboration. If it weren't for the support of my editor, my cover artist and my beta readers, it would be less than it is. All mistakes, as usual, are mine and no other's.

About the Author:
Connie Suttle lives in Oklahoma with her husband and a conglomerate of cats. They have finally banded together to make their demands, which has proven disconcerting to all humans involved.

You may find Connie in the following ways:
Facebook: Connie Suttle Author
Twitter: @subtledemon
Website and Blog: subtledemon.com

ALSO BY CONNIE SUTTLE

Blood Destiny Series:

Blood Wager

Blood Passage

Blood Sense

Blood Domination

Blood Royal

Blood Queen

Blood Rebellion

Blood War

Blood Redemption

Blood Reunion

Blood Recall

Blood Alliance

Legend of the Ir'Indicti Series:

Bumble

Shadowed

Target

Vendetta

Destroyer

High Demon Series:

Demon Lost

Demon Revealed

Demon's King

Demon's Quest

Demon's Revenge

Demon's Dream

God Wars Series:

Blood Double

Blood Trouble

Blood Revolution

Blood Love

Blood Finale

Saa Thalarr Series:

Hope and Vengeance

Wyvern and Company

Observe and Protect*

First Ordinance Series:

Finder

Keeper

BlackWing

SpellBreaker

WhiteWing

R-D Series:

Cloud Dust

Cloud Invasion

Cloud Rebel

Latter Day Demons Series:

Hot Demon in the City

A Demon's Work is Never Done

A Demon's Due

Seattle Elementals Series:

Your Money's Worth

Worth Your While*

BlackWing Pirates Series

MindSighted

MindMage

MindRogue

MindMaster*

Black Rose Sorceress Series

The Rose Mark

Rose and Thorn

Black Rose Queen

Queen of Thorns and Roses

Other Titles from SubtleDemon Publishing:

Malefactor

Transgressor

Underhanded*

by Joe Scholes

*Forthcoming

CHAPTER 1

F*alchan*
Randl Gage

"That's not scary." Salidar DeLuca shook his head as I used a finger to turn the three-dimensional image I'd created. "I've never seen anybody touch their images, and I know plenty of powerful people."

"Maybe they've never tried. This is my dream from last night," I added, surveying the image from all angles, searching for a clue as to what actually happened.

The scene was from Bornelus—the same place where nearly a year earlier, a massive, concrete block, filled with the skeletons of sacrificed humanoids, had been removed from the planet. The following night, the empty pit had been filled in, as if by a giant, magical hand.

Today, that same pit had been almost half-emptied of the dirt that filled it. There was no explanation for it. No reason for doing it, either, unless the Prophet wanted to announce his return.

That made no sense, either. Why would he advertise his presence anywhere, especially if he wanted to attack the Joint Alliances Conclave again?

For me, nearly six years had gone by, as I'd ended up on Falchan five years in the past after facing off against the Prophet. Salidar was waiting on Falchan for me, to train me in the art of the blade and many other disciplines, before sending me after the Prophet again.

I'd been ill-prepared the first time I'd gone against the Prophet, and only luck and Zaria's medallion had kept me alive.

Salidar had focused my time and energy most of these six years, but I'd searched for the Prophet and honed my mage skills in any free time I had.

I still considered the Prophet a sorcerer, who also held the skills of a necromancer. That would frighten even the bravest among us. Somewhere in Queen Lissa's dungeon on Le-Ath Veronis, two reanimated corpses were held inside an impermeable glass prison.

They hadn't moved after the Prophet's disappearance.

They also hadn't decomposed. Not only had I asked Salidar for that information, but I'd searched for it mentally, finding it easily enough.

As a result, I found myself hoping that the Prophet couldn't see those bodies so easily. It could make Queen Lissa a target. She was powerful, but the Prophet was an unknown, and I had no idea whether he could harm her or those about her.

If he were determined enough, he could find someone to harm; I understood that quite well.

"Your time is winding down, you know," Salidar interrupted my thoughts.

"I know." He'd taught me much in the time we'd been given. "My concern is how to explain this to Director Griff, Travis and Trent." I deliberately left Sabrina off that list—I'd come to realize she wasn't for me, and did my best to let that heartache go.

"I don't think it'll be hard," Sal shrugged. "It may be harder to explain those blades you forged for yourself."

"You were the one to tell me the tale of the hero whose weapon nobody else could carry," I pointed out.

"But that's fiction—a fairy tale of sorts. You made it real, and I still haven't figured out how."

"How many advancements started out as fiction?" I turned a steady gaze on him.

"True," he conceded with a shrug.

BlackWing X

Sabrina Kend

"Captain Anderson," I dipped my head to BlackWing VII's commander. She'd been transported aboard X to discuss recent events on Bornelus.

"Dori," Travis grinned as he swooped into the Captain's cubby, where Captain Anderson and I waited for Travis and Trent.

"Good to see you, Trav," she grinned back at him.

"What's happening with Bornelus?" Travis asked her.

"Micro-drones transmitted disturbed ground where the concrete block used to be," Dori replied. Her short, curly blonde hair suited her, and with blue eyes, I figured she drew plenty of looks.

Something about her, however, felt dangerous. As if she had claws and was prepared to strike if anyone made an improper move.

"Dori," Trent folded into the Captain's cubby, rather than bothering to walk from his cabin.

"Hey, Trent," Dori nodded at Travis' twin.

"Dori's telling me that the ground has been disturbed around the concrete block's former resting place on Bornelus," Travis brought Trent up to speed.

"Anything other than disturbed ground?" Trent asked. He pulled a chair closer to the Captain's desk and sat, flipping his long, black braid over a shoulder.

"It's ah, really disturbed," Dori explained.

"In what way?" Travis asked.

"As in the hole is more than a third empty, now. Images from last night show the hole filled in and grass and weeds growing over it. This morning, a big chunk of it is gone, along with grass, weeds, tree roots—everything."

"That's a disturbance, all right," Travis rubbed his chin. "No explanation, I take it?"

"None. We've been ordered not to approach the planet. Kooper wants bigger drones sent tomorrow."

"It's been almost a year since the concrete block disappeared," I pointed out. That wasn't the only thing that had been gone almost as long.

Travis held out hope that Randl was alive. I wasn't so sure, and as more time passed, any hope I'd had dwindled to nothing.

Trent stood with his brother on this, and I'd learned to stop arguing with them. Randl wasn't coming back; they merely refused to admit it.

"Does this mean the Prophet is back?" Dori asked the question we were all pondering.

"That would be a logical assumption," Travis rumbled. He wasn't happy; I could hear it in his voice. "Kooper asked us to meet with you and proceed to Bornelus. Larger drones will be sent to the surface then to take samples. XII is on the way, too, in case we need backup."

XII had a science crew aboard—it made sense that they'd come if they were available.

"I talked to Mom," Trent said. "So far, not a twitch from Akrinn and Lorvis' bodies—they're still crumpled where they fell after the Prophet was blown off Pyrik."

"Maybe he's forgotten them. I would have," Dori shrugged.

"I was hoping that those bodies would be the gauge for the Prophet's returning strength," Trent shook his head. "As long as they were unmoving, it gave me hope that the Prophet hadn't recovered. I suppose it's too much to assume he'd never recover." That statement was followed by a heavy sigh. "They never decomposed, though. Mom says so."

How Lissa found time to report on Akrinn and Lorvis' undead existence baffled me—she was a Queen with council meetings and two new babies to keep her busy. I'd seen images of Wayne William and Willow Wynter—they were as cute as any babies ever, but they were a handful, no doubt.

Travis and Trent were googly-eyed—their term, not mine—over their brother and sister, and showed me new images whenever they got them, which was often. Winkler sent them more frequently than Lissa, if I understood things correctly.

During the past year, too, I learned that Travis and Trent had asked someone to mute their attraction to me, so we wouldn't carry things too far. The explanation was this—that they didn't want disruptions on the ship, or the possibility that there could be accusations of favoritism.

That meant I had more than two years to go on my stint for the ASD, which included forced celibacy.

I'd been offered a *mute on my affections*, as Karzac the physician termed it, but I'd refused.

I was beginning to regret that decision.

A lot.

I wished for Randl during the worst times—to talk to. To get me through the worst of my physical cravings.

David, of all people, told me how wrong that would be, if Randl were still alive. Randl had been in love with me, and I'd completely missed that about him. I felt guilty, too, that he'd experience the same pain I felt.

It's a moot point, I scolded myself. *Randl is gone.*

Bornelus

Randl

I'd waited until Salidar was asleep before transporting myself to the deserted planet. Night was just falling on this portion of the planet, with a weak sliver of moon hanging low in the sky.

Insects and night birds were singing and calling—I had myself shielded so well they'd never realize someone had come. Wind moved tree branches not far away, their hushing sounds adding to what should have been a peaceful night on Bornelus.

Sometime during the second year of my training with Salidar, I'd learned to fold space. He'd urged me to try it, after I'd demonstrated other skills only a warlock or a wizard might achieve.

Folding space was terrifying at first until I became used to it, because there is a moment of the darkest dark, where even my mindsight won't reveal anything. I'd never been in such conditions before, and it still unsettled me.

Nevertheless, folding space is now a part of my gifts.

Kneeling on the ground beside the unusual excavation, I placed my hand upon the dirt and plant detritus at the edge. Like the graves the Prophet had emptied, this was precisely cut into the earth, as if he couldn't bear the concept of a ragged removal. Every root and stray twig had been excised as if by a laser.

Snorting softly to myself at the imagined obsessive foibles of a mass murderer, I reached out with my mind to discover what I could about his unusual revisiting of this killing ground.

Yes, I could sense that he'd been here the moment I arrived. It had been too optimistic to hope that he'd disappeared forever.

I blinked as the images came to me—of him, spreading his arms and commanding the dirt to disappear—neatly, of course. Nothing more came, however. I was still as confused about this act as I'd been before my arrival on Bornelus.

Deep in the ground, however, and not far away, lay more of the creatures that attacked us when we'd first come to Bornelus. They were waiting for someone—anyone—to arrive. I'd hidden my presence from prying eyes, or they'd have sensed me.

Standing and stretching, I considered that perhaps there was a reason for this after all. Director Griff would surely send someone to examine this new twist in the Prophet's plans.

It was a trap.

I had a decision to make. Reveal my continued existence to him and those coming to Bornelus, or let them walk blindly into the death or subjugation the Prophet planned for them.

Just in time to throw the ASD into chaos before the rescheduled Joint Alliances Conclave.

Reaching out with my senses, I searched for Director Griff's current location, then folded space to Le-Ath Veronis.

~

New Fangled Bar and Restaurant, Le-Ath Veronis
Kooper Griff

"What do you think it means?" Kell asked. He and Opal had joined me for a drink at New Fangled, to discuss the latest events concerning the Prophet and Bornelus.

"No idea. There's no reason for it, as far as I can see." I tossed back the shot of bourbon and waited for it to burn a path to my stomach. "I have three ships on the way now; X, VII and XII."

"Probably a good idea," Opal agreed. She'd settled for a glass of wine, while Kell and I had our favorite bourbon. I barely paid attention to the man who settled on the barstool next to mine; I merely put up a shield to make our conversation private.

"It won't do any good," he said while nodding to the comesula bartender to give him the same thing I was having.

I went still with shock. He'd been gone nearly a year, and most people thought he was dead.

I slammed back another shot of bourbon before turning toward him. "Why are you here?" I croaked. "Now?" I added.

"Had some things to learn," he shrugged. He looked older, somehow. I began to have suspicions that he'd been gone more than ten months—in *his* existence. I wished I had a way to contact Zaria, because she'd surely known where and when Randl had been. "Besides, I had to come now to warn you," he went on. "Sending those ships to Bornelus is sending them into a trap."

"Fuck." I pulled my comp-vid from a pocket and began tapping messages. Randl set a clay container in front of me while I warned the ships to stay well back from Bornelus' orbit—and sent mindspeech at the same time to those aboard the ships who could receive it.

"What's this?" I asked, once I'd gotten replies from all three BlackWing ships. I nodded at the clay pot.

"Soil samples I just took from the hole. Won't be any different from the many other soil samples you've taken during the past year or so." Randl thanked the bartender and lifted his glass of bourbon to me.

"A trap. I should have guessed," I let my shoulders sag.

"He wants your ships, Director," Randl's sightless eyes bored into mine. "And your people—dead or alive, it doesn't matter."

"Fucking, bloody, ass-scraping hells," I cursed.

"Agreed." Kell said. He'd been listening carefully with Opal at his side. Both nodded at me before raising their glasses to Randl.

"Wait—you can fold space?"

"Yes." Randl emptied his glass and thumped it on the bar, letting the bartender know he wanted another shot. "And a shit load of other things, too," he added.

"You learned a lot from Travis and Trent," I observed. *Shit load* was one of Lissa's favorite terms, and most of her children used it regularly.

"Didn't learn it from them," Randl lifted his second shot and tossed it back.

"Who, then?"

"Can't say. Sorry, Director."

"Are you back, then?"

"I think so. I sent mindspeech. Haven't heard back, yet."

"I'll put your back pay in your account."

"Thank you. I probably need clothing."

"I'll have uniforms made."

"Then I'll buy the civilian clothes I need."

"Can I ask you to report to X in three days?"

"If there isn't a problem. I'll let you know if there is. By the way, can we reverse the trap?" He lifted an eyebrow at me.

"How?" I frowned at him. That thought hadn't occurred to me.

"You send in old junkers disguised as the newest model ASD cruisers. Set them to detonate the minute anybody sets foot on them."

I held my breath for a count of five. "How soon?" I asked after slowly releasing a sigh.

"Two days should do it. It'll piss him off, but we need to let him know we won't fall for all his shit."

"I'll see what I can do." My words were dry.

"Thanks. I have errands to run. I'll let you know whether joining X is an option."

"Make it soon," I said as Randl rose, dropped a credit chip on the bar and walked out.

Avii Castle, Le-Ath Veronis

Quin

"Brandl?" Dena and I walked into the office he kept at Avii Castle. He'd spent most of his time here after Randl disappeared. He'd never given up hope that Randl was alive, however.

He and I shared that notion.

Brandl looked up from his comp-vid—he was working late, as he usually did. His light-brown hair was sprinkled with more silver than it held a year earlier, and his eyes were clouded by a deeper sadness.

"Queen Quin," Brandl rose quickly from his chair and dipped his head respectfully.

"Brandl, you're a friend and you don't have to do that," I pointed out for perhaps the hundredth time. "Besides, I have good news."

"What good news?" he blinked curiously at me.

"I heard from Randl. He'll be here in an hour."

Brandl went still with shock, his mouth open. I think he forgot to breathe for several moments. I was prepared, in case a short bout of healing was necessary.

"Pap?"

Randl arrived early, surprising all of us.

CHAPTER 2

Quin and Dena left when Pap started crying and wouldn't let me go. After a few moments, I felt my own tears dripping onto my cheeks.

I hadn't seen Pap for nearly six years. At least I'd known he was alive; he hadn't known that about me. "I'm so sorry, Pap," I apologized, my words cracked and whispered.

"I'm happy, Son," he squeezed me again before letting me go. "Probably look like a mess," he wiped wetness from his cheeks.

"You look like my Pap," I said. "And I love you, no matter what."

"Are you hungry?" It was the standard parent's question for a child, I think.

"Yeah. I just had two drinks on an empty stomach, so food wouldn't hurt."

"Come on, let's go to the kitchen, then, to see what we can get."

What we could get turned out to be a hot roast-beef sandwich, an idea which Avii Castle's cooks had borrowed from Queen Lissa's kitchen. It consisted of toasted bread, topped with plenty of shredded roast beef and covered with delicious brown gravy. I hadn't realized how hungry I was until my first bite.

Quin and Justis found us there and sat down to share a small plate of fruit and cheese while we ate and talked.

"Can you tell us where you've been?" Justis asked.

"I can't," I shook my head. "I made a promise, I'm sorry."

"Don't worry about it. My Quin disappeared for five years. I was grateful to get her back."

"Five years your time," Quin pointed out before popping a grape in her mouth.

"Yes. Five years my time," Justis sighed. He'd suffered during that time, just as Pap had suffered during my absence.

"If there comes a time when I can tell you, I will," I said. "But for now, I have to keep the secret." I didn't want the Prophet to turn his gaze—and his wrath—upon Falchan for any reason. After two years of training with Sal, he'd sent me to help the current Warlord and his General on Falchan, while I continued to train with blades. Evidence of the help I'd provided was now tattooed across my back.

Salidar would be safe enough, but Falchan could be placed in danger if it was discovered I'd spent time there, learning a great many things so I could stand against the Prophet when the time came again.

Time would tell whether I'd learned enough to stand against him, because I knew as surely as I knew anything that he had plans to attack the Conclave and this time, it was on the Founder's home planet of Campiaa.

Teeg San Gerxon had security measures in place, but there was no reliable method of predicting what the Prophet could do when presented with such a challenge.

The Prophet would know in two days that the gauntlet had been thrown, as Salidar was fond of saying.

So far, no more had been seen of infected humanoids, but that could be a temporary ruse. I had no doubt that those soldiers—living and dead—merely waited to serve the Prophet's whims.

"How long can you stay?" Pap asked. He understood that Kooper still needed me; it wasn't necessary to tell him.

"I have three days before reporting in," I said. "I want to pay a visit to Queen Lissa's dungeons tomorrow, and then I need to do some shopping for clothes. What I have now isn't suitable."

After five years of training, all I had was Falchani-style leathers, and those were a dead giveaway to anyone as to where I'd been. I'd left the leathers with Salidar in his mountain cabin, choosing to wear the clothes I'd worn at the time of my disappearance.

Those clothes were now so tight across the shoulders I could barely fit into them, even after I'd made alterations with power.

So many things had changed while I was gone.

I'd changed while I was gone.

You have my blessings, Salidar's voice sounded in my mind. *I always knew you'd choose the time to leave. Kick ass and take names, all right?*

Thank you, I replied. *For everything, including those cheesy Kung-Fu vids.*

Just trying to make you into a well-rounded individual, he sent a mental smirk.

Right.

Send mindspeech anytime, he ended our conversation.

Right.

"Do you want company when you visit Lissa's dungeons?" Quin asked.

"I'll have to shield you if you go," I said, pushing my last piece of toast through the remains of brown gravy on my plate. "I'm going to visit Vrak."

"Why?" Pap didn't sound convinced that I should do anything of the sort.

"I have to know something about him," I shrugged.

"You learned how to shield?" Justis asked the question the others wanted to know.

"I sort of taught myself," I said. "I taught myself several things, actually."

"Isn't that unusual?" Justis asked.

"It is, but my ability isn't like a wizard's or warlock's, or so I've been told." I didn't add that Ilya Ironsmith told me so. I'd awakened the talent in myself, too, which, according to Ilya, wasn't possible with wizards or warlocks. Someone else had to do it for them, when they were young. He said the talent would remain out of their reach, otherwise.

My talent had been hovering in my mind all along, waiting for me to grasp it. And, as my father didn't have anything like it, I knew it had to come from my mother.

How I had it and she didn't, however, I had yet to figure out.

"We'll go with you to Queen Lissa's palace," Quin interrupted my thoughts. "We just won't go to the dungeon with you."

"I'd appreciate that," I said. "Pap, you want to go?"

"I need to speak with Lissa anyway about an event at the beach palace. I'll come," he agreed.

"You have a suite here to stay the night," Quin smiled at me. "It's still yours if you want it."

"That sounds great," I said. "I've had a long day."

Later, I pulled covers back on the bed inside a private suite not far from Pap's. Sitting on the edge of the soft, sheet-covered monstrosity, I leaned over to pull my boots off. They were Falchani-made, and I'd get rid of them the moment I bought other boots that could be found at a shop in either Alliance.

I undressed slowly as I considered events surrounding the last Joint Conclave, which had been postponed and relocated.

I also considered a piece of evidence that I'd asked Kooper for and hadn't gotten before I'd been sent to Falchan more than five years in the past.

Holding out a hand, I brought the coin to my fingers. The way I'd done it—with power—wouldn't set off any alarms in the ASD evidence warehouse.

Perhaps I'd put it back there the same way. For now, I wanted to examine it more thoroughly. I hoped it had the residue of the spell about it, because I wanted to study it.

I also wanted to search its history, and I had to hold it to do that.

Just not now. Now, I was more than weary and needed sleep. Setting the coin on the small, bedside table, I finished undressing and lay back on the bed. Time to meditate—just enough to fall asleep.

Kooper, I sent before beginning my meditation. *I have the coin from Vogeffa II.*

All right.

Good-night.

~

BlackWing X

Travis

"No, I've had several drinks already," Kooper held up a hand when I offered a glass of bourbon. He'd met me in the Captain's cubby not long after he'd ordered X, VII and XII to reverse course.

"What's going on with Bornelus?" I asked, offering a chair to Kooper before sitting down behind the desk.

"Well, I have it on good authority that any ships that show up will be flying into a trap."

"That's—interesting," I said after hesitating a few seconds. "Can you expand on that thought?"

"The source says the Prophet likely has designs on the ships and personnel that show up to investigate his hole-digging. I have a preliminary sample of the soil from the site and so far, there's no difference in it and any other samples we've taken."

"I'll ask who took that sample later," I said. "A trap sounds logical, now that you've said it. It would be in the Prophet's wheelhouse, I believe, after the attack he planned on Cord'ilus last year."

"I think that, too. Tell me, who do you think might have gone to take the soil sample?"

Kooper was hiding something, but his face was set and revealed nothing to me. "No idea," I admitted. "Someone with folding skills and power, I assume. Did Mom send somebody?" She'd be my first guess, if she weren't tending to two three-month-olds.

"Your mother had nothing to do with this."

"Wow." I flipped my braid over a shoulder and lifted the bottle of bourbon to pour a glass for myself. Who'd know anything about Bornelus—enough to sense that something had been disturbed and then have sufficient wisdom to take a soil sample for Kooper. "I don't have a clue," I shrugged.

"Randl," Kooper's voice was flat. "He's back—and—different."

I let that information soak into my mind for a moment. I'd just described who could take a soil sample. Randl couldn't fold space. Did he magically appear out of thin air and convince someone to give him a ride to Bornelus?

"I'm sorry," I pinched the bridge of my nose. "This isn't making sense."

"My entire evening has been filled with stuff that doesn't make sense."

"Where is he now?" I thought to ask.

"Asleep at Avii Castle, according to Quin. I'm giving him three days before sending him here to BlackWing X. Be prepared. This isn't the Randl you knew before."

I toyed with my empty glass for a few moments before lifting my eyes to Kooper's. "When should I let the crew know?"

"Tomorrow is good enough. I have to get some uniforms together for him—for official business, you understand. You're going back undercover from here on out." Kooper rose from his seat, preparing to leave.

"Different how?" I asked the question foremost in my mind concerning Randl.

"I had a shield around me, Kell and Opal at New Fangled earlier. Randl breached it to include himself."

Kooper's admission made me draw in a breath. *Who could do that?* Shields created by the truly powerful couldn't be breached, to my knowledge. I couldn't breach one of Kooper's shields if I tried.

"No, I have no idea how he did it and trust me, I've been working on that since it happened," Kooper waved a hand. "Three days and he'll be here. I want full reports, Captain Tetsuya. If you can, find out where he trained and with whom. We may need that information."

"Yes, Director."

Kooper folded space while I pondered Randl's return—and the conundrum of what he'd become.

~

Queen's Palace, Le-Ath Veronis
Randl

We'd been invited to have breakfast with Queen Lissa, once she learned that we were coming. Wellend and Warlend transported us to her palace after I'd risen and dressed.

Pap couldn't stop smiling at me, and clapped me on the back when we landed in Lissa's private dining room. Several of her mates were there, including Winkler, Drake and Drew.

Winkler gave a low laugh and rose from his seat to engulf me in a hug.

"I hear you have some babies, now," I grinned when he pulled away.

"Sure do. Come take a look before you leave." He was as proud as any father could be of his twins, and wanted to show them off whenever possible.

"That sounds great," I said.

"I hear you want to visit Vrak," he said, his voice lowering.

"Yes. I want to do an experiment."

"Anything dangerous?"

"No, sir. Just a brief change of appearance, that's all."

"You want to see if he'll recognize you as the Prophet, don't you?" Winkler was a very smart werewolf.

"Yes. I'm the only one who's seen past the Prophet's hood, I think. I want to see if Vrak knows him by sight, or whether he has another way to identify the asshole."

"That's an interesting idea," Lissa said. As a vampire, she'd hear a whisper clearly. It didn't matter, I needed her permission anyway to visit Vrak in her dungeon.

"Come take a seat," she invited. "Sit next to Winkler so you won't have to talk over so many people," she added.

I took the indicated seat next to Winkler. "We heard you were back last night—from Kooper," Winkler said as plates of food were set in front of us. "I was hoping we'd get to see you before you took off into to the wild blue yonder."

The unusual phrase made me smile. What he referred to was occasionally wild, seldom blue and certainly yonder.

"I'm just glad he's alive," Lissa said. "It's good to see you, Randl."

"I feel the same way," Pap raised his cup of tea.

"Our boys will be happy, too," Drake said. "They've missed you and your sage advice."

"Some days I don't feel very sagacious," I said. Most of those days involved bruises and sore muscles from intense training with Sal. I wasn't going to admit that to anyone, however—except Travis and Trent. If they wanted to tell their mother and fathers, that was fine. The secret would be safe enough with them.

BlackWing X

Travis

"I asked you to this meeting to make an announcement," I said. We'd just finished breakfast, so Susan and Bekzi could join the rest of us at galley tables to hear the news.

"Does it involve the reason we're not going to Bornelus now?" David asked. The crew only had sketchy information on Kooper's reasons to reverse course. While David was an Amterean by naturalization, he had enough curiosity to be an Amterean Dwarf by birth.

"Yes, but that's not the most important thing," I said, waving off his question. James and Nathan, pilot and navigator, were here, too, and I didn't want to keep them away from the bridge for long.

Pulling in a breath, I blurted the news. "Randl's alive, and he's joining us aboard ship in two-and-a-half days."

For a crew of ten, they made enough noise to fill the entire galley. "Hold off on the speculation so I can tell you the rest," I raised my voice to be heard. Things quieted immediately.

"Thank you. Randl met with Kooper last night, who was just as surprised as the rest of us by his sudden appearance. He told Kooper that the Prophet removed dirt from the hole to pull us into a trap. Instead, Kooper's sending a few old ships to the area on auto-pilot, and setting them to detonate if anybody boards them."

"So, we fire the first volley instead of the Prophet," Jayna said quietly.

"That's the idea. Kooper says it will send a message to the Prophet —that we won't fall for all his tricks."

"That will just make him more devious next time," Sabrina pointed out. She'd learned a lot in a year; she'd made the decision to remain an ASD agent rather than become a liaison. She'd also immersed herself into her lessons after Randl's disappearance, and passed all her tests in near-record time. She was a full-fledged member of the crew, now, sexual frustration aside.

Kooper had readily agreed with Sabrina's decision to become a regular agent; I think she had some idea of avenging Randl's death. Nothing Trent or I could say would dissuade her so here we were; all of us waiting for her three-year stint to pass.

"Yes, but we'll have Randl back, and I hope that helps," Trent took over for me. "Conclave is coming, and Kooper wants all of us on alert. The Prophet has plans again, and nearly a year has passed for him to make them better. We have to be prepared for any attack."

He didn't say what we all knew, however. Without Randl's help last time, we'd probably be dead or enslaved by the Prophet. Not a pleasant thought, by any means.

"Where has Randl been?" James asked.

"I don't have that information. You can ask him yourself in a couple of days. That's all for now. Back to your duties, everyone." I dismissed the crew.

"Need tea?" Bekzi came forward as the others filed out of the galley.

"Yes. Please."

"I get," he nodded and walked away while I sat heavily at a galley table to consider everything I'd learned in the past day.

"Bro, stop worrying about it. We'll deal with things as they crop up," Trent sat opposite me.

"Yes, but what things? We already know the Prophet is as devious as they come—maybe more so."

"I'll feel better when Randl gets here," Trent blew out a breath. Bekzi arrived and set a mug of Falchani black in front of both of us.

"Be good to see Randl," Bekzi said. "He friend. Good help."

"You're right as usual, Bekz," Trent nodded to the lion snake shapeshifter. "I just hope we make it through the next round with the Prophet."

"That make two," Bekzi agreed. "We stand strong. As should."

Queen's Palace, Le-Ath Veronis

Randl

"Are you sure you don't want Winkler and me to come in with you—as mist?" Queen Lissa attempted to hide her worry.

"I'll send mental images," I said, hoping to put her off without upsetting her. "I think I'll be all right."

"Open the door," Lissa nodded to the dungeon guard, a vampire with a century of experience at handling unruly prisoners.

"No need," I said. "I can get myself inside."

"It's shielded," Lissa began as I bent reality and walked through it— and the cell wall—at the same time.

Lissa

Holy, fucking hell. It was all I could think as Randl did something I hadn't known was possible. Sure, I could mist through walls, but he'd been *solid* when he passed through the walls *and* my shields. *Holy, fucking hell*, I mentally repeated.

That's when Randl began transmitting images to Winkler and me as we stood outside the cell door. Winkler's hands dropped to my shoulders and he pulled me against him as we watched the scene unfold.

~

Randl

At first Vrak didn't know I was there. He sat against a wall, arms draped over bent knees, staring at the floor. My disguise was in place, hood and all, when he looked up. Vrak scrambled to his knees and almost prostrated himself before me.

"Please," he wept, "Tell me my children are alive."

~

"I didn't get much from him—he only babbled about his children, Varok and Perill. I figure they're in deep with the Prophet, and subject to his whims, just as Vrak is."

Kooper had joined me in Lissa's private study to hear what I'd learned from Vrak. Winkler, Drake, Drew and another mate, Rigo, were also there.

"Director, I need information on Vrak's past."

"You think this is another Phorde Gaster, don't you?" Kooper sat back in his chair, shaking his head.

"I'm concerned, yes," I told him. "Whatever the Prophet did to Phorde's replacement convinced him in every way that he was the real Phorde Gaster. Down to the fingerprints and DNA, if your testing procedures were correct."

"That's how we identified him," Kooper sounded grim.

"Do you think the Lyristolyi drug is involved, somehow?" Lissa asked. "That's the only way I know to make clones that are indistinguishable from the original."

"Do you know about the Lyristolyi drug?" Kooper turned to me.

"I'll do research," I said. "This sounds as if it may be the base the Prophet works from to produce these doppelgangers."

"This means he could have his sycophants planted everywhere," Lissa didn't sound pleased. "I thought that shit died out with Vardil Cayetes."

"I was hoping it was gone for good," Kooper agreed.

"We still don't have an idea how he's placing obsessions," Winkler growled. "He has a Sirenali stashed away somewhere, you can bet on that."

"Probably keeps him nearby most of the time, so we won't find him," Lissa grumbled. "Has he ever appeared with anyone else in your dreams?" Her question almost made me jump.

"No," I said.

"That's too bad. Whoever this Sirenali is, the Prophet is hiding him very well," Kooper sighed. "Randl, use your code word to research the Lyristolyi drug in the ASD database. You'll find most of what you need there."

"Are there others that we know who've had the drug?" I asked.

Kooper and Lissa stared at one another for several seconds.

"Only Zaria," Lissa whispered.

Sun City, Le-Ath Veronis

Quin

Randl wore a frown as he joined us for lunch at a popular restaurant in Sun City, the major city on Le-Ath Veronis' light half of the planet. Le-Ath Veronis rotated on its side, keeping half in darkness and half in light.

It kept the vampires safe on the dark half, while tourists and others could safely travel from one hemisphere to the other with ease.

I was happy to get a day out; Justis seldom offered to come with me on shopping trips, although this one was for Randl. Dena, Ardis, Wellend and Brandl were with us at the table when Randl pulled out his chair to join our party.

"What sounds good?" Randl asked as he flipped through the projected tabletop menu.

"The prime rib is very good," Justis said.

"I'll have that," he said, tapping the item.

"How was the—ah—visit?" Wellend asked.

"Informational—up to a point," Randl replied. "Still plenty of mystery to go around, however."

"That's too bad," Wellend said.

Randl

Drinks were brought to the table by two servers who couldn't stop smiling at us—I could easily see they were excited to have the King and Queen of the Avii at their restaurant. It was a tale they could pass on to their friends.

I'd done research on humanoid servers as opposed to robotic ones —the interaction between humanoids and other races was rated far above that provided by a server-bot, even the most sophisticated of them.

Bots were employed at some fast-food restaurants, as Sal called them, but in the better places, those things were relegated to the kitchens, where they peeled and prepped vegetables, washed dishes and cleaned floors and counters.

Many of the best restaurants still did all that by hand, however. Sal had taken me once to Dee's on Tulgalan. The food had been incredible, there, and everything in the restaurant was done by a real person.

The prices were quite high, but worth every credit.

"What are we looking for today?" Pap asked.

"Everything," I shrugged. "I have what I'm wearing, and it really doesn't fit very well."

"I recognize it," he nodded. "It was what you were wearing when you, well. You know."

"Yeah." He didn't add that it fit me before I'd disappeared. It didn't fit now. "I need several pairs of boots, I think," I said. "Along with the other stuff."

The meal was good, although we only engaged in idle conversation. Shopping took longer, and felt more grueling than hours spent working out or sparring with Sal or under his supervision.

I had enough clothing, boots and shoes afterward, though, to do me for a while. When Wellend transported us back to Avii Castle, I found six uniforms lying on the bed inside my suite. Kooper had them delivered while I was out.

He'd assessed my size employing his own power to be assured of a proper fit, and I was grateful. *Dress casually for dinner—Justis wants to eat on the terrace,* Quin informed me in mindspeech. *Your new denim pants and a comfortable shirt will do.*

Thanks, I returned. *Eating outside sounds wonderful.* It did—it was warm enough outside. I'd left the beginnings of a harsh winter behind on Falchan.

Randl, the decoy ships have almost reached Bornelus, Kooper informed me.

Thank you for letting me know, Director. I have something to do before they arrive.

What's that? Kooper asked.

Plant a false reading of life forms aboard each, I replied.

Kooper went silent for several seconds before responding. *That's good,* he said. *Very good. And good to know. We're monitoring the sensors aboard each ship. I'll let you know if they detonate.*

Thank you.

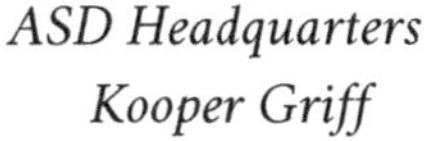

ASD Headquarters
Kooper Griff

"Link me to all the readings from the sensors," I ordered.

"Yes, sir," the agent replied via comp-vid. In seconds, the images of all sensor readings aboard three decoy ships displayed on my comp-vid. The life-form reading was non-existent.

Until it wasn't.

I held my breath and counted to ten before blowing it out again. Not only were there life-form readings, but those life forms appeared to be moving about each of the ships.

How the bloody hells did Randl accomplish that?

Whoever told him that his power wasn't like that of a warlock or wizard hadn't been lying. This was far outside those parameters. More than ever, I wanted the name of the person who'd trained him to do these things. In all the records in the ASD and CSD archives, there'd been no reports of power wielders doing this level of wizardry.

I borrowed Sabrina's idea of creating echoes, Randl's mental voice informed me, as if I'd actually asked him that question. *I've taken real life-form readings from other ships and duplicated them aboard your decoys, that's all.*

That's genius, I began.

Thank Sabrina, she's the real genius. I'm merely adapting her idea to fit our need.

May I have a meeting with you tomorrow? I'd like to discuss plans for the Conclave.

Yes. What time?

Ten bells tomorrow morning?

I'll be there.

He didn't know it yet, but I had a meeting on Campiaa with Teeg, Wyatt, Dormas and Tybus at ten bells in the morning. Randl would be joining us.

~

Randl

In the past five years, I'd been taught not to reveal my thoughts in facial expressions. Kooper was taking me to Campiaa; I knew it the moment I met him in his office at ASD Headquarters.

He grinned at me before folding both of us to Teeg San Gerxon's private study. Wyatt, Jett Riffler, Dormas and Tybus were there, and wise men that they were, didn't outwardly register their surprise at my unexpected arrival.

Good to see you, Wyatt sent.

He didn't add that he worried that I was truly dead, like so many others did. *Good to see you, too*, I replied to his mindspeech.

"Please, sit," Teeg San Gerxon, Founder of the Campiaan Alliance, indicated chairs for Kooper and me.

"I have three decoy ships about to enter Bornelus' orbit," Kooper announced after he sat and made himself comfortable.

"I thought you were sending," Teeg began. "Ah," he said after a moment's consideration. His eyes turned toward me, then. "I take it this is at your advice?"

"Yes, Founder," I dipped my head to him.

"Call me Teeg. Nothing's changed, Randl. How soon will we know whether the trap has been sprung?" He turned back to Kooper.

"I'll get a message from those monitoring the situation," Kooper replied. "Now, who, in your opinion is among the most vulnerable of the attendees, so I'll know where to place undercover agents?"

"Cloudsong," Teeg said immediately. "They've only been members of an Alliance for a short while and are still coming out of their isolationistic shell, so to speak. I know Revalus can mostly protect itself, but I worry that the Prophet will view it as another new world with little knowledge of how to protect itself. It could be vulnerable for that reason alone. I have a list of six others," he passed a comp-vid to Kooper. "Jett will provide additional guards, but you have access to —shall we say—more talented agents than he does."

"If they're armed and professional, that's all we need," Kooper said absently while thumbing through the list on Teeg's comp-vid.

An alarm went off on Kooper's comp-vid, then, and I stiffened.

The Prophet's army had just boarded the ships, and all three exploded at once.

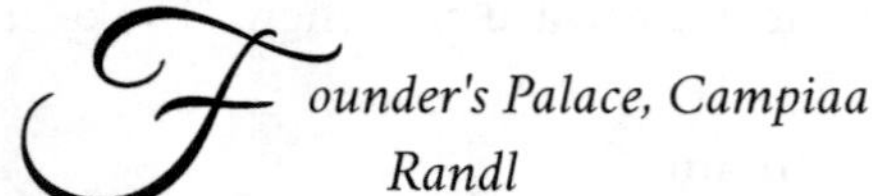

ounder's Palace, Campiaa
   Randl

Lunch was brought to us, after which we viewed the images recorded and sent by the vid-cams aboard the decoy ships until they were destroyed.

Only brief images of ten enemy soldiers boarding each vessel were recorded before the explosions occurred.

Whether the men died or were pulled away at the last moment, we had no idea, although Kooper was considering it a temporary victory.

"We've made our challenge, I think," Jett Riffler said after watching the images a third time.

"Has security been increased at every space port in both Alliances?" Wyatt asked.

"From the moment Randl told me Bornelus was a trap," Kooper confirmed. "They've been warned to watch for anything unusual, and to double and triple check every ship coming or going."

"What about freighters and passenger ships in the shipping lanes?" Teeg spoke his fears.

"All have been warned that there may be an increase in attempted piracy, and that their lives could be on the line as a result," Kooper said. "I assume you've gone over every bit of Campiaa, to check for irregularities?"

"Twice," Jett sighed. "And we're still looking. We don't have an abandoned nuclear waste site, or a city destroyed by a nuclear accident—Campiaa was solar-powered from the start. That doesn't mean we don't have difficult-to-reach places that would be ideal hiding spots for the enemy; we have drones combing those sites and transmitting data to CSD Headquarters."

"I have Quin going through images," Kooper sighed. "In fact, she's buried in images as of this morning. Anybody who's in charge of anything the Prophet could target is on that list."

"Do you have the information I requested on Vrak—the original, anyway?" I asked.

"I sent that to her. I'll send a copy to you when we get back to Le-Ath Veronis. I think I'll put X in charge of Cloudsong. As far as the list goes, I think they're the most vulnerable world that the Prophet could target. Besides, there's enough talent on X to get any of you elsewhere in a hurry, if it's necessary."

"Agreed," I nodded. My senses had pinged the moment Teeg said Cloudsong earlier.

Avii Castle, Le-Ath Veronis

Quin

I had enough images to look through to keep me busy for days, with barely enough time for meal breaks and sleep. My wings drooped about me as I considered yet another face on my ASD-issued comp-vid.

"Hi, baby."

"Mom?" My head jerked up immediately when Zaria appeared before my desk.

"I can help with that pile of images," she smiled at me. "If you'll help me first."

"What can I do?" I stood, the comp-vid on my desk forgotten. I'd help because she asked and not for the promise of a return favor.

"I need your healing skills," she said. "We need someone, but first, he needs us."

"When?" I asked, suddenly sounding breathless. This was important; I could almost see it in my mother's eyes.

"Now, and in the past." Her reply was cryptic.

"I will give whatever you need," I said.

"We need your best healing," she said. "Come. It's time we rectified a wrong."

∼

ASD Headquarters, Le-Ath Veronis
  Randl

"I'm sending one more agent with you to BlackWing X," Kooper informed me when he folded me back to his office. "He's a veteran agent with fourteen years' experience, completely trustworthy and has success in the field tracking down and eliminating security threats. He's an uncanny judge of people, too, and is very accurate in detecting a lie when it's told."

"His name?" I felt it was prudent to know who'd be sent to the ship with me.

"Vik Roth," Kooper replied. "At least X's ceilings are high enough that he won't have to duck his head when he walks through the ship."

"So—he's tall, then."

"We see eye to eye," Kooper laughed. Kooper was quite tall, and many were forced to look up to him. Most of the time, he secretly enjoyed that. "This will bring the crew's number to twelve, and I figure with babysitting Cloudsong's King and his advisors, you'll need an extra hand."

"Because you may be pulling me off the ship regularly," I said.

"I knew you'd see that," Kooper nodded. "It's true. You'll be in high demand, and Jett has my permission to contact you for special circumstances, too."

"All right. I like Director Riffler. He's a credit to his people and his work."

"Teeg and I think so, too. Look, go spend some time with your father. I expect you back here at eight bells tomorrow morning. Vik will be here, too, and you'll both report to Captain Trent aboard X."

"Thank you, Director," I said.

"Don't thank me. We're going to wear you out with this Conclave business."

"We'll see about that."

∼

Hotel Chessman, Le-Ath Veronis

Vik Roth

I shut my packed bag with a sigh, remembering Zaria's words to me fifteen years earlier.

I also recalled what she'd done for me—she and Quin.

I'd been prevented from committing a heinous crime; one I'd have extreme difficulty reconciling since I'd survived it, thanks to Zaria's interference.

I'd taken a mortal wound, too, in the process, but Quin had healed that and many other maladies I'd borne through the years.

My appearance was changed, as was my name, but inside, I knew who I was. I also knew what I'd been saved from, and I would forever be grateful for that. For so long, I'd limped along, feeling mostly useless and a burden to those who knew me.

Now I had purpose and hope—both gifts from Zaria. I also wore a small, gold medallion around my neck, that she'd also given me. I intended to repay her as well as I could, by doing my best in the coming months.

Tomorrow, I'd meet another agent, and we'd be transported aboard BlackWing X, one of a secret fleet of pirate ships operated by the ASD. The ship would bear a disguise while we made our way to Cloudsong, the newest member of the Campiaan Alliance.

I hoped the King wasn't as paranoid as many of the records said.

That was difficult enough to deal with, without a nameless enemy walking through his door unannounced.

Kooper Griff said the other agent could see through most disguises, and read whether an obsession was placed on someone, in addition to dozens of other troubles infecting them.

I'd also been informed of the problems dealt with during the Conclave ten months earlier—in fact, those problems had precipitated the rescheduling of the Joint Alliances meeting.

My stomach growled, reminding me it was time for dinner. I headed for the door; there was a restaurant downstairs that served good steaks. One of those was in my near future.

~

Avii Castle
   Quin

I had a very short list of images to consider, thanks to Zaria. I was tired after our trip to the past and back again, but Zaria had saved me many days' work by tapping my comp-vid and providing a list of names and images that needed my attention.

The others, she'd said, were fine for now.

"Time for dinner—stop working," Dena walked into my study, rustling her multi-colored feathers. It was another way to scold me for spending so much time on this project—or so she'd thought.

Zaria had brought me back to the moment after we'd disappeared, so to Dena, it appeared as if I'd never been gone.

In reality, I'd been gone for several hours, so this would be a long day for me. I didn't mind. Time with my mother is always a blessing, no matter what form it takes. She and I, however—we had a secret to keep, now.

"I'm hungry," I said as I stood and folded my red wings against my back.

"Good. I hear they cooked your favorite noodle and mushroom dish."

Randl

"Send messages when you can," Pap said. He and I were having dinner together at Lissa's beach palace. It was good to have a meal with him only, so we could talk freely. In my pocket, I carried the coin from Vogeffa II—soon enough I'd handle it, hoping to find information in it from the past.

Pap had a gold coin like it in his pocket—from my mother. It was older and more worn, but he'd held onto it all these years as something to remember her by.

Perhaps I'd ask to examine it one day, to see if I could find images of my parents in it.

"I'll send regular messages, I promise," I told Pap.

"I'll write, too, but my notes will be boring," he grinned.

"Pap, boring sounds great. Tell me all about the boring stuff. It'll be welcome, I assure you."

"I know you won't be able to tell me much, once you get there," he said. "But tell me how you are anyway."

He wasn't saying it aloud, but he was terrified I'd disappear again— or be killed, as he'd believed during the time I was missing.

"Pap, have you ever considered—well, asking someone out?"

"Hmmph."

"It's been a long time. Having somebody beside you isn't the worst idea, you know."

"I know."

"Think about it, all right?"

"I will."

Pointing out the reality of that lie would only bring excuses, and I could see through those, too.

"Is there anything else?" Our comesula server appeared at Pap's elbow.

Fuck being a realist, I thought. "I'd like a beer, please. Refizani Blue, if you have it."

"Of course."

~

BlackWing X

Trent

Once Randl and our newest crew member, Vik Roth, were aboard, we'd set a course for Cloudsong. In two weeks, the King of Cloudsong, his assistants and a few Council members would be shuttled to Campiaa aboard X.

As one of seven recent additions to the Alliances, Cloudsong and the others would attend newly-created orientation meetings, to bring them up to speed on Conclave history, activities and best practices on dealing with the politics surrounding a conclave. They'd be approached by special interest groups, although that was an illegal practice in both Alliances. Many times, payment or favors changed hands, but those schemes were often difficult to prove.

BlackWing X, during this operation, would bear Raptor II's name and ID numbers. Devarr, King of Cloudsong, would know little about us, except that the ship was provided by Teeg San Gerxon, since Cloudsong's space station was still under construction and had little in the way of security to protect the King.

Devarr would also be accompanied by Captain Lenk of the Palace Guard and Hulce, his Chief of Sciences, who was also Devarr's husband.

Six other worlds would be escorted early by BlackWing ships in disguise, while the remaining five ships would haunt the shipping lanes as usual. I'd heard from Dori, Captain of VII earlier—she'd been assigned to escort Revalus' contingent.

Travis and I'd discussed the new orientation meetings—we'd decided that there was also another reason for bringing in the new worlds early—they could become targets for the Prophet and his army.

That threat hung over both Alliances' security details, like the blackest of clouds concealing a tornado of terrible force. We merely waited for it to hit us. Until then, we wouldn't be able to gauge its strength or the extent of its destruction.

"We have visitors," Travis poked his head inside the Captain's cubby door. A wide grin accompanied that announcement. "They're in the galley, waiting for you."

"Tell them the Captain is on his way," I grinned back. I'd be more than happy to see Randl, and I'd read Vik Roth's dossier. He'd be a welcome addition to the crew, I think.

~

BlackWing X

Randl

Vik turned to look about him—I'd transported us to the galley, as it was one of the few places aboard ship that could hold all the crew at once.

I figured Trent, who was acting Captain for the day, and Travis, his brother and co-Captain, would want most of the crew to gather and meet the new member together.

As Kooper said, Vik was tall, strong and capable.

I wasn't sure Kooper knew everything there was to know about him, though. Zaria would expect me to keep those secrets, and I would.

Travis and Trent arrived first, grinning as they strode into the galley. I was engulfed in one hug after another, with plenty of back-slapping in between.

They went to Vik, next, offering handshakes and introductions. Then, the rest of the crew began to arrive; David, first, followed by Terrett, Jayna, Bekzi, Susan, James, Nathan and—finally—Sabrina.

I won't say my heart didn't flutter slightly because it did, but at least the sight of her didn't send me into immediate depression.

"We're overdue for a few beers," David declared after pretend-punching me in the gut.

"I hear that," I agreed as the others surrounded us. Travis and Trent let us do informal greetings and introductions for several minutes before asking everyone to take a seat in the galley. We were about to be advised of Kooper's plans for BlackWing X.

~

"Cloudsong," Jayna sighed as Vik and I followed her to our assigned cabins. I thought about asking her how she and Wyatt were doing, but I already knew Wyatt wanted to ask her to marry him—after the Conclave mess was over.

I didn't want to tip my hand by broaching the subject—this should remain a surprise for her, until the proper time came.

"Have you been before?" Vik asked. "To Cloudsong, I mean."

"No, but I've read the information. Have you been?"

"Once or twice, before and after it was populated by the displaced peoples from Carek Prime."

"They're lucky they had someone powerful on their side," Jayna huffed. "They'd be dead without that help."

I had a very good guess as to who'd provided that help, but didn't voice it aloud. "How long will we be in transit?" I asked instead.

"It takes four days to reach Cloudsong from our current location. Trent plans to get under way in two hours."

"Gives me enough time to unpack," Vik said.

"I was thinking the same," I agreed. "After that, I hope I can get tea in the galley and watch stars flash past."

"I'm amazed by the gift you carry," Vik said. "Kooper says it allows you to see everything."

"It does."

"Heard you were a good hire," Vik grinned as Jayna stopped in front of his cabin first.

"Remains to be seen," I grinned back.

"See you in the galley in a few." Vik walked inside his cabin, the duffle he carried scraping the side of the door as he passed through it.

"Yours is the same as last time," Jayna said as she and I continued our journey. "Randl," she added, "I can't tell you how happy I am that you're not dead."

~

"We have you set up to train with Bekzi again, starting tomorrow," Travis said. He held a mug of Falchani black in his hands as he and I sat at a galley table. We'd just gotten underway to Cloudsong, and I'd gotten my mug of tea from Susan, who'd been happy to hand it to me.

"That's fine," I said. "Although I have a special request."

"What's that?"

"I'd like to get some blade practice in two or three times a week, with either you or Trent, it doesn't matter."

Travis went silent for a moment, as he absently tapped the side of his mug with a finger.

"You've been gone for a while, haven't you?" He lifted dark, unrevealing eyes to mine.

"Yes. I can tell you and Trent where and how long, but nobody else —if you want to know."

"I think I know where, just from your question," he said. "Keep the information to yourself. I think it's important that you do so."

"As do I."

"Someday, I may ask who gave you blade training," he added.

"And I may tell you," I said before lifting my mug to sip tea. I'd gotten used to Falchani black, but still preferred other kinds of tea—if they were available.

"Mind if I join you?" Vik walked in.

"Sit," Travis nodded toward an empty chair.

"Thanks." Vik folded his long frame into a galley chair and scooted it toward the table. Susan appeared as if called to ask him what he wanted.

"I'll have what Randl's having," Vik said right away.

"Having a meeting and didn't invite me?" David walked in. Susan waved at him—she knew he wanted coffee.

"You like meetings?" Vik asked.

"No. I just don't like being left out. And I like coffee."

"So you'll suffer through a meeting, rather than be left out of it?"

"Especially if there are pastries and coffee," David said. "The good kind, not that cheap shit."

"I hear that," Vik agreed.

"What do you have planned when you finish your tea?" Travis asked me.

"I have plenty of research to keep me busy," I said. "I have a report for you on Vrak, too. I visited him recently in his dungeon, and learned a few things. I'll probably get more information from Quin regarding him, too, and I'll add my assessment to her findings."

"Meet Trent and me in the Captain's cubby before dinner, then," Travis said. "I'll be spending my afternoon there, writing reports and doing grunt work."

With that, Travis rose, saluted us with his mug and walked out of the galley.

"I have a few things to do, too," David said. "The engine is scheduled for a routine check. You know where to find me if you need anything." He followed Travis out of the room.

"Your little brothers grew up just fine," I told Vik, who almost spit tea across the table.

~

Vik

I needed an ally. I found him under the most unusual circumstances. I'd already attempted to contact Zaria, who miraculously replied to my mindspeech.

You can trust Randl with your life, she'd informed me, but no further information was given.

Who the hell was Randl Gage, that Zaria trusted him like that? Most people who were born blind had electronic eyes, which enabled them to see almost as well as a sighted person.

This man saw everything anyway, including what was hidden behind the best of masks. As a test, I sent mindspeech to Randl.

May I join you in your training session with Bekzi tomorrow?

Even Bekzi wouldn't recognize me; that's how good the disguise was. Randl had seen past it immediately.

Absolutely, came the reply. *Any time you want. I figure David and I will have a few beers before bedtime tonight. If you'd like to join us, you'd be welcome.*

Yeah. I'd like that, I agreed.

My cabin at twenty-three bells, then.

Thanks.

~

Gungl, Vogeffa II

V'dar

I'd been plotting revenge for nearly a year, and the taking of ASD ships should have occurred without difficulty. The crew should be under my command, too.

Instead, I'd lost more than thirty of my own, when the decoy ships were boarded by the crew I'd sent to Bornelus.

As if someone—well, I knew who it was. It could only be the one who'd faced me on Pyrik, after all. He'd taken information from me— what little I hadn't bothered to hide, anyway.

I'd announced myself when I removed the soil from Bornelus. As I'd heard or seen nothing of him in the past ten months, I was cautiously hopeful he was dead or debilitated.

Neither of those things proved true.

Perhaps he hoped I'd be angry enough to act rashly in return.

Yes, I was more than angry enough. As for acting rashly, that was not my plan. There were other ways to get what I wanted. "Varok, attend me," I shouted.

"I am here, Prophet," he said quickly.

"Good. We have plans to make. Do research now. I wish to contact Adarr Gramm, Rale Linn and Jewl Yarro."

"The Big Three?" He called them by the name these criminal masterminds had gained for themselves. Word had it they collaborated at times and shared in the spoils of this illegal act or that plotted murder.

"Yes. Should we find them, we find everything we want and more to make our plans work. They have ships and wealth. We'll take what they have, and they will obey me or die."

"I will begin the search immediately," Varok dipped his head to me and left the room.

~

Captain's Cubby, BlackWing X
Randl

"Randl, this is Captain Dori Anderson of BlackWing VII," Travis introduced the woman to me. "Her ship is the one that reported the soil taken from Bornelus."

Short, curly blonde hair framed a lovely face. Behind sky-blue eyes lay a will of iron and a determination that many aspire to and would never attain.

"Captain Anderson," I dipped my head to her in respect.

"I've heard a lot about you," she said. "Travis says you were the one who told Kooper that Bornelus was a trap, and to have our ships reverse course. Thank you for that."

"You're welcome," I said.

"Sit," Travis said. "Trent will be here in a minute."

"Your eyes," Dori began.

"Bother me not at all," I said. "I don't use them to see anyway."

"That's really unusual—and amazing."

"I'm used to it."

She laughed. I liked the sound of it. I'd already seen many things about her, and an interesting fact had surfaced; she knew Salidar.

Not only did she know him, she'd gone to school with him, and he'd been her first crush—until they'd had a falling out.

Since then, she hadn't gotten serious about any man. Her focus was on her ship and crew, now. I admired that about her.

Salidar, I sent, *I met Dorilou Anderson.*

She has claws, he returned.

I've seen that already. I didn't hide the amusement in my voice.

"Did I miss anything?" Trent spared a grin for all of us as he swept inside the Captain's cubby.

"Waiting on you, bro," Travis said. "Randl is about to tell us what he found on Vrak."

"What has our prisoner been up to?" Trent settled in a chair and waited expectantly for me to explain.

"I went to see him, disguised as the Prophet," I said. "The first thing he did was ask about his children."

"That's not frightening," Trent sighed, sarcasm evident in his words.

"Quin and I have looked at the images of the real Vrak—when he was young," I said.

"This is another Phorde Gaster?"

"Funny, that's exactly what Kooper said," I acknowledged. "Somehow, these people are made exact replicas of other people. Kooper and your mother suspect that the Lyristolyi drug may be involved somehow, but my research on that isn't complete, yet."

"That would explain the cloning effect—right down to DNA and fingerprints," Travis agreed. "That filth is an abomination, and we hoped it was gone when Vardil Cayetes was killed."

"Maybe not," I shrugged. "But remember, if the drug is involved, then Phorde and Vrak were given that substance years in the past, before Vardil's death."

"That's true," Travis turned to his brother. Mindspeech was exchanged between them—I didn't listen in.

"We've had a really hard time with this sort of thing in the past," Dori covered the brothers' mindspeech by speaking aloud.

"I understand that," I agreed. "Don't worry—they're not upsetting me," I leaned my head in the twins' direction.

"Sometimes they get so wrapped up in their own world they forget other people are in the room," Dori raised her voice.

"Huh? Did you say something?" Travis turned to Dori with a grin.

"Jerk," Dori teased him.

"When do you think you'll have research done on the drug?" Trent asked me.

"I have a lot to get through—from Kooper and your mother, so in three or four days," I said.

"About the time we reach Cloudsong," Travis said. "I'd like a full report at that time, barring unforeseen difficulties."

"I should have it ready for you."

"Will you copy me?" Dori asked Travis.

"Sure. Kooper probably wants all the BlackWings to have it, but I'll double check with him."

"Want to stay for dinner? It's pot roast night," Trent asked.

"Pot roast? Absolutely," Dori agreed.

"So then, the pirate captain complained that we bruised his wrist when we cuffed him, and tried to file legal action against us," Dori said. "We caught him transporting a kidnap victim, and all he has to say is his wrist is bruised."

"Did the suit go forward?" Travis grinned.

"Are you kidding? The kidnapped victim was a minor royal from Moor'Kin. His family pointed to the bruises and cuts on the victim. If the original suit was accepted, the subsequent suit would have to be accepted, too. The captain withdrew his complaint. He was facing enough jail time as it was, without adding a civil complaint to the rest of his charges."

"Attempting to draw attention away from his own guilt," I said with a smile. "People with a weak character do that a lot."

"It would have been different if we'd actually harmed him—the laws protect prisoners taken in space. The physician said the bruise likely came from an attempt to escape the cuffs, because they're padded enough to protect the skin under normal circumstances."

"Now that's funny," Trent grinned and pointed his fork at Dori. "He wanted to file charges for an injury he caused himself."

"You think that's funny? You should hear the one about the crow shapeshifter," Dori laughed.

"How did that turn out?" Travis' eyes gleamed in anticipation.

"Oh, we had to write a full report on the ocelot that escaped and grabbed the crow with her claws, with only minor injury to the crow, I might add."

"What did said crow do?" David set his beer on the table. It appeared he loved good stories.

"Oh, he liked shiny things, like most crows," Dori said. "He had a cargo hold full of jewelry and valuable ancient coins to line other peoples' nests."

"Where did the ocelot come from?" Sabrina asked.

"There," Travis and Trent pointed at Dori, who laughed again.

Sabrina

I'd gotten the idea that Captain Anderson had claws—I just hadn't imagined the physical kind. I reminded myself to get better at identifying shapeshifters; it appeared there were plenty of them sprinkled throughout the BlackWing fleet.

"You should meet Amos Thompson, he captains BlackWing I," Travis told me. He'd read my expression easily concerning shapeshifters. "Amos is a white buffalo, and his wife, Flossie, is a swan."

"Flossie's a damn good cook," David said.

"As are Bekzi and Susan," Dori countered.

"That goes without saying," David grinned.

"Then we're all on the same page."

"How will we fit? Must be a damn big page."

"Are we having an argument?" Dori asked. "You're an owl, remember? Ocelot here," she added, tapping her chest.

"Are you saying ocelots are better than owls?"

"Shapeshifter logic, here we come," Trent hid a smile.

"As if we could all be dragons," Randl intervened.

"Are you dissing dragons?" Travis tossed his napkin on the table in mock fury and glared at Randl.

"This is your Captain speaking," Trent stood and held up both hands in surrender. The entire table of diners dissolved into laughter.

CHAPTER 4

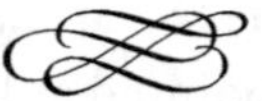

*R*andl

"Good beer," Vik said, wiping sweat off the label of his Refizani Blue.

"I've had plenty of it while doofus here was missing," David pointed his bottle toward me.

"I've had a few, too," I admitted. "Whenever possible. Thanks for calling me doofus, man."

"Insults are a free service I provide," David grinned.

"Can't argue with free." I raised my bottle to him and drank.

"You need a better desk chair," Vik slapped the arms of my chair.

"Look, tall dude, it fits him. I don't fit in it either—not really." David, who sat at the end of my bed while I leaned against both pillows at the top, made a face at Vik, whose lanky frame looked ready to spill out of the chair that wasn't suited to his height.

"We're like a bad set of bookends," Vik grinned at David.

"Right on, man," David clinked his beer bottle against Vik's.

"I need to turn in, soon," I said. "Bekzi won't appreciate a hungover trainee."

"Back to that, huh?" David asked.

"I'm joining him," Vik said. "To brush up, you understand."

"Well, hell, why don't I come too—to keep you in line?" David lifted an eyebrow at Vik.

"Sure. Bekz won't mind."

"Bekz is awesome," David agreed before emptying his bottle. "Get your beauty rest, Goldilocks," he told me and slid off the bed. "Papa owl needs sleep."

BlackWing VII

Captain Dori Anderson

"It's drifting," Phillip, my second-in-command informed me. He'd taken the conn when I retired to my cabin, and I'd gotten roughly three hours' sleep before he sent mindspeech, asking me to come to the bridge.

A freighter, with no signs of life aboard, had been left to drift in the shipping lane. No identification was on the hull; Phillip had already checked for that. Its erratic movement could spell trouble to smaller vessels barreling through who weren't looking for such anomalies.

"I've already sent images with the notification to headquarters," Phillip said. "They have no record of a missing ship, or anything that resembles this one."

"Did they have instructions for us?"

"Approach with caution," Phillip replied.

"The standard answer from the night crew at headquarters," I huffed. "This doesn't make sense to me," I added. "It shouldn't make sense to the eggheads at headquarters, either."

Phillip snorted a laugh at my description.

"Bring us closer—slowly," I ordered our helmsman.

"Yes, Captain."

BlackWing X

Randl
First, I realized I was dreaming.
This dream reflected reality, and that concept almost occurred too late.

~

BlackWing VII
Captain Dori Anderson
We'd covered roughly half the distance between us and the ship when it exploded. Our shields were up, but they were no match for this.

A part of me understood that the ship—and our bodies—were flying apart.

Until they weren't.

I heard Phillip's shout as our bodies were stretched to the limit and pulled away with the rest of the crew while VII continued to explode behind us.

~

BlackWing X
Travis
"What happened?" I knelt beside Dori's chair in the galley, where she and all her crew sat in stunned silence. Her hands shook slightly—some of the others were having quiet meltdowns. The rest of my crew were doing their best to console and care for our new passengers.

Randl, his back toward us and dressed only in sleep pants, stood at the galley windows, gazing at the stars we flew past. Tattooed on his back was a strange image. A large, quarter moon cradled a sun within its center void, and within the sun lay an Udjat—the eye of Horus.

The Udjat was a symbol from Ancient Egypt—on Earth, far in the past. How had he come to get it, and why?

That question had to wait. I placed a hand on Dori's shoulder to steady her. "We found an abandoned freighter in the shipping lanes,"

Dori worked to keep a quaver from her voice. "We sent the information to headquarters, since we found no evidence of lifeforms aboard. They told us to approach cautiously to investigate, because they had no record of a missing ship like that one. We got halfway to it when it exploded. Tore right through our shields. Should have killed us all."

"Here. Drink." Bekzi arrived with a cup of calming tea with plenty of whiskey laced in.

"I can call for a physician," I offered.

"No, we're just shook up—and without a ship," she whispered.

"I give others same," Bekzi said and walked away to get more tea and whiskey.

Randl

"Hey, bro," Trent approached me carefully.

"Captain Trent," I acknowledged with a slight nod.

"Want to talk about this?"

"I barely got them away," I stated flatly.

"I don't think that's the problem," he said. "You got them away. That's what matters. I'm still wondering how you did that. Some of them say they thought they were dying at first, until they found themselves here and whole."

"I don't want to talk about it," I replied. "Not that part, anyway."

"All right. What can you tell me?"

"This has turned into a game of Irzu," I said. "The Prophet made the first move. We countered. This is his second move. He thinks he scored a hit with this one, because there's space debris of VII and the abandoned ship all over that shipping lane, now."

"How would he know to target VII?" Trent asked.

"Look at it this way—there have been three BlackWing ships in orbit around Bornelus from time to time. X, VII and XII."

"And now he's targeting all three." Travis' words reminded me of cold steel. "I need to alert Kooper," he turned to go.

"I've already sent a message. For now, the Prophet can't find us, because Terrett is aboard. There are no Sirenali aboard XII, and none were aboard VII."

"Not good," Trent cursed under his breath for a moment. "I'll see if I can't change that." He folded away instead of walking.

~

Travis

Kooper's on his way, Trent sent mindspeech.

Let me know when he's here, I replied.

Bring Randl and Dori with you, he added.

Will do.

"Thank you for saving us," Dori said before drinking the last of her whiskey-laden tea.

"Don't thank me. That was Randl."

"Huh?" her head jerked up immediately.

"He's more talented than most people think," I admitted. "Come on. Kooper's on his way and he wants a meeting."

"I feel cold," Dori said as she stood to follow me.

"Here." I *Pulled* in a blanket for her. "Wrap up in that, and if you need something warmer, just say so."

"It's just shock," she mumbled and followed me out of the galley. I sent mindspeech to Randl, who folded space instead of walking.

~

"What the hell happened?" Kooper demanded the second we walked into the Captain's cubby.

He was pacing and frowning at Randl, who stood against a wall with arms crossed over his chest.

"The Prophet, who wanted to treat us with our own medicine," Randl replied calmly. "He's seen X, VII and XII in orbit around Bornelus in the past. He's hunting those three ships."

"He sure as hell hit VII," Kooper fumed.

"The crew are all alive," Randl said. "It was the best I could do with the time I had."

"I'm sorry," Kooper continued pacing, but now his forehead wrinkled in frustration. "We lost a valuable ship to that lunatic."

"I know that. For now, he thinks you lost its crew as well."

"I've already sent BlackWing I toward Revalus, to take VII's place," Kooper growled.

"I think you should send a ship to Pyrik, too."

"What?" Kooper jerked his head to stare at Randl.

"He may have a beef, as some people say, with them as well."

"Fucking hells," Kooper sighed. "Captain Anderson, you're welcome to go on shore leave with your crew until a replacement ship is commissioned," Kooper told Dori.

"With your permission, I'd like to stay aboard X," she said. "The others need time to recuperate. I want to get this bastard."

"Captains?" Kooper asked Travis and Trent.

"She'd be a welcome addition," Travis agreed. "An extra hand is always appreciated."

"Good enough. Anderson, I'll keep you posted on the status of your next ship."

"Thank you, Director Griff."

"Randl, keep me advised," Kooper said and folded space.

"That went well," Randl mumbled. Trent barked a laugh.

Randl

"I'm sorry about your ship," I said.

"Me, too," Dori sighed as she and I followed Jayna toward Dori's assigned cabin.

"I'll see you at breakfast?" I asked before turning down my passage.

"Maybe. Trent gave us permission to sleep late, so I may do that, and then send messages before heading for the galley."

"Good enough. Good-night," I said and walked away from her and Jayna.

I'd had a second—maybe two—to make the decision to take the crew and leave the ship, to distract the Prophet.

Let him believe he'd gotten his revenge for soldiers killed—at least for now. Kooper was already working to get Sirenali aboard XII, and reassigned I to Revalus. I hoped he'd warn them to keep a watch for unusual activity around that planet.

Randl?

Quin's mental voice reached me.

Hey, Quin, I replied.

I heard there was some excitement, she said.

Yeah. A real mess.

Everybody all right?

Everybody's fine. How did you find out?

Terrett.

Ah. Your Sirenali mate. He's keeping us safe, you know that?

He's good at it.

And I'm grateful.

I think BlackWing VII should be grateful to you.

I don't need thanks. I need my hands around the Prophet's throat.

A lot of people feel the same way.

No doubt.

Are you going to bed now?

Yes.

Pleasant dreams.

Any dreams would be more pleasant than the last one I had, but thank you.

You're welcome.

~

"Where'd you get the tattoo?"

Travis set his plate on the table I occupied. Breakfast was hash, eggs and toast, one of my favorite meals. I'd almost finished my food when Travis joined me.

"It was a gift—from the Eagle Warlord. That's a secret, by the way."

"Back tattoos denote extreme bravery, or services rendered to the Warlord that none other could accomplish," Travis said and cut into his eggs.

"It's the latter, I assure you."

"I'm impressed with the workmanship."

"Thank you. It isn't dragons, though. Any girl will be more impressed by dragons."

"Who's more impressed by dragons?"

Sabrina set her plate down next to Travis, while Dori, who walked behind Sabrina, was forced to take the chair next to mine.

"Everybody," I said.

"He's dissing his tattoo, when it was earned," Travis said.

"Where is it?" Sabrina asked.

"It's a full back tattoo," Travis told her. "Someday, Trent and I will explain what you have to do to earn one of those."

"What *did* you do to earn it?" Dori asked before biting a corner off a piece of toast.

"I delivered pizzas on time," I said. She'd get the reference; like Sal, she was from Old Earth. Sabrina sighed because she had no point of context for my words.

Dori ducked her head to hide a smile.

"You deserve an arm tattoo for last night, at the very least," Travis pointed his fork in my direction.

"Nah, that's all right. I think one is enough," I replied. "Where did they take your crew?" I asked Dori, hoping to change the subject.

"Le-Ath Veronis. Kooper has housing reserved on both hemispheres for emergency situations. Phillip supervises them for now."

"Anything new on the Prophet after last night?" Travis asked.

"I've not gotten anything. He's probably gloating, because he views the attack as a complete success," I said. "Let's hope he continues to think that, and that Kooper finds Sirenali to round out Captain Anderson's crew and the crew of XII."

"That has been arranged," Terrett pulled an extra chair to the table to sit at the end.

"If you helped with that, I'm grateful," Dori nodded to him.

"You are welcome. There are others who will be more than happy to join ships' crews, to keep them safe. They are very determined in this matter."

"Where will the Prophet go from here?" Dori asked.

"No idea. I have plenty of research to do. I'm not convinced that the logging industries didn't have something to do with this, even with no other evidence found to the contrary. Something is going on, there, and I want to know what it is."

"The ASD did a thorough investigation," Sabrina pointed out.

"Like the thorough investigation of Bornelus before the giant worms attacked us? I'm sorry, that didn't come out the way I meant it," I apologized.

"With the Prophet involved, we could miss a lot and not realize it," Travis agreed. "Randl, let me know if you find anything that warrants further investigation."

"I will."

I really am sorry, I sent to Sabrina.

"I know," she mumbled aloud.

We'll talk later, I said. She and I—we needed to clear the air between us, as Sal would say.

She had no interest in me; I understood that. During my absence, David revealed to her the secret I'd carried a year ago—that I'd cared for her. She didn't want to say how she really felt now, because she didn't want to hurt me.

That was and wasn't a good thing. It was time for both of us to move forward—with the proper understanding, of course.

We could be friends—that's what she wanted, anyway. Perhaps it would be easier to go on with my life if we weren't working together, but that felt like the coward's way out. I'd deal with this and get past the tiny ache that remained in my heart.

"Randl, Trent's calling us to the bridge," Travis pulled me away from my thoughts.

"All right." I stood when he did and followed him out of the galley.

"Tell me what you see." Trent placed a comp-vid in my hands.

"Shella Karp," I began. "She's ah, got a growing obsession," I breathed as I studied her image closely. "I need to see her in person," I added.

"Where is she?" Travis asked. He peered over my shoulder so he could see Shella's image better.

"In the group coming from Pyrik," Trent said. "I just got this from Kooper, who says it came from Quin. Kooper says she's the new President's assistant in charge of scheduling and events."

"What does Kooper want to do about this?" I lifted my eyes to Trent's.

"He says he wants to keep her under observation. Therefore, Kell and Opal will be aboard the ship carrying the contingent from Pyrik."

"Do you think she could explode like some of the others?" Travis asked.

"No idea. Quin gave Kooper what she had; Randl needs to see her, too, and Kooper figures nothing will happen until she gets to Campiaa anyway."

"So the first of the Prophet's soldiers makes her presence known," Travis sighed.

"Or it could be another trap—a distraction, this time," Trent pointed out.

"I'll add her to the list of things I need to research," I said. "Will you ask Kooper to forward all her records, from birth until now?"

"Sure thing," Trent said. "We're still on course to reach Cloudsong in three days. That gives you time to investigate her thoroughly."

"Yeah." I handed the comp-vid back to Trent.

Dori

I was writing my report on the destruction of BlackWing VII and the rescue of the crew when someone knocked on my cabin door.

I was surprised to find Sabrina on the other side.

"What can I do for you?" I asked after inviting her in.

"I need some advice," she said.

"What advice would that be?"

"Well, I wanted to come to you, because you're a Captain and a woman," she said.

"I may or may not be able to help until I hear the question," I responded.

"How do you—tell someone that you like them, but don't love them—at least romantically."

"That's a good question," I said. "I've found honesty usually works best."

"But what if that hurts their feelings?"

"Then be nice about it. There are some assholes out there who can fly off the handle when they're rejected, but normal people generally don't react that way."

"That's not helping," she mumbled. "I thought it wasn't a problem, since he'd disappeared and was presumed dead. Now he's back and says he wants to talk."

"You're referring to Randl."

"Yes."

"The way I understand things, he knows exactly how you feel about him. You won't be revealing any secrets to that man when you tell him you don't want a romantic relationship. At least he's willing to talk to you—if he fell into the asshole category, he'd be vindictive and insult you every chance he got. If I were you, I'd hear him out first. Then, if you still need advice, come see me."

"That makes me feel awful," she admitted.

"That's what happens in situations like these. Everybody feels awful—at least for a while. Work this out and get past it. That's my temporary advice."

"I really liked it when we were friends," Sabrina sighed. "I could take my troubles to him and he'd make me feel better every time."

"Then don't use him as a crutch unless he offers," I said. "It isn't fair to him, you know."

"I know."

She walked out of my cabin without another word, her shoulders sagging as if I'd delivered the worst news in the world to her.

She might be a genius, but she still had growing up to do.

Randl

"Can we talk now?" Sabrina waited outside my cabin when I reached it.

"If that's what you want," I said, although that was mostly a lie.

I left the cabin door open and walked inside; she followed me and took my desk chair while I settled on my bed.

"Tell me what you see when you look at me," she said.

"That eerily reminds me of my previous boss," I said.

"No—I didn't mean it that way. You can see that I don't have romantic feelings for you—can't you?"

"Yes. I've come to the realization that it can't and won't be. I'm all right with that. Mostly."

"I wish we could go back to the way things were after we first met, but I've been told recently that it wouldn't be fair to you to ask for or expect that."

"I'm coming to terms with all this, but it will take time," I said. "Someday, maybe we'll be like that again. I'll do my best in the meantime, if it will make things easier for you."

"That gets me off the hook completely, as Travis would say." She sighed and stared at her hands, which were folded in her lap.

"This was one-sided from the start, so there's no reason for you to bear this burden," I said. "You never offered more than you were willing to give. I wanted to take it further, but it just wasn't happening for you. I can understand that."

"You know who I love," she said, her voice husky with emotion. "I hope this doesn't interfere with that friendship."

"It won't. That's separate. Travis, Trent and I get along very well, and I appreciate their willingness to work with me."

"Randl, anyone would be privileged and honored to work with you. You've done so much, while I feel useless most of the time."

"Don't feel that way. I still have the pistol you made for me," I forced a smile. "Never had to use it, thank goodness, so it's still good."

"Can you tell me where you were?"

"No. Not now, anyway."

"You've changed a lot. You got a tattoo. You look—stronger, I guess."

"Let's hope I'm strong enough to face the Prophet next time," I said. "Because he's waiting—looking for me. If he discovers who or where I am, things could go very wrong in a hurry."

"Yeah. So we're all right then?" She blinked at me.

"Yes. We're all right. We can even sit at the same table and joke and tease and drink beer," I agreed.

"That sounds good. Well, I have designs waiting, and they won't create themselves," she said and rose from her chair. "Thank you, Randl. We missed you, you know."

"I know."

She closed my cabin door behind her, the latch making a soft, snicking noise as it engaged with the jamb. I released a shaky breath.

Thank you, I sent to Captain Anderson.

For what? she replied.

For giving good advice to Sabrina, I returned. *Things worked out well enough, I think.*

Then you're welcome. Any time.

❧

Queen's Palace, Le-Ath Veronis
Winkler

"You have Randl working on this now?" I handed Kooper's comp-vid back to him.

"Yes. For now, we'll let her travel to Campiaa with President Lebbon. Quin has already reviewed him and the rest of his party—

they're unaffected for now. Shella will be watched carefully, and that's where you can help."

"Because this is Harifa Edus' first Joint Conclave," I said. "You want me to go with Lukas, like before."

"That's right. I'm considering who to send with Amlis, now that he's back on the sanity wagon."

"Halimel may be available," I suggested.

"That's a good idea. Perhaps one other, since Amlis and Rodrik are in uncharted waters, here?"

"Then approach Aurelius. He has more experience with politics than anybody else I can think of."

"I can see that," Kooper considered my choice. "Both those vampires have leadership experience. I'll ask them. I'll also ask them to help keep an eye on Ms. Karp, while she's hobnobbing with other assistants and their planetary leaders. We don't need a spreading infection this time, but we sure as hell want her to lead us to her boss, and I'm not talking about President Lebbon."

"I got that the second you opened your mouth," I observed.

"See, I knew you'd be helpful from the beginning."

"Well, you scheming old bastard, why don't you go conscript two vampires, then?" I laughed. "At least I offered tea instead of coffee. See what you get from them."

"I hate that blood substitute shit," Kooper rose and grinned at me. "Thanks for the tea."

BlackWing X

Randl

Shella Karp was still Shella Karp—the original and not a substitute. Somewhere, somehow, she'd encountered the Prophet or one of his minions. The Prophet still had his hands on Pyrik; that much was evident.

I pulled up the CSD report on the progress made in Lee'Qee, the site of a nuclear accident long in the past, which had been taken over by the Prophet's army—or a good portion of it, anyway.

Stores of packaged food had been found in underground rooms and passages—most of it traced back to pirated goods from ships attacked by small-time pirating factions.

Both the ASD and CSD were paying more attention to those small-time attacks. The BlackWing fleet was stretched to the limit as a result, and I understood Kooper's anger at losing VII much better, now.

Lee'Qee was slowly being demolished by construction bots. The few humanoids involved in the operation wore suits appropriate for blocking radiation.

Across Pyrik, too, some had fallen ill from the leaking radiation caused when the shields fell around Lee'Qee. As if the planet hadn't suffered enough already from heavy fines levied and the cost of cleanup.

It made me wonder if Pyrik would remain in the Campiaan Alliance. It would be cheaper to cut its losses and drop out, although the population would suffer greatly from such an act.

Alliance-mandated health care would likely be eliminated with no replacement provided, and those already suffering from radiation poisoning would die unless they could afford the expense of hospitalization.

"What a fucked-up mess," I mumbled before getting back to the records on Shella Karp. Kooper had even provided her spending records, and those showed she'd taken a vacation shortly after the cancellation of the previously scheduled Joint Alliances Conclave.

She'd been hired as one of Lebbon's new assistants when she returned from her time off.

I looked for images before and after that happened, and found several. At the beginning of her vacation in the mountains outside the small city of Ba'Moru, she didn't have the obsession.

In the image taken on her last day of vacation, she had the beginnings of obsession. Somehow, she'd been approached by the

Prophet or his minions during her time off, and they'd probably researched the applicants for Lebbon's assistants before targeting her.

Kooper, I sent, *we need a list of all the people who applied for positions on Lebbon's staff, before he gave the job to Shella Karp.*

I can get that for you. Do you want a copy sent to Quin?

Yes, please.

I'll get someone on it right away.

Thank you.

Setting Shella Karp's records aside for a moment, I turned to Vrak Falken. First up were two images—that of a young Vrak Falken at eight years of age, and a more current image.

Two different people, as suspected. How had the Prophet selected him for replacement, and what had happened to the original?

I couldn't see his death in the boy's image—that meant the original Vrak could be alive somewhere. Kooper had already done an image search in both Alliances, and no true match had been found.

The real Vrak could look much different, now, thanks to the Prophet's manipulation. How many others had been killed or changed in some way, to suit the Prophet's machinations? Did the Prophet take the original Vrak and place him in his army? If so, how and why?

I was back to one of my original questions—*what did he want from all this, and why did he want it?*

Time to examine the coin from Vogeffa II.

Pulling it from the drawer of my tiny, bedside table, I flipped it in my fingers a few times before settling back on my bed and closing my eyes. My fingers tightened about the gold disc as I searched for images in its past.

The first image made my body jerk—a woman lay on a bed, her back turned toward me. The coin flipped through the air and landed on the bed beside her as the shadow at her back turned away.

It took a moment for me to realize she was weeping.

CHAPTER 5

lackWing X
Travis

"What else did you learn?" I asked Randl during dinner. He'd already told me as much as he could from his research on Vrak Falken and Shella Karp.

"I learned that the coin from Vogeffa II was once used to pay for sex." That upset him in some way. He didn't explain why.

"Was there anything else?"

"I haven't gone past that point, yet. This will take time, I'm afraid."

"Did you contact Kooper with your findings?"

"On everything except the coin. I didn't think he'd be interested in what I've found so far."

"True."

"He's sending more information on the applicants for the job Shella got with President Lebbon. She had to get her obsession somehow, and I'm attempting to see whether they reached the other candidates, too."

"How did they get to her?" I asked. "In your opinion?"

"They had to approach her while she was on vacation—the image I saw of her when she first arrived showed no obsession. Just a day or two before she left, she had the beginnings of it."

"Is there a way to retrace her steps? To determine a location?" Dori asked. She, Terrett, David and Sabrina sat with us at the same table, and they'd listened while Randl spoke about his research.

"I don't know. I think several days were spent hiking up the mountain, which is covered in forest for the most part," Randl shrugged. "That would be a strange place for the Prophet or one of his soldiers to approach, mostly because she hiked with her fiancé and a group of other people. It was a guided tour, as I understand it."

"Does it list the tour guide's name?" Dori asked.

"I can get that, I think."

"Good. I think I'd like to visit Ba'Moru and sniff around."

"You have permission to go, as long as you're back before we reach Cloudsong," I said. "I'll advise Kooper, if that's your plan."

"Randl?" Dori turned toward him.

"I was thinking of going on my own," he confessed. "If you want to go, then we'll go."

"We'll go," Dori turned back to me. "We'll figure out who the hiking guide was and talk to him."

"I only need to see him," Randl pointed out.

"Then we'll see him," Dori grinned.

Ba'Moru, Pyrik

Randl

"A friend recommended him as a guide," Dori told the hotel desk clerk. Before leaving BlackWing, I'd found the name of Shella's hiking guide. Caille Morr had served as a trail guide for more than five years, and was regularly requested by vacationers.

"I think he's taking a group up the mountain tomorrow," the clerk replied. "They meet outside the Greenever Lodge before heading toward the mountain."

"That sounds great," Dori said. "We'll meet him then, and ask about a reservation for his next hike."

"So, one room?" the clerk asked.

"Sure," Dori agreed. We'd brought clothing for an overnight stay, although I hadn't counted on rooming together. Dori was playing the couple card to its maximum effectiveness, however.

It didn't matter—all I needed was a blanket and a floor to sleep on.

"Here's the door code," the desk clerk handed Dori a comp-vid chip. "You have a nice view of Greenever Mountain outside your window."

"Thank you," Dori offered a smile before turning toward me.

As the dutiful boyfriend, I lifted both our bags and followed Dori toward the trans-vator.

"You can have the bed," she said the moment the door shut behind us. "My ocelot can sleep on the sofa."

"That doesn't sound fair," I protested. "I can sleep on the floor."

"I'm the Captain in charge, here," she said. "You take the bed. My ocelot will be happy on the sofa."

"Then it'll be that way," I agreed. "Where do you want your bag?"

"In the bathroom. I think we're dressed well enough to find dinner and a drink somewhere. You can scope out the locals and have a meal at the same time."

"That sounds fine," I agreed. "I was planning to go out and see things for myself anyway."

"And I'm going out with you, in case I need to reel you in."

"I usually don't need reeling in."

"You know—I could see that early on," she agreed. "But you can never tell for sure about these things."

"Whatever you say, Captain Anderson." I rubbed the back of my neck with a hand while attempting to deal with my current situation. She barely knew me, and had little to go on regarding my reliability and reluctance to be anything other than invisible most of the time.

"Come on, then. I'm hungry."

I followed her from the room.

~

The Greenever Resort was Dori's choice of places to eat. There was a large restaurant and a smaller pub that sold sandwiches and lighter fare. She chose the pub as it was full, while the restaurant only held a few diners.

She picked a table near the bar, in a location where we could survey the room without being obvious about it. "I'll have the Mergis white," she ordered wine for herself. I ordered my usual beer.

Our waiter could have been a standard-hire for any pub, with a white cloth tied at his waist and a comp-vid in his pocket. I focused on the pub's patrons once he walked away to fill our order.

What I found was troubling.

Captain Anderson, I sent, *there are seven people in this crowd with growing obsessions.*

Are you sure? And call me Dori, she replied.

I'm sure, Dori.

Can you get anything from them?

I'm linking with Travis and Kooper right now, to transmit images. These can barely recall their names and what they should be doing.

That takes talent, to transmit images, her mental words were dry. *Are they locals or from somewhere else?*

Locals.

I'm on my way, Travis responded.

I'm sending Kell and Opal, Kooper sent.

We can't just arrest them, Dori pointed out.

No, but we can have them followed tonight, and send someone to observe the situation tomorrow, Kooper returned. *I'll have identification on them soon enough.*

I was only half-listening to Kooper's mindspeech at this point, because Caille Morr walked into the pub.

The description provided by our hotel desk clerk failed to do Caille justice. He was a mountain of a man; tall, with wide shoulders and bulging muscles, topped off by a full, dark head of hair and a bushy beard that covered much of his face and ended mid-chest. He was obsessed, too, but that was the least of my worries at the moment.

He focused on Dori and me the moment he walked through the door, and was now charging like a bull in our direction.

Things are about to get nasty, Dori shouted mentally at Kooper and me before rising from her chair to meet our new adversary head-on.

Caille roughly shoved a patron off a barstool before he reached our table. After lifting the barstool high, he stalked forward, intending to break it over my head. Caille roared as he charged, but I was prepared to send a blast of wind at him to force him backward.

I'd taken my eyes off Dori for perhaps two seconds.

It was long enough for her to shift to ocelot and launch herself at Caille, spitting and hissing, with claws extended. Reeling the spelled blast back so I wouldn't hit her with it, I watched in horror as Dori buzzed his head and upper torso like a furred tornado, clawing Caille's face to shreds before using her hind legs to push off his body and leap away.

Caille, like a wounded bear, roared again while attempting to wipe blood from his eyes. Focusing on Dori now instead of me, he rushed toward her.

Like any cat, she'd fluffed her fur as high as it would go and crouched, ready to spring at him again.

What the hell? Travis' voice reached me—he stood near the doorway, taking in the situation.

A few terrified patrons were struggling to get out of the bar while others, interested in the outcome of this fight, crowded against a wall to give Caille and Dori space to fight.

Dori's ocelot yowled and spat at Caille, who didn't seem to care that she'd shredded him enough to require sutures.

"Hey, stupid," I shouted at Caille, who stopped in his tracks before turning toward me.

Jerking a chair up with my right hand, I tossed it at Caille and put power behind it. It smashed against his body, shattering the chair and momentarily confusing him.

Dori launched herself at him again, clawing his shirt and chest to bloody ribbons before kicking off his body a second time. He screamed this time at the pain she'd caused with her back claws.

I was ready to toss another chair when I saw it. The Prophet was watching, and Caille—well.

Get Terrett, I shouted mentally at Travis, before encasing Caille in an impermeable shield. When he exploded, the shield contained his grisly remains and the green mist he'd blown outward.

The others—those I'd noticed first who'd borne obsession—they'd melted from the pub, leaving no trace.

Caille had covered their disappearance by attacking Dori and me. By the time Travis arrived, the others were already gone.

I considered that the Prophet could have pulled them away, too, but I hadn't noticed that they bore the same cellular recording devices that Caille and Vrak did, which allowed the Prophet to see everything from their perspective.

"What do you want to do with this?" I flung a hand at the shielded remains of Caille. Kooper had come with Kell and Opal, once he saw what was happening.

Dori sat at our table; Travis had helped clean her claws with power before she changed back to her humanoid self.

"I'll send it to Karzac's bots; they can examine it in a leak-proof environment later."

"Let me know when you want the shield released, then," I sighed and raked fingers through my hair.

"We have as much information as we could gather," Kell approached Kooper and handed him a comp-vid. "Terrett took care of the accident explanations."

"Good. I'll have images of every resident sent to Quin. We'll find out if any other locals have been infected."

"Have her send what she finds to me," I said. "Why here?" I asked the question that troubled me most.

"Do you think this is just incidental to Shella's infection?" Kooper asked.

"I have the idea that Caille's infection is much older than hers."

Kooper stared at me for a moment. "That doesn't make sense," he huffed. "Look, I'll do research on my end, and get back with you."

He intended to look into the reason why Shella chose this vacation spot over others on Pyrik. I wanted an answer for that, too.

In the meantime, I worried that we'd forced the Prophet's hand again, and things could go very wrong as a result.

Whether the Prophet understood that we knew about Shella, the investigation had gone sour the moment we asked the desk clerk about Caille. At least we'd never mentioned Shella's name at any point.

This game was now tied, and I worried how the next round would go.

~

Queen's Palace, Le-Ath Veronis
  Winkler

"Kooper?" He'd stalked into my office without knocking or announcing himself.

"Tell me I'm an idiot. That's an order."

"Why?"

"No. Wrong. Tell me I'm an idiot."

"Okay, you're an idiot. What idiotic thing did you do? You look like you've been rode hard and put up wet."

"I'm a snake, not a horse," he waved a hand at my obscure reference. "I told Kell and Opal to look for the seven who disappeared last night after daybreak. They're not the only ones missing from Ba'Moru this morning."

"How many?" I thought to ask.

"More than three hundred, out of a population of fourteen hundred locals. It's not a big place, until you count the tourists who visit."

"Let me guess—you think they just joined the Prophet's army, don't you?"

"Oh, yeah. I sent their images to Quin after we got a head count with names and faces. So far, every one of them shows signs of the infection. If Randl hadn't placed a containment shield around the one who exploded last night, we'd be in even more trouble today."

"Do you think Caille recruited them?"

"That's all we have in the speculation department—that he managed to infect them somehow."

"What about others like Shella—the tourists?"

"Big problem," Kooper grimaced. "I've got somebody on those records now, but that will take time. Plus, we don't know exactly how long Caille has been infected, or whether he targeted other tourists aside from Shella Karp."

"Are you saying that Shella Karp could be an incidental infection, rather than a specific target?"

"I still think she was targeted for a purpose, to get close to Lebbon."

"And the mess just keeps getting bigger," I growled.

"We'll be looking carefully at every attendee to the Conclave. If there are others infected, we have to know names and faces soon."

"Or it can blow up in our faces, like it almost did last night," I said.

"Exactly."

～

BlackWing X

Randl

"He had a face full of angry, spitting, giant ocelot," I told Vik as we lifted weights in the exercise facility on the ship the following day. "It was funny—afterward."

"Most shifters are larger than their normal counterparts," Vik grunted. He lifted six-hundred-pound weights easily enough while I did leg-presses. "Winkler's wolf is huge. Probably stands about shoulder-high on you."

"She didn't have to attack him, but it was fun to watch," I admitted. "Her back claws are like razors."

"She isn't a BlackWing Captain because she's a wimp," Vik grinned.

"I understand that."

"Where were the remains sent, after Caille exploded?"

"Karzac has them."

"Good."

"Having fun without me?" David walked in dressed in workout pants only. Broad and muscled across the chest, I considered that David's owl could score a hit against anyone, if he chose to do so.

"We were just discussing the advantages of having shapeshifters for friends and co-workers," I said.

"And don't you ever forget it," David said before selecting hand-weights and beginning his workout.

~

Queen's Palace, Le-Ath Veronis
Winkler

"Didn't I just see you?"

Kooper frowned at my words before nodding absently. Karzac had been busy from the moment he'd received the blasted remains of Caille Morr hours earlier. He'd called a meeting with Kooper, Lissa and me, inside Lissa's office.

She and Karzac hadn't arrived yet, so Kooper and I were waiting.

Karzac walked in, a comp-vid in one hand. Lissa arrived seconds later. "What do we have?" Lissa asked. "We're taking a break from the meeting, so I can see this."

I could tell she wanted to drop her tiara onto the desk and unpin her hair, but she didn't.

"I was able to examine skin cells closely from Caille Morr's remains," Karzac began, while tapping his comp-vid. "What I found is a work of frightening genius."

"What's that?" Lissa peered at the comp-vid in Karzac's hand.

"I'll create a three-dimensional image," Karzac said. "Sit. Please."

"Well, I'll be skinned and made into a hat band," Kooper swore as the image appeared.

Two images appeared side-by-side. On one side was an insect, whose eyes were multifaceted and could see in all directions. It was something taught to young children, and fascinating enough on its own.

The other image reflected what Karzac had found in Caille's skin cells.

Organic, microscopic insect eyes had covered him head to toe, employing the same ability to see in all directions.

"He was a hybrid?" Lissa blinked in horror.

"It would take some power and imagination to create this," Karzac informed us as the images grew larger. "The eyes experience a symbiotic relationship with their host, and it appears the images are retained unless or until they are transmitted directly to a waiting recipient."

"That's not fucked up," I mumbled my sarcasm.

"The good news is that I think a scanner can be created that will reveal this anomaly," Karzac said. "I wish to employ Sabrina Kend for this project." He turned to Kooper then, who'd remained silent while he gaped at Karzac's images.

"She's yours," Kooper breathed. "How fast do you think," he didn't finish—he was back to examining the images.

"Soon, I hope, although it may not be in time for the Conclave."

"Unless time is bent," Lissa snapped.

"Are you saying?" I asked her.

"Yes, I'm saying," she replied. "We need this gadget as of yesterday."

"It won't detect all those infected," Karzac pointed out. "Just these hybrids."

"These hybrids look to be the Prophet's army officers, so anything we have to identify them is a step in the right direction," Lissa said. "Kooper, go collect Sabrina. I can bend time if it's necessary."

BlackWing X

Travis

"We need Sabrina to work with Karzac," Kooper said before I could greet him properly.

"All right. Did you find something important?" I asked.

"We did. Or rather Karzac did. That fool found a way to make hybrids out of some people, by implanting microscopic insect eyes into their cells."

"You're joking."

"No. I saw the images myself. Those eyes can see in all directions, and either record or transmit images directly to a recipient. In this case, it's the Prophet."

"Fuck," I said before sitting heavily at the desk in the Captain's cubby.

"The project will be done in secret on Le-Ath Veronis, and your mother has offered to bend time if necessary, to get this ready for the Conclave."

"Sounds like we need it," I agreed. "I'll get Sabrina packed up and bring her in a few."

"Thanks. This is top secret—make sure she understands that."

"I will."

Sabrina

"You'll be staying at the palace when you're not working on the project," Travis said. His dark eyes begged me to understand that this was not only top secret, but that my presence on Le-Ath Veronis had to remain secret, too.

"He knows you," Travis pointed out. He meant the Prophet; I was well aware of that. "He's taken you once, because he had alternative plans in place. Don't reveal your location and make yourself a target again."

"Believe me, I never want to be in his clutches again." I suppressed a shudder—without the medallion Zaria had given me, I'd have been killed or raped by the Prophet's jailer.

"Mom may provide a disguise, but that only goes so far. If somebody discovers what you're working on, it'll tip our hand."

"That's scary," I pointed out.

"Baby, I don't like scaring you, but this is scary business. You should know by now that Randl and Dori walked into a trap last night. If they hadn't had the talents they do, they'd be dead or infected right now."

I went still when he called me *baby*. With the mute in place, that seldom happened. "I love you," I blurted.

"I know. Trent knows, too. It'll kill us if you get hurt or kidnapped again. Don't let it happen, all right?"

"All right." I lowered my head—I couldn't bear to look at him any longer. My cheeks burned, too, at my admission of love.

"Hey," he tipped my chin up with a finger. "We love you, don't ever forget that." Travis leaned in to kiss me, and I savored every second of that seldom-offered affection.

Randl

"We'll reach Cloudsong shortly after lunch tomorrow," Trent announced at the crew meeting he and Travis called. "Sabrina is on special assignment, so I hope I don't have to remind any of you to keep that to yourselves."

"Any advice on approaching King Devarr?" Dori asked. "I heard he was something of a recluse."

"Isolationist," Travis corrected her. "His husband, Hulce, is better at meeting strangers than the King, per the dossier Kooper provided."

"He feels as if he's in a fishbowl since Cloudsong joined the Campiaan Alliance," I said. "As yet, Cloudsong hasn't signed the agreement to send troops to the army for training." I'd read the King's dossier after asking Travis for the information. Devarr's image was included in the material.

"Then we need to make Devarr feel comfortable," Jayna offered.

"Any ideas on how to do that?" David asked.

"He's about to be a father—he and Hulce found a surrogate for their child," I said.

"What? That must be a well-kept secret," Trent exclaimed.

"It is," I agreed. "That doesn't keep me from knowing about it. He doesn't want to make the announcement yet, since he and Hulce will be away from the planet for several weeks. They'll be forced to leave the surrogate behind with palace security. I think if Teeg offered additional guards for the surrogate during Conclave, Devarr would be more than happy."

"How do we approach him with this?" Travis asked.

"I can handle it," I offered.

"Then you're in charge of that. As for the rest of you, remember that you're acting as CSD employees. I trust you're well-versed in all things CSD?"

"Yes, Captain," we said.

"Good. That's how to refer to me during this mission. Trent is acting as my second-in-command, and he will also be addressed as Captain. If our guests prefer meals in their cabin, they will be delivered, and all things will be handled professionally, understood?"

"Yes, Captain."

"Good—you're dismissed. Dori, I'd like you and Randl to remain behind."

After the others were gone, Dori and I waited for Travis to tell us what he wanted. It didn't take long.

"I need you both to set aside your title and status for this mission," he said. "I need a representative from Teeg—an ambassador, if you will. I think Randl will fit that position very well. Dori, he needs an assistant. Are you willing to do that? If not, I'll ask Jayna or Terrett."

"That sounds fine," Dori shrugged. "I'm sure it'll get me into meetings and briefings that I normally wouldn't be a part of, because of my temporary title. Just don't let it go to your head," she lifted an eyebrow at me.

"No," I held up a hand in mock surrender. "I saw what you did to Caille's face. I will not let this go to my head, I promise."

She surprised me with a grin, which revealed a dimple in her right cheek. I doubted many people were fortunate enough to see it.

"Good, that's settled. We'll have proper CSD uniforms and clothing appropriate to your station brought to your cabins before we reach Cloudsong; Teeg had it delivered earlier, via special courier. Put your ASD uniforms away; you can keep any civilian clothes you have, provided they're suitable for the place and time."

"What about after we reach Campiaa?" I asked. "Will someone else take over as a liaison for Devarr?"

"That's the idea. Teeg will have someone in place to handle those duties, so we can concentrate on the Prophet and his plans."

"And I can get back to bossing you around," Dori teased me.

"Yes, Captain," I dipped my head to her. She laughed.

"Feel like a beer? I understand you didn't get your drinks last night before all hell broke loose in that pub." Trent stood and stretched.

"Sounds good," I said.

"I'll have a beer," Dori agreed. We left the meeting room behind and headed for the galley.

Avii Castle, Le-Ath Veronis

Quin

"All of them were infected," I told Kooper. It was late at night, and I was thinking about how good the bed would feel when I climbed into it. That's when Kooper arrived, asking about the images of all those who'd disappeared from Ba'Moru.

I'd gone through all of them quickly—it was easy enough to find the growing affliction in all of them.

"Are there any that appeared worse off than the others?" Kooper continued his questioning.

"A few. I've set those aside for Randl to study."

"It's really a moot point, since we have no idea where any of them are," Kooper sighed. "I'll have their images loaded into the security bots in both Alliances, but that may or may not do any good at all, considering the Prophet is well-versed in disguises."

"We have to try," I said. "These people could infect others. Where would we be if we didn't at least attempt to stop them at security checkpoints?"

"You're right as always," he agreed. "I'll go and let you get to bed; you look exhausted."

"As do you. Get some rest, Director. Healer's orders."

Kooper rose from his seat in my study and turned toward the door before turning back again. "I have a favor to ask," he said.

"What is it?"

"I have people working on a special project, and they need privacy and space to work. I thought there'd be something suitable at Lissa's palace, but it isn't working out so well. Too many distractions, I think."

"We have some empty workrooms on the other side of the bowl," I said. "Who needs the space?"

"Karzac and Sabrina. Mind you, I'm serious about the privacy thing. Make up some inane excuse that they need to have a laboratory set up there. Tell your people that they're studying a new disease. That ought to keep the curious away."

"I'll have it ready for them by lunch tomorrow."

"Thank you. I appreciate that more than I can say."

CHAPTER 6

*B*lack *Wing X*
  Randl

Dori and I were dressed in modified CSD uniforms, identifying us as Teeg San Gerxon's liaisons when we reached an orbit around Cloudsong.

"Cloudsong is hardly recognizable from what it used to be," Dori said as we watched the planet's surface race past our galley window.

Less than twenty years earlier, it had been a dead husk of a planet, with only a few weeds and stubborn bushes struggling to grow in dry soil.

Something happened to change all that, when King Devarr's original world, Carek Prime, was destroyed by Vardil Cayetes.

He and his people were transferred to Cloudsong, which had made a miraculous recovery in very little time.

"Zaria do this." Bekzi arrived to watch the planet with us as forests and farms slid past our view. While he'd answered my question, he was just as amazed as I at Cloudsong's transformation, and the ultimate kindness of a woman I still didn't fully understand. She'd saved an entire population from genocide.

Devarr and his people had received the gift of life. I hoped they were properly grateful for it.

"We'll dock at the unfinished space station and take the shuttle to the surface," Dori sighed. "It looks so pretty from up here. Every planet does, until you get to it and learn that the people there are no different from people anywhere else."

"Feeling cynical today, assistant Dori?" I turned to lift an eyebrow at her observation.

"Cynical Dori still has claws and we haven't reached the planet yet," she retorted, although she smiled when she turned away from me.

"Ah. I'll take that under advisement."

"Travis was right to name you the ambassador," Dori sighed. "I'm not suited to those things."

You're suited for what you do, Captain Dori, I informed her in mindspeech. *I think you enjoy it, too.*

She drew in a breath and squared her shoulders before dipping her head in a slight nod. She loved her work and missed her ship.

You'll get another ship soon, I told her. *Even if I have to steal it myself.*

She snickered aloud.

~

Founder's Palace, Campiaa
Wyatt

"If Devarr accepts Randl's offer of additional security for the surrogate, who should we send?" Dad asked. He, Tybus, Dormas and I were in a private meeting inside Dad's study, attempting to sort this new turn of events.

None of us had known that Devarr had a surrogate in place so he and Hulce could be parents. Usually those things were publicized.

Devarr was such a paranoid recluse that he was holding the information back from everyone, including his own people. Only he, Hulce and a handful of palace guards were aware that a royal child was on the way, until Randl saw Devarr's image on a comp-vid.

"I worry that Devarr will turn into Amlis—or the Amlis of the past," I pointed out.

"I'll take that under advisement," Dad said, steepling his fingers as he leaned back in his chair. "He certainly shouldn't pass those fears to his child, or we'll have another generation of it to deal with later."

"Can Quin help with that?" Dormas asked. He seldom offered advice or disagreed with the rest of us, but he usually had everyone's best interests at heart when he did.

"I don't know that Devarr will allow it, and it would be unprecedented in this case," Dad frowned.

"It's better than forcing him to get treatment for his fears and anxiety later," Dormas pointed out.

"We'll work on that," Dad said, "if an opportunity presents itself. We haven't heard anything from the Prophet lately, and that has me more worried than Devarr's predicament."

"Agreed," Tybus said. "Have we heard from Director Riffler?"

"Not since yesterday, and he didn't have anything then."

"Do we have a full report on the incident in Ba'Moru?" Tybus asked.

"I'll request it from Kooper. I'm sure he'll release it to us, especially since it involves Shella Karp in some way. We're taking a risk by allowing her to come to Conclave in the first place."

"I'm worried that we've tipped our hand where she's concerned," Dormas observed. "He's on alert; we knew that when his servants disappeared from the resort village."

"True enough," Dad blew out a frustrated breath.

P'loxett

    V'dar

"They're ready," Varok informed me. "Three hundred soldiers, ready to take their assigned places within the logging industries."

"Good." We'd chosen employees from each of the six major logging concerns suitable for replacement—unmarried men and women who were in supervisory positions and kept to themselves most of the time.

Six of those held high positions in each of the logging concerns, and I had specific plans for each of their replacements. The rest would take orders from those select six, as they knew more of my plans than the others.

We'd administered the altered drug, combined with blood from the selected employee, to create successful replacements. None, including those closest to the actual supervisor, would realize they dealt with a replacement instead of the real thing.

For the special six, we'd added the DNA of insects to the altered drug, not only to make them look like the humanoids they replaced, but to make them more useful to me at the same time.

Those they'd replaced had also been treated with the altered drug, at my command. In a few days, once the drug became fully effective, we'd have another batch of hapless humanoids to sacrifice to our cause—once they were fully infected with the growing obsession.

At first I was concerned that my secrets and plans would be revealed when Ba'Moru was chosen for an investigation.

I should have known they were on the wrong track the whole time. My plan would remain safely out of reach of both Alliances, and soon enough it would be too late for them to do anything about it. P'loxett held secrets of its own, and I intended to use those secrets to full advantage.

I was grateful that those who'd shielded P'loxett had kept parts of it in stasis, so little on the surface was changed. Therefore, the planet presented no enticement for investigation by anyone, including the Alliances.

Our new base of operations suited my purposes perfectly.

"Make arrangements for the final transfers," I commanded while holding back a laugh. How would the last of the enemy feel, when they realized the shocking answers to their questions had been right in front of them all along?

King's Palace, Cloudsong

Randl

"You're the liaison?" Hulce had come to greet us on the palace grounds when our shuttle landed on Devarr's courtyard.

"Yes, Prince Hulce," I nodded and addressed him properly.

"Please, follow me," he allowed a smile to cross his features. Few recognized him or gave his correct title when they met him the first time.

The others fell in line behind me as Hulce led us toward the palace.

"King Devarr," I bowed properly to him when Hulce brought us to the throne room. Devarr wasn't sitting on the throne; he stood several feet away, as if he were waiting for the King to appear and was dressed more plainly than most royals. He awaited our reaction, and to see whether he'd be recognized or not.

The others behind me copied my bow and remained that way until permission was granted by the King to straighten ourselves.

"Please rise and make yourselves comfortable," Devarr was pleased and surprised that he'd been recognized so easily.

"My King, this is Randl Gage, Founder San Gerxon's liaison for our journey to Campiaa," Hulce introduced me first. "He also recognized me," he added with a smile.

"Ah. Liaison Gage, may I ask about your eyes? I would say you could be blind, except that you recognized me so easily. Is this some new technology, perhaps?"

"No, your majesty, I am blind. The Founder will tell you himself that I suffer from occasional clairvoyance. In most cases, it enables me to recognize people and not much else."

That small lie would serve me well with Devarr. I didn't wish to create another Amlis on Cloudsong.

"Then you have a gift," Devarr proclaimed. "Shall we have a meal while you tell me about our journey and what will be expected of us when we arrive on Campiaa?"

"Of course, your majesty," I agreed. "Thank you for your generous hospitality."

Travis

Damn, he's good, Trent sent mindspeech. *They'll be eating out of his hand by the end of the day.*

He had several years' experience smoothing things over between Amlis and others, I replied. *It isn't what he wants to do all the time, but he's perfect for assignments like this. They think his blindness makes him harmless enough. Even Kooper doesn't know what he's capable of doing if he sets his mind to it.*

It would be a tough choice as to who's better at this—Randl or Wyatt.

Randl has an edge, because he can see what they want right away. Wyatt has to feel his way along; he's just really efficient doing it. Besides, Wyatt is needed on Campiaa, so we conscripted Randl for babysitting duties.

I'm surprised Dori is doing so well as Randl's assistant.

I think she's mesmerized by Randl's ability to smooth the way. Just wait— she'll ask for him the next time she needs that sort of thing on a mission.

She'll owe us a favor if we loan him out.

That sounds intriguing, I hid a smile as we followed a servant toward the King's dining hall.

Randl

"This is exceptional," I complimented Devarr on his selection of our after-dinner brandy.

"Thank you. It came from Carek Prime, when we ah, made the move."

"Your choice to bring it with you was an excellent one."

Travis, Trent, Dori and I sat in the King's private study to have our drinks, after the others left to return to the ship.

"We ah, have a concern to bring to you," Hulce cleared his throat and changed the subject. I already knew what it was, I merely waited for him to tell us.

"What is that? Is there something amiss?" I set my drink down, feigning concern.

"No, nothing is amiss, it's just that—Devarr and I have wanted a child for several years, and we recently selected a surrogate who satisfied our requirements. We didn't expect her to conceive so quickly, however."

"Our concern is this," Devarr sighed. "We worry about leaving the surrogate and the unborn heir behind, with only the palace guards to protect them."

"That's perfectly understandable," I said. "How may I help allay your fears?"

"We ah, would prefer the surrogate be protected by the best in either Alliance—those who won't have an interest, perhaps, in changing the course of Cloudsong's history?"

"I see your meaning," I nodded my understanding. "Shall I consult with Founder San Gerxon? I'm sure proper security can be arranged while you and Hulce are away."

"That would be a welcome relief," Hulce breathed. "How long will it take to contact the Founder?"

"I should have an answer for you in the morning, and, as always, you have the option of rejecting any or all of the Founder's choices. This is your child and a royal heir. You deserve the best we can provide."

"Thank you," Devarr said. "We will look forward to speaking with you in the morning."

BlackWing X
  Travis

Mom and Wyatt found three guards each, and I hoped Devarr would accept at least four of those, so two could be on guard all the time. All six would be better, as that would mean shorter shifts, but Devarr would make that decision.

Randl approved of all six when Wyatt brought them—I wasn't surprised. Neither Mom nor Wyatt would send anyone who couldn't be trusted.

"Do you think Devarr has a credible threat from his own people?" I asked Trent as he walked into the Captain's cubby carrying his comp-vid.

"Randl would be better at answering that question," Trent dropped the comp-vid on our shared desk and rolled his shoulders. I was Captain for the trip to Campiaa while he filed our reports and reviewed those completed by the crew before sending everything to headquarters.

"Susan says the VIP suite is ready for Devarr and Hulce, and a cabin across the passage is reserved for Lenk and another guard. The Council member and an assistant are down the passage and within easy reach if needed."

"I hope that makes Devarr feel secure enough," I said.

"It's only four days," Trent reminded me.

"Too bad we can't fold space with them."

"True, but the less these people know about us personally, the better off we are. Traditional travel is what we're forced to deal with— it makes writing reports so much easier."

"And it doesn't present a gap in ship's logs and records," I agreed. We had a hard enough time fixing those problems when they occurred. We didn't need to make more work for ourselves or Kooper, if we could help it.

We'd already had a conundrum to deal with regarding BlackWing VII's destruction and the fact that the crew had been pulled from one sector into another, so we could keep them safe.

"I know what you're thinking," Trent said. "None of us are listed in the official records as a warlock or wizard, because we're not. It's tough keeping your ability to fold space out of everything."

"Face it, the BlackWing crews are a special bunch," I grinned. "I need tea. Have fun crunching numbers, bro." I rose from the desk chair and walked out, leaving Trent with the worst duty of the day.

King's Palace, Cloudsong
Randl

Dori and Vik came with me to present our choices for surrogate guards to Devarr, then escort him and his party to the ship, so we could get underway.

Devarr invited us to his study; we stood there while Devarr examined the six guards we'd brought.

"Are all of them trustworthy?" Devarr asked, as if the guards were things instead of people, who could hear his words clearly.

"I would place my life in their hands, your majesty."

"Good enough. I have one request, however."

"What is that?"

"May I have this one, too?" He pointed at Vik. Vik stood at least a head taller than the tallest of the guards, and looked as if he could handle the worst anyone could bring against him.

Devarr had no clue what Vik could do if pressed.

I knew.

"What do you think?" I turned to Vik. The choice would be his to make.

"I can handle it," he shrugged.

"Good. Very good," Devarr declared. "I wish to place you in charge of the others. Is that acceptable?" Devarr turned back to me.

"It is," I agreed. "I believe Vik will do well in that role."

"Good. Then I accept all these. Lenk, advise them of the schedules, while Hulce and I make final preparations for our journey. Liaison Randl, please make yourself comfortable. If you have need of anything, let one of my attendants know."

"I will."

Vik and six guards followed Captain Lenk from Devarr's study, while Devarr and Hulce walked through a hidden door behind Devarr's desk. It was a narrow passage that would take them to the royal suite, with a few twists and turns along the way.

You'll let me know if you see anything coming our way? Vik sent mindspeech.

You got it, I replied. *Devarr isn't completely paranoid,* I added. *There is a faction on Cloudsong that blames him for the destruction of Carek Prime. If they become a problem, use everything you have to keep the surrogate safe. Send mindspeech if things start to go wrong; I'll ask Jett Riffler for a CSD ship to shadow the planet, in case troops are needed to keep the peace.*

Thank you.

Not a problem.

~

BlackWing X

Travis

Devarr wanted Vik to stay and take charge of the other six, Randl sent. *I allowed it. I hope you don't mind.*

I don't mind, as long as he's all right with it.

He is, I asked him.

Good. It's only for a few weeks, then he can go back to business as usual.

Just what I was thinking.

When will your party be ready to board ship? I asked.

Devarr and Hulce are still making preparations, so it could take some time. Be ready for some delay.

Roger that.

Roger? Oh. Never mind.

"Prepare for a delayed departure," I informed James and Nathan. "If you want a break or a snack, I'll take the helm."

"Thank you, Captain," James grinned. He and Nathan left the bridge.

~

Avii Castle, Le-Ath Veronis

Sabrina

"I can tune the scanners to look for something specific, but it will only look for that, instead of anything else a scanner would normally search for," I explained to Karzac.

"Is it possible to create a scanner that will do both?"

"It'll be bigger and more obvious than what people are used to," I said. "It'll take more time to get the proportions down to an acceptable size."

"Build a prototype, then see if one of our warlock or wizard friends can reduce the size for us."

"I—hadn't thought of doing that," I confessed.

"The option isn't available to the public, engineers and scientists included," Karzac gruffed. "We have time constraints and an enemy who could be anywhere," he added.

"I know." I didn't hold back a sigh. He and I had spent long hours in our makeshift lab at Avii Castle—I learned just before our move there that palace comesuli were already gossiping about my presence at meals with Queen Lissa.

Lissa had arranged through Kooper to get our lab moved, so the gossip would stop. She'd made vague references to troubles in the past that were generated by careless gossip. She didn't want to add to that list.

Someday, I intended to ask Travis and Trent about that. Meanwhile, I had a design to build to keep as many people safe from the Prophet as I could, and I only had days to do it.

~

BlackWing X

Randl

"This is quite fine," Devarr said as he surveyed the VIP suite. It was elegantly furnished and quite large, even compared to the Captains' cabins.

"I hope you will find it comfortable enough on your journey," I dipped my head to him and Hulce. "Captain Lenk is nearby, as are your other subjects and Council members. If you need something, all you have to do is ask. You are also welcome in all parts of the ship, although the Captain asks that you send a request if you wish to visit the bridge."

"Understandable," Devarr smiled.

"There is a comp-vid beside the bed. It will link you to the galley and to me, if you're hungry. You are also welcome to eat in the galley, as it has the best views from the windows, but we will deliver meals to your suite if that is your desire."

"My King, I would like at least one meal in the galley each day," Hulce breathed.

"Then we shall do that," Devarr smiled and humored his husband. "Your choice, of course."

"Let us know in advance, and your table will be waiting," I said. "Is there anything else I can do for you?"

"I think we are quite fine," Hulce said. "Thank you for your assistance."

I left their suite, knowing that Hulce was overflowing with excitement; he and Devarr had never had a vacation together, and the four days aboard ship presented an opportunity for such.

Our guests are comfortably established in their cabins, I reported to Travis.

Good. We're officially underway.

My cabin felt confining, so I chose to sit in the galley to continue my research. Ba'Moru and the events there still troubled me, in ways I couldn't define. Quin had gone through all the images of those who'd disappeared, and they were all affected by the growing obsessions.

She'd then gone through images of those left behind, and none of those were anything other than normal. As a result, Quin and I had asked Kooper for records on all visitors to Ba'Moru in the past five years.

Quin, who'd received the images and information from Kooper, was going through the first of those records.

So far, there'd been nothing to report.

"You look like a man on a mission." Trent set his cup of Falchani black on the table and pulled out a chair to join me.

"Ba'Moru is still bothering me," I admitted. "Quin is going through the visitor records for the past five years, but so far, nothing has turned up to warrant my uneasiness on the matter."

"Dude, I would never discount your feelings on any matter," Trent said. "We know more than we did about Ba'Moru, and we need to know more before Shella is loosed on Campiaa."

"I've looked into her records and at her images—she's as loud and shrill as they come," I said. "If somebody doesn't follow her slightest whim, they get dressed down in front of everybody else. She has no real friends; what she has are followers who are afraid of her, so they stick close and kiss her ass."

"Never a good thing, that," Trent sighed and sipped tea. "Those people tend to have no concept of what their shortcomings are. Deep down, she's probably as insecure as they come."

"How did you know?" I teased.

"I know this may come as a surprise, but I was already an adult when you were born, man. Trav and I have been to at least three institutions of higher learning, earning degrees from all of them. We've seen all kinds."

"You know, I sort of knew that about you," I chuckled.

"Now see—I knew that you knew," he pointed his mug of tea in my direction. "I just wanted to hear myself talk."

"Whatever you say, Captain Trent." I didn't bother to hide my grin.

"Feel like blade practice tonight? Trav and I wouldn't mind working off a few frustrations."

"If whacking me with a practice blade will accomplish that for you, then I willingly volunteer."

"Good. Nineteen bells in the exercise facility?"

"I'll be there," I agreed.

~

Queen's Palace, Le-Ath Veronis

Winkler

"They reserved the space for this conference last year, shortly after the announcement was made to reschedule the Conclave," Kooper took a seat in my study.

"Why is this coming to light now?" I asked. Kooper's comp-vid was in my hand as I studied the information put out by the six largest logging industries.

"The casino hotels aren't obligated to share this information; they can rent their rooms and meeting facilities to anyone, as long as those groups aren't convicted criminals. If we'd known or suspected, we could have asked about it. We didn't, and now we have a logging conference going on during the first five days of Conclave."

"Because they want to push their agenda with every leader they can approach, no doubt."

"That's not legal, but you know they'll try. Some will succeed, too, because they have plenty of money to buy dinners and offer valuable perks—all under the table, as you're so fond of saying."

"The Eclipse is one of the smaller casinos, at least, at the end of the half-moon bay. Conclave will be housed at the Sandswept, near the other end and closer to Teeg's palace," I pointed out.

"It's not a great distance to travel, and attendees will end up in every casino along that strip of sand. How the hell will we keep tabs on the royals and planetary leaders, look for interference by the Prophet and watch the logging industries at the same time?"

"Have you spoken to Teeg and Jett about this?"

"I have a meeting with them this afternoon. Want to go with me?"

"Sure."

"I was hoping you'd agree."

~

King's Palace, Cloudsong
 Vik

Two of Devarr's guards troubled me. They watched me and the others, suspicion behind their eyes.

They'd been absent when Randl and the others visited the palace, and that also troubled me.

In fifteen years, I'd never used the medallion Zaria gave me. Focusing on the guards in question, who stood at the wide doorway to the throne room, I touched my chest, where the medallion lay beneath my shirt.

Randl, I sent, *can you see these two through my eyes?*

I see them, he responded immediately. *They are allied with the dissenters, and have passed the information on the surrogate to their hidden colleagues.*

Are they planning to strike in the King's absence? I asked.

Yes.

If they attempt a coup, Devarr will demand that you bring him back immediately, I said.

I know that. Look, why don't we be proactive in this? I'll come in tonight to meet with you—they're not planning anything for another two days. That gives us time to deal with this and keep Devarr where he is.

I sure hope you come up with a good plan, I informed Randl. *I don't like the looks of this one bit.*

Neither do I.

I'll keep you advised about our two friends, then, and see you tonight in my suite.

I'll be there.

Thanks.

~

BlackWing X, Captain's Cubby
 Randl

"Please say you're joking," Travis moaned.

"They're planning a coup, and it will begin with their attack on the surrogate and her guards," I said. "Once the surrogate and heir are out of the way, they intend to take the palace and institute martial law. They know what happened with Kifirin fifteen years ago, so they'll drop out of the Campiaan Alliance right away, leaving Devarr without a throne."

"And the people aren't armed, so they can't fight back. The only thing we can do is pull Teeg in on this, and bring the ship Jett sent into play. How many are involved in this?" Travis asked.

"They have more than two thousand ready to go. They've spent the last few years making or hoarding what weapons they could—not all of that legally, as you can imagine."

"This alone will ensure that they stand trial," Trent observed.

"Do you think we can prevent the coup from happening by leveling weapons charges against them?" Travis turned to his brother.

"That's a question for Teeg, Jett and Wyatt, I think."

"I'll send mindspeech to Wyatt, and let you know what he says," Travis breathed a heavy sigh. "This certainly puts a crimp in all our plans."

"It'll be worse if Devarr doesn't attend Conclave, and far worse if this reinforces his isolationism," I said.

"True. Nothing about this is going to be easy."

"How do most of Devarr's subjects view their king?" Trent thought to ask.

"The majority enjoy their membership in the Alliance," I replied. "They have benefits now they never had before, and Cloudsong, under the partnership between King and Alliance, is thriving and more industry is being developed, along with crop exports and such. Merchants have a much larger market than they ever had before. The dissidents want things the way they used to be, when it was only them and nobody else."

"So, nobody who's forward-thinking in that bunch, then?" Travis frowned.

"They don't like the prospect of the influx of visitors, once the space station is completed," I explained. "They'll probably destroy that, too, if their coup is successful."

"Idiots," Trent rumbled.

"You called?" Wyatt appeared in the Captain's cubby.

"Yeah. Have a seat," Travis pointed to the empty chair beside mine. "We have a problem, and we need your help."

CHAPTER 7

*B*lackWing X
Travis

"Let me get this straight—they're planning a coup with only two thousand or so?"

"They can take the palace with that number, and once they take that, the rest of Cloudsong won't know how to fight back." Randl shook his head. "Especially if they execute a few civilians who think to stand in their way."

"They're that vindictive and evil-minded?"

"I think their leaders are, and they've fanned the flames of fear and racism—once Cloudsong is opened to tourism and such. They believe others will arrive to take their jobs and farms. They haven't looked into the Alliance laws that protect the sovereignty of each planet." Randl shook his head.

"You saw all this from two guards?"

"I saw most of it, yes. I also saw their leaders. That's where the rest of my information came from." Randl offered his comp-vid to Wyatt.

"So, you have names." Wyatt took the comp-vid and began tapping the information.

"Not all of them, I didn't have time to research two thousand or

90

more. What I have are the main components of this coup. If I had more time, you'd have the whole of it."

"Look, Dad, Jett and Kooper are having a meeting in half an hour. I'd like you to join us," Wyatt told Randl. "And Trent, if he can be spared," he added.

"I'll handle Captain's duties, and explain Randl's absence if necessary," I waved a hand. "Go now. Teeg should probably hear this first."

"He and Tybus are having a private lunch at the moment. I'm sure we can fit in."

"Good. Keep me updated. This is making me itch," I complained.

"That makes two of us," Wyatt declared. I watched as he folded Trent and Randl away, leaving me alone in the Captain's cubby.

"If it isn't one thing, it's four others," I mumbled and reached for my comp-vid. I could do research, too; I just wasn't as efficient at it as Randl was. Something else concerned me about this, too—Randl had received his information through Vik, and that puzzled me.

Founder's Palace, Campiaa
   Randl

"I hear from Wyatt that trouble is brewing on Cloudsong," Teeg said the moment we sat at the table with his near-twin, Tybus.

While the people of Campiaa and the Campiaan Alliance would never know there were two who ruled their Alliance, I would never have difficulty sorting one from the other.

"A planned coup," I acknowledged. "I have the information from two palace guards, who are secretly aligned with the dissidents."

"You have names of the leaders of this operation?" Tybus asked. Wyatt handed his comp-vid to Tybus, so he could see the names and information I'd found.

"What do you think?" Teeg asked Tybus.

"I think Jett needs to see this, and perhaps we should consider the arrests of all those in charge of this rebellion," Tybus handed the comp-vid to Teeg. "It shouldn't be hard to do—there are less than a hundred we'll have to arrest initially, and then work on taking the others later—after we've announced on all the news programs that more dissidents are being sought."

"I've been thinking about how Devarr will react," I said. "I think he needs to be a part of this, so he'll know first and foremost that his safety and his position on the throne are our priority, where Cloudsong is concerned."

"Not a bad thought," Tybus said after thinking about my words for a few moments. "It's no secret to us how paranoid he could become, since he was an isolationist on Carek Prime, and it took us more than seven years to convince him that joining the Campiaan Alliance was in his best interest."

"Most of Cloudsong's residents like the benefits of being Alliance members," I said.

"But there are always troublemakers," Teeg agreed. "Wyatt, take Astralan and Stellan with you when you go back to BlackWing X. That will provide a legitimate method of getting Devarr from the ship to Campiaa, so we can talk with him. Randl, I want you in these conversations with Devarr. Travis tells me you've developed a rapport with him."

"I just did my job," I said.

"Then keep doing your job. This could turn into a delicate situation, as you likely already know."

"It could, Founder," I agreed.

"You know to call me Teeg," he grinned.

"Of course, Teeg."

"While you're here, I'd like you to attend the meeting I'm having with Kooper and Jett, in case they have questions about the dissidents on Cloudsong."

"I'll be happy to stay for that."

"Good. Are you hungry? I'll have three more places set if you are."

That's how Trent, Wyatt and I came to have an unplanned meal with Teeg San Gerxon and Tybus, his co-ruling doppelganger.

~

Founder's Palace, Campiaa

Winkler

Kooper hid his surprise at finding Randl and Trent in Teeg's study when we arrived. Something was up; that went without saying.

"Well, it looks like something's going on with Cloudsong, unless I miss my guess," Jett's deep voice announced shortly after his arrival. He'd been surprised at the extra people he found at the meeting, just as Kooper and I were.

"Unless we do something to stop it, there's a coup planned during Devarr's absence," Teeg said.

"What's the plan, then?" Jett took a seat and waited for Teeg's thoughts on the matter. Kooper nodded to two chairs close together; he and I sat down to hear what Teeg had to say.

"We have a list of the leaders in this mess. The plan is to arrest them first, and make it public that we're hunting the rest."

"At that point, they'll be too scared to stick their noses out their front door—or they should be," Wyatt added.

"Don't forget they're armed," Randl spoke up.

"Yeah. That's something to consider," Kooper drawled.

"How are they armed?" Teeg turned to Randl.

"A lot of homemade weapons—some stolen or acquired illegally."

"Homemade? By whom?" Jett asked.

"I need to hold one or two to give you an idea—it wasn't any of the leaders, so it must be some of their underlings."

"Shall we lay plans to get Randl what he needs, then?" Jett asked.

"Yes," Teeg agreed.

"There's something I'd like to present while Randl is still here," Kooper held up a hand.

"What's that?"

Instead of watching Teeg, I watched Randl. He was drinking in Kooper's information more quickly than he could drink water.

"The logging industries are having a conference here, which coincides with the first five days of Conclave," Kooper replied to

Teeg's question. "Now, I don't have to tell you what kinds of problems that could present, do I?"

"Perhaps we didn't scrutinize them well enough before," Teeg growled. "Fucking hell."

"Is there a way to get a list of attendees for their conference?" Randl asked.

"I'll get one, if I have to choke it out of somebody," Teeg promised. "Give me until tomorrow, and you should have it then. Wyatt, make sure that happens."

"I will," Wyatt said.

"Now, back to handling Devarr and company, as we deal with unhappy subjects who want to throw a coup at the palace while their king is away," Teeg said.

~

BlackWing X

Randl

It was decided that Astralan and Stellan, two of Teeg's four warlock guards, would arrive aboard ship the following morning with Wyatt, who'd inform Devarr of what the plans were to protect Cloudsong.

I was grateful for the delay—I needed rest, so blade practice with Travis and Trent had to be put off.

Meditation, on the other hand, was a welcome respite, because it enabled me to slip sideways into sleep.

~

Avii Castle, Le-Ath Veronis

Sabrina

My headache worsened as I stared at the melted mess that used to be the latest version of my design. Bel Erland, Lissa's grandson and Quin's warlock mate, shook his head at the mess covering my worktable.

I'd built a working model of our scanner, and it had performed well enough. When Bel arrived to miniaturize it, we discovered that the power source I'd used was far too strong for the tinier version.

It had zapped, fried itself and then melted in front of me.

"I'm too tired to curse, as much as I want to," I confessed.

"What sort of power source can you use for something that small—that will still make it effective?" Bel asked.

"That's the problem," I rubbed my forehead. "It requires sufficient power to run the scanner at a cellular level, and something this small may not handle that load. Ever. I have no idea how to fix this in so little time."

"Don't give up," Bel encouraged. "We need this. Gran and Dad say so."

"I'll keep working on it," I said, although that was the last thing I wanted to do at that moment. What I really wanted was to crawl in bed and sleep for two days.

"I see it didn't make it through the surge of power," Karzac appeared in the lab and studied the melted puddle on my work table.

"Yeah."

"I will heal your headache and have food brought," Karzac said. "Then we will begin again."

BlackWing X

Travis

"While you believe this to be your worst fears come to life," Randl soothed Devarr, "Consider this—before you joined the Campiaan Alliance, you'd be forced to deal with this on your own. The guards we placed in your palace uncovered the plot quickly, and notified CSD Director Riffler. We now have a plan in place to take the leaders of this attempted coup before they can act, and eliminate the threat against you, your throne and your child. That's one of the benefits the Alliance offers—military assistance when it's needed."

Devarr, still in shock at the news we'd delivered during a breakfast meeting, jerked his head from Randl to Wyatt and the warlocks and back again.

"Will this force you're providing be sufficient?" Devarr's voice cracked.

"Yes. We have another ship on standby, too, if those troops are required. This will be as bloodless as possible, and these prisoners can be held at a holding facility on another world, if that will ease your worries."

"Yes. Keep them as far away from Cloudsong as possible. My child is of the utmost importance, you understand."

"I do," Wyatt dipped his head. "My father says that he stands with you in that sentiment."

"Do you think that they would have still attacked, had we stayed home?" Hulce asked.

Randl drew in a breath before answering. "Prince Hulce," he said, "had you stayed at home, their plan was to kill you, the King and the child, too, in their desire to remove Cloudsong from the Alliance. Most of your subjects like their Alliance citizenship and the benefits it provides. These dissidents fail to understand the full scope of their actions."

I watched as Hulce's fingers gripped Devarr's. It hadn't mattered whether they remained on Cloudsong or not. While Randl was reluctant to reveal this truth to both, it had become necessary.

"Hulce and I wish to be there when the leaders are captured and brought to the palace—before they are transported elsewhere," Devarr stated. "I want to see them, so their image will be in my memory from now on."

"If that is what you wish," Wyatt agreed. "I'll provide a special detail to protect you and the Prince, in addition to those who guard the surrogate while the raid is happening."

"Who will guard us?" Hulce asked.

"I will be with you, and will ensure the ability of those sent to protect you," Randl offered. Hulce blinked for a moment before nodding his agreement.

If it were just him, he'd want to be in the middle of this, Randl informed me in mindspeech. *The child changes the equation.*

Understood, I replied.

Captain Lenk should be included in his guards.

I'll see to it.

What should we do about the palace guards who are involved in the coup?

Trent and I wouldn't mind a little exercise. Dori can take the conn while we're away.

Randl

Hulce and Devarr were dressed in more practical clothing when we gathered for transport to Cloudsong. Teeg's warlocks were ready and waiting for Wyatt's permission. Lenk, dressed in his work uniform, was also ready to go.

The other passengers would remain aboard ship; none except the senior Council member were aware of the mission. He could be trusted, and I told Devarr so.

"You're going with us?" Hulce asked when Travis and Trent, dressed in black leathers and two blades strapped across their backs, joined our party.

"We're part of your personal guard, King Devarr," Trent bowed properly to Devarr.

"Black leathers. That means you are proficient with your blades," Devarr sighed.

"Yes."

"I hope they're not needed."

"As do we."

"Ready?" Wyatt asked.

"Yes," Devarr replied. The warlocks transported us to Cloudsong.

Founder's Palace, Campiaa

Kooper Griff

"Did you suspect something like this on Cloudsong? Is that why you requested BlackWing X for that world?" I'd joined Teeg for an early breakfast.

"I was concerned we'd meet with some difficulty getting Devarr off the planet—it was hard enough convincing him last time," Teeg replied. "I had no idea he'd found a surrogate for his heir, though, and that complicated matters this time. He wasn't aware that the dissidents had carried their takeover plans this far, either."

"And neither were you," I pointed out.

"Neither was I. I can't say how happy I am that Randl came back when he did. Without him, we'd be neck-deep in big trouble right now."

"We could still be neck-deep in big trouble with the Prophet," I reminded him. "We don't have any idea what he has planned, and I'll be honest, I have people watching graveyards everywhere. We don't need another army of the dead marching down the streets of this city."

"Mom says to stay the hell away from misting inside their heads to blow them apart," Teeg admitted.

He seldom referred to his mother, Queen Lissa, with anyone, although I knew who his mother was. Every citizen of the Campiaan Alliance thought he was an orphan, who'd wrestled the worlds of the Campiaan Alliance away from the criminals who ran them and formed a viable Alliance from a group of mostly lawless planets.

"Face it, we've never seen anything like this before," I said. "I'd suggest not doing it, too."

"Astralan and Stellan say they can place a power-dome over something like that, but we need the dead army, for lack of a better term, all in one relatively small space to make it completely effective. If they're spread out, or the Prophet sends more than fifty, that will render useless any attempt at a power dome."

"That's the plan? To hope the Prophet puts them in a small enough space and only has fifty dead troops?"

"It's what we have right now. You had a group of people fighting those things on Cord'ilus, and the majority of that group were of the powerful variety," Teeg said. "We don't have an army of powerful troops, here. My warlocks are the only option I have to successfully combat these things for now. Fighting them with Regular Campiaan Alliance troops will release that green mist you keep talking about, and people will either fall under its influence or die from the blast when the dead explode."

"Have you asked for backup from King Rylend?"

"We've discussed it, yes. He's willing to provide as many warlocks as we need, but I have no idea how many that will be, and we're not even sure the Prophet will attack us that way. Besides, Astralan says we need Fifth-level warlocks, and there's a limited number of those available." Teeg's frustration was evident in his voice.

"What about your mother—has she offered help?"

"Of course she has. Dad wants to get in the middle of this, too, because he was on Cord'ilus, remember? He knows what these things are capable of."

"I've never known Gavin to shy away from a fight," I agreed.

"And he won't; you can bet money on that."

"My concern is how that army will arrive, if it does arrive."

"How did it get onto Cord'ilus?" Teeg asked. "The Prophet has power. Jett showed me the images when he went against Randl. I still don't know how Randl survived."

"We're not sure, either, but we're grateful. Randl may have talents that haven't been explored, yet. Let's hope we don't need them."

BlackWing X

Dori

"The cameras are working," I informed Travis. He, Trent and the others were inside Devarr's palace, setting up their defenses in case they were attacked. They'd placed multiple cameras throughout the palace, and the images from those cameras would be sent to recording devices aboard the ship.

This was for the official record and was standard protocol with all ASD ships, including the BlackWing fleet.

"Boots are on the ground," I heard Trent's voice coming from behind Travis. The CSD troops had arrived and were on their way to arrest the dissident leaders.

"Stay safe," I sent my last verbal message before breaking off that part of our communication. The vid images would be my information from now on.

"Maintain course," I told Nathan and James.

"Maintaining course, Captain," James replied.

King's Palace, Cloudsong
Randl

The surrogate had been brought to the small ballroom chosen by Captain Lenk as the best defensible portion of the palace—one that could hold the number of people who stood guard at both entrances.

Hulce knelt by the surrogate's chair and patted her hand while Devarr hovered—they not only cared for the child she carried, but for her as well.

Vik stood by the ballroom's large window, which overlooked the courtyard below the palace. He watched for any unusual activity. He and I were connected again; I could see what he saw, if I chose to do so.

Travis, Trent and Lenk were connected through com-links with squad leaders of the CSD troops, and they'd know when the ones targeted were captured.

"Two in custody," Travis informed us.

My breath froze in my lungs.

The Prophet couldn't have planned his next move better if he'd known about the Cloudsong maneuver ahead of time.

He hadn't known—I was sure of it, or he'd have capitalized in a bigger way. Pulling in a breath after seconds ticked by, I bellowed

Vik's name and pulled him away with me to a planet none had visited for a very long time.

⁓

BlackWing X

  Dori

"Where is he?" I shouted at James and Nathan, before realizing they were as much in the dark as I was.

We'd all watched as Randl disappeared from Cloudsong, taking Vik with him. Travis and Trent were pressed to reassure Devarr and Hulce regarding the disappearance of those two.

They had no real explanation for any of it, and Randl hadn't bothered to send a message. I sent mindspeech. *Randl, you'd better have a fucking good reason for this*, I growled into his mind.

Captain, if you could see what we see, you wouldn't be asking about a fucking good reason, he responded.

Where the hell are you? I demanded.

My mind was suddenly filled with visions—Randl had found a way to send what he could see. I went still with shock.

⁓

ASD Headquarters, Le-Ath Veronis

  Kooper Griff

You're where? I was ready to explode from pent-up anger at Randl after hearing from Travis that he and Vik had disappeared from Devarr's palace.

Kev'Ril, Randl replied. *See?* I was suddenly linked with him and with Dori Anderson, aboard BlackWing X.

Kev'Ril? I did explode this time. *Get the hell out of there*, I began, before cutting off my sending.

Randl and Vik had to be shielded, otherwise the people surrounding the hole filled with liquid concrete would surely have attacked. Kev'Ril was a world destroyed by radiation—not from a nuclear plant meltdown, but from nuclear warfare. They'd built so many weapons, and employed all of them in a great war that killed nearly everything on the planet long ago.

Trees and plants were slowly growing back, but it had been a long, weary process. Currently, Kev'Ril was off-limits to anyone from either Alliance, because of the contamination still present.

What are you planning to do? I sent, my words wary.

We're waiting for the victims to arrive, Randl replied.

And then what?

You'll see.

I cursed aloud, sending several underlings running in my direction to see if I needed something.

~

King's Palace, Cloudsong

Travis

Lenk had taken Vik's place at the window, to watch for attackers. "There's a crowd pouring into the courtyard," Lenk shouted.

Jerking my head at Astralan, he folded us to the window.

"They're carrying weapons and don't look friendly," Astralan advised.

"They're coming," I announced. "Be prepared. Backup troops are on the way."

~

Kev'Ril

Randl

Here. I tossed my ranos pistol to Vik, who caught it without blinking. It was the weapon Sabrina made for me, but I'd modified it somewhat with power. It would allow someone I designated to fire it.

What are you going to fight with? Vik's sending was dry. Across the wide square of liquid concrete, the people lining three sides of that filled excavation began to chatter.

Their victims were approaching.

With these, I held up my hands. *We just have to wait until the sacrifices get here.*

He wanted to ask about sacrifices, but wisely kept his question to himself. He'd see soon enough, as would Kooper and Dori.

~

King's Palace, Cloudsong

Travis

"Our troops are coming in behind the enemy, but the enemy will reach us first," I warned the others. They were already past guards posted on the lower levels of Devarr's palace, and I wasn't optimistic about the guards' survival.

"Bro," Trent nodded to me and pulled his ranos pistol from its holster.

"Yeah. Weapons at the ready," I snapped. "For King, planet and Alliance." Trent and I killed the first enemies who broke through the door.

~

Kev'Ril

Randl

The scene was eerily familiar to me. *Don't fire yet,* I warned Vik. *I'm hoping the Prophet is here with them, and we can get a clear shot.*

They're coming, Vik said. I could see them almost as easily as he could—the victims chosen for this sacrifice.

I only had to read the first few to realize who they were and that they were infected with the growing disease. They hadn't been infected long, and although their appearance was no longer the same, there were remnants of their former selves still there. The Prophet had no idea that I could temporarily tell this about his victims.

That made my work much more difficult. *Kooper, we'll need a safe place for these, away from anyone else,* I sent.

Looking now, he replied. *There's an abandoned village on Karathia—I just have to clear it with Rylend,* he returned. *Got it,* he said after a few seconds passed. *They're placing a heavy shield around Didge, now.*

All right. Things are about to get weird in a hurry, I informed him.

I'm watching. I can bring help if it's needed, he began.

Stay away from this mess, Director, I told him. *I have us shielded, but I can still taste the poison in the air.*

You know I can take care of myself, he began.

Sir, the Prophet isn't here, but I feel him watching.

Ah. Kooper finally understood my reluctance to bring anyone else to this fight.

Ready? I asked Vik. The first of the sacrifices had almost reached the pool of liquid concrete.

Ready.

~

King's Palace, Cloudsong
Travis

If we hadn't had Astralan and Stellan with us, the fight would have gone on longer and more would have died.

After the first few had fallen, the enemy rushed the wide doorways, coming through in a huge mass. It was designed to get at least some through to kill the King, the Prince and the Heir.

Astralan and Stellan, fifth-level warlocks that they were, prepared for such an onslaught and together, formed a river of flame that engulfed the dissidents. Trent threw a shield around the King and those close to him, blocking out the sight and sounds of screaming, dying men and women.

There were only a handful of dissidents left alive outside the ballroom doors, and they dropped their weapons immediately after the burning slaughter, raising their hands in surrender.

We had casualties, however. Three of our guards died and Lenk was injured when the backup troops arrived to secure the palace.

Devarr, Hulce and the surrogate were whisked to Devarr's suite, where they were checked by med-troops and guarded closely by hand-picked member of the CSD. Someone else tended Lenk, who'd taken a laser-shot to his shoulder.

Kev'Ril

    Randl

Understanding that something significant could happen when I pulled the Prophet's intended sacrifices away, and the actual experiencing of such an event turned out to be an incident outside the realm of my imagination.

The moment I transferred more than three hundred sacrifice victims to Didge on Karathia, Kev'Ril exploded around Vik and me.

lackWing X
Dori

"Astralan and Stellan are with Devarr," Travis announced as he flopped onto a chair in the Captain's cubby. "They'll transport him and the others straight to Campiaa. Teeg gave permission for them to bring the surrogate with them, because they don't want her out of their sight."

I hugged myself as I listened to Travis' rambling. He knew something was wrong right away.

"What is it?" he demanded. "Tell me."

"I was linked to Randl. Kooper, too. He took Vik with him to Kev'Ril."

"What? That place is almost as bad as Tiralia," he snapped. "Trent," he shouted.

Trent, looking tired and out of sorts, folded into the room. "What's going on?" he asked.

"Dori says Randl and Vik went to Kev'Ril."

"Bloody, nose-wiping hells," Trent swore. "What happened?"

"I think they're dead," I hugged myself tighter. "Kooper and I were linked with Randl and suddenly, Kev'Ril blew up. I've already had

James and Nathan double check. Kev'Ril isn't there anymore, and we lost contact with Randl."

"Because we were in Didge, making sure the survivors were all right, and recording their real names on a comp-vid for Kooper," Randl said as he and Vik appeared just inside the door. "They're all scared to death, in addition to having that filth in their bodies," he added. "Travis, I know you're tired, but we need a meeting with," he didn't get any farther than that, because I'd launched myself into his arms and scared the hell out of him by kissing him. Hard.

Travis

Kooper folded aboard the ship roughly an hour after Randl arrived. He'd been to Didge, too, and he and Ry had arranged to have food, water and other necessities delivered to the Prophet's intended victims.

"Do you think the Prophet knows where they are?" I asked.

"I hope not, but Randl knows better than I do, I think."

"He and Trent went to clean up," I explained. "They'll be here shortly. Vik's available, too, if you need him."

"I need his report," Kooper sighed and took a seat in the Captain's cubby. "And coffee or tea—whatever's ready and available."

"I'll have it delivered," I said and sent mindspeech to Susan.

Avii Castle, Le-Ath Veronis

   Sabrina

"It's just not possible." I dropped my head in my hands, resigned to the fact that miniaturizing the scanner just wasn't to be, and it all came down to the amount of power needed to make it effective.

"What's wrong?" Quin and Dena arrived, bringing lunch for Karzac and me in a basket.

"The power source," I said. "It takes so much power for the new scanner to work, and something tiny enough to fit inside the other scanners just can't handle it."

"Too bad Quin or Randl can't just fly overhead, looking for the people you want," Dena said, setting the basket on my desk. "We have soup and roast-beef sandwiches for you."

"No joke," I lifted my head to blink at the two winged women. "Flying over the crowds would solve everything, except it wouldn't be uh, practical—wait."

"Do you have an idea?" Karzac asked.

"I went to a party once," I said, "and they had these mechanical drones flying over people's heads and dropping party hats," I said.

"The attendees will be very suspicious of drones," Karzac pointed out.

"But," I held up a hand, "If Quin, or something like Quin—say a bird or another creature that flies, can provide entertainment for the crowd and carry a scanner at the same time—would that work? Do you think Bel Erland can spell a replica of an exotic bird to fly overhead?"

My question was pointed at Quin, because Bel was her mate and a powerful warlock.

"He could make dozens of them fly overhead," Quin shrugged. "With no trouble."

"Let me get Lissa," Karzac breathed and disappeared.

"Dena," I said. "I think you earned ten years' wages today."

BlackWing X

Randl

I admit that I had to shove thoughts of Dori and her kiss out of my mind before meeting with Kooper and the others. By the time I arrived, I found Kooper, Wyatt and Jett Riffler in the Captain's cubby, waiting with Travis and Trent.

I barely had room to squeeze in and take a chair in front of the desk, which Kooper had commandeered.

"I've had time to get further identification on some of those people on your list," Kooper said. "You know who they are, don't you?"

"Yes, and I have a feeling the Prophet has arranged to have all of them replaced with his own, who now look exactly like them. I also think that the Prophet hasn't guessed that I can tell, at least at first, who these people were before he infected them. As for them and the Prophet's replacements, whoever they look like now is who they'll be in a few days to everybody, Quin and me included. Past that, we'd have to see images of the original to know there's a difference."

"You think this is what he did with Phorde Gaster, don't you?"

"It is what he did—there's no guessing about it in my mind."

"So, the logging industry is clueless about this?"

"I'd say yes, unless there are a few that he's gotten to since Quin looked at them last."

"That's worrisome," Jett said.

"It should come as no surprise that the number of sacrifices matches almost exactly the number of people who disappeared from Ba'Moru," I went on. "We may have forced him to act on this quicker than he planned, but things match up too well, Director."

"You're saying that those who disappeared from Ba'Moru are now acting as employees for the logging concerns?" Jett asked.

"Yes."

"Add that to the fact that the logging industry is having their conference on Campiaa, which coincides with the first few days of Conclave. That spells big trouble for us," Kooper grimaced.

"We can't force the issue," I said. "You saw what he did to Kev'Ril."

"How *did* he do that to Kev'Ril?" Jett wanted to know.

"I'm sending a robotic research pod to gather information," Kooper said. "No ships—he could be waiting to take those."

"I'm surprised he didn't take those freighters hauling food, instead of stealing their cargo," Trent spoke up.

"Last resort, I think," Kooper pointed out. "He wants faster ships with a decent weapons system, plus, taking the whole ship meant we'd be more diligent in searching for it and the crew he kidnapped. He wasn't ready, and the Conclave wasn't being held then."

"So, we're back to the Conclave. He really wants to disrupt or destroy it, take your pick," Jett said.

"We're also back to the logging industry and what, if anything, they have to do with it," Travis offered. "The Prophet infiltrated their ranks last time, and he's done it again, if what we've seen with the sacrificial victims is any indication. There must be a reason for that, or he'd pick another industry, don't you think?"

"I thought he was looking to grab the employees the loggers sent to abandoned planets and deserted places, to assess the quality of the trees available and how much trouble it would be to ply their trade in those places," Wyatt spoke up.

"That's possible," Kooper agreed.

"That may only be part of it," I said. Everybody turned in my direction, then. "Phorde Gaster was a frontrunner in this plan. How long ago was this set in motion? Phorde—the real one—died more than twenty years ago, and his replacement took his job with WildTree Industries. Vrak—the real one, disappeared thirty years ago or more. I haven't sensed his death, so the real one is probably under the Prophet's thumb. The version of Vrak sitting in Queen Lissa's dungeon? Because of his obsession I can't find his real name, but by his own admission, he has children that are under the Prophet's command."

"We still don't know why Vrak was targeted, either," Kooper sighed. "He worked in a factory that produced telescope lenses. It makes no sense."

"I'll tell you what doesn't make sense—those mutant Ra'Ak," Trent complained. "They almost took us down."

"What I'd like to know, too," Wyatt began, "is why all the theatrics surrounding the intended deaths of those victims, and why bury them in a river of concrete?"

"Whatever it was, I believe he was worried we'd learn the answer, and blew up the planet instead," I said.

"Captain," Dori's voice sounded on Travis' communicator. "We have early information from a sat-bot six light-years away from

Kev'Ril. Scientists on Bennall say Kev'Ril was fired on from the outside. Their initial guess is that it was done with a ranos cannon."

"Do they have images?" Kooper was on his feet immediately.

"Already sent to your comp-vid," Dori replied. "I'm sure I don't have to tell you that Bennall is scared to death, now."

This was good news and the worst of news at the same time. I was grateful the Prophet's power wasn't sufficient to destroy a planet, but learning he had a ranos cannon at his command could be just as bad.

Kooper was now shouting orders at someone from headquarters, telling them he wanted to track any signs left behind by a ship carrying a deadly, planet-killing weapon.

"The last time we saw one of those things was when Vardil Cayetes and his loyal sidekick, V'ili, were the biggest criminals in or out of the Alliances," Travis said. He, Dori and I sat at a table in the galley, which was empty except for us.

We were discussing the ranos cannon. Kooper had sent information back to us after investigating the images he'd received from Bennall. His experts in weaponry had all but confirmed it as a hit from a ranos cannon.

"Do you think he found something that Vardil used to own?" Dori asked.

"That, or he was lucky enough to find the plans to build one."

"I wouldn't call that lucky," I said. "Not for us, anyway."

"Randl, did the Prophet kill his own people, there?" Dori turned sky-blue eyes in my direction.

"I don't know," I confessed. "I was concentrating on getting the victims away and not paying attention to the crowd who came to watch."

"You're saying that he could have gotten them away before he blew Kev'Ril to bits?" Behind those calm words, Travis was worried.

"It's possible."

"Fuck." Travis rumbled. His dragon, usually calm and restrained, was near the surface.

"There's one thing I know for sure," I added.

"What's that?"

"Wherever the Prophet is, he's pissed."

~

P'loxett

V'dar

"Find replacements." I waved a hand at Varok and Perill, who rushed from my side to fulfill my command. Sixteen of the two hundred I sent to Kev'Ril had failed to see my adversary. I punished them.

The others were terrified and more than willing to do anything I said. Sixteen dismembered bodies littered the floor about me. I could clean the detritus away with little effort, but I was resolved to leave it where it lay—as a reminder.

"Where are you?" I whispered aloud. For now, my adversary and I were trading blows, and the ranos cannon my subjects cobbled together would require extensive repairs before I could use it again.

My enemy hadn't seen the cannon, as I'd been aboard the ship that carried it. So much worse for him, should I find *his* hiding place.

It would be destroyed as quickly as I could make that happen. As for the sacrifices, they couldn't be cured and would die eventually, unable to reveal any of my secrets—including who they were before. The drug I'd given them had altered everything about them. Still, it made me angry that he'd taken them from me, as their deaths would serve a purpose. A replacement for Kev'Ril would also have to be found. He'd taken that away, too, with his bothersome meddling.

Therefore, I resolved to take something from him—if I could find what he cared for. To do that, I had to know who he was and where he came from. He, like Campiaa and the Conclave, had climbed to the top of my obliteration list.

~

Avii Castle, Le-Ath Veronis

Sabrina

"I thought I'd have to bend time just to get the scanner finished," Lissa studied our combined handiwork with hands on hips. "I had no idea it would be done so we could create rainbow birds."

These weren't real rainbow birds, but they looked like them and sounded like them. Bel Erland had spelled two of them, and now they flew in an intricate pattern overhead, calling out to one another.

These massive birds were life-sized, and the creatures they were patterned after were an endangered species living in the jungles of Avendor. Word had it that all of them lived near gishi fruit groves and were protected zealously by the owners.

These replicas each had one of my new scanners hidden in its belly, and was solar-powered by a panel on the bird's back—large enough to power the scanners, which were suitable to handle the power source and do the job without anyone the wiser.

Multi-colored wings swished as the replicas flew; long, multi-colored tail feathers streamed behind these copies of the real thing. Their size was perfect for this operation and their calls as haunting and beautiful as their replicated feathers.

"The attendees will love this," Dena breathed. She and Quin stood next to Bel Erland, who studied the birds' flights with a critical eye.

"The registration takes place in an outdoor courtyard lined with trees and flowerbeds," Lissa agreed. "These are perfect."

"I'll have the other eighteen spelled and ready to go by tonight," Bel Erland said. "Does Teeg know they're coming?"

"I just sent the information," Lissa replied. "He's looking forward to this."

"The scanners are programmed to send images and information of suspects to Kooper, Jett Riffler and both their headquarters," I said.

"Well done," Lissa smiled at me. "I think you can be transported to Campiaa when the birds go. Travis and Trent will be docking BlackWing X there soon."

"Thank you," I said. "I think I need a nap."

Lissa laughed. "Go ahead—you've earned it."

BlackWing X

Randl

"We'll be docking at Campiaa's space station in six hours," Dori informed me. She'd arrived at the table David and I chose to have lunch, after a morning workout. "Sabrina is supposed to be waiting at the Founder's Palace for us, although I doubt we'll be staying there during the Conclave."

"Did she get the secret weapon built?" David asked.

"I heard it exceeds expectations, but that's all I know for now," Dori shrugged.

My mental eyes followed every movement she made, plus my mind recorded the slight flush of pink in her cheeks as she fussed with her plate of food.

She's got it bad, bro, David informed me mentally.

Is there something wrong with that? I returned.

She's a Captain, he reminded me.

Oh. Right. She, Captain. Me, grunt. Got it.

Sorry to put a damper on your libido, but that's the way things are.

You couldn't wait until I wasn't sitting across from her to tell me this?

You were giving her calf-eyes. Now you only look mildly irritated.

You know I can send you to a deserted island somewhere, don't you?

You've been upgraded to pissed status, now.

Dude, I may see a swim with sharks in your near future.

Now you're a fortune-teller. That's two steps above pissed. Congratulations, man, you just won a weekend at a one-star resort, although you have to attend a sales pitch to fully qualify.

What the bloody hell are you going on about?

Major frown! Major frown! Abort, abort, abort!

"Ahem," Dori cleared her throat. It was obvious David and I were having a mental conversation and she'd been excluded. That was extremely rude.

"I'm sorry," I apologized. "Dave thought it the proper time to point out that you're a Captain and I'm not."

"Seriously? You couldn't lie?" David pretended offense.

"Not to her," I said.

"Oh, we're being serious, now." Dave sighed.

"David, I understand your concerns—probably better and more deeply than you do," Dori pointed her fork at him. "If Randl wants, he and I can approach Kooper about this. Later."

"All right. I just don't want the bro here getting in trouble."

"That trouble will fall on me before I'll allow it to fall on him." Dori rose from the table and stalked away.

"Damn," David swore. He sounded impressed.

Dori

Yes, I was sulking in my cabin. Writing a report was my excuse, but little had been written, yet.

The knock on my door startled me. "It's open," I called out. I hadn't expected it to be Randl walking into the room.

"I got this from Susan," he placed a warming box beside me on the bed. "You didn't eat earlier."

My breath caught. Sure, I'd dated before. Nobody ever lived up to my expectations. I'd gotten to the point where I believed I was just too picky, or too high maintenance.

This man baffled me and squeezed my heart at the same time.

"Hey," he said and reached out to touch my cheek. "Thanks for defending me." He walked out of my cabin swiftly, closing the door with a soft click behind him.

Cori, I sent to my older sister, *I think I found the One.*

BlackWing VIII
 Co-Captain Cori Anderson-De Luca

Marco was acting Captain, leaving me with the reports for today. President Lebbon of Pyrik and selected staff were aboard. We were less than a day away when I received mindspeech from Dori.

She and I had traded mindspeech more often than usual since BlackWing VII was destroyed. She'd had a difficult time explaining how she and the crew survived while the ship was left behind to be blown to bits.

She'd asked to stay aboard BlackWing X with Travis and Trent, and just today informed me that she'd found the *One*.

Once, when she was young, she'd had a huge crush on Marco's younger brother, Salidar. Sal had disappointed her, and she'd broken it off with him.

Yes, she'd gone out with others, but none of them ever measured up. She and Sal were civil to one another, still, but there would always be an uncomfortable distance between them.

Are you sure about this? I sent back to Dori.

You'll meet him soon enough, she informed me. *You can tell me then whether he's worth it or not.*

Is he good enough to introduce to Daddy?

If Daddy's not impressed, then he never will be.

When are you getting to Campiaa? I thought to ask.

In a few hours.

How about dinner tonight? Bring him with you.

I'll see—he may be stuck in meetings—with Teeg. That's happened a lot, lately.

Must be special, then.

You'll see.

~

Founder's Palace, Campiaa
 Sabrina

"Make yourselves comfortable," Wyatt grinned at Bel Erland and me. We'd been set down in the Founder's library, which few people ever got to see in person. "Drinks and snacks are on the way," Wyatt added.

Nearby, in an empty space between massive bookshelves, lay the enormous crate that held our rainbow bird replicas. Bel had packed it and spelled it himself, so no damage would be done to the scanners.

"I can't wait to see these things, bro," Wyatt said. "Gran says they're amazing."

"When will BlackWing X arrive?" Bel asked. I wanted to know the same thing, so I waited for Wyatt's answer.

"In less than two hours," Wyatt grinned. He was waiting for Jayna to arrive, while I waited for Travis and Trent.

"Where will we be staying?" I asked instead.

"Well, Ry has a cabin in the mountains," Wyatt replied. "Although it's big enough to house an army. We've decided to put you there; somebody can transport you back and forth when necessary."

"It has an amazing view of the ski slopes farther down," Bel said. "I've stayed there plenty of times."

"Someone will get you and the BlackWing crews that are transporting people to Conclave up to the cabin, but the Captains will be meeting with Dad and a few others before they can join you there," Wyatt said. He understood the waiting part—he'd be included in the meeting, while Jayna went to the cabin with the rest of us.

"Don't worry," Wyatt held up a hand—you'll all have roles to play while you're here, but there are still a few things we have to figure out, first."

"Like what to do about the mess with the logging industry conference," Bel grumbled.

"You heard about that too, huh?" Wyatt asked.

"Yeah. Big mess. Dad says we need a spy in their ranks, but who do we send, and how do we accomplish that?"

"I don't have an answer, but that's on the agenda for our meeting."

By that time, a servant arrived with a tray of drinks and small sandwiches. "Let me know if there's anything else you need," Wyatt said and turned to leave.

I knew what I needed—Travis and Trent. The snack tray was set on the table in front of the sofa Bel and I occupied. He reached for a mug of tea first; I followed suit with a sigh.

≈

BlackWing X
Randl

"Astralan says that Devarr and the rest of his entourage were just delivered to their hotel suite," Travis announced. We were in a holding pattern to dock at Campiaa's space station, so a staff meeting was in progress while we orbited the planet, waiting for our berth to clear.

"Most of you," Travis continued, "will be taken to the mountain retreat owned by King Rylend of Karathia. It's large enough to house us and the other BlackWing crews that are bringing new attendees to the Conclave. Some of us—ships' Captains and Randl—will be expected to attend a security meeting with Teeg, Jett, Kooper and a few others. Once that's over, you'll be given your assignments for the duration of our stay on Campiaa."

"Is there speculation as to what those assignments could be?" Susan asked. "And is there a full moon happening while we're here?"

"There is—in three days. Flyer has already made arrangements to be here with you for several days," Travis grinned at her. "You'll have the day of and the day after the full moon off. David, too."

Susan turned bright pink and tried to hide a smile.

"We're cleared to dock," James' voice sounded through the ship.

"Take us in," Travis responded.

"Leaving orbit for space station now."

≈

P'loxett
V'dar

Images and information were transmitted by one I'd conscripted at Campiaa's space station. He was a lowly employee who entered names of ships and their docking fees.

Those aboard each ship had no knowledge of his existence, he was so invisible.

He'd also had no choice whether to serve me or not—it was a command; therefore, he did as I bid him.

All the ships carrying new members of each Alliance had arrived; the last one, *Gloria I*, had just docked and was charged appropriate fees.

These—they weren't important enough to initiate my plans, although Pyrik's transport ship and crew was included in their number.

No—when my newest replacements arrived for the logging industry conference, which began on the first day of Conclave—*then* I would set my plans in motion.

"Have you found new information on Adarr Gramm and the others of the Big Three?" I asked when Varok set a cup of tea before me.

"The last information was correct, although the ones you seek were no longer at those locations. They hide themselves well by moving often, my lord."

"Then keep searching. I wish to include them in my plan."

"The search continues, my lord."

Founder's Palace, Campiaa
  Randl

I'd felt eyes on us when we left the ship and walked through the security gates before getting a shuttle to the surface.

That meant I'd have a question for Jett and Teeg when I arrived at their meeting. Another shuttle had waited at the Founder's Palace, waiting to whisk the rest of the crew to a mountain cabin, leaving Travis, Trent, Dori and me behind to attend the security meeting.

Squaring my shoulders, I walked beside Dori; she and I followed

Travis and Trent into a side door of the palace; we'd been guided there by one of Teeg's palace guards.

"We were being watched at the space station," I said once we were inside a trans-vator and rising to the top of the palace, where Teeg's meeting rooms were.

"Who?" Trent turned quickly and gave me a frown.

"I don't know, but if I can get a list of employees from Teeg or Director Riffler, it won't be difficult to find him or her."

"We'll do that first thing, then," Travis said. "Damn, this is one foul thing after another."

"I sent mindspeech to Wyatt—he's working on the list now," Trent said.

"Thank you."

Dori, whose head came to my chin, looked up at me, questions swimming in her blue eyes. "I think it's just somebody ticking off arrivals," I said. "But I'm concerned that the space station comps won't be the only recipient of this information."

"You think the station has been infiltrated?" Travis asked. He didn't need to ask by whom—only one would truly be interested in this.

"It's possible."

Wyatt waited outside the trans-vator when the doors opened. He shoved a comp-vid in my hands, containing a list of all the space station employees on duty when we arrived.

I wasn't interested in those who worked security or management. This was a low-level employee in the bowels of the station itself.

I chose that subsection while we walked toward the meeting room. "Him," I pointed to the image of Cleaster Leech.

"What do you think we should do?" Wyatt asked. "Do you suppose he'll explode if we approach him?"

"I don't see that in him—he doesn't have what Phorde Gaster did, or Caille Morr. He has a growing obsession—that's what I see."

"You think we can work with where he's sending information? Tap into the comp system and see where it goes?" Travis asked.

"We can try that, but we risk losing the connection," Wyatt advised.

"Is that a bad thing?" Dori asked. "If we treat this as system maintenance, it's easily explainable."

"We have nothing now—what do we have to lose? Plus, if Cleaster gets found out by routine maintenance, then we have an excuse for sticking him in the pokey," Trent said.

"I'll hand this to Dad and Jett—they'll make the final decision," Wyatt said. "Here we are; the others are already here."

Dori

When Wyatt said the others were already here, I knew Cori and Marco were in the meeting room, waiting for our arrival.

Cori would get to see Randl before she thought she would. Perhaps we could still have dinner after the meeting—provided it didn't last forever and we were still awake.

Four chairs waited for us at the huge table, near where Teeg sat. He wanted Randl close, that was evident.

I saw Marco and Cori farther down. Both saw Randl at the same time.

This is him? Marco spoke first, and his mental voice wasn't complimentary. *Dorilou, he's fucking blind.*

CHAPTER 9

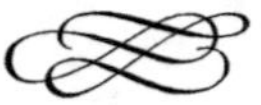

ecurity Meeting, Founder's Palace, Campiaa
    Randl

"We'll run a maintenance check on the comp system," Jett agreed with our assessment. "And we'll fabricate a reason to arrest Leech if we can't pinpoint this problem."

I was only half-listening to his words; I'd found Dori's sister Cori, and Cori's husband, Marco, sitting at the table. They were co-Captains of BlackWing VIII and Marco's opinion of a blind man as Dori's love interest was less than complimentary.

Sal, I expected more from your brother, I sent mindspeech.

Marco? What's he got to do with anything?

So far, he's called me fucking blind in mindspeech and scolded Dori for being interested, I replied.

Fucking hell, Sal swore. *Do you want me to set him straight?*

No, I'll handle it.

So—you and Dori. I'll be honest, I did not see that coming, he said. *She's, well, she's shied away from serious relationships for a really long time. I may be partly to blame.*

Sal sounded sheepish, and he never sounded like that.

It hasn't reached the serious stage, I said. *I'm letting her set the pace—because she's still unsure of her footing in this.*

Plus, there's the whole Captain-lesser being thing, Sal added.

That, too. Look, I have to go, they're about to ask questions.

See ya.

"In addition to other measures we're putting in place," Teeg said, "we need a way to infiltrate the logging industry conference, and someone who can fit in who won't be suspected."

"Can we send in an outside gambler—somebody who can keep an eye on those people?" Amos Thompson, Captain of BlackWing I, asked.

"Who will we send?" Teeg asked. "It'll have to be one of ours to do any good at all, and I worry they'll be refused a room because the conference has pretty much filled up the Eclipse Casino's entire hotel."

"Then send in a big spender, with a retinue who can do spy work," someone else suggested.

"We don't have any recognizable names, in case you haven't noticed, and it would have to be a recognizable name to get into one of the tower penthouses, because those rooms are pretty much all that's left."

"Zanfield Staggs," Wyatt said.

"Seriously?" Teeg blinked at his son. "Zanfield is as eccentric as they come. Even if we could dress somebody up like that kooky bastard, we'd have make sure the real Zanfield didn't show up and blow everything straight to hell."

"I think I can convince the real Zanfield that we need his help," Wyatt said. "You know how he loves to play dress-up. How many times have you seen him in a fake ASD uniform?"

"He can only get away with that here, because CSD uniforms are different," Jett pointed out. "If he impersonated one of my agents, I'd have him arrested."

"Funny, that's what I say every time he comes to Casino City on Le-Ath Veronis, dressed as a CSD agent," Kooper said.

"You think you can convince him to cooperate?" Teeg asked Wyatt.

"If I can't, I can take Terrett with me."

"Now there's a thought," Kooper pointed a finger at Wyatt. "Take Terrett anyway. This is too important to let go of the idea, and Eclipse will fall over itself if Zanfield makes a reservation."

"They'll give him the room for free, just for showing up," Wyatt said. "We only need to copy his tendency to win occasional big jackpots."

"And find a costume and a retinue and an interesting way to arrive," Teeg nodded. "Wyatt, see if you can make an appointment with Zanfield between now and when Conclave starts."

"I'll get it done," Wyatt agreed. "What's next?"

"How about a late dinner at the Sandswept Casino?" Wyatt asked me later, as the meeting was breaking up. Dori stood next to me, waiting for me to say yes.

She wanted to introduce me to her sister. It wasn't difficult to tell she was angry with Marco, who'd made disparaging remarks about my blindness in mindspeech.

Except for the few times Teeg had deferred to me on matters concerning the Prophet, Marco had no clue that only my eyes were sightless.

"Anything will be fine," I agreed. "Dori's hungry."

"Are we going out?" Cori arrived with Marco, her arm linked with his.

"Sandswept Casino," Wyatt said. "I can get us there, and into their best restaurant."

"Then let's go," Cori smiled. "Marco is about to cave in."

"Hello, Cori," I held out my hand to her. "Marco," I nodded to him.

"Has Dori been talking about us?" Cori asked, taking my hand for a shake before letting it go.

"No," I said. "Nothing other than she wanted us to meet."

"Be careful, Randl probably knows the color of your underwear by now," Wyatt teased.

"What?" Cori took a step back.

"What I'm saying is that he's a clairvoyant, and can pretty much see whatever he wants, including your images. He sees with his mind," Wyatt tapped his temple. "If you think he's really blind, then you are very wrong."

"See—I'm not so fucking blind after all," I turned to Marco.

"Holy shit," Marco sighed.

"You're the one who killed the mutated Ra'Ak on Bornelus with a ranos rifle," Cori breathed. We sat at a corner table in Sandswept's best restaurant with Wyatt, who'd used his influence as the Founder's son to get us in.

"I wasn't there, but I wish I'd seen it," Dori said. "I heard the story, but nobody ever said who'd done it."

"Well-kept secret," Wyatt said and sipped his wine. "Kooper keeps most of that information quiet. The Prophet, you know."

"We can keep secrets," Marco growled.

"Look, we got off on a bad note," I said. "Can we call a truce?"

"Marco, you owe me," Dori huffed. "Be a decent person, all right?"

"Fine. I'm just trying to look after Cori's baby sister," he held up both hands.

"Cori's baby sister is a ship Captain, and gets to make up her own mind," Dori said.

"Look, if it makes you feel any better, Dori's in charge, here," I said. "Nothing happens without her say-so."

"I just want to know she's safe," Marco said.

"Marco," Cori scolded him.

"She'll be fine," I said.

"I'll be fine," Dori echoed my words and glared at Marco.

"Well, as potential family gatherings go, this one is a near-disaster," Wyatt said. "Look, I'd trust Randl with my life. Dori probably does, too, although after I saw the bar fight on Pyrik, I'd say Dori seldom needs saving. Shall we? It's time I took you to the mountain retreat so you can find a place to sleep."

~

King Rylend's Mountain Retreat, Campiaa
Travis

Sabrina sat between Trent and me. We'd chosen a wide chaise on the front porch of the cabin, although the porch would hold two normal cabins on its own. The cabin steps were cleared of snow, but deep, white powder lay across the yard—deep enough to reach the tops of my boots. Snow had begun to fall again in quiet, large flakes, dusting cleared spaces like powdered sugar on sweetcakes.

We were content to watch the flakes fall from our covered space on the porch, although it was very cold where we were. An occasional, icy breeze lifted a dusting of snow and spread it across the eastern end of the cabin, where a drift almost chin-high had already formed.

Below us, the lights of the ski slopes twinkled. Far below those lights lay the crescent-shaped capital city of Campiaa, which looked like stars floating on a calm lake from our vantage point.

"Cold?" Trent wrapped the padded jacket Sabrina wore closer about her. Where we were, it was freezing. In Campiaa City far below, the weather would be fine and warm enough for lying on the beach when the sun was out.

So far, Randl, Wyatt, Dori and Dori's sister and brother-in-law hadn't arrived. They'd gone to dinner, but I hadn't missed seeing the tension that developed quickly between Marco and Randl.

We didn't need dissension in the ranks, as Kooper would put it. Perhaps Marco saw himself in a protective role for Dori, when nothing of the kind was needed—especially where Randl was concerned.

"We're here," Wyatt announced as he and the others appeared on the porch not far away.

"About time," I drawled.

"Has Jayna gone to bed?" Wyatt asked. I wasn't surprised that he'd ask about her—he'd been on and off the ship several times and hadn't gotten to see her.

"I think she said she was going to bed to read," Sabrina said.

"Good." I caught the flash of Wyatt's smile before his boots scuffed across the polished wood porch, heading for the door.

"Do we have assigned rooms?" Marco asked.

"There's a comp-vid with a layout on the kitchen table," I said.

"Thanks." I turned to watch Marco and Cori follow Wyatt into the house.

"It's so peaceful here." Randl wasn't looking at the door; he studied the falling snowflakes and the view below with an audible sigh.

Dori, standing beside him, slipped her arm through his and wrapped fingers around his forearm.

"You cold?" He smiled down at her.

"A little."

"I can fix that."

The porch was suddenly flooded with warmth. It wasn't too hot; it was just enough to convince us to take off our jackets after a few moments. The snowflakes that were blown onto the porch by an errant wind were unaffected, however, and continued to pile up on the porch, as if the warm air were held back specifically from each one.

"I'm not even going to ask," Trent grinned and tossed his jacket onto a nearby chair.

"Probably just as well," Randl replied before leaning down to kiss the top of Dori's head.

Randl

I was awake early the next morning, and found Travis sitting at the kitchen table nursing a mug of Falchani black. He wore his frustration well; most people would never see it.

I saw it.

He and Trent were having difficulty with the mute on their affections for Sabrina. It was also impossible for Sabrina to hide her naked desire and love for both of them.

This was a collision course, with fireworks at the end of it.

"Tell me," Travis said as I pulled a mug from the cabinet and went about making tea for myself.

"Tell you what?" I asked. I could almost predict his question, even with my back turned toward him.

"Who awakened your wizard abilities? Who trained you to use them."

"Strange that you'd ask that question now," I said, setting my cup beneath the tea maker and tapping the button. He'd held it back from me, after Kooper ordered him to find an answer. I imagined—perhaps wrongly—that he considered it an imposition on our friendship and refused the order.

"It's not strange at all," he insisted. "Every wizard, witch or warlock has to have someone awaken their power, or it lies dormant."

"I have a question for you," I said. I set my mug of tea on the table and pulled the chair out across from his.

"Mine first," he said.

I settled onto my chair, pulling it forward and scraping legs across the stone floor. "My question is connected to yours—in a way," I said.

"All right, I'll bite. What's your question?"

"Who did that for the Prophet?"

Travis leaned back in his chair, but his dark eyes never left mine. "I have no idea," he finally admitted. "Who did yours?"

"I did. Oh, Zaria pointed me in the right direction, but I did it myself," I held up a hand to fend off more questions.

"But no wizard or warlock can do that," he blew out a breath.

"Who said I'm a wizard or warlock?"

"What about the Prophet, then?"

"I've already called him a sorcerer with a penchant for necromancy. I stand by that."

"Are you a sorcerer?"

"I think I prefer the term mage."

"Why?"

"Because I believe a mage would think before he acted, while a sorcerer may not. A mage may have the common good as his goal. A sorcerer may not."

"I think I'd like to discuss this with Ry or Bel—with your permission and when you're present," Travis said. "I'm not sure what they'll say about this, or what their definition of what you are will be."

"Am I something that has to be categorized to keep everyone happy?" I asked. "Are you questioning my motives, if I don't fit neatly into an accepted definition?"

"No," he held up a hand. "Not at all, and I sure didn't mean to upset you. It's just that after last night—damn, man, that would take anybody ten years to learn how to do properly—to get the proper temperature and hold it within a set of specifications, to allow the snowflakes to fall through it unharmed. Did somebody teach you that?"

"No. I did it myself."

"I don't understand this," Travis massaged his forehead.

"Look, if it will make you happy, and by extension, make Kooper happy, because I see him behind this, I'll talk with King Rylend and Prince Bel."

"Kooper was here earlier; that's why I'm up before you."

"I will say this," I said, ignoring his last remark because I knew it already, "I dislike people discussing me behind my back. You should know better, because I'll see it every time." I folded space to get away from the tension that had developed between Travis and me.

Founder's Palace

Wyatt

"We have an appointment with Zanfield Staggs," I informed Dad.

"We arrested Cleaster Leech last night," Dad countered. "We found irregularities in his reporting, but before we could follow the information trail back to the Prophet, it disappeared without a trace."

"Charged with dereliction of duty?" I asked.

"And conspiring to release classified information, plus half a dozen other things," Dad confirmed. "When are you and Terrett meeting with Staggs?"

"He invited us to lunch."

"I hope you don't end up eating toasted insects or something," Dad teased.

"I've never heard of him ordering food that strange and exotic," I pointed out.

"There's a first time for everything."

"You're not making me feel better about this."

"I didn't intend to."

"How about I stay here and run the planet, while you go talk to Staggs and eat bugs?"

"No way."

"Why not?"

"Because I'm your dad," he grinned.

"Right. Play the Dad card."

"Have fun with Staggs, Son."

"Right."

~

Mountain Retreat

Travis

He disappeared and hasn't come back, I informed Kooper.

What the hell happened?

I probably messed this up, somehow, and made it sound like you and I don't trust him or what he can do.

Kooper swore. *I just wanted to know where he learned all that. He slid right past my shield when he showed up at New Fangled. Somebody had to teach him how to do that—or that's what I thought.*

I already talked to Bel Erland. He consulted with his grandfather, and neither of them have ever heard of somebody learning this on their own.

"What if it's in his DNA?"

Zaria's sudden appearance made me jump. Somehow, she'd gotten the message to Kooper, too, because he folded onto the cabin porch to join us.

"What the fuck are you talking about?" Kooper half-shouted at

Zaria, before reeling his anger in. Zaria wasn't someone you could fly off the handle with, as Mom would say.

"Tell me, Master Lion Snake, how the Larentii come to their power? They're born with enough to destroy an entire galaxy, you know." Zaria's eyes narrowed at Kooper, who ducked his head. He didn't have an answer and she knew it.

"Well, my work here is done," she turned a frown in my direction, next.

"Sorry," I apologized to empty air; Zaria was already gone.

Randl

I'd never walked a beach before. This one served double duty, as I had some anger to wash away. With shoes and socks in both hands and my pants rolled up, I stepped through the surf and considered my place in the universes and the ASD.

Where are you?

Dori's mental voice was terrified.

Walking the beach, I replied and sent an image with my words.

Thank goodness. When I heard you'd disappeared, it scared me.

I'm fine, I told her. *I'm sorry I worried you. I'll be back shortly, after I work through a few issues.*

Marco didn't get to you, did he?

No, Marco had nothing to do with this. Neither did you.

Will you tell me?

Maybe sometime. Not now.

Because you're upset about whatever it is.

Yes.

Why won't you tell me now?

Because I've seen you shred somebody, remember?

So, you're protecting them, not me.

Possibly.

It's probably a good thing we're not together right now, she informed me.

Why?

Because I'd be kissing you again.

The woes of being an underling, I lamented.

You make me laugh, Randl Gage, she said.

Glad to be of service, I replied.

~

Felarku, Wib'burne

Zanfield Staggs' Private Residence

Wyatt

"No. I will not agree to someone taking my place," Zanfield snapped.

"What will you agree to, Master Staggs?" I asked, although my hopes of gaining his permission were dwindling.

"I wish to do this myself," he waved a hand in the air, as if he were summoning the cosmos to the dinner table. "No other can do me as *I* do me."

I made a mental note to let Dad know Zanfield hadn't served toasted beetles for lunch.

It was half-cooked squid, instead.

"Then how do you propose we work around you doing you?"

"Why, your agents will serve as my retinue. I'm sure they can be out and about the casino without raising many eyebrows. I'll spend money as I usually do, drawing attention away from all of *you.*" His eyes, a dark green, settled on me then, as if to punctuate his statement.

His hair, an unnatural yellow with purple tips, rippled over his head like a ripe wheat field. Only a naturally-born Wib'burnee could do that, and it drew my attention away from his eyes and the matching green suit he wore.

"I'll have to discuss this with my father," I began, imagining the withering look Dad would level against me before saying no.

"I don't care who you discuss it with. This will work, and you know it."

"It will work," Terrett spoke for the first time during our visit.

"See—your friend knows," Zanfield clapped his hands and laughed.

"You will never tell anyone else about this conversation, or what our intentions are, unless I release you to do so," Terrett said.

Zanfield went still for a moment while the obsession settled in his mind. "This will be so much fun," he laughed moments later and slapped the table, making me jump.

~

Founder's Palace, Campiaa

Wyatt

"Rich people can afford to be eccentric," I told Dad, who'd been frowning at me for at least ten minutes.

"Terrett placed obsession?" Dad asked.

"He did."

"Good. Set this up and tell Kooper and Jett to choose their agents carefully. They need to be somewhat on the flamboyant side, or they'll never fit in as Zanfield's employees. Arrange for Zanfield to arrive in a manner that will fit his outlandish ways. If we play this game, we may as well play it to the hilt."

"I think I want Randl to look at Zanfield before we make those decisions," I said. "He should have gone with us, but decided to go on walkabout instead. I still want him to see images of Zanfield before the arrival."

"Probably not a bad idea. Make it happen," Dad said.

"How are the initial orientation meetings with new members going?"

"Those are going well."

"What isn't going well?" I could tell he was withholding something.

"That shrew Lebbon hired—the affected one? She's been yelling at everybody, including people she has no business yelling at. I was there to greet Lebbon as expected, and she just couldn't stop herself from making a scene with the people behind him."

"Maybe she's trying to impress you."

"I sure as hell hope not. I asked Dormas to do research—seems she's always been that way. Even Lebbon is afraid of her, when he should just fire her. I'd never have hired her to begin with."

"You think strings were pulled somehow to get her in his employ, or has the Prophet interfered in this the whole time?"

"Jett says his people haven't found evidence of anything yet, but he's still looking."

"It may be something you can't see," I said. "Or scent, maybe. Randl says she's affected, but what if it's more than that?"

"I didn't get close enough for either of those things, and I don't want to. Her screech hurts my ears." Dad grimaced at remembered pain.

Few people know how sensitive our ears are, and they won't ever know that Dad is the child of two vampires, and I am the child of a vampire and a High Demon. The truth is this; I have more of my Dad's talents than my mother's. Lexsi is the only one of my siblings that got Mom's talents in full measure, plus a few from our vampire grandmother.

"You don't want Astralan to arrange a happy accident, do you?" I named Dad's chief warlock guard. He knew I was teasing. His answer was serious, however.

"No, we have research to do, and we don't need the Prophet plotting revenge—more than he already is," Dad grumped. "We already have one space station employee in jail. We don't need the Prophet commandeering more employees to spy on us."

"This is fucked up, isn't it?" I sighed.

"I wish fucked up was all it was. This—defies imagination. Look, you have plans to make regarding Zanfield Staggs, and I have to make a speech at an orientation meeting. Alliance etiquette and protocol classes begin for them tomorrow, and the newbies have lots of studying to do before the Conclave starts. Go do your job, and I'll do mine."

Mountain Retreat

Randl

"I don't understand why you waited as long as you did to ask that question," I said. "Honestly, I thought it was trust and mutual respect that held you back before. You know the things I've done since my return. Why spring this on me now? Did Kooper ask you to watch me, in case I got out of hand?"

Travis sat behind the desk King Rylend used whenever he visited. I sat on the opposite side, employee-like while Travis acted as Captain.

"He didn't tell me to watch you, so much as find out—if I could—who trained you. Where you learned how to do the things you do. Some of the things you've done would take a warlock or wizard years to perfect, and even then, some would never be powerful enough to do those things. Other things you've done—no wizard or warlock would be capable of. Kooper wants the name of your teacher, because he doesn't know anyone who can train this type of thing. There's nothing in the ASD or CSD archives to account for it."

"And when I said I trained myself, everybody got their underwear in a twist."

"That's not all that happened," Travis stared at the desktop for a moment.

"What else happened?"

"Zaria popped in for a few seconds, chewed my ass and Kooper's ass, then left. I think we know not to ask any more questions," he admitted. "I'm sorry for my part in this. Really."

"I think I'll accept your apology—just not now. I'm still angry about this."

"I'll accept your acceptance later. I'd still be upset, too. What I need to talk to you about now is Zanfield Staggs."

"What about him?"

"Wyatt and Teeg still want you to evaluate him. He's made a bargain with Wyatt to participate personally in our charade. He'll be himself, but we have to place our agents in his retinue—the odder the better, actually, and that will gain us access throughout the Eclipse."

"Are we only intending to watch the affected ones, or take action?" I asked.

"Kooper says watch them initially, and continue investigating the Prophet's plans. Once we locate their rooms and place a few hidden devices, we can track their movements better."

"That sounds sort of lame," I pointed out.

"I know. We have nothing to go on, except those replacements. For now, they're our only true link to the Prophet, and they're already under surveillance at work and at home. As for the Conclave itself, we have the new scanners Sabrina designed. We have to pinpoint all the Prophet's players, and make plans on the fly."

"Because we still have no idea what he's planning or what he wants."

"Yes."

"When will I meet Master Staggs?"

"In a few days. Wyatt has a meeting set up to finalize plans with him. That means we need a list of agents who will accompany him, and his method of arrival."

"Do you have images of Zanfield Staggs?"

"Everybody has images of Zanfield."

"I'll take a look, and we'll go from there."

~

Meeting Hall
  Sandswept Casino
  Teeg San Gerxon

The speech was routine—how good it was to see fresh faces in Alliance rule, how happy Campiaa was to host the orientation meetings, and that I looked forward to seeing them at the upcoming Conclave—yada, yada, yada, as my mother would say.

President Lebbon of Pyrik had come, as he'd been invited.

Unfortunately, he'd brought shrew-woman with him, along with several others. Most of the attendees only had an assistant or guard with them—here they were safe, and Alliance guards were not only outside the doors, but several were stationed along the walls of the meeting hall.

If the Prophet had some connection with the shrew that we were unaware of, then he was watching my speech right along with everyone else.

If she were armed in some way and we weren't aware, then my life was in danger. While I spoke, Astralan and Stellan stood behind the podium, watching the crowd as only experienced warlocks could.

Both were prepared to throw a bubble shield around the shrew if it became necessary.

Life as the Founder of the Campiaan Alliance is never dull.

"Thank you for coming, and listening to another dull speech," I said. "And now, lunch in the adjoining dining area is waiting for you. Enjoy."

I allowed my shoulders to sag as everyone rose from their seats and headed for the double doors along one wall, which were now open. Tables waited inside the dining hall, covered in white cloths, the best tableware the hotel had to offer, and servers were prepared to direct attendees to their tables before taking food orders.

"Want us to fold you home?" Astralan spoke beside me.

"I'll wait until they're all in," I said. "Once the doors are closed, then you can get me the hell out of here. Frankly, I'm too tired to do it myself."

Lebbon of Pyrik and his entourage were the last to reach the doorway. Shrew-woman was busy giving another of Lebbon's employees the sharp end of her tongue when I saw a male server approach them.

I thought he was going to direct them to an open table.

Instead, he pulled a laser pistol from a pocket and shot Shella the shrew in the head.

CHAPTER 10

ounder's Palace, Campiaa
    Wyatt

"She didn't explode—that's the good news. Her body is in a tightly sealed biohazard room and Karzac is on the way." I sat heavily at the meeting table, where Travis, Trent, Dori and Randl waited to hear the rest of the unofficial statement.

"What about the shooter? The news-vids are going crazy, saying a Campiaan citizen killed a Conclave attendee."

"That's not true, and Dad will make an official statement in a few. We know who the killer is, and he isn't Campiaan."

"It was Shella's fiancé, wasn't it?" Randl asked.

"It was. We're in the process of sorting out many communications between the two via comp-vid, but it looks as if this is an act of jealousy. Shella had sex with someone else while they were on vacation together, sneaked around to do it and didn't tell her intended. He got pissy about it when he found out."

"How did he get here?" Travis asked.

"Paid for passage like anybody else," I said. "There wasn't any reason to stop him. He had no criminal record—until now."

"Has anyone questioned him—about who she had sex with?" Randl asked.

"How is that relevant?" Trent asked.

"No idea, I just get a creepy feeling when I think about it."

"That someone besides her murderous fiancé wanted to have sex with the humanoid tsunami alarm?" Travis frowned at Randl.

"No, it just bothers me."

"Then I'll make sure somebody asks," I said.

"I want to see him," Randl said.

"I can make that happen. Come on, I can get you into the holding facility now, if you want to go."

"We all want to go," Travis said.

I transported the four of us into an empty office, before walking down the hall and showing the guards our credentials. We went through the heavy door separating offices from cells, and it swung shut and locked behind us.

"That always creeps me out," Trent whispered as the heavy bolts slid into place.

"Come on, he's down here."

Randl

Shella's fiancé, Melton Timble, was still angry and far from happy. If he could have reincarnated Shella Karp, he'd try to kill her again.

And again.

I studied him through the glass and bars of his cage. There would be no simple cell for his future—I'd see to it myself.

"Shella had sex with Caille Morr," I said. "Melton here found out about it shortly after Lebbon's party left Pyrik. They had a few less than complimentary conversations regarding her duplicity, and here we are."

"What do you think the Prophet will do?" Travis spoke softly.

"Nothing," I shrugged.

"What?" Wyatt blinked at me in confusion.

I was glad all the cells about us were soundproofed, but to make sure, I placed a soundproof shield around the four of us anyway. "The Prophet didn't have anything to do with this. Shella was infected when she had sex with Caille," I said. "Then, she passed the favor along to Melton, here." I jerked my head toward the prisoner, who seethed inside his cage.

"Fucking, blood-letting hells," Wyatt swore.

"Do you think the Prophet is aware of this new twist?" Kooper paced inside Teeg's private study. He, Jett and Teeg were in attendance, once Wyatt informed them through mindspeech about the latest danger concerning the infection.

"I doubt it," I said. "If my assessment is correct, the Prophet is an obsessive-compulsive. He doesn't like loose ends, or things outside his control—especially things he doesn't know about."

"And any sex his subjects have with normal people may be outside his control?" Jett asked.

"I'd say yes."

"This keeps getting worse," Teeg growled. He wanted to take something apart with his deadly vampire claws, but that would have to wait.

"This means we have to keep an even closer eye on those fuckers with the logging industry," Travis pointed out. "You know these conferences are an excuse to get sex wherever and whenever."

"Why do you think the Prophet is an obsessive-compulsive?" Kooper went back to my previous statement.

"The two square holes filled with concrete? If you measured those, you'd find they weren't a micrometer off—in any part of them. They were perfect. Even when he removed the concrete from the first one, the hole left behind was perfect. There's really no reason to make any of it perfect, when your intention is to kill people by drowning them in liquid concrete."

"So aside from the Prophet's murderous tendencies, he's also a neat freak?" Wyatt shook his head.

"I think so," I responded.

"I wish there were a way to tag these people," Kooper said. "So we could keep tabs on them."

"Maybe there is," I said.

"How's that?"

"Either identification bracelets or badges, or, failing that, tagging their credit chips."

"That's illegal—tagging credit chips," Jett began.

"Unless the target has committed a crime, and the Prophet has already committed a crime. These people are impersonating others, so they're committing crimes, too. I've seen the CSD vids and read the regulations. You can tag someone who's committed a crime, to track their movements. Can't you?" I stared at Jett—he knew as well as I did what the legalities were.

"I'll make that happen the second they step off their ships and go through security. Nobody will even know it happened—those tags will go straight to CSD comps."

"We can give the traces to the agents working with Zanfield," Wyatt suggested. "They'll be able to tell where they are and when. Anything that looks suspicious is passed up the chain of command."

"We need to know if they're fucking like bunnies," Teeg snapped. "Not just being in the wrong place or plotting the demise of the Conclave."

"Then you'll need me in Zanfield's group," I said. I wasn't looking forward to that assignment, however. I'd walked through one casino already, after my earlier conversation with Travis. The noise of the casino and the press of bodies set my senses on edge. That's when I'd gone to the beach instead—to do my thinking and deal with my anger.

I assumed the casino experience was overload—like that I'd felt before when my mental sight had taken time to adjust and too many people were shoved in front of me at once.

"We have one volunteer for the Eclipse to watch the Prophet's doppelgangers," Wyatt tapped his comp-vid. "Anyone else?"

"Why don't you let me put the team together?" I asked. "I think I can do well enough at this, and get a few extras in with none the wiser."

"I want the list first thing in the morning," Kooper gruffed. "And I have final approval."

Zaria did get your underwear in a knot, didn't she? I sent to him.

I can charge you with insubordination, he replied.

Do it, then. I don't like threats.

Neither do I.

Who threatened you?

Nobody yet. He didn't sound happy. I didn't alter my previous statement, but it was becoming clear that Zaria handed his ass to him, and he didn't like it.

And there I thought you were a great boss, I said.

We'll discuss this later. Much later.

Are we good until then?

Yes.

~

Kooper

I should have apologized and I didn't. Randl managed to stay a step ahead of everyone else, and he'd also pointed out things that I should have noticed myself and didn't.

I had images from the first deep hole on Bornelus after the Prophet removed the concrete block. The dimensions were available for me to read, and I hadn't noticed that they were perfect, when there was no real reason for them to be perfect.

Randl then handed me CSD law, when I should have been several steps ahead of him on tagging the credit chips of known criminals.

I took a moment to chastise myself over recent failures, my run-in with Zaria and how my anger and shortcomings could affect Randl. Like it or not, he was the best chance I had at getting to the Prophet.

It just bothered me that someone was outthinking the Director on this, and I needed to point my anger at myself rather than toward someone else. We sure as hell didn't need to scare the public with a sexually transmitted disease—one that no medical test would detect and only a few had the talent to recognize.

Travis, I sent, *I want to have dinner with the BlackWing bunch tonight. I really need to speak with Randl and Sabrina, but I need input from the rest of you, too. Ask Randl to have his list of agents for Zanfield ready, too, so I can make arrangements.*

Will do, Travis replied. *Want me to handle catering?*

Please. Set it up for twenty-one bells—I should be available then.

"Want to have dinner with the pirates and me tonight?" I asked Jett aloud.

"Sure thing. I learn more when I talk to them than from talking to the entire list of CSD agents."

"Good. Let's visit with Karzac and our prisoner, then, to hear what the physician has to say about sexually transmitted obsessions."

Randl

Karzac didn't tell Kooper, but he'd asked to link with me while he explained his findings to Kooper and Jett. He'd been working on this problem since the first infected body had been delivered to him, and, with the assistance of med-bots, had reached some conclusions in the matter.

I could see Kooper and Jett through Karzac's eyes, as he welcomed them into a small office, connected to the sealed glass room where Shella's body was quarantined.

Through the glass wall, I could see that the med-bots had already proceeded with an autopsy, and were still working on Shella's body.

"What can you tell us?" Kooper asked.

"I believe I've discovered changes in the amygdala of other bodies, and I'm hoping to find something similar in this one," Karzac replied.

"That tiny part of the brain?" Jett asked.

"Yes. Those two small parts may be tiny, but they have a great effect on how we react to many things. It is tied to our emotions and memory, so it isn't a far stretch to imagine that an obsession would affect it in some way."

"Is there anything we can do about it?" Kooper asked.

"Removal of the amygdala is unpredictable, and I believe it is only a part of a greater problem. The infection, for lack of a better term, also seats itself in the organs of those affected, and will still infect another if someone comes in contact. Therefore, removing the amygdala of an infected individual may only prevent the obsession from activating, while leaving them fully capable of infecting another —through sex if nothing else."

"We're still left with a serious problem," Jett shook his head as he watched the med-bots work.

"Yes. Definitely a serious problem. It's too bad we didn't find Shella after she was first infected—it could give me an idea of how quickly the infection spreads after intercourse."

"Are you working on a possible cure, then?" Kooper asked.

"I have considered it, but for now, that could be far down the road. By the time a cure is developed and tested, too many people could be infected and it would be too late to administer a preventative. I'm unsure as to whether a cure can be found for anyone after they are infected, Director."

"If I didn't know better, I'd say this was connected to the God Wars," Jett grumbled.

"That has yet to be disproven," Karzac turned to him. "At this point, we can rule nothing out. The Prophet may be a servant of the dark ones, left behind to create chaos and destroy, in his masters' absence."

"You're not making me feel any better," Kooper snarled.

"You do not outrank me in the Hierarchy," Karzac snapped back. "Hold your anger back, Director, especially from those who are only attempting to help you and your cause."

"You're right," Kooper admitted, before pinching the bridge of his nose. "I've already barked at Randl, when I should have been listening to him instead."

"You have a very good team around you, Director. I suggest getting more sleep in the future, and allowing others to keep watch during that time. They will not let you down, I believe."

"Yeah. I'll work on that."

Mountain Retreat

Randl

"We have to present this to Zanfield in a way that he'll consider it sufficiently noteworthy," I said, handing a comp-vid to Kooper after dinner.

Travis and Trent had found a type of pot roast somewhere to feed all of us, and we were having after-dinner tea and coffee while I went over my list of choices for Zanfield.

"You want Dori to be the ocelot?" Kooper frowned at me.

"She will walk in at Zanfield's side. He'll be dressed as his favorite high-ranking ASD Director, but with a retinue worthy of his eccentricity. Travis and Trent, acting as his bodyguards, will follow, both dressed in ASD uniforms. Then comes David, as the favored shorter person. As for who will be walking beside David—and I'm still working on this, by the way—I've decided to have a female snake charmer, with Bekzi's lion snake wrapped around her shoulders and torso."

"Who comes after that?" Kooper asked.

"I do. The blind man dressed in black leathers with two Falchani blades strapped to his back. As I'm blind, who will think the blades dangerous?"

"How do you arrive? Have you thought of that? Zanfield always likes to make a statement when he exits a vehicle."

"I've borrowed something from Bekzi and his brothers," I grinned at Kooper.

"What's that?"

"A nineteen-twenty-five Rolls-Royce Phantom," I said. "It has been modified as a hover-car, so Zanfield will arrive in style."

"Who will be the snake charmer?" Jett asked.

"I was thinking either Jayna or Susan," I shrugged. "I don't know which one can be more comfortable wearing a snake around their neck. Neither are fond of snakes," I added, "so we may have to convince them."

"Sort it out," Kooper said. "I don't care which one ends up going; they're both competent. We'll go with your decision in that role and consider it the final list," Kooper tossed out a hand. "Randl, you're in charge of this."

"Thank you, Director," I dipped my head to him.

❧

Kooper

I considered that Karzac was correct, and it was time to allow someone to hold the reins while I rested.

Two came to mind immediately—Kell and Opal. Opal held a place in the Hierarchy, and I figured Kell would get there soon enough.

I sent mindspeech while having a drink in Teeg's massive palace kitchen. Kell and Opal arrived seconds later.

"You'll be taking over for me when I'm unavailable," I announced before emptying my glass of bourbon.

"Good," Opal breathed a ragged sigh. "We thought you were trying to kill yourself by refusing to rest."

"Thanks for noticing," I said, my words dry. "I'd offer you a drink, but you're officially on duty now. Coordinate with Jett and his people, and we'll work out a schedule tomorrow. Don't wake me unless a bomb goes off or you see the Prophet in person."

"If we see the Prophet, we'll wake Randl first," Kell said, his words equally dry.

"Sounds good." I poured another glass. "Go forth and manage," I said. "I'm getting drunk."

❧

Felarku, Wib'burne

Wyatt

"This is pure genius," Zanfield hooted as we let him watch the parade of images cooked up by Randl and Sabrina on my comp-vid. Sabrina had provided graphic images of what Zanfield's arrival and entrance to the casino would look like, and it was indistinguishable from the real thing.

"The ocelot and the snake are tame, aren't they?" Zanfield thought to ask.

"Both are shapeshifters," Randl informed him, "and both work for the ASD. They are agents, Master Staggs."

"Outstanding," Zanfield said. "I see you at the back, dressed as a Falchani," he told Randl, before restarting the images again. "I've never heard of a blind man working for the ASD."

"He's the first—an experiment," I said, attempting to divert any worries Zanfield could have.

"I do well enough," Randl agreed. "You'll see."

"I'm already booked at the Eclipse," Zanfield sighed. "I can't wait to arrive like this."

"It will be the spectacle of a lifetime, guaranteed," I said.

"Good. When will my uniform be delivered?"

"Today. We've had it tailored specifically for you, and it will be authentic, right down to the buttons and ribbons."

"Excellent. I can't wait!"

Sandswept Casino

Randl

"This is the ballroom where the Conclave will be held," Wyatt took me on a tour of the facility after our meeting with Zanfield.

The massive ballroom, which would be covered in tables and chairs in only a few days, was currently empty and our footsteps echoed as we walked across marble tiles. *Do you think Zanfield will cause us any trouble?* He asked mentally.

I think Zanfield is too excited about being this close to actual ASD agents, and close enough to being one himself to mess it up too badly, I replied. *He's as giddy as a schoolboy going on holiday.*

I get the giddy part, Wyatt chuckled softly. *That's Zanfield when he's excited about something. But Bekzi,* he began.

Yeah. I understand about Bekzi and Zaria—that they're together. Bekzi told me himself, or I wouldn't have known it.

It's better for him if not many have that secret, Wyatt admitted. *He's powerful enough, but what if he's targeted because of her? She doesn't want that, I don't think.*

You're right.

And the same goes for the rest of her mates. Do you know who they are?

I saw them in someone else, not Zaria, I said. *And those secrets I will keep.*

"Here's the security area, where badges will be checked before the attendees enter," Wyatt said aloud. "This time, the Kings, Queens, Presidents and other rulers will come through first, instead of through a separate entrance, like the one on Pyrik."

We'd walked out of the ballroom and into a wide pergola, with exotic plants, trees and flowers spaced throughout.

This is where Sabrina's rainbow birds will fly, checking the crowds before they pass through security, Wyatt informed me.

There's plenty of room for them to operate, I acknowledged. The pergola was quite high and supported by carved columns resembling equatorial trees from many worlds.

Bel says he's even spelled the rainbow birds to land on one of the trees now and then, to complete the ruse. I think the most lavish parties from now on will be crying to get rainbow birds for their events.

It could be another moneymaker for Sabrina, I agreed. "Will everyone show up at once, or will they have assigned arrival times?" I asked aloud.

"There will be assigned arrival times," Wyatt said. "That way, nobody will be waiting overly-long to enter." *You think someone's listening in, too, don't you?* he asked.

Yes. I feel eyes on us, too. Very much like the occurrences on Pyrik and Jaledis.

I'll have Astralan and Stellan check it over for spells, Wyatt said, *to see if they can detect anything.*

Let me know what they say. I could do some checking of my own, but I worry that the eyes will see what I do, and that will identify me to someone I'd rather stay hidden from.

Understood. Want to go with me to visit Dad? I think he'll want to hear this.

Of course. I like your father.

I think he likes you, too.

"That's all of it," Wyatt said aloud. "How about a snack and a drink?"

"I like that idea," I replied.

When we were several feet away from the pergola, the buzzing sensation of someone watching us dropped away and I sighed in relief.

"How do you suppose they got in there to place a spell, or whatever this is?" Teeg San Gerxon asked. He and Dormas, his ancient vampire assistant, were the only ones in Teeg's study besides Wyatt and me.

"I don't know," I confessed. "I still don't know how they got into Sabrina's lab on Jaledis, either. I only felt the presence, if you can call it that, and called a halt to our entry. They still managed to get to her later, after we had her equipment moved."

"Who are they targeting, here?" Dormas asked. "Or is it the entire Conclave?"

"If your warlocks don't put them on notice by searching for the spell, it could be everybody," I said. "If the one who laid the spell doesn't retract it the moment he feels he's been discovered, then he'll be going against the norm, I think. If that's the case, and we can't get rid of it somehow, I suggest having a High Demon contingent available during Conclave."

"I'll certainly consider that," Teeg agreed. "I think we can borrow a few guards from my wife."

He meant Queen Reah of Kifirin, who ruled the High Demons.

I didn't mention Vik—it would be hard enough for him to see her again, although she wouldn't recognize him now.

Neither would Teeg, for that matter.

I felt bad for Vik—he was still being punished in some way, in my opinion. *I hope you know what you're doing,* I sent to Zaria.

I believe I do, she replied, surprising me with her response. *Although nobody is ever one hundred percent accurate one hundred percent of the time,* she added.

I felt the smile in her mental sending.

Then Vik may be our hidden asset in protecting the Conclave, I said.

Exactly my thoughts, she agreed.

"What do you think, Randl?" Teeg drew me away from my conversation with Zaria, to ask about beefing up security in addition to adding a few High Demons.

"I think you should discreetly position all the BlackWing crews either in the pergola or inside the ballroom," I said. "You have plenty of talent there, and adding them to the existing guards wouldn't hurt."

"A sound recommendation, and one I'd already considered taking to Kooper," Teeg nodded. "I'll present it to him and Jett tonight at dinner."

"That's great, Dad," Wyatt said. "Can I have a private dinner with Jayna, tonight?"

"Have a good time, Son," Teeg grinned.

I considered that I ought to have dinner with Dori—or at least ask if she wanted to have dinner with me. She could invite others if she wanted, but time alone sounded nice. I also considered that there was a long list of things I should attend to, and one of those things was the coin from Vogeffa II.

After my first experience with the object, I was reluctant to hold it again, and I couldn't define the misgivings I felt at those images.

As if I'd see something eventually I didn't want to see.

Vehicle is here, Bekzi sent.

I'll be right there, I replied. I really wanted to see the Phantom again, because it was a beautiful thing.

I'd never considered applying for a vehicle operator's license, and wondered how the Alliances would feel about a blind man driving anything.

Dori and a few others were outside the mountain retreat, admiring the car when I arrived. Without thinking, I went straight to her first, draped an arm around her shoulders and squeezed.

Dori's head dropped against my shoulder while she released a happy sigh. She'd been waiting for me to do this. It could create another rift between Kooper and me, but for the moment, I didn't really give a reptagator's ass if it did.

"Want to go to dinner with me after this?" I breathed against her hair before dropping a kiss there.

"Yes." An arm stole around my waist, and I was more than happy to have it there.

"This way, we can kill two birds with a single stone," Dori smiled at me across the small restaurant table.

We sat near a window, which gave us an uncluttered view of Greenever Mountain above the small village of Ba'Moru on Pyrik.

"Something about this place bothers you, too?" I asked.

"Yeah. I can't really say what it is, and I sure can't see what you can when you look at people, but it gets my tail in a knot every time I think about it."

"I worry that Caille was having sex with anyone who'd say yes," I voiced my concern. "He apparently didn't care whether the woman was engaged, so we could be looking at half the women in the village."

"Involuntary soldiers for you-know-who's army," Dori said. "He just doesn't know they signed up yet."

"And if he finds out, he could exert his power over them and send them running in his direction."

"He didn't send the others running, he pulled them out instead," Dori pointed her fork at me. We talked over salads and glasses of wine while waiting for our main courses to arrive.

"True—good point," I said. "So, if he discovers them and pulls them away, we have no idea where he'll take them. Kooper's been looking for him for almost a year, and I—well, I've been looking longer than that."

"I can't believe he doesn't have ties to somebody in the logging industry. He keeps going back to that, you know. Otherwise, he wouldn't have placed more of his soldiers in their ranks and made arrangements to influence the location of their conference."

"We don't have proof that he did that, only strong suspicions," I said.

"Come on, you know he had a hand in this."

"Yes. I think you're right, we just don't have proof of it."

"Do you think it's because they're so easy to infiltrate—the logging industries?" Dori asked.

"That could be part of it, plus, I think pseudo-Phorde Gaster was unwittingly giving information to the Prophet about suitable places to set up his pirates and troops, or where he could bury those confounded concrete blocks that he uses to sacrifice people."

"And we still don't know whether that's just a sick fantasy or if there's a purpose behind it."

"Also true. I haven't had much time to do research lately, but I really want to get to the bottom of how the Prophet creates exact replicas of other people. The original Phorde Gaster is dead, and was replaced by a replica. He did the same thing with those who worked for the logging industry—it's why we're going into the Eclipse with Zanfield Staggs—to watch them and what they do."

"Any theories on that?" Dori smiled at me before sipping her wine.

"One or two have suggested the Lyristolyi drug, and I have information that Queen Lissa sent to me, but there's been no time to absorb any of it."

"Sounds about right, although they'd have to modify the drug to get it to do this—in the past, only someone who could survive the drug to begin with could be cloned—by giving their blood to another person with the same blood type. Whatever metamorphosis the drug went through in their system was then able to create an exact replica of the original survivor. That happened with Vardil Cayetes," Dori said.

"Well, you seem to know a lot about this," I said. "Tell me more."

"Vardil contracted the disease that affected so many worlds after Siriaa was destroyed, sending that planet's deadly affliction into space and eventually dropping onto other planets. It made the planet and its people sick."

"I know about that—tell me what Cayetes did." I knew most of it, but wanted Dori to tell me what she knew, in case I'd missed something. Also, Cayetes ended up using the Lyristolyi drug, and I certainly wanted that information.

"Cayetes hired a warlock and a witch to do a transference—it's a black spell and illegal everywhere. Those two transferred Cayetes' spirit from one body to another, trying to outpace the effects of the disease, and of the transference itself, because a transference only lasts for a few days before the body begins to die and a new one has to be provided. He went through countless people before his assistant found a cache of the drug and they administered it to twins who survived, and then cloned numerous copies of the same bodies so Cayetes would look the same instead of changing appearances every few days. Eventually, the drug was manipulated and a spell cast that enabled Cayetes to be rid of the disease and keep the same body, although he was a broken, mindless fool for quite a while after that— until Quin healed him. She had the best of intentions, understand, but it released that prick into the world of crime again, and what followed wasn't pretty."

"So, the Lyristolyi drug is perhaps the worst kind of drug imaginable."

"Yes. It was outlawed long ago, and even the Lyristolyi people consider it a capital offense for anyone to have it in their possession."

"The death sentence isn't levied on most worlds, but I knew that world still held it in reserve," I nodded. "Now I know why."

"Most people think drakus seed is the worst drug, because they've never heard of this one. Imagine what it would sell for on the black market."

"Why is that?" I asked.

"Because of the saying, once a survivor, always a survivor. In other words, the Lyristolyi drug will ensure that you can live forever—if you survive it the first time and can get a supply of it when your current body dies. That doesn't include the number of clones you could make of yourself, either, by giving blood to others who share your blood type."

"You just scared the pants off me," I frowned.

"I don't want to scare the pants off you," she said. "I want you to take them off willingly."

"We'll get to that," I laughed.

CHAPTER 11

Mountain Retreat, Campiaa
Randl

We talked about work if you must know, I replied to Kooper's mindspeech. *We discussed the Prophet, his possible motivations and the Lyristolyi drug.*

Don't get defensive, that's not what I intended, Kooper said. *Did you find anyone else in Ba'Moru who Caille infected?*

One of the servers at the restaurant was infected—I could detect her interaction with Caille, and only had to dig a little deeper to see her affliction from that contact. That means there could be many, many more, each of them passing their own version of the infection along to their unwitting partners.

Fuck. Kooper's frustration came through clearly in his mindspeech. I didn't point out that the word itself was how people were now sharing the Prophet's encroaching disease. *How do we stop this?* he asked after a moment's silence.

Unless you intend to tell every person living in and out of the Alliances that they either have to practice abstinence or go back to long-outmoded methods of sexually transmitted disease control, then there's not much to be done. You already know this can't be found with any existing medical test, so everybody will be suspicious from the get-go. If you explain exactly what it is that they have, the Prophet will realize his army is likely much larger than he ever dreamed it could be. All those people, just waiting for his commands, once he learns of their existence.

Wait, I'm coming to you. Give me a few seconds.

Kooper arrived in the library of the mountain retreat where I sat, going through information on the Lyristolyi drug on my comp-vid.

The Director took a seat and stretched out his long legs, while allowing his arms to dangle over the sides of his cushioned chair. He didn't speak for a while, because he was considering what I'd said to him.

"You said they're waiting for the Prophet's commands."

"Yes."

"Can anyone else command them?"

"Not likely," I shrugged. "Unless he clones himself, and I doubt he's willing to do that. Even an exact replica of himself would mean he'd have to share power, and he doesn't strike me as the kind of individual who would do that."

"Then we have to kill him as soon as possible. No commands mean the disease will lie dormant in all those people infected through sexual contact."

"I know you don't want to hear this, but we have to find him, first," I said.

"You found him the last time," Kooper began.

"No, Director. He found *you*. He wants you dead, remember? You and Jett. I was fortunate enough to see him through Phorde Gaster— fast enough that I could tell a few things about him, such as where he was and what his immediate plans were. I was able to stop him last time, because he wasn't expecting anyone to come against him. I won't have the element of surprise a second time."

"You think he's looking for you, like we're looking for him?"

"Undoubtedly. He wants me dead, just like he wants you, Jett and who knows how many planetary leaders dead or under his thumb. He doesn't like losing, Master Lion Snake. He lost the first round to us.

He's planning something even more malicious, and this time, he's not tipping his hand."

"Someday—it doesn't have to be today, but someday, I'd like to hear good news from you, Agent Gage."

"Let's hope that day comes, then. For now, I'm as much in the dark as you and everyone else. We can't find him, even when we employ power to do so. Wherever he is, he's plotting nasty things and nobody will know what they are until he springs his traps."

"Conclave starts in an eight-day," Kooper sighed. "I'm sorry I barked at you, and frankly, until this is over, I don't care what you and Dori do with each other. The worlds could end and I'd be forcing you to abide by rules that may not make a damn bit of difference in the long term. We survive this; we'll discuss things afterward."

"Thank you, Director."

"Whenever you have information, keep me apprised. Notify Opal or Kell if I'm unavailable."

"I will."

"Good. That's settled." Kooper rose from the chair, nodded to me and folded space. The weight of two Alliances sat on his and Jett Riffler's shoulders, and I didn't envy them their burdens.

Queen's Palace, Le-Ath Veronis

Winkler

"I'm saying that Randl is as much or more of a target than anyone else," Kooper paced inside my office. "That means that his father, Brandl, could become a target, too, if the Prophet ever learns who Randl is."

"Easy enough to do," I agreed. "What do you intend to do about this? Brandl travels to and from Avii Castle and the beach palace all the time. Anybody could get to him while he's traveling; it wouldn't take much, you know."

"Either Brandl has to accept guards—who have power—or he

allows someone to be disguised as him during travel times, while he's transported back and forth by someone who can fold space."

"Which is your preference?"

"A disguised replacement, who won't be easily taken down," Kooper said. "Brandl wouldn't want someone captured or dying in his place. We either need a vampire, werewolf or someone else who can defend themselves, to act as Brandl during his regular travel times. Get the real Brandl back and forth by folding space."

"Have you discussed this with Randl or Brandl?"

"Not yet. It just occurred to me after Randl and I talked earlier. He says he's a target because the Prophet doesn't like losing, and he lost to Randl last time."

"Megalomaniacs are so predictable," I said dryly.

"And so dangerous," Kooper said, his tone grim.

"Do you think Randl can go against him again? Since the Prophet will be expecting something of the sort?"

"Randl's worried about the same thing. He says he no longer holds the element of surprise, so we're dealing with the unknown, now."

"We were dealing with the unknown when he attacked us with the exploding dead," I pointed out. "You think he has more of those things waiting?"

"There are no reports of newly-vandalized cemeteries," Kooper replied.

"Hmmph." I didn't like that answer, and neither did he.

"Will you arrange for someone to take Brandl's place when he commutes from one palace to the other?"

"I'll have it done in an hour," I said. "Erland's here, so he can provide the disguise," I said, naming Lissa's warlock mate. "I just have to choose which person would be best suited for the job."

"Let me know who and when," Kooper said. "I need to get back to Campiaa."

"Have fun," I waved as he disappeared.

～

Mountain Retreat, Campiaa

   Randl

"Are you going to read all night and starve, or are you coming with us?" David and Vik arrived in the library, where I was still researching the Lyristolyi drug. Lissa had extensive records on it, including what Dori had given me.

To say it was dangerous was putting it in the mildest of terms.

Vik, whose head wasn't far from the ceiling, stood beside David, who was less than half Vik's height. They really were mismatched bookends. "I'll come," I shut off my comp-vid. "I think I need a couple of beers, too."

"We can manage that," Vik grinned. "Either come now or I'll carry you out of here."

"I'm not incapacitated," I said. "Just hungry." My stomach rumbled, giving credence to my words.

"Then let's go. We have a table waiting at the Glitz."

The Glitz, short for Glittenganz Casino, was on the higher end of places to stay, and held a number of good restaurants. Many catered to the less than well-dressed, so I wasn't worried about being in casual clothing.

"Lead the way," I gestured toward the door. I'd never been skipped anywhere by a High Demon. Vik skipped us in, so I knew he'd informed David of his hidden talents, at least.

I hope you know how to keep secrets, I sent to David as we were led to a table near the back.

Owl shifter, remember? David responded.

Right.

"Drinks?" Our server, a perky young man, asked after arriving at our table.

"Refizani Blue Label," I said immediately.

"Make that three," David said.

"Very good, sir," the waiter acknowledged. "I'll be back with your drinks, and I'll take your order then."

"Hear that? He called me sir," David teased. "I think everyone should call me that."

"Have you been knighted by the Queen?" Vik asked.

"No."

"Then I'm not calling you sir."

"Somebody went to clown school," David pointed at Vik.

"And I have the big shoes to prove it," Vik agreed.

It took a moment for the meaning to sink in, but it did and I laughed.

"Where's Dori tonight?" David asked.

"With her sister and brother-in-law," I said. "Cori wanted to go to a particular steakhouse, and, as things aren't so cordial between Marco and me, I said to go on without me."

"Marco's usually better than that," David said as the waiter set our beers on the table.

"Marco's never been presented with a potential addition to the family," I pointed out. "As far as he's concerned, I'll have to earn my place."

"I'd like the prime rib, please, thick cut, rare," Vik said, ignoring David and me so our server wasn't kept waiting.

"Very good, sir," the young man smiled. "And you?" He turned to David.

"Roasted fowl, please, with the fruit sauce."

"Excellent choice. And you?" he had no idea how to deal with me, because he, like most people, could only focus on my white eyes.

"I'd like the seafood pasta, please."

He blinked, because I hadn't ever lifted my menu to read it.

"That's a new item, but it comes highly recommended."

"I'm looking forward to it," I said.

"Your orders will be out shortly. Let me know if there's anything else I can get for you."

"Another beer," Vik said before emptying his bottle.

"Right away, sir."

"Now who's being called sir?" Vik set his empty bottle down and lifted an eyebrow at David while the waiter hurried away.

"Tall people are always insufferable," David sniffed in pretended annoyance.

"Do I need to get between you two?" I asked.

"I can still reach him, even if you do," Vik grinned.

"Whatever you do," David turned to hiss at me, "Do not let him pat me on the head."

"But you're so cute when you're an owl, I just want to pat your head," Vik laughed.

"You see what I've had to put up with while you've been galivanting around?" David frowned at me. "The least you could do is take me with you sometimes, just to keep him at arm's length."

"I want to go, too," Vik said.

"It's going to be a long night," I sighed.

Vik

When I said I wanted to go with Randl and David, I had no idea I'd end up in Melton Timble's cell, while Randl studied him. We'd received permission from Kooper and Jett, and had to promise that we'd be shielded against any attack from the prisoner before they allowed it.

They were also watching from an office nearby—the cell had several vid-cameras placed inside it.

So far, Randl hadn't said a thing, while Melton snarled at us from his seat on the cot. At least he knew he was outnumbered, although he eyed David from time to time.

Melton thought he was selecting the easiest target.

David could take him apart if he wanted. Melton Timble had never trained to fight, and David trained or worked out every day.

"Where did you get the weapon?" Randl spoke abruptly, making Melton jump.

"Not telling," Melton turned his head away, refusing to look at Randl.

"But you just did," Randl said, a smile lighting his face. "Thank you. I learned something today."

"What the hells do you think you learned? I told you nothing," Melton hissed.

"Perhaps someday, you'll figure out that you can, in fact, be wrong about something. Later, you may discover you can actually admit it. Good luck with that, by the way," Randl said and folded David and me out of the cell.

~

Randl

"I know where he got the weapon," I said, once we appeared inside the office where Kooper and Jett waited.

They or their agents had asked that question continuously after Melton's arrest, but they'd gotten no answers.

"But he has a growing obsession," Kooper pointed out.

"He still has the memory, and there's been no activation of the obsession—we discussed that already. Therefore, when I asked him a direct question, the memory of where he got the weapon surfaced and I could see it. If we'd waited a few weeks more, I probably wouldn't have seen it; it would be swallowed up by the encroaching affliction."

"Where did the weapon come from?"

"He purchased it from Poll Endicut. I understand he's a small-time criminal, with suspected bigger-criminal ties. We need to find Poll, I think, so I can see what he knows about the bigger fish."

"What does that have to do with anything?" Jett asked.

"I'm concerned there may be connections we don't know about. Remember, the Prophet can infiltrate legitimate businesses. Can he not also infiltrate not-so-legitimate ones, too? He's had a year to work this out, and he may hit us in ways we haven't even considered."

"Randl, when I asked you to keep me informed, I had no idea it would be all bad news," Kooper growled and rose to his feet. "Come on, let's visit Teeg. I'll contact Opal and Kell on the way."

~

Kell and Opal dragged Poll Endicut in for interrogation just before dawn. It didn't matter—I hadn't slept much anyway.

I left David and Vik at the mountain retreat—no need to wake them for this. Kooper was waiting for me inside the interrogation room when I arrived. Jett, Kell and Opal were in an adjoining room to watch and listen.

"Hello, Poll," I said, sitting down opposite him at the small table inside the room. "Do you know why you were brought in?"

"Whatever it is, I'm innocent."

Poll had small eyes, pursed lips, wispy blond hair that was combed over a balding patch atop his head, and an attitude that would have befitted a much larger, infinitely more honest man.

"You sold a laser pistol to someone who paid you several thousand credits for it," I said. "That laser pistol, which has no registration, I might add, was used to commit murder."

"I don't know anything about that. I was with my family at the time."

"You were with a woman whom you paid for sex at the time of the murder," I pointed out. Poll was so easy to read, there was nothing subtle about his mind—everything floated near the surface and was easy to extract.

"See, not guilty."

"I said at the time of the murder, not that you committed the murder. You sold the laser pistol the day before. That's the crime you've committed recently, anyway."

"I committed no crime. The murderer shot that woman."

"Oh, so you do know about this, then."

"I don't know anything. I know my rights and I'm leaving."

"You're not going anywhere."

"I want my advocate, then."

"Fine. I have everything I need from you already." I rose and walked out of the room, leaving Poll to his fate.

Agents were already going through his home and hiding places, and I figured they'd find enough evidence to keep Poll incarcerated for a very long time.

~

"The names I pulled from him are Adarr Gramm, Jewl Yarro and Rale Linn."

"Three of the worst that manage to elude us every time," Jett grimaced. "We think they're working together, but there's no substantial proof. Drugs, weapons, whatever you want that's not legal, they can sell you—through middle-men like Poll."

"Poll has seen the employees of all three, although he has no idea where they're based; they send him information on where to meet their servants, who provide the contraband, take the credits, then disappear."

"That doesn't help us," Jett began.

"I have another name—that Poll certainly doesn't want anyone to know."

"Who's that?"

"The woman he loves, who also sells contraband. She got him into the business, actually. Her name is Charla Dare."

~

Travis

"Charla Dare lives here," Kooper pointed to the three-dimensional map of Campiaa City. "It's on the northern side, where the wealthiest of the citizens live."

"That's a fortress, not a house," Trent said. "How do we get in to take her? Assuming, of course, that she sits there, waiting for our agents to bust in and drag her out. If she doesn't have a tunnel or a warlock to get her out of there, I'll be much surprised."

Kooper and Randl both looked weary, after spending most of the night and early morning working on this angle of Prophet interference.

We didn't have solid proof of it, yet, but after consideration, it made terrible, twisted sense.

It's what other criminals had done in the past—they'd send their spies to infiltrate the ranks of their rivals, to either take them out or take them over.

It wasn't just the logging business, now, and we should have seen this long ago. I realized we were playing three-dimensional chess with a two-dimensional board. Our view of things hadn't expanded to take in the nuances of the game, and we should have been prepared for that.

"We need a mister," I said. "We need Wyatt to take us in and set us down in strategic spots, so we can get this done."

"I'll see if Wyatt's available," Kooper sighed. "I agree—that's our best bet for doing this without risking her getting away. If my guess is correct, she's in deeper with the Big Three than we thought."

The Big Three. Agent speak for Gramm, Yarro and Linn. They'd rushed in to fill most of the void left behind when Cayetes died. They'd had more than fifteen years to establish themselves as some of the current worst on everybody's list, in or out of the Alliances.

Trent and I had a theory, that involved piles of Sirenali bones either bought or stolen from Cayetes' stash after his demise.

Sirenali bones were more valuable than the most priceless jewels—to criminals, anyway. It enabled them to hide from the powerful, as a Sirenali's talent for doing such didn't end with their deaths.

Zaria was the one who'd pointed out that whatever magic the Sirenali had, it resided in their bones and not their flesh.

Bones were easier to carry and keep, as they never needed feeding or care. Both Alliances destroyed the bones whenever they were found, so nobody could use them again.

The difficulty was often finding them in the first place. "They can be hidden in walls or buried in concrete and they'll still do their work."

I hadn't realized I'd spoken aloud until Kooper interrupted his plans to ask me what the hell I was talking about.

"Nothing," I waved a hand. "I was just thinking about Sirenali bones, and wondering whether Charla has any."

"We suspect that's true, because we can't get a lock on her inside the house, although all indications say she's there. That's why we have to go in, rather than allow Randl to just *Pull* her out. He can't get a fix on her, either."

He did that for me and my crew, remember? Dori's voice filled my mind.

Yeah. I remember.

"How many are in the house?" Vik asked. "Any idea?"

"Word is that she keeps eight bodyguards on duty most of the time," Kooper replied. "That doesn't include servants, groundskeepers or anyone else she employs. The place is massive enough to house all of them."

"And they could all be armed," David observed.

"Most likely that's the case. She's bigger than we suspected and so far, has managed to look as if she's legitimately wealthy. She wasn't on Jett's radar until Randl told him."

"That doesn't sound good," Dori grumbled.

"Somebody call?" Wyatt appeared in the retreat's library, where our meeting was being held.

"We need a mister," Kooper said. "Kell is busy elsewhere, so you're the prime suspect."

~

Randl

We had six hours to rest and plan before descending on Charla Dare's residence at nightfall.

Kooper had already pointed out likely places for Wyatt to drop each pair of agents—I wasn't surprised when Vik and David asked to go in together. Sabrina and Jayna would be paired with Travis and Trent, while Dori and I would go together. Susan, Bekzi and Terrett would form a triangle outside the fortress walls, in case anyone attempted to escape.

James and Nathan would monitor everyone's movements from Teeg's palace—each of us had a chip embedded in our dark clothing so they could track us, should anything happen to warrant backup.

Jett had agents on standby, but they'd be hidden farther down the hill, waiting for a signal from us if help were needed.

My hope was that I'd be able to see what Charla knew. A part of me was terrified I'd find her affected, just as so many others were, and that it would be too late to see anything in her.

Poll loved her—that was true.

She'd never had sex with him, however, so he'd been left to grovel in her wake, hoping that she'd change her mind someday. He had to content himself with paid sex in the meantime, and wasn't infected.

My other worry—that Charla could be one of the Prophet's chosen mutations, and that he could see us coming through her, caused me to warn the others to disguise themselves or have someone else do it.

I had no desire for the Prophet to target any of us because he knew our faces or names.

Travis and Trent had changed their last name slightly to work with the ASD, so they wouldn't be connected immediately with the Queen of Le-Ath Veronis and her Falchani mates.

Tetsuya instead of Tatsuya. Easy enough for the Prophet to make that leap, however. He wasn't stupid—I knew that better than anyone, I think.

Bel Erland will do it for us, Wyatt replied quickly.

Thank you, I said. Those two were as close as half-brothers could be. If one asked, the other answered, and if help were needed, it was provided. And, as Wyatt was close in age to Travis and Trent, they were more like brothers to him than uncles.

They had a large, close-knit family, and while I loved Pap more than anything, he was all the family I had.

I hoped that Dori wouldn't mind being added to it someday, but we had work to do before that could happen. Meanwhile, I could only watch Wyatt's large family in envy, and wonder what it would be like to have more family members.

Three hours, Travis sent a mental warning to all of us. With a sigh, I considered that I wouldn't get any sleep between now and then if I didn't lie down right away.

~

Two-and-a-half hours later, I wiped sleep from my eyes and rose, wondering if anything could bring me to full wakefulness after such a short period of sleep.

By the time I made it to the kitchen, fully dressed, there were only a few minutes remaining before Wyatt would transport us to Charla's fortress.

"Here." Trent shoved a cup of Falchani black in my hands. I couldn't say I liked the stuff, but I'd drank it before.

I gulped most of the tea, forcing the strong brew down my throat before setting the mug in the sink. "Thanks," I told Trent. "That will certainly keep me awake."

"Us, too," he agreed before slapping me on the shoulder. "Come on, man, we have damsels to throw in jail."

~

Good luck, Wyatt whispered mentally as he dropped Dori and me outside Charla's personal study. There was no light under the door, so I imagined she was elsewhere in the house.

So far, none of the others had sent mindspeech as to Charla's whereabouts, so I folded Dori and me inside the study to look around. Only a muted solar lamp lit the large room, where a massive, antique wood desk—something seldom seen in either Alliance—took up a great deal of space at the center.

Beneath the desk lay a priceless, ancient Serendaan carpet. No expense had been spared throughout the house, so crime was quite lucrative for Charla Dare.

Atop the desk, however, lay a comp-vid.

Dori snatched the device off the desk and shoved it into a pocket of her dark trousers before nodding to me. Nothing else caught our attention in the room, so I folded us back to the hallway outside to continue our search for Charla.

Travis

This must be the guest wing, I sent to Sabrina, who walked slightly behind me, as if she were afraid something was about to jump out at her. Bedroom after bedroom, suite after suite, lined a very long hallway inside the massive, multi-storied mansion. While passing an open door, a tree outside, blowing in the wind, cast shadows against a wide window.

Sabrina smothered a gasp and almost ran into me before she realized it wasn't anything to be afraid of. This was her first real stealth mission, and she wasn't used to it.

I stopped dead when the voices came—someone was heading toward our hallway, which turned a corner ahead.

They were coming toward us.

Quickly, I pulled Sabrina inside the open bedroom door and pressed her against the inside wall next to me. My ranos pistol was in my hand immediately and I sent mindspeech, letting the others know that someone was coming our way on the second floor. I was prepared to either fire my weapon or fold space—whatever it took— as neither of the voices was female.

These were Charla's guards, doing a routine check of the house unless I missed my guess. The alarm hadn't been raised or they'd be heading our way in silence, rather than talking and laughing.

Stay safe, Trent sent to Sabrina and me.

Roger that, I replied.

Randl

I smell food—there's a kitchen up here, Dori sent. We'd taken the third floor, where Charla's suite and her private study lay.

I knew another, large kitchen was on the first floor, but the plans Kooper had given us didn't show a second kitchen anywhere else.

Charla had done some renovations, altering the original house plans from twenty years ago. Either it was done for her convenience, or for that of her personal guards, so they wouldn't have to go downstairs for a break.

I held a strong shield about us as we made our way toward the smell of food; we'd be hidden from sight, sound and scent, unless someone accidentally bumped against us.

Let's see who's in the kitchen, I sent to Dori, who nodded. At least these hallways were well-lit and easily navigated—we'd had dim lighting during most of our trek through the massive third floor.

The renovated kitchen held six guards; four male, two female, all of whom laughed and talked over a massive amount of food laid out on a wide kitchen island. Once I got a good look at all of them, I pulled Dori close against me.

All of them were infected.

All of them.

CHAPTER 12

harla Dare's Fortress, Campiaa
    Vik

When we received mindspeech from Randl, telling us that six guards on the third floor were infected, David and I both pulled our weapons. We'd taken the first floor and had skipped past four guards between receiving mindspeech from Travis and Randl.

Neither of us had Randl's gift of seeing the infection in any humanoid, and it was safer to assume that everyone in the house could be infected, too, Charla included.

If we found her.

So far, nobody had.

Bekzi, have you seen any movement outside? I sent.

Guards. No others, he replied.

Where the hell is Charla? David asked.

She could be a million miles away and we wouldn't know it, I replied.

Fuck. David didn't mince words.

Keep looking, Travis' voice was stern. *Our guards didn't even bother to stick their head inside the room,* he added. *We'll move again once they're gone.*

Moving on from the third-floor kitchen, Randl reported.

Keep us posted, Travis told him.

We're blinder than Randl in this, I told David. *He can see that shit and we can't. This could go badly in too many ways to count.*

You're really smart for a tall guy. I may have to reconsider my opinion of you, David replied.

Thanks. Coming from you, that means so little, I said.

Don't start with the short jokes, man.

Are you implying that I'd stoop so low?

Oh, it's on, bro.

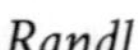

Randl

I smell perfume, Dori said after grabbing my arm to slow me down. We were approaching a door at the end of a corridor, a long way from the kitchen where Charla's guards were eating and talking. *Too much perfume*, Dori added.

I didn't consider the weight of her words right then—what I did think was that we'd probably found Charla.

We need to get past that door, Dori said, nodding to the door in question.

There were no other doors near it, which indicated that it could be the only entrance to a massive suite.

Charla's suite.

We may have found something, I sent, along with a visual of where we were on the third floor.

Be ready, Travis barked at the others. *Proceed*, he sent to Dori and me. I folded us inside the suite, never expecting to see what we found there.

Founder's Palace
  Kooper Griff

We may have found Charla, Travis sent the update. *Randl and Dori are going in now.*

Keep me advised, I said. *If you need backup*, I didn't finish.

Randl says that six guards on the third floor are infected. We don't know about the others, but we've encountered more than twenty guards and servants inside the house. So far, we've kept clear of any contact.

I swore softly. At least six of twenty or more infected with the Prophet's filth. Randl was right—the Prophet did want to infiltrate the criminal element. There was no way to tell what he planned to have them do during Conclave. The Big Three had access to weapons and money—enough to buy off or kill almost anyone they wanted.

Stay on target, I said. *I want Charla, infected or not. We need to know what's going on between her and the Prophet.*

Understood, Travis said.

I pinched the bridge of my nose after Travis cut off mindspeech. This was giving me a massive headache, and Kell and Opal still hadn't returned from Pyrik, where I'd sent them on a special mission.

Randl

That's disgusting.

Dori didn't mind voicing her distaste at the scene in front of us.

I knew it wasn't Charla but the Prophet's doppelganger of Charla, who was busy having sex with the real Vrak Falken. Both of them were members of the Prophet's mutants, who could transmit everything they encountered to the Prophet.

If Dori and I weren't shielded, they would transmit our images to the Prophet, although we were both disguised.

The Prophet didn't need to know anyone was inside the house whom he hadn't allowed there.

Where is the real Charla? I sent mindspeech to anyone listening, along with a reluctant vision of what Dori and I were witnessing firsthand. While I couldn't see past years of heavy obsession in the couple fornicating on Charla's bed, I couldn't sense Charla's death, either.

That troubled me.

Are you telling me that's not her? Kooper's voice demanded.

That's not Charla, Director. They're both mutants belonging to the Prophet, I replied. I wanted to swear, too, but held that back.

Dori jerked beside me at the soft whine coming from against a wall.

Look, she sent.

I turned my eyes away from the couple on the bed to find a small, fluffy white dog shivering against the wall.

Scratches covered the wall at his back as he lay there, obviously in distress.

What the hell did they do to him? Dori was ready to scratch eyes out, I think.

Show us, Travis demanded. I sent him the mental image, just as a terrible thought hit me.

Hold your positions, I said. *If things go south, get the hell away from here.*

What are you saying? Travis barked.

That's Charla's dog, I replied. *He's trying to find Charla. Hang on baby,* I sent to Dori. *We're going through a wall.*

~

Mer'bali, Pyrik

    Opal

Kooper's hunch was a good one, but we'd had to twist the non-interference rules to get what we needed.

At first, Kooper suspected that Shella Karp could be related to President Lebbon. She was related, although not directly.

He'd sent us to Pyrik, looking for the answers to his questions—regarding Shella's employment by Lebbon, and why he'd keep her in his employ after learning she was disturbing his staff and creating a terrible working environment.

We'd eventually tracked down Lebbon's first cousin, Bella Karp. Lebbon and Bella had been having an affair since their teens, and they'd kept it quiet. Not even their legitimate spouses knew, and it was against Pyrik's laws anyway, to have an intimate relationship with such a close relative.

Shella was Bella's daughter with her legal husband, and Bella asked Lebbon to hire her daughter because Shella was incapable of keeping a job anywhere else. Instead of finding a therapist or someone suitable to calm Shella's frequent tantrums, Bella foisted her daughter onto the one person who'd never fire the woman.

It no longer mattered, of course, because Shella was dead.

Kell had placed compulsion on Bella, to learn the full story before taking our information back to Kooper.

The Prophet had no hand in Shella's infection. Like Randl said, it was transmission by sex and nothing else.

"Ready to go back?" Kell pulled our bags off the hotel bed.

"Yes. More than ready," I said. I wanted away from Pyrik—to me, the whole planet was unsettled and half-poisoned. I hadn't felt comfortable during any part of our stay.

Kell felt the same; he just wasn't complaining about it.

"I'll buy you dinner someplace nice on Campiaa," he promised.

He had no idea we'd have to put that plan on hold.

Charla Dare's Fortress, Campiaa

Randl

I held Dori against me while she and I hovered several inches off the floor.

We'd almost walked into the Prophet's trap. If we'd set our feet on the floor, it would have worked, too.

He'd laid a displacement spell on the secret room adjoining Charla's suite. There, he'd stuffed all of Charla's servants and guards, while he'd sent his own crew in to take over her business.

Charla herself, looking emaciated, sat in a corner with two female guards flanking her. Above their heads, and fitted into the walls, were the poison gas pipes the Prophet had set to kill the inhabitants of this room if anyone attempted to rescue them.

It was easy to see in these prisoners that they'd been trapped in the room for several days. Due to lack of water, some of them were near death. None of them were infected, however, and I considered that for a few seconds before transmitting images to Travis, Kooper and the others.

What are we going to do? Trent's voice whispered in my mind. He understood that if we moved anyone inside the room, or set foot on the floor, the Prophet would know and he'd kill anyone inside the room with a poisonous blast of gas.

I'm calculating the weight of everyone in the room, and their placement, I replied absently.

What good will that do? Kooper demanded.

I can send Dori out of here with these prisoners, I said. *While maintaining their proper weight and placement on the floor.*

You should get yourself out of there, too, Travis said.

I can't do that without alerting the Prophet, I replied. *We need a more legitimate way to destroy the house. Any ideas? The Prophet doesn't need to know we've figured out this part of his scheme.*

If I can find the solar panel connections, I may be able to create a short in the system, Sabrina offered. *It could cause a rush of power throughout the house, frying all the connections and starting a huge fire.*

Do it, Kooper said. *Now. Randl, you said yourself that the Prophet is a perfectionist. Make damn sure you have that weight and placement down to the micron and milligram before sending those prisoners to the holding facility. I'll have physicians on standby when they get here.*

Sabrina, can you short out the system in such a way that it will lock all the exits and entrances? Vik asked.

They're all locked now, Sabrina said. *I can see they stay that way. It won't be a stretch, I don't think.*

Good. Better. Go, Kooper barked. *What are you waiting for? I'm developing an ulcer, here.*

Hold on, I cautioned.

What now? Kooper wanted to know.

He's a perfectionist.

And?

He has their weight and placement down, but they're breathing. Drawing in air. That means their weight fluctuates by the tiniest of amounts. Bloody, fucking hells. Give me a minute. Sabrina, are you and Travis at the solar panels?

Yes.

Can you do everything up to the final point and hold off until I tell you?

Yes.

Good.

Randl, what are you doing? Kooper asked.

Resetting the spell, so it will fluctuate like living, breathing bodies, while maintaining DNA and every other fucking variable in this equation, I snapped. I'd apologize later, and doubly so if what I was doing had no effect on any part of this. I couldn't take a chance on this one, though; I felt it in my bones.

Tell me when it's time to take them, Dori said, her voice calm.

Founder's Palace

Kooper

"You're joking." Kell and Opal had arrived, and I'd allowed them to see what I'd gleaned from Charla Dare's fortress so far, including the most frightening thing of all—Randl calculating weights of bodies and air in and out of the lungs.

"What if," Kell began.

"Don't," I held up a hand. If anybody knew that breaths could be interrupted, Randl would. I had no idea how he was calculating this, or providing a spell to duplicate all of it, and my biggest concern was that the people in that room would die, and then the house would explode.

The result was that the Prophet would know we'd discovered this part of his plan—as little as that was for the moment.

I needed the people in that room to tell me what they knew—and I certainly needed Randl to tell me what those people weren't willing to tell me.

Vrak Falken—the real one, this time—how did he figure in all this, while his double sat in a sealed cell in Queen Lissa's dungeon?

At this point, I doubted that Randl or anyone else could tell me whether he'd gone to the Prophet willingly or had been taken by him.

No matter; if all went according to plan, he'd be toast soon enough.

"I really do think I'm getting an ulcer," I breathed.

"Then stop it," Opal said.

~

Charla's Fortress

Travis

Sabrina had already disabled the transformer outside the house, making it appear as if it had failed on its own—or as much like that as she could. A working transformer ensured that a surge of power into the house wouldn't occur. They seldom failed, however, unless they were neglected or damaged in some way.

We were now inside the house again, where the power panel was affixed to an inside wall. *She hasn't had this checked for several years—here's the last inspection tag*, Sabrina pointed out the tag in question. She was right—the date was six years earlier. *That gap between inspections will make this so much easier*, Sabrina said, before pulling the outside panel open to examine the comp-like wiring and connections to every part of the house and grounds.

It will only take the smallest of metal filings, she said, pulling a small laser cutting tool from her utility belt.

I watched as she removed three long, metal slivers the width of fingernail parings off the back edge of the panel, near a hinge. *Now,* she went on, *I only have to attach one end of each sliver to the inside of the metal panel door*, she worked at connecting the tiny slivers to the door as she sent mindspeech to me.

What then? I asked.

I wait for Randl to say when. I slam the panel door shut and the ends of the slivers hit these corresponding connections. She pointed out the proper circuits. *That will cause three simultaneous short-circuits that will burn out the entire panel. A non-functioning panel and a broken transformer will open everything up to a surge of power from outside, which will cause appliances and the lights connected to solar power inside the house to either spark or explode. That will start a fire in every room and we get the hells out of here. This is why it's Alliance law to check these things yearly, to make sure nothing like this happens. And, as I'm about to disable the emergency fire alarms and the sprinkler systems, the whole place will go up.*

I love you, I told Sabrina. *Randl, how's it coming?*

Randl

This has to be a gradual removal, I told Dori.

Like filling a tank, only in reverse? She asked.

Yes. Very much like that. Almost ready, I replied to Travis' question.

Wyatt? Travis called out.

Here, Wyatt replied.

Evacuate non-essential personnel, Travis commanded.

Moving in, Wyatt said.

Ready? I turned to Dori.

Ready. She leaned in to give me a quick peck on the lips. I nodded. Whatever happened, I'd make sure she got out of this alive.

I began trading actual weight for virtual, spell-driven weight. It would take a few seconds to accomplish, and those seconds were slow in passing.

Vik

Wyatt had a big task, collecting all the people from the house that didn't need to be there. David and I were last on his list, as Wyatt started on the upper floors first. David had already sent our location, so we were forced to wait where we were.

Someone's coming, David's voice hissed into my mind.

It took a few seconds to realize that a guard was heading for the restroom across the hall from our hiding place.

All this time, and he has to take a piss now? David grumbled.

Stop breathing, I commanded. If I ended up skipping us out instead of waiting for Wyatt, then explanations to the Director would be in order, and I wasn't prepared to explain my true nature or my continued existence. For now, only Randl knew the full truth. David knew part of it. Kooper had no idea and I wanted to keep it that way.

What the hell is he doing in there? David pulled me away from my thoughts. *He's jerking off, isn't he?*

Please stop. I can't laugh, remember?

Now! Randl's sending hit both of us at the same time, and an explosion sounded at the other end of the massive structure.

Wyatt practically sucked us into his mist as rooms began to catch fire all around us.

Randl

I didn't leave immediately—I wanted to make sure Dori and her charges arrived at the holding facility safely, and that the poison gas wasn't released as an indication that the Prophet was aware of our infiltration and rescue effort.

In the adjoining suite, I heard Charla's replacement scream and Vrak's shout as their stolen boudoir caught fire.

Pulling Charla's dog into my arms with power, and then adding the photograph I'd seen on her bedside table to one of my pockets, I watched the gas pipes for barely one moment more before flinging myself away from the inferno that engulfed Charla Dare's home.

Holding Facility, Campiaa

    Kooper

Nearly half of those Dori delivered to the holding facility needed to be in a hospital. I had them sent to Le-Ath Veronis, so their names wouldn't appear on any lists in Campiaa. The Prophet could be checking, and I was determined to follow Randl's example and work to outthink that devil.

The rest, Charla included, were being treated by medics inside the holding facility, where they were being given water, fluids and nourishment.

There was no sense trying to talk to any of them now; I waited for Randl to come and tell me what he saw in them.

"I'm here," he said, appearing beside me in an office, where I watched the proceedings through a vid-screen. Randl looked and sounded more tired than I was, and that was admitting a lot.

"You smell like smoke," I pointed out.

"You would, too, if the room next to you was on fire," he said. "I waited to make sure the gas wasn't released."

"Good. Did anybody get out of the house?"

"No."

"While that's a terrible way to die, it was the only way in this situation," I shook my head.

"I know."

"How long will it take Charla to come around?" I asked, changing the subject.

"She isn't just Charla Dare," Randl said, setting a photograph on the desk in front of me.

"What's this?" I asked, lifting the frame to study the two images depicted.

"Charla and her mother—Jewl Yarro," Randl replied.

"Get Jett for me." I was up and at the door talking to a guard faster than most people could see my movement.

"Right away, Director."

"This—how could anybody see this?" I slapped the photograph on the desk, cracking the glass in the antique frame.

Without a word, Randl reached out and pulled a finger down the crack, repairing my mistake.

"You may need that, Director," Randl observed.

"Yeah. I guess I will."

Mountain Retreat

Travis

"What's this?" I stopped halfway into the kitchen, where Susan was ruffling the fur of a small, white dog while he voraciously drank milk from a bowl.

"This is Barkins, according to Randl. He hasn't eaten in days, poor fellow."

"He got Charla's dog out?" I blinked at Susan, who was on her knees beside the dog, soothing him as he finished the milk and licked the bowl clean.

"I believe so," Susan replied. "I didn't want to make him sick, so I'm only giving him milk and water first."

"What are we going to do with a dog?" I asked.

"Give him back to Charla," Randl appeared in the kitchen and headed for the cold-keeper. "At a price," he added and opened the cold-keeper door.

"You want to make a trade? But you can get all her information already," I pointed out.

"That's not what we'll aim for," Randl pulled the makings of a sandwich out and set them on a nearby counter. "What we need is a deal with Charla's mother."

"What good will that do?" Susan stood and blinked at Randl.

"It'll get us a meeting with Jewl Yarro, Charla's mother," Randl shrugged. "We'll see how willing she'll be to help us get to Charla's would-be killers."

"I admit, I never saw that coming," I blew out a breath. "Jewl Yarro and Charla Dare. Wow."

"Is there enough for me?" Dori walked into the kitchen.

"I'll make a sandwich for you," Randl said. "Sit down, sweetheart. You look tired."

Wow, indeed, Susan's voice filled my head. *Is he allowed to call her that?*

"You fixing?" Vik walked in with David right behind him.

"Have a seat," Randl's grin was tired but genuine as he gestured toward empty seats at the island. "We need sustenance, dammit."

Holding Facility

Opal

Kell and I watched the news-vids buzzing through both Alliances. Normally this would attract the most attention in the Campiaan Alliance, but as Campiaa was the location of the upcoming Conclave, all the news outlets in the Reth and Campiaan Alliances had images of Charla's house burning down. They also reported the early information gleaned from the local inspection crews—that Charla's transformer and solar power panel hadn't been checked in six years or more, because Charla refused to allow anyone inside the house.

Kooper was sleeping at Teeg's palace, but only after Kell threatened to place compulsion if he didn't go to bed.

For now, those rescued from Charla's home were barely coherent and still receiving medical care.

While we watched the news-vids and the speculation floating throughout all of them, I toyed with the comp-vid Dori had taken from Charla's fortress. I didn't have the code to open it and didn't want to pass it to the team who handled those things.

If anyone would know the code, Randl would.

If it were Charla's device, he'd see it. If the device belonged to one of the Prophet's people who'd died in the fire, the code could elude us, still.

Kell and I really wanted to know what was on the comp-vid. Kooper would too, when he woke.

The news that Charla was Jewl Yarro's daughter put Jett into a frenzy, and he had some of his most trusted agents working on that connection, now.

I wondered if the Prophet knew of the connection, but if he had half the smarts Randl did, he'd have known about the photograph in Charla's suite, too.

"What will we do if the Prophet has already infiltrated the Big Three?" Kell asked, echoing my thoughts. "We won't know, really, unless we convince Charla to contact her mother."

"The news outlets are reporting Charla's death," I pointed out. "How will that initial contact go, when Jewl thinks her daughter died in that fire? The images of charred remains being hauled out of the rubble is already spreading everywhere."

"At least the Prophet's game is working against him in this case," Kell sighed. "The replacement clones will match DNA and the other markers of Charla and her bunch. It won't help us any at all when we approach Jewl. Not unless her daughter is willing to convince her in some way."

"Kooper may need to leak false information about the possibility of other remains found, or the Prophet may notice," I said.

"I agree. Let's put a plan together for him, so he'll have a course of action when he wakes."

"How will we explain the one set of DNA that wasn't supposed to be there?"

"Which one?" Kell wasn't thinking along the same path—yet.

"Vrak Falken—the real one, according to Randl. He was in bed with Charla's clone. I wonder how Jewl will receive that news, along with that of her daughter's supposed death?"

"No idea. Let's hope she listens to her daughter, though. Kooper should convince Charla to speak with Jewl the moment she's able."

Randl

Dori, in ocelot form, was sleeping beside me on my bed when I woke. "Baby, are you warm enough?" I raised up and leaned on an elbow before touching her head and stroking around her ears. She wasn't covered by the blanket, but I was.

She lifted her head and blinked at me with wide, gold-and-brown eyes. Then she sneezed on me.

I dropped onto my back and laughed out loud. Dori's cold nose nuzzled my cheek before she slipped off the bed and padded out of my suite, tail tip low and curling suggestively. *See you in the kitchen*, she sent. *I'm hungry.*

I was learning that a shapeshifter's metabolism was higher than that of a human. I liked women with healthy appetites.

Especially one woman with a healthy appetite. *Right behind you*, I sent to her. *Don't eat it all.*

Then hurry, she said.

I did.

⁓

"How's Barkins?" I asked the dog, who turned his head at a quizzical angle as he looked up at me.

"Begging for food," Dori said. "Want eggs and bacon? You fixed last night; I'll get this one."

"Yes," I said. "Scramble an egg for Barkins, too, all right?"

"Already on it," she replied. "He was tapdancing on the tile until I told him I'd fix him an egg. I think he recognizes that word."

"A criminal who loves her dog can't be all bad, can she?" Susan walked into the kitchen, followed closely by Flyer. Both appeared happy enough to me. Flyer was shirtless and showing off his full set of Falchani tattoos. Hawks covered all of his upper torso and flew in spirals down both arms.

"It's a point in her favor," I agreed. "We'll see how willing she is to cooperate with us, since she's officially dead to everyone else."

"Tea?" Flyer grinned at Susan.

"Not that stuff you call tea," she swatted at an arm. "I want proper tea."

"Proper tea on the way," he teased and busied himself at the counter where the brewer sat.

"You remember Chief Markus, from Jaledis?" Travis, Trent and Sabrina walked into the kitchen. Travis asked the verbal question before nodding to Flyer's unspoken one—of whether they wanted tea or not.

"Yes," I said. I had a feeling where this was going, but waited for Travis to explain.

"He's on the way. Kooper's pulling in agents and supervisors he can trust to help with this. There'll be a meeting this afternoon to bring them up to speed."

"Good. We're going to need them," I said.

CHAPTER 13

andswept Casino
        Vendor Ballroom

Randl

"This is where the tourism departments from each attending world will set up their displays during the Conclave," Kooper announced to a crowd of two hundred agents and ASD supervisors. "You should have a list of names and associated members on your comp-vids already. Each of you has an assigned world to investigate, and be sure to listen carefully while you guide them through the process of setting up in here. You know already that most worlds will be represented, so make sure you act appropriately and be knowledgeable about their tourism industry and displays. Any information you find pertinent will be sent to the command center we set up upstairs."

"You suspect that some of them may be associated with the Prophet?" One of the supervisors asked. Kooper had already gone through that information. It had taken two hours to bring everyone up to speed, too.

"At this point, anything is possible. You know he's infiltrated one criminal element, and we're still working on whether he has connections to other legitimate interests. If you see or hear anything suspicious, send the information to the command center. Discreetly, of course."

"What's his endgame? This Prophet person?" someone else asked.

"That's something we'd all like to know. Figure it out and I'll double your salary and hand you a promotion."

"Does Randl have anything to say about this?"

I recognized that voice—Chief Markus.

"What do you want to know?" I asked after Kooper motioned for me to come to the front of the gathered crowd.

"What you know, I suppose," Chief Markus said.

"This is what I have," I said and formed a three-dimensional, life-size image of the Prophet, complete with hooded cloak, before me.

I heard Kooper's intake of breath behind me, but I wanted these agents to know what they were dealing with. "You can come close and touch," I said. "I can't say for sure what his skin feels like, so I've extrapolated, somewhat. You can believe me when I say, however, that you never want to come this close to the real thing. You'll either die or become ensnared."

"Are those fine scales on his skin?" One of the first agents to approach the image asked after looking closely at the lower half of the Prophet's face. The rest was covered by the hood of his cloak, and wouldn't be seen by most.

"Yes. I have no idea whether he is a mutant or some race I haven't seen before."

"My guess is mutant," Kooper rumbled beside me. "Think about Lee'Qee," he added.

"I was thinking about it, Director. That doesn't mean he came from there, though. He could be from elsewhere."

"True." He was thinking the same as I—that I had a coin from Vogeffa II that was supplied by the Prophet. It could be a coincidence. More and more, I didn't believe that.

I'd seen him on the streets of Gungl in a dream. Whether that had already happened, or had yet to happen, I didn't know. I only knew that he was familiar with the city and at least one of its residents.

That's when it hit me. I would recognize the place of that

meeting well enough. All I had to do was locate it and place my hand on a nearby wall or other structure to see what I wanted to see.

When this meeting is over, I need to visit Gungl, I informed Kooper.

Take someone with you, he warned. *Don't stay gone too long.*

No worries, I repeated one of David's favorite phrases. I'd take David with me—Vik and Dori, too, if they wanted to go. They could stand guard while I did my business there. As it turned out, Travis and Trent insisted on going with us, too, and Travis asked to be included in my visions, if any came.

With a reluctant sigh, I agreed.

Gungl, Vogeffa II

Travis

David grumbled at Randl when we arrived in Gungl—a heavy rain fell and our breaths plumed outward in the subsequent cold as we huddled against the wall of a building. Half the roof was gone, but a slight overhang above our heads kept some of the rain off.

The pounding of the rain against broken street stones became so loud after our arrival that I couldn't hear Randl's reply.

What are we looking for? Trent sent.

He says it's a place he saw in his dreams—where he saw the Prophet speaking to another man.

This place looks even more decayed than when we were here last time, Trent observed.

He was right—in part. The rain wasn't helping our view or opinion of the place. Gungl was falling quickly.

I can do this alone, Randl said.

No, Trent and I sent at the same moment. Our orders from Kooper were to stay with Randl the entire time.

Then I'll have to shield and warm us while we search the city, Randl cautioned.

He still hadn't forgiven me for taking information to Kooper last time. *Then do it*, I said. Trent and I could warm ourselves, but David, Vik and Dori couldn't.

The effect was immediate. No rain dripped on us and we were dry and warm. *This is what I'm looking for*, Randl sent, while an image accompanied his words.

All of us saw the place—and the Prophet's meeting with another man, whose back was turned toward us. I struggled to hold the image long enough to recognize the street location again—because the Prophet and his minion wouldn't be there when we arrived.

I worried, however, that what we might see in Randl's vision afterward would be frightening.

There's a chunk out of that nearby wall that looks like a face, Dori pointed out.

She'd looked more carefully than I had.

And a cross-pattern in the empty spaces between street stones, Vik added. Clearly, he'd been the outstanding agent Kooper said he was. Vik's observation skills were excellent.

There was something else to this, however. My attempt to use my *Looking* skills failed.

Looking was a gift Trent and I received from our mother—that of focusing on a single thing and either finding it or discovering more about it. I had a feeling that if we'd been *Looking* for anything else in Gungl, we could have found it.

This—the Prophet and perhaps a Sirenali or their bones were involved somehow. That meant we had to search for it like anyone else—by walking the streets to find it.

I had a feeling Randl knew the same thing—and had the same sort of talent, whether he called it that or not.

The rain hadn't let up, and still sent rivers of water down the streets we walked, since any bare patches of ground were already filled to the brim and overflowing. Even though I was warm enough and dry enough beneath Randl's shield, I still hunched my shoulders and trudged beside my comrades, looking for elusive signs of a place where the Prophet had met an unnamed man.

Avii Castle, Le-Ath Veronis

Quin

"You asked to see me?" Brandl stepped onto the library balcony, where I sat on a comfortable bench, reading a book Daragar had brought to me. It was a history book, written by his father, Nefrigar, about an ancient world that had died long ago.

"Yes," I set the book aside and smiled at Brandl. "My mother left a gift for you. She gave a similar gift to Randl—to protect him."

"I already have plenty of protection," Brandl began. I knew all about the disguises and the ones charged with impersonating Brandl, to throw anyone off. Those protections would work—against normal evils.

The Prophet wasn't a normal evil, or so Zaria told me when she left the small box with me at breakfast.

"I will be leaving soon to attend Conclave, and it's important that you have this now," I lifted the small box from the bench beside me and held it out to him.

"What is it?" he asked, taking the small box in hands that were used to hard work.

"It's a medallion. Randl wears his always, as should you, even in the bath. Never take it off. Please. It will protect you—and the knowledge of your son."

"It has my name on it," Brandl pulled the medallion and chain from the box. The gold glinted in the late afternoon sunlight as he studied it. "I've never worn jewelry," he added, his eyes focusing on me again.

"Wear this no matter what, I beg you," I said.

"Very well." He pulled the chain over his neck and allowed the medallion to slide beneath his shirt. "How does it work?"

"I have no idea. Zaria does. Perhaps you should ask her," I smiled at Brandl. "Be safe—always. You are family to us."

"Thank you—and thank Zaria."

"You are welcome."

~

New Fyris, Harifa Edus
  Morrett

"Morrett? When did you arrive?" Amlis rose from behind his desk and blinked at my sudden appearance in his study. If Quin hadn't healed him from his madness, in addition to his mortal wounds, Zaria would never have asked me to perform this errand for her.

I signed to tell Amlis my arrival was recent. He nodded his understanding. I was grateful to be communicating with a sane man instead of what he'd been a year earlier. Pulling two boxes from my trouser pocket, I set them on Amlis' desk.

What's this?" He studied the boxes for a moment before lifting his eyes to mine again.

Gifts, I informed him in fingerspeech. *From Zaria,* I added. *For you and Rodrik.*

"Why would she send anything to us?"

I shrugged. *Open,* I signed to him.

He opened the one bearing his name and pulled out the medallion. It was quite fine and fit enough for any Prince to wear.

Wear always. Never remove, my fingers moved deftly. *Zaria says so. Protection.*

"Protection from what?"

Evil. Death. Many other things.

"I suppose this has something to do with the upcoming Conclave?"

Yes. I nodded to emphasize my signing.

"Very well." He slipped the chain around his neck. "I suppose I'll have to convince Rodrik to wear his, now."

Yes. I nodded again.

"Thank you, Morrett. I don't suppose I could convince you to work for me again?"

No. That sign indicated my final answer. *I enjoy working with King Rylend and his son, Prince Bel Erland.* My fingers flew through the spellings of their names.

"I understand. A little, anyway. Thank you for bringing these," he tapped the boxes. "Will I see you at Conclave?"

I gave a half-nod. I would accompany the King of Karathia to Campiaa. I was sure we'd see Amlis in passing—somewhere.

~

Gungl, Vogeffa II
Randl

It took nearly two hours to find the place, and by that time, we were all weary of the rain, the search and the rising tension, which I hadn't contemplated yet. At least I didn't feel eyes on us this time, but that absence also worried me.

Where *had* the people of Gungl gone?

Travis echoed my thoughts as we approached the cross-shaped gap in street stones, not far from the wall where Dori had pointed out the hole resembling a face.

Where is everybody? he asked, squaring his shoulders as if warding off a chill.

That worries me—that I don't feel anyone watching, I replied, before stopping short several feet from the empty, cross-shaped gap.

Let's get this over with, David complained. He felt it, too, whatever it was.

Follow me, I told the others, giving the cross-shape a wide berth. Something about it bothered me, but I couldn't explain why.

Not yet.

With Dori at my back, Travis and Trent beside her and Vik and David two steps away from the twins, I set my hand on the wall next to the face-shaped gap, before including my companions in what appeared in my visions.

~

Holding Facility, Campiaa
Kooper

"The one who saved you and your crew also saved your dog," I handed the photograph from the bedside table to Charla. "Now, why would you have a photograph of Jewl Yarro beside your bed?"

Charla's face paled when I mentioned her mother, but other than that small sign, she didn't show any reaction.

"Barkins is all right?" she asked instead.

"Yes, he's fine and being cared for by someone who loves animals. Now, what I need from you is the reason someone posing as you took over your home."

"I don't have an answer," she lied.

"Yes, you do."

The IV was still taped to the back of one hand, delivering much-needed fluid to her body, and she'd eaten solid food for the first time at breakfast that morning. The physicians on duty said she was well enough to answer questions.

She sat in a chair beside her infirmary bed, while I sat in another, brought in for the purpose of questioning her.

There would be no regular visitors for this patient. "Most people believe you're dead—that you died in the fire that consumed your house, instead of the one posing as you."

"I don't care about that." Her voice was sullen.

"I believe your mother cares about that."

"My mother is dead."

"Your mother is Jewl Yarro. The last I checked, she wasn't dead."

This time, my accusation caused her body to jerk—a reaction to the hidden truth I'd spoken. "We have Poll Endicutt in custody, too," I added. She turned her head away before I could see the recognition in her eyes.

"What do you expect me to do about that? I don't know anybody by that name," she snapped.

"He knows you," I said.

A hissing breath escaped her lips. If she weren't in custody herself, I imagined that Poll's life would be over quite soon. If she couldn't accomplish that feat, her mother surely would on her daughter's behalf.

"I'd like for you to contact your mother," I held out an unregistered comp-vid. "Tell her what you refuse to tell me—that someone kidnapped you and tried to kill you, to take over your criminal empire. Tell Jewl we want to make a deal with her regarding these usurpers."

"Hmmph."

"Don't you want her to stop grieving? For Barkins to stop grieving? He saved your life, you know, by scratching on the bedroom wall and leading my rescue party right to you."

"How the hell did you even find out I'd been replaced?" Charla demanded.

"I have resources you have no knowledge of," I replied. "Some of them—let's say they defy the imagination."

"I'll bet you do. Why is the ASD even here? This is the jurisdiction of the CSD."

"Jett and I know one another very well. I doubt you'd prefer to be talking to him right now. He's extremely upset, and may not be so willing to cut a deal with you—or your mother."

Jett was upset—that part was true. As for his willingness to cut a deal, we hadn't really discussed it yet. Charla had been operating as a legal, upstanding citizen of Campiaa, so he was certainly angry about that. He and his team were only now beginning to make discoveries and assumptions regarding what Charla's and Jewl's relationship could accomplish without anyone the wiser.

Charla knew I couldn't charge her with a crime in the Campiaan Alliance—I had no real jurisdiction over Campiaan citizens. I was here as a go-between, to convince Charla to cooperate.

"At least tell me about your kidnappers. Anything could be helpful," I coaxed.

"Hmpph. That filth? I'm glad they're all dead. Losing my house was worth it, just to kill all of them."

"Did they say what they wanted? What their purpose was? Did they ask for money?"

"They wanted my contacts in Campiaa City. I gave them that and they still locked me in that room."

"Now we're getting somewhere," I said. "I need those contacts, too. Give them to me and I'll see that Jett doesn't charge you for concealing information regarding known criminals."

"I want to see Barkins, first. You could be lying about him."

"Susan?" I tapped the comp-communicator on my wrist.

"I'll be right there, Director."

Moments later, Susan walked into the infirmary room carrying Barkins in her arms. He was as happy and healthy as could be expected. He yipped and struggled to get out of Susan's arms when he saw Charla.

Susan set him down and let him run to his mistress. Susan stepped forward and held out a small container of treats for Barkins.

Charla reached out for them, before rising to her feet and striking out at Susan. My chair was sent flying backward as I rose to my feet, but what came next I had no explanation for.

Susan became the buff orpington hen that she was; her clothing dropped to the floor and she squawked and flapped her wings in Charla's face before pecking her on the nose.

"Make it stop! Make it stop," Charla shouted, while Barkins began to bark at both his mistress and the offended hen.

"Bakaaaww," Susan squawked again.

"I'll tell you everything, just make it stop," Charla begged as Susan continued her assault.

"Susan," I snapped. Fluffy, golden feathers floated in the air about me as Barkins continued to bark.

Susan, who'd been flapping furiously to stay aloft and continue her attack, dropped to the floor and ruffled her wing and tail feathers as only a chicken could, before stalking out of the room, her chicken toenails ticking on the tiles indignantly.

"You'd better tell me everything," I said as Charla snatched Barkins into her arms and retreated to her chair. "Or I'll bring back the hen."

Mountain Retreat

Wyatt

"Randl told her that Charla was afraid of birds—all kinds of birds," Flyer grinned at Jayna and me as he carried Susan the buff orpington into the kitchen and set her down on the island.

"My love, are you all right?" Flyer touched a gentle finger to Susan's comb atop her head.

She clucked the affirmative, and ruffled her feathers. "Of course," Flyer responded to her mindspeech. "She wants to get dressed and have some fruit," he said, before lifting Susan in his arms again and disappearing.

"That was useful information," I turned to Jayna and leaned in for a kiss. "When this is over, will you marry me?" I bumped my forehead against hers.

"But I," she began.

"There are no butts that matter—just ours," I teased. "Dad keeps wondering what's taking us so long."

"But you're royalty," she pointed out.

"And you will be, too. Say yes, baby."

"All right, then. Yes. And may the gods help you," she smiled at me.

Gungl, Vogeffa II

Travis

At first we only saw the back of the unknown man as the Prophet approached him, his face hidden as usual by half the hooded cloak he wore.

Randl moved—it broke contact with the vision for a moment, before it cleared again and we saw the stranger's face.

It was the scarred man we'd given food to almost a year earlier. This had happened sometime after that, because Randl hadn't seen a meeting with the Prophet in the scarred man before.

I itched to ask Randl whether the man had been infected with the Prophet's spreading disease, but I worried I'd interrupt the images.

Before, Randl had only seen this meeting from behind the scarred man. Now we watched from the side as the Prophet stabbed a finger in the scarred man's chest.

Did that just go through his skin? Trent sounded half-spooked. The Prophet removed his finger. No blood covered it, and the man's chest remained whole. I didn't think his spirit was whole, however.

I knew we were watching past events, but the terror I felt was real.

That's when I felt Dori's hand grip mine, and somehow, I knew to grip Trent's. Randl peeled the four of us away from the wall, and still inside his vision, we walked toward the cross-shaped pattern of missing stones.

The Prophet and the scarred man disappeared, leaving only a shadowy Gungl behind—the Gungl that was neither now, nor the time when the Prophet met the scarred man. We were between those times, somehow, and I couldn't say how I knew that.

Randl placed a foot on the cross-shape. I was grateful my hand was locked with Dori's and Trent's, because we were flung far away from Gungl amid silent screams.

~

Randl

We dropped onto a hillside, on a planet that was making its way back to life after centuries of poisoned existence.

Like Bornelus and many other worlds, plant life was returning to almost barren ground. Across from us, forests of stunted evergreens struggled to thrive.

In the distance, a stand of young deciduous trees grew. Something was odd about that, as there were no other trees like them anywhere else—only in that one place.

There was no sound of birds, animals or anything else—just the wind sweeping thin, knee-high grasses that grew between boulders. Those boulders were scattered about, as if a giant had played a game with marbles and then left his playthings behind when the planet died.

Around the edges of this vision, if vision it was, things fluctuated, as if they hadn't finalized their materialization. Something about the unusual stand of trees beckoned, however.

"No," Travis said aloud, and reached out to drop a hand on my shoulder.

I shrugged it off.

A sound came in the distance. I knew that sound, now. It began as a soft rumble, until it gathered in noise and intensity.

Mutant Ra'Ak were here—on this abandoned world, just as they'd been on Bornelus.

"They're coming," Travis shouted, before tossing Dori onto a nearby boulder. He and Trent—I could feel their change as they became dragons and lifted from the ground behind me.

One of my blades formed in my left hand as I gazed at the ground between me and the trees ahead. Beside me, atop the boulder, Dori's ocelot hissed a warning.

Five of the massive worms broke through the ground with a terrible roar. Above me, Travis and Trent's dragons sounded their own challenge to the Ra'Ak.

I didn't have a ranos rifle with me now, and considered it luck that Vik and David had been left behind on the deserted streets of Gungl.

My second blade appeared in my right hand and I stalked forward, as more mutant Ra'Ak burst from the ground in front of me.

Travis

There is a tale the Falchani tell, of Caylon Black and a small band of warriors, who were attacked by more than a hundred enemy warriors in the distant past.

That tale says that Caylon and fifteen Falchani fought the enemy, killing as many as they could until Caylon's men began to fall.

Until only Caylon was left.

When he fell, surrounded by the enemy, he and his men accounted for more than ninety enemy lives.

Because of Caylon's bravery and talent on that day, he was chosen by the gods to become a member of an elite race that protected worlds from the Ra'Ak.

Trent and I called him Uncle Caylon, and neither of us could defeat him in a battle of swords.

I almost wished Caylon could have seen Randl on this day, fighting mutant Ra'Ak with two blades and the power he held. When they lunged toward him, he lopped off their heads, his blades slicing through those terrible, horned and crested monsters like a hot knife through soft butter.

I knew as well as anyone how difficult any Ra'Ak was to kill, and more than once, the teeth of a monster met with the unbreakable shield Randl held about himself as he fought.

If it survived the encounter, the monster jerked away, roaring in pain and fury before attacking again.

When the Ra'Ak began to dust, blasting huge chunks of dark, stone-like clumps everywhere, we were grateful that Randl could shield himself so well.

Somehow, he'd shielded Dori, too, although I had no idea how he managed to do that and concentrate on fighting giant worms with sharp, poisonous teeth.

One would leap in, followed by four or more of his companions, only to be rebuffed by the shield, a power blast or a slice by a deadly blade. No Grey House wizard had made these blades—our older sister would have told us if they had.

I attempted mindspeech with Kooper while Trent and I flew above the battle, but it failed to arrive at its intended destination.

That confirmed my suspicions—that Randl had somehow deposited us between times. I'd never seen anyone do this sort of thing before, although I suppose if one were powerful enough, one could do it.

Powerful enough.

It took a mighty power to bend time; that much I knew.

A huge Ra'Ak roared and died beneath me as I flew across the battleground, watching for other monsters to arrive.

Randl

I'd fought my way forward, toward the trees, as more mutant Ra'Ak appeared to drive me back. For whatever reason, they had no desire for me to reach that stand of trees.

My strength was failing, along with my power, when I removed the head from the largest of the monsters who'd come to attack me.

Three remained—the large one had been their leader.

Now would be the time to help, I sent to Travis and Trent, who'd been content to fly across the battlefield while I worked.

Dragons descended from the sky, and vicious claws and fiery breaths tore and burned two creatures while I, with one last effort, launched one of my blades at the third, where it pierced one of its eyes.

The second blade followed the first, taking out the monster's other eye. It screamed in pain before falling to the ground, writhing, tossing clouds of dirt and rock in the air and then dying and dusting.

I almost didn't have the strength to maintain the shields about Dori and me, before the dusting stopped and I collapsed on the ground.

Travis

"Randl, please wake up," Dori patted his cheek desperately. We couldn't leave unless he took us out of here, because we'd already tried that.

Our folding skills had been neutralized, and I had no idea how that was.

"Huh?" Randl mumbled before blinking his eyes and struggling to focus on Dori's face.

"Randl, I sure hope you can get us out of here," Dori said. "This place is creepy and there's Ra'Ak dust everywhere."

"Oh, uh, all right," he sat up, rubbing his head. "Come on, let's get you out of here, sweetheart."

Dori helped him stand, and once upright, he swayed on his feet. "Ready?" His question to us was slurred.

I hope he can get us back, Trent's voice breathed in my mind.

He did, but barely.

David shouted and Vik reached out to catch Randl as he collapsed in front of them on the streets of Gungl.

CHAPTER 14

*M*ountain Retreat, Campiaa
Dori

"Drained."

That was Karzac's diagnosis. Randl was still unconscious, although he was now in a healing sleep the physician had placed.

"He killed nearly fifty of those things," Travis said, sounding ashamed. He and Trent had watched while flying above the battle, and I—my ocelot wouldn't have been a mouthful to any of those monsters.

"How many did you kill?" Karzac asked.

"One."

"Ah."

He didn't say that it was after Randl asked for help.

"Lafe will have to strip some of these tattoos off us," Trent mumbled and stalked out of Randl's bedroom.

Randl

What I recalled about my extended bout of unconsciousness, was

203

the fever-like dreams I'd had—particularly of the trees I'd struggled to reach while fighting mutant Ra'Ak.

In my dreams, something kept pulling me away, and I'd fight my way forward, my feet sticking in deep, watery concrete.

The trees began to scream, then, and I saw that they had faces—two of the faces belonged to the scarred man and his friend who limped.

When I woke, I found myself shouting at them to get away.

"You should not be dreaming in a healing sleep," Karzac's voice was calm as he sat beside my bed.

"Right." I croaked and fought to calm my pounding heart. Closing my eyes, I hoped to find some peace from my nightmares by attempting to meditate.

Sometime during my meditation, Karzac left me alone and I slept peacefully for a time. When he came back, he told me I should rise and eat.

I followed him to the kitchen willingly.

~

Travis

"You can't make us feel worse about this than we already do," I said. "We thought he had things well in hand—or well enough. Turns out he was exhausting himself and didn't ask for help until it was almost too late."

Kooper wore a deep frown as he listened to my words. So many things had gone through my mind while Trent and I had flown above Randl, not least of them that we should have taken Dori with us, so Randl wouldn't have to shield her.

A part of me was angry at Randl, too, because he'd done the foolish thing of taking us between times anyway, without consulting me or anyone else.

"Do you know where you were?"

"No idea. Gungl is empty, though. I think the Prophet took all the people for one of his sick sacrifices."

"Does Randl know where you were?"

"Maybe. I don't know," I said, turning to Trent. He shrugged, indicating he had no idea.

"Tell me again how Randl just walked through time with all of you."

"I don't know how he did that. I've gone with Mom a few times when she bent time—this felt nothing like that."

"You say the Prophet stabbed a finger through the man's chest without leaving a mark?"

"Yes," Trent and I both answered.

"It was the scarred man we saw before?"

"Yes."

"This just keeps getting more bizarre and much, much worse," Kooper's voice lowered to a rough growl. "Karzac says Randl is up and eating, but it may take a few days before he's at full strength."

"That's not good," Trent rumbled.

"Agreed. Look, I've never seen either of you back away from a fight, so I'm going to chalk this up to experience. I'm not sure what I would have done if I knew I was somewhere—what did you call it— between-time?"

"It felt weird," I admitted. "Afterward, we found out we couldn't fold space to get away, either. Something negated that in us. Have you ever seen that happen before?"

"No. This bears thinking about," Kooper grimaced. "Go get some sleep. I assume Vik and David are all right, since they didn't end up there with you?"

"They're fine, and probably wondering what the hell happened, just like we're wondering."

"Explain it as best you can, and I want a report. Mark it for my eyes only."

"We will, Director." I rose and dipped my head to him. Bed sounded good—if I could keep the willies away, as David always said.

Randl

"You should have taken me with you," Vik said. He and I stood on an outcropping high above the retreat, so we could have a private conversation.

"And out you to your brothers?"

"There's that," he nodded. "My Thifilathi wouldn't have held back when the Ra'Ak showed up—even if they were mutants."

"And you'd be outed to your brothers."

"Yeah. Damn." He shook his head and hunched his shoulders against the higher-elevation cold. "You know you were only gone for a few minutes—my time."

"I suspected, but I'll be honest, I haven't been awake much since we got back."

"True. Do you think you killed all of them?"

"I don't know. Unconscious, remember?"

"Where were you, do you know that, at least?"

"Tem'Bek II."

I waited for Vik to stop laughing.

"It's a place," I said.

"Yeah, but," he chuckled again.

"Go ahead and talk to me about Old Earth. I'll wait," I said.

"Nah, I'm done," he said. He was still grinning, though.

"I should go talk to Kooper—he's wondering about it."

"Can you get yourself to the palace?"

"I don't know. I let you get me up here, remember? I feel—drained, like Karzac said. Empty."

"What if it had something to do with where you were and when you were?" Vik asked, his deep voice thoughtful. "I've never heard of anybody splitting time like that, to get somewhere."

"Splitting time?" I turned to blink at him before turning away to gaze down the mountainside. Far below, I could see the roof of the retreat. It looked tiny from our high perch. "Splitting time," I repeated and nodded slowly as a few snowflakes floated past. "I think you're right."

"Feel strong enough to visit Kooper?"

"I suppose. I can only answer questions, though. If he needs anything else, he may have to wait."

"Want to be folded in by one of the others, or take mundane transportation?"

"You know, I think I'll take the mundane method. I haven't seen what's between here and the city, yet."

"Mundane it is," Vik agreed and skipped me back to the retreat.

The ride to the Founder's Palace took more than an hour at the hover-car's best speed. I enjoyed it, though, and found the scenery restful as the images settled into my mind.

Vik and David acted as my guards when we climbed from the vehicle and were escorted through a back entrance. Teeg's guards were everywhere, and one of them was Galaxsan Starr, a member of his four warlock guards.

Galaxsan was bursting with questions, but held those back while he led us inside the palace and toward a trans-vator. Again, I'd never seen the lower levels of the palace—I'd always been transported directly to Teeg's study or his library and meeting room.

My boots echoed on polished tiles as we walked onto the trans-vator. Galaxsan could have folded space with us, but I think he wanted to take the long way himself, this time.

I was a curiosity to him—I understood that. He wanted to know about a new kind of power wielder, because that's how he saw me—neither warlock nor wizard—*something different.*

"If you think I'm different, it's because you haven't met the Prophet, yet," I informed the warlock as we stepped off the trans-vator three levels up.

"They told me you'd see it," he laughed. "I have a million questions, but they'll wait."

"How about a beer or three later tonight?" I invited him.

"I think I can squeeze that in."

"Good. Send mindspeech when you're available. We can drink at the retreat, or meet somewhere in the city. Your choice."

"Retreat sounds good. Here we are. Enjoy your meeting," Galaxsan grinned before folding space.

He'd left us outside the doors to Teeg's library, which stood open. Inside, Kooper, Wyatt and Teeg stood near a table, talking and waiting for my arrival.

"And so the inquisition begins," I sighed and squared my shoulders. David snorted at my comment, but didn't say anything. He, Vik and I strode into the library.

~

"You're calling it splitting time." Kooper made a face, as if he were struggling with the term.

"Want more tea?" Wyatt asked after consulting his comp-vid. He was in contact with someone from the kitchen.

"How about a sandwich to go with it?" I asked.

"I'll have them send a tray," Wyatt agreed and tapped an answer on his device before setting it down again.

I was hungry; Vik and David were half-starved. They'd been listening patiently while Kooper and Teeg asked questions. They'd already told their part of the story, which included waiting for only a few minutes before we popped out of the air right in front of them on the streets of Gungl.

"Splitting time fits best," I agreed. "It was—difficult. Travis and Trent couldn't fold space to get away because they were stuck in time where we were. Dori, too. Only I and the inhabitants of Tem'Bek II could do anything with power during those moments. Travis and Trent had to use what their dragons had, because they have that naturally, without power to force it."

"You're saying you split time, and forced a moment to last for however long it took to kill at least fifty mutant Ra'Ak?" Teeg asked. He was quite calm about it, actually, and I appreciated that.

"I think so, yes."

"That's rather unnerving," Teeg sighed. "And amazing, at the same time."

"It drained me—I couldn't push your teacup half a finger-width with power right now."

"Early arrivals are already coming in for Conclave," Wyatt pointed out. "We still don't have a reply to Charla's message to Jewl, either."

"I'm not sure things can get any worse," Kooper growled.

"Jett's increasing security around the Sandswept Hotel," Teeg said. "Your people are in place already, and the displays are being brought in. I have one of my warlocks checking everything delivered for the tourism tables and spaces."

"If they notice anything unusual, will you let me take a look?" I asked.

"Of course," Teeg agreed. "Do you have someone who can transport you wherever you're needed? Until you have your strength restored?"

"I'll have someone assigned," Kooper agreed. He intended to order Travis or Trent to do it, because he was miffed at them, still, for their perceived inaction.

"Director, I wouldn't have asked them for help at the last if I hadn't needed it. This is an unknown—like an empty space between one second and the next. We have no idea whether there will be adverse effects from this—for them or anyone else."

I'd spoken my fear aloud—that repercussions could come and I couldn't predict them accurately.

Kooper drummed his fingers on the polished-stone table for a moment and refused to look at me. Finally, he nodded before meeting my eyes. "All right. You'll be kept in the informational loop. If you have advice or an opinion, I want to hear it. Understood?"

"Yes, Director."

P'loxett
V'dar

My guardians had been killed on Tem'Bek II in a fraction of a second, and I failed to understand how that could be.

I'd seen none of it happen—only the aftermath.

At least the concrete block hidden in the stand of trees was still intact, and held the sacrifices from Gungl secure in its depths.

I'd searched for evidence of an enemy's encroachment, but found nothing other than a few patches of charred weeds and grasses, and creature dust lying in chunks everywhere.

I would sort this out later; other things demanded my attention, not least of which was my newly-acquired servants on Campiaa, who were ready to do my bidding. It aggravated me that Charla Dare hadn't had her solar power panel and transformer inspected for six years or more—that was an accident waiting to happen and had cost me many important servants.

I had new ones to fill that void, however, and Charla had paid with her life. Regardless, I now had contact information for Adarr Gramm and Rale Linn. Jewl Yarro could come later; with the first two, the third could be brought in easily.

Once the first two saw what I could do, they'd come along quietly or die by my hand. Things were falling into place for the Conclave and soon enough, I would hold both Alliances in my grip.

Besides, I now held new information—information that would enable me to exact a revenge that had been fermenting for a year. I looked forward to it with great anticipation.

Mountain Retreat, Campiaa
Randl

"There was a response to Charla's message, but it wasn't exactly what we hoped for."

Kooper arrived and sat down with Vik, David, Galaxsan and me to have a beer. He needed six more, in my estimation.

Galaxsan floated a bottle out of the keeper and popped the top off with power before sliding it in front of Kooper. Kooper nodded his thanks to the warlock and lifted it to drink.

"Let me guess; she was unenthusiastic about her daughter's survival," David offered.

"Yeah," Kooper set his bottle down after drinking half its contents.

"Actually, she doesn't believe her daughter survived. She thinks the ASD and CSD are—what's the phrase—pulling her leg?" I offered.

"Nice." Vik clinked his beer bottle against mine.

We'd chosen what David called *the man cave* for our drinking session, as it had the best night view of the city below. It also had a fully-stocked bar and cold-keeper, a sink and comfortable, overstuffed chairs and sofas throughout, placed so any visitor could watch the multiple vid-screens hanging on each wall.

I'd asked Dori to join us, but she wanted to have a night with her sister Cori, so I told her to enjoy herself and sat with the others in the man cave to drink. That's where Kooper found us, and I was thankful we hadn't finished our first beers yet.

"Do you think you can convince Charla?" Kooper asked me.

"I can try," I said. "When?"

"Tomorrow morning. We need to get a meeting with Jewl, find out if she's infected, and if not, guarantee immunity—at least during Conclave, so we can deal with the shit coming our way. Jett has managed to pull in a handful of people from the list Charla gave us. I have it with me."

Kooper rummaged in a pocket and drew out his comp-vid. "Images are on the first screen," he handed the comp-vid to me so I could look.

Three of the seven images showed me infected individuals. The remaining four were petty thieves and likely beneath the Prophet's notice. I tapped the three I'd chosen to add to a new file for Kooper— to have them quarantined.

It was anybody's guess whether they'd infected anyone else by having sex. Frankly, I refused to look for *that* in them. Not tonight. I wanted to get drunk and not think about it.

"Not good," Kooper shook his head as he surveyed the list I'd created. "Nearly half. I wonder if that percentage will hold for the rest."

"Get the Director another beer," I said. "He needs to chill."

Queen's Palace, Le-Ath Veronis
   Winkler

Lissa and I had just put the twins to bed when we received word. Aurelius came to tell us himself.

The vampire we'd disguised to act as Brandl's replacement was dead, his ash scattered across the waters between Avii Castle and Lissa's beach palace. Half the boat he'd been aboard was little more than floating rubble, after being hit by a strong blast of power.

This vampire was one of the few who could walk in daylight, given blood by Lissa herself for worthy service to the crown. He was now dead and she was sad and angry.

The crew on the boat was also dead, although they weren't vampire. Their charred remains were brought back to land by Sun City's Shore Patrol.

The real Brandl was now in Lissa's library, waiting for us to arrive. He had no enemies except one, and that one was Randl's enemy, first.

"Send someone to make sure Amlis is protected," Lissa snapped at two guards as we strode into the library. "Send Drake and Drew with them if necessary."

They would have run if that were allowed in the Queen's presence; still they walked away as fast as they could without being obvious about it.

"I thought you and Quin were being overprotective—all these measures you took," Brandl's hand shook as he shoved hair away from his face. He was in shock, that was easy enough to see.

"You asked to see me?" Bryan Riley, Le-Ath Veronis' news administrator and journalism magnate, was ushered into the library.

"Bryan, thank you for coming on such short notice," Lissa sighed. "We need an official announcement made—that Brandl Gage and all the crew aboard the *Gray Swan* are dead. Renée will give you names of the others aboard the vessel."

"So, it's official," Bryan nodded. He knew as well as anyone that Brandl was there in the library with us. Dipping his head respectfully to Lissa, he turned and walked out with his accompanying guard.

In minutes, the official report would be given, along with images of the damaged ship.

"What can I do?" Brandl asked. He was lost, that was easy to see.

"We're sending you to Campiaa," Lissa said. "You can help Randl get back on his feet."

"Something happened to him?"

"More like he happened to something," Lissa snorted. She had the report from Kooper, just as I did. "He just drained his energy, that's all. He'll be fine in a day or two."

"Will you let me know how things go in New Fyris?"

"Of course. Winkler, will you transport Brandl? Tell Kooper you're on the way."

"I will."

Mountain Retreat, Campiaa

Randl

"Pap?" I was drunk enough to believe I might be hallucinating. Staggering to my feet, I blinked at my father and Winkler, who stood beside him.

"Somebody killed the vampire who was disguised as me," Pap said and almost broke down.

"Oh, no."

My drinking buddies left the room quietly while Pap and I hugged each other. Somehow, the Prophet had learned my name, and had gone after my family.

It was a sobering thought, in every sense.

New Fyris, Harifa Edus

Amlis

"Drake, Drew and two others are waiting in the vestibule," Rodrik strode into my private study. He sounded angry. It was very late at night where we were, and normally I'd be in bed reading.

Instead, I was studying the voting topics for Conclave, so I'd be ready before we left in a few days.

"Calm down, Rod," I said and scooted my chair back. "Did they say why they're here?"

"Something about your life being in danger," Rodrik grumbled. "Look around you—we aren't in danger."

"Rod, you should know that things can change quickly," I said. "I hope you recall the visit from WildTree?"

"Illusion. You know they can do it," he said.

I realized that I could have a problem on my hands, now, if Rodrik wasn't dealing well with reality.

I should know—I'd traveled that path.

"Let's go downstairs and be civil to our guests," I said, walking toward the door. Rodrik fell in line behind me, as he usually did.

≈

Prince Amlis' Castle, New Fyris

Drake Tatsuya

What's the holdup? Drew sent. He and I backed Aurelius and Flavio, who'd come as ambassadors from Le-Ath Veronis. The news we bore was grim; our intention was to tell Amlis and Rodrik that they could be targeted, merely because Randl had worked for Amlis in the past.

We'd been asked to wait in the castle vestibule while Rodrik, who wasn't pleased by our appearance, stalked away to inform the Prince that he had visitors.

Rodrik's dragging his heels, apparently, Aurelius supplied an answer. Aurelius, the ancient vampire with the mane of shaggy, blond hair and wide shoulders, looked more like a bear than a vampire at this late hour.

He wasn't happy with the delay, either. We bore important news, and Rodrik chose to waste time getting Amlis around to meet with us.

He could have offered refreshments and a more comfortable place to wait, too, but that was neither here nor there, as Lissa would say.

I hear them on the hidden stairs, Aurelius sent.

In moments, Amlis appeared in a doorway designed to blend in with the curved wall of the vestibule, Rodrik right behind him.

"I'm sorry to keep you waiting," Amlis said, just before the entire vestibule exploded around us.

CHAPTER 15

Queen's Palace, Le-Ath Veronis

Lissa

"I told him to wear the medallion. I watched him put it on. His wife found it lying on the dresser in their bedroom." Amlis was grieving for Rodrik, who was the only casualty in the trap the Prophet laid for him.

Amlis was fortunate to be alive—Aurelius, Flavio, Drake and Drew had formed shields at the last moment to protect themselves, but only the medallion Zaria had given him saved Amlis' life. Rodrik had been gifted with a device, too, and had chosen not to wear it.

The front portion of Amlis' castle now lay in ruins, and six servants were in a hospital with severe injuries. It was luck that dictated the event take place late at night, when few would be in that part of the castle.

Regardless, we now had a conundrum on our hands. If Amlis were reported dead, he couldn't attend Conclave. If he survived, the Prophet would continue to target him in his efforts to take revenge against Randl.

"We can't report his death," Ildevar Wyyld appeared and sat on the sofa next to me. He and I watched Amlis on the sofa opposite mine in my library. Amlis held his head in both hands, fingers gripping hair tightly as if they wanted to tear it away from his head. Rodrik wasn't just Amlis' heir—he'd been a lifelong friend and confidant.

Zaria tried to save him; he'd refused her help. There would be no second chance for Rodrik. His wife and child would have to learn to live without him.

"Amlis will need someone to go with him to Conclave," I sighed. "In addition to Halimel and Aurelius."

"Then I suggest asking Berel Charkisul to stand in for Rodrik. Berel is an outstanding ambassador," Ildevar replied. "He is also familiar enough with New Fyris to advise the Prince."

I suppose it wouldn't matter that Amlis would be backed by a blue-winged Avii when he attended Conclave. Wherever they went, the winged Avii drew attention and admiration.

Berel will be protected, Zaria's voice sounded in my mind. *He is a good choice in this matter.*

If Berel didn't already have one of Zaria's medallions, I figured he'd have one soon enough. Edden, Berel's blue-winged father, could advise Quin and Justis at Conclave—he was the best, in my opinion, with Berel a very close second.

"Thank you, Founder Wyyld," Amlis mumbled.

"You are a ruler in good standing in the Reth Alliance," Ildevar rose from his seat and patted Amlis' shoulder. "Make time to grieve for the fallen when Conclave is done. For now, your people must be represented. We will provide as much help as you need."

With that, Ildevar was gone.

"We have troops surrounding the castle in New Fyris," Drake announced as he and Drew arrived.

"Thank you. We'll let the Prophet believe the Prince may be dead—at least for tonight," I said.

~

Mountain Retreat, Campiaa
Dori

"I can't believe you let Marco spill the beans," I accused Cori, who looked guilty. She'd waited until we got back from having dinner out, too, before dropping the bombshell.

Marco had told Mom and Dad that I was seeing someone. They probably thought I was hiding him from them. Now, they were planning a trip to Campiaa during Conclave, just to see what I'd gotten into, in Marco's words.

Marco hadn't been with me when Randl transported Travis, Trent and me to Tem'Bek II. Yes, the name was a joke to those of us from Old Earth. What happened there wasn't a joke, though. Marco thought he was so tough. If he'd seen Randl fighting Ra'Ak mutations armed only with two swords, he'd change his tune in a hurry.

So far, Marco was being thick-headed about this, and I failed to understand why.

"Dori, they'd have to meet him sometime anyway," Cori said.

"When I chose to do so, not when Marco decided to tell on me, like he's nine or something."

"I think they only want to make sure you're—well, safe enough," Cori fumbled. Trust Marco to leave us alone in the kitchen and go hide in their bedroom so I could have it out with my sister. He deserved the blame for this, not her.

"Marco's jealous." Someone else appeared. I drew in a breath. I'd never seen her up close, I'd only heard about her and seen her from a distance—years ago at SouthStar. Zaria was here, and I had no idea why.

"What are you doing here?" Cori snapped at Zaria.

"Cori," I mumbled. I didn't think it wise to yell at Zaria for any reason.

"Well?" Cori's arms crossed over her chest and she glared at Zaria. Zaria wasn't wearing her white wings—not that I could see, anyway. And her skin wasn't blue, but with Zaria, that didn't mean anything. She could appear as a winged Larentii if she wanted. For the moment, she looked mostly human, except for the gold glints covering her skin.

"Marco—and you, for that matter, weren't elevated into the

Hierarchy for a reason," Zaria said. She didn't sound angry, but she didn't flinch or blink at Cori's anger, either.

"And what reason was that?" Cori huffed. I could see she was upset about it, too—that others joined the ranks of the powerful all around her, including Marco's brother Salidar, while she and Marco were left out. I'd been left out, too, but I'd never pointed that out to Cori. It wasn't my due—I hadn't done anything to deserve a place in the Hierarchy.

"Those of the powerful seldom are granted children," Zaria stated. "Have you felt more irritable than usual, lately?"

"Why would you care about that?" Cori wasn't backing down.

"Because in a few days, your daughter is going to upset your stomach, and you'll lose your breakfast for a couple of weeks."

My mouth dropped open, just as Cori's did.

"But-but," Cori stuttered.

"There was a reason. I just told you what it was. Don't be assholes for the next few years and you may get what you wanted after all."

"That's—what am I supposed to do?" Cori whispered.

"I think you should go home with your parents when they leave here, eat healthy, get plenty of rest and take care of the baby when it comes. You can go back to work later if you want—there's plenty of time for that. And, if Marco isn't happy about this news, I can have a talk with him. His brother may never get children. Think about that, all right?"

"Wow," I breathed. "Just—wow."

"I have something for you," Zaria turned to me then, and held out a hand. A small box appeared there. "Wear it. Never take it off. If you don't know why, ask Randl what happened to Rodrik earlier tonight."

With that, Zaria disappeared. "I don't know what just happened," Cori mumbled. "All this time, Marco and I were pissed."

"And you decided to take it out on Randl and me?" I turned toward her.

"I," she began. "I don't know," she dropped her eyes and stared at the floor. "Sali—you used to think he was what you wanted. I guess Marco thought," she didn't finish.

"Whatever was between Sali and me ended a long time ago."

"But you were never really interested in somebody else," Cori defended herself. "That's why Marco thought." She tossed out a hand, struggling to make me understand.

"So. I find Randl, whom I care about as an adult, and you try to ruin it for me. Thanks, Sis. Thanks a lot."

Tightly gripping the small box Zaria had given me, I turned away and stalked out of the kitchen.

Randl

Dori's ocelot was sleeping beside me when I woke the next morning, fighting a hangover.

Reaching out, I ruffled the fur around her chin before encountering a gold medallion.

Zaria had come to see my girl.

The parents are coming to visit. What happened to Rodrik last night? Dori raised her head and blinked sleepy cat's eyes at me.

I closed my eyes while my brain fought off information.

Rodrik's dead, I replied. *Killed by the Prophet.*

Amlis?

He's fine—he wore his medallion and wasn't hurt.

That's what it's for, then. She sounded smugly satisfied.

I think so. You must be special, I grinned and leaned in to drop a kiss on her head. "Now, what's this about your parents?"

After I consumed several painkill tabs, two cups of tea and scrambled eggs for breakfast, Travis and Trent transported Dori and me to the holding facility. It was time to see what could be done about making Jewl Yarro believe her daughter was alive.

"She's getting her strength back," Jett Riffler met us in a makeshift office in the facility. "We've restrained her with the wall cuffs. She can walk to the toilet and back, but that's all she's allowed. Kooper's on the way, but he said you can take a look at Charla before he gets here."

Wall cuffs were a sort of invisible chain—a connection between a device on a wall and a cuff wrapped around a prisoner's wrist. It couldn't be removed without the proper electronic keys, and those devices were kept elsewhere until needed.

The cuffs effectively kept the prisoner within a set perimeter, and the perimeter could be adjusted as needed, so the prisoner couldn't approach guards delivering food or cleaning infirmary rooms.

Charla had already attempted to attack Susan when she brought Barkins in; Susan's hen had subsequently retaliated against Charla.

In fact, Charla still bore a red mark on her nose where Susan pecked her. I saw it when Jett and I walked into Charla's infirmary room to see her.

"Well, Director Jett Riffler," Charla's voice held deep sarcasm. "Come to make me more miserable?"

"He didn't, I did," I told her.

"Who the hells are you?" she demanded.

"I'm the one who pulled you the hells out of your house before you and your people died in it," I said.

"You're fucking blind. How am I supposed to believe anything you say?"

"Director," I turned to Jett, "I know how to convince Jewl that her daughter is alive."

Kooper

My opinions of Charla and Jewl were already low, but Randl's information sent them to the bottom of the Campiaan Sea.

"She was mad at her mother, so she stole a piece of jewelry?" I asked Randl.

"Yes. Afterward, she accused a servant of taking the necklace. Jewl had the servant killed and Charla buried the necklace outside Jewl's compound so she wouldn't be found out."

"How does that convince Jewl that Charla's alive?" Jett asked.

"I know where the necklace is. All we have to do is tell Jewl to look there," Randl replied.

"Write the message," I scooted the comp-vid across the desk toward Randl. "I'm assuming you can add other things to make her believe the message is actually from Charla?"

"No worries," Randl said and began tapping a message on the comp-vid. "I'll use her personal code this time, too. Charla didn't use the proper one last time."

"I should have known," Jett growled. His opinion of Jewl and Charla hadn't improved, either.

Our offer of immunity—at least during Conclave, didn't sit well with Jett or me, and I ground my teeth in frustration over it. This could be the only way we had of making sure the Prophet didn't get to all members of the Big Three, however. I hoped that once Randl laid eyes on Jewl, he'd know how to contact the other two.

Even Charla didn't know that; Jewl always acted as the go-between in those dealings. Charla also didn't know her mother's location at any given time; Jewl moved constantly so she couldn't be tracked by the authorities.

"Message sent," Randl tapped the screen with a finger and handed the comp-vid back to me. "We'll see how long it takes Jewl to respond."

"How do you know she will?"

"She will. Trust me."

~

Mountain Retreat

Randl

"It wasn't just any piece of jewelry," I said. "It was a piece given to Jewl by Charla's father—before he was killed by CSD agents. Charla still doesn't know that—Jewl never told her."

Vik and David found Dori and me after we made our way back to the retreat. My headache threatened to return, but I was staving it off with more tea and painkill. Kooper had already sent a message, telling me that Jewl contacted Charla, and a deal was in the works.

Kooper didn't like the idea of offering immunity during Conclave, but that's all it was—a short period to sort out the trouble coming with the Prophet.

We knew he was coming, we just didn't know how or when. I hoped that finding Adarr Gramm and Rale Linn would tell us the how, or at least part of it.

When Jewl arrived on Campiaa, as she surely would, I'd be there as part of the greeting party to see what, if anything, I could glean from her. As for my power, I felt it stir, but it was still mostly dormant.

It wasn't a good feeling, knowing that in a few days, I needed to be more ready than I'd ever been, because the Prophet certainly wouldn't have drained himself days prior to the execution of his plans.

Tension was getting to some of the others, and I mentioned that to Vik and David. Dori sat beside me in the retreat's library, having tea with me while the four of us talked.

"Kooper may blow a gasket if he doesn't calm down," David observed. It took a moment for me to understand what a gasket was. Dori hid her smile against my shoulder as I worked out the meaning of the unfamiliar phrase.

"Randl, you need to come," Sabrina rushed into the library.

"What?" I asked, rising swiftly. I could see what caused her fear, however. With my heart racing, I and the others followed her as she made a hasty retreat to the kitchen downstairs, where Travis and Trent were waiting.

Travis

Trent and I washed our hair two or three times per eight-day. This surprise had waited until the evening before, when we'd done our usual and hadn't bothered to look closely as we combed and re-braided our hair.

A white streak—mine just to the right of center, and Trent's slightly to the left, now threaded its way through our black hair.

Sabrina, almost in a frenzy, had rushed to find Randl, to see what he could tell us. As for a cause, we'd never experienced anything like this, and neither had our fathers or grandfathers.

Randl skidded into the kitchen, closely followed by Sabrina, Vik, Dori and David. He blinked at me as I held up a mug of Falchani black in a mock salute.

"Fuck," Randl sighed and came closer to get a better look at our hair. Color washed out of his face as he sat heavily on the chair next to mine and shook his head.

"This is my fault," he said. "For asking you to help me during split-time."

"But," Trent began, his gaze landing on Dori.

"Dori didn't interfere, and I had her shielded," he explained. "I am really, really sorry."

"But I thought," Trent reached beneath his shirt and pulled out his medallion. A grim expression settled on Randl's face as he studied it.

"It worked, I think," Randl admitted. "If it hadn't, I believe things could be worse."

"How much worse?"

"I don't know. I just have that feeling, that's all. I thought I could take all those monsters out without your help, but it didn't turn out that way. If you'd joined the fight early on, well, you could have a full head of white hair, at the very least."

"That's not good news," Trent went back to his tea. "I have to say, though, this is sort of cool. I like it."

"You're joking," Sabrina snapped.

"Not joking. It's an inch-wide hunk of hair. Easy enough to change if I want to do it," Trent shrugged. "Like I said, it's like a battle scar or something similar—to show I've engaged in something nobody else may have ever done."

"I don't believe this," Sabrina tossed out a hand.

"It changes nothing," I frowned at her. "It's as Trent says—it's a small price to pay to keep Randl alive. Face it, he's done more than that for all of us already."

"Men," Sabrina huffed and stalked out of the kitchen.

"I think she's in a snit," David said, looking up at Vik.

"You think?" Vik said.

They didn't touch on what concerned me, however. Was Sabrina so shallow that a few strands of white could affect more than how our hair looked to her?

It was something to think about.

P'loxett

V'dar

One success, one partial failure. The latest word was that Prince Amlis survived, but his heir didn't. A partial victory, to be sure, but the main objective—Randl Gage's father—was dead, confirmed by official reports.

Perhaps that would teach him not to come against me again—I could hurt him in ways he couldn't imagine.

"The reports on Adarr Gramm and Rale Linn—both are taking the bait," Varok set a comp-vid beside my chair and backed away.

"Who knew that ancient gold and precious artifacts from Vogeffa II would tip the balance in our favor?" I chuckled. "It did us no good, as it could be traced back to us in inconvenient ways. It is good to find a use for it, no?"

"It is as you say, Prophet," Varok bowed his head to me. He didn't like giving up treasure that he'd collected, although in this case, it was a brief necessity.

"No need to worry," I waved a hand. "Once we have those two criminals in hand, all of it will come back to us, should we desire it."

"Of course." Varok bowed again, but not before I saw the light of relief in his eyes.

"Leave me now, I must attend to personal business," I waved Varok from the room. He scuttled away quickly, determined not to arouse my anger.

No, my anger was at a simmering point for now. To celebrate my victory in killing the only living relative of my enemy, I resolved to visit the catacombs beneath my makeshift palace.

So much was in store for the Alliances, and none of it was good—for them, anyway.

~

Founder's Palace, Campiaa
Travis

"What happened?" Kooper studied the white streak in my hair before turning to examine Trent's.

"Randl says it's the effect of interacting in the split-time he created."

"I don't understand that in the least," Kooper waved off his concern. "We have a meeting scheduled with Jewl on Avendor—she agreed to connect with our people there. I want BlackWing X to rendezvous with Jewl. You'll bring her and two guards to Campiaa, for a reunion with her daughter and to work out a temporary deal during Conclave. She is to be treated as an ambassador, with complete immunity during her travels and while she's here."

"Great. Are we taking the entire crew?"

"Yes. You can fold space to get into Avendoran orbit, but you can't do that on the way back for obvious reasons. You'll have to hurry, too, to get back here in time to meet up with Zanfield Staggs before he marches into the Eclipse. Wyatt intends to go with you, in case a real diplomat is needed."

"All right. I'll pull the troops together and we'll leave shortly."

"Do it," Kooper nodded. "Keep me informed."

"We will."

~

Randl

I understood that I'd be sending information to Kooper after we met Jewl and her escorts at Avendor's space station. Jett had already cleared her arrival, since Avendor was a member of the Campiaan Alliance.

If Jewl or her escorts were infected, that information would go immediately to Kooper and Jett. BlackWing X would be traveling under her third disguise—Gloria I, which was registered in the Campiaan Alliance. The hull identification numbers and ship's frequency were already changed by the time Dori, Vik, David and I walked on board.

Wyatt and Jayna were the last to arrive. After that, the ship's doors were sealed and we were on our way. Pap was left behind at the mountain retreat, but he wasn't alone; the other BlackWing crews, depending on their current assignments for Conclave, were there to keep him company.

Travis

We transported the ship to a place mere hours away from the Avendor space station. We made our way toward Avendor under more normal speed until we settled into an orbit there, waiting to dock when we received word that Jewl's vessel was arriving.

They just received clearance to approach the space station, Kooper sent mindspeech. *They'll arrive in two hours.*

We'll be there, I replied before ordering James and Nathan to take us in.

At least the scanners should detect any weapons on board—if they were the usual sort. That was part of the agreement—Jewl could bring no weapons, only her guards.

Nathan announced through the ship that we would be docking soon. *Prepare yourselves*, I sent. *We're about to meet with one of the most wanted criminals in the Campiaan Alliance.*

~

Kooper should have gotten identification on the guards. Trent stated the obvious.

Jewl had two Blevakians flanking her. Blevakians were four-armed behemoths who reportedly had six brain lobes instead of the usual, humanoid four. They wouldn't need weapons if they had extensive training in hand-to-hand combat.

They're brothers, Randl informed us as we studied Jewl and her guards across the space that divided us. Electronic motors whined as a walkway was being moved into place; it would allow us to cross to Jewl's berth at the station.

Only Trent, Wyatt, Randl and I had left the ship to greet Jewl and her party. Her ship would be leaving shortly, while we transported her to Campiaa.

We didn't wear our uniforms; the agreement was to travel on a neutral ship provided by the Campiaan Alliance. Jewl wanted nothing to do with ASD or CSD troops. Therefore, we dressed in a transport ship's uniforms instead.

Jewl bore little resemblance to Charla, so Charla must look like her father. She was also shorter than I expected—perhaps four inches taller than Mom, who was only five feet tall.

Black hair hung in waves down her back, while gray eyes flashed her displeasure for where she was. The stone-faced Blevakians beside her looked like giants in comparison.

The metal walkway clanged into place between us and the gate on both sides lowered, indicating it was safe to cross.

Jewl approached us; the walkway was barely wide enough to accommodate her and the Blevakians, who refused to allow her to walk ahead of them.

Just what we needed—loyal servants protecting criminals. Wyatt stepped forward to greet Jewl; Randl moved behind Wyatt's left shoulder. Trent and I stood back, hoping we wouldn't have to fight our way out of this.

"Welcome to the Gloria I," Wyatt spoke first. "We'll make your trip as comfortable as possible."

"Who are you to address me?" Jewl's tone was haughty.

Don't, I sent, but my word of warning wasn't needed.

"This is my servant," Randl stepped smoothly in front of Wyatt. Randl realized quickly that Jewl didn't need to know that Wyatt San Gerxon had come to greet her.

"And who are you?" Jewl demanded of Randl. Wyatt took another step backward, away from Jewl and her guards. The situation had become cold and strained without warning.

"I see you found the necklace," Randl said, as if he didn't feel Jewl's anger and the threat of intimidation from the two Blevakians.

Jewl's hand went immediately to her throat. The necklace had to be beneath the black, raw silk tunic she wore; it wasn't worn on the outside.

"Greetings, Mak and Jak," Randl nodded to the Blevakians. "I trust your families are well and thriving?"

It was a standard Blevakian greeting, because both responded before they were even aware that they did so.

"Madam Yarro, your trip will be pleasant, I assure you, and your daughter is waiting anxiously for your arrival. Your safety is guaranteed by both Alliance Security Directors, and you will be allowed to leave Campiaa when Conclave is over." Randl focused on Jewl again.

"With nobody following me?" Jewl's left eyebrow lifted.

"Of course. Now, time is short, but sufficient for you and your guards to inspect the ship and your quarters before we sail," Randl continued, his voice smooth and sure.

"Are you blind?" Jewl asked.

"In some ways, Madam," Randl confirmed. "In others, not blind at all."

And that's putting it mildly, Trent's voice huffed in my mind.

"We have refreshments waiting, when you are satisfied with your transport," Randl held out a hand toward the ship.

"We will certainly inspect it," Jewl said, although the anger and ice in her had decreased dramatically.

"Then come, we have gishi fruit and tea aboard," Randl said.

And that's how you handle a criminal—give them gishi fruit, Wyatt's mental chuckle made me force back a smile.

Although Jewl remained haughty, the Blevakians went about their business of inspecting the ship with a more casual attitude. Who knew that greeting them the proper way would smooth those wrinkles?

When our three guests were settled into the VIP berth, and a tray of tea, tiny sandwiches and gishi fruit was provided, we disembarked from the Avendor space station and got underway.

Randl

You're sure she's not infected? Kooper asked.

She isn't, and neither are her Blevakian guards.

Blevakian guards—plural?

Yes.

It's difficult to entice them away from their homeworld for any reason. Why are they working for her?

There's a recession on Blevakia right now. They're supporting their families this way.

Well, dip me in caramel sauce and serve me in a cone, Kooper grumbled. I could hear the wheels turning in his mind, though. He was considering whether any Blevakian could be lured into working for the ASD.

It depends on the Blevakian, I said, letting him know I understood his thoughts.

Right. Get out of my head, Gage.

Out now, sir.

At least you called me sir.

Of course, sir.

All right, now you're just annoying.

Randl out, I sent.

Thank the gods.

That's funny, sir.

~

Campiaa

Kooper

"Consider it house arrest while your mother is here," I told Charla, who eyed me warily before surveying her surroundings.

Teeg had an empty suite in the San Gerxon Hotel and Casino—although he no longer had any dealings with the management of it; Wyatt and Dormas did that.

It took up much of the top floor, and only a fourth of it was allocated to Charla and Jewl. It was guarded and would be, day and night. I'd also placed a shield around the quarters they'd occupy—in case anyone had thoughts of escaping.

I was waiting to tell Jewl about the Prophet and his machinations after she arrived; the information could cause her to panic.

She thought that ordinary kidnappers had almost killed her daughter.

That idea would change soon enough. I needed contact information on Adarr Gramm and Rale Linn—as of yesterday. We had a narrow window of time to get things done before Conclave began.

So many thoughts ran through my mind. What if the Prophet had already taken Gramm and Linn? How could we combat the full force of both criminal elements, in addition to whatever the Prophet could do?

"You're a thousand light-years away," Charla said. Her sudden speech made me jerk in her direction.

"Before this is over, you may wish you were a thousand light-years away, too. The ones behind your kidnappers are still out there, and they're gunning for all of us."

<h1 style="text-align:center">CHAPTER 16</h1>

ounder's Palace, Campiaa
Zanfield Staggs

I'd never been invited to the Founder's Palace before. It wasn't quite to my taste, but it wasn't mine to decorate or furnish.

Nevertheless, it suited Teeg San Gerxon, who'd invited me to stay for two days, until it was time to check into the Eclipse.

The Eclipse also wasn't my first choice of places to stay, but it would do. I quite looked forward to walking in with my appointed entourage, merely to hear the shrieks and whispers that would surely come.

I'd worn a yellow silk jacket to this meeting with the Founder, with a purple shirt, which quite matched my hair.

"This way, Master Staggs," Dormas, Teeg's personal assistant, led me into Teeg's private study.

There was a smoothness to Dormas' voice and words, as if he'd had centuries to practice the art of putting people at ease. I liked the fact that I'd be one of only a handful of civilians who'd been invited to this hallowed office.

Teeg San Gerxon waited inside for my arrival. He looked better in person than he did in the vids, but then most people do. Dark hair, dark eyes, a suitably handsome face that many women fussed over—I wondered briefly if he'd had any surgical work done.

I'd never ask that question, however—I didn't want to tempt him to opt out of this agreement. It was a delightful opportunity to play at a mystery, without having someone supervise me at every turn.

"Good afternoon, Zanfield," Teeg greeted me as I swept through the door. "Please, make yourself comfortable."

"Thank you," I said, waving a hand. "I'd be telling my closest friends what an honor this is—if I had any."

"That's—surely that's not true," Teeg sounded surprised.

"Hmmph. You have no idea," I waved the other hand after choosing a chair and sitting on it. "I have acquaintances at best—most of whom only see the money and nothing else about me."

"I've had experience with that—on a certain, political level," he agreed. "But that's not important," he said, sliding away from the topic, as any good politician would.

"I've gambled beside many politicians and a few criminals," I shrugged. "They're pretty much the same."

"Surely you jest," he said, although I saw a hint of agreement in his dark eyes. I'd read his biography—he was a carpenter and then a contractor, before he took over the San Gerxon empire and wrested it into an Alliance that closely mirrored the Reth Alliance.

Anyone who could tame the lawless bunch that ended up as members of the Campiaan Alliance certainly had my support and respect, although I didn't say that. I let most people come to their own conclusions about me. It made life more interesting to do so.

Plus, I could afford any eccentricity I wanted; therefore, I had many.

"What I wanted to discuss with you is your entourage, and their positions as ASD agents," Teeg said. "You realize that they have to follow the laws and protocol set out for them at all times."

"Say no more," I held up a hand. "I've studied the ASD and CSD laws extensively. I believe I know all of them by now."

"Then I can trust you won't ask any of them to do something they shouldn't?"

"Oh, I never said that, Founder San Gerxon," I waved a hand expressively. "I never said that at all."

~

BlackWing X

Randl

Why didn't you tell us he wasn't susceptible to compulsion? Kooper demanded. The subject was Zanfield Staggs and a meeting he'd had with Teeg San Gerxon.

He's susceptible to obsession, I pointed out. *Terrett's orders are holding. You didn't tell me you intended to place compulsion, too.*

You know what this means, don't you?

That he'd make a King Vampire if he's turned? What's the likelihood of that?

We aren't communicating, Kooper accused.

Yes we are, you're just not listening. How do you know there aren't dozens like Zanfield out there? Each one could become a King Vampire in the unlikely event that a vampire just happens to have permission to turn them when they're near death, or even on a whim. It's not something you can control, Director.

Fuck. I hate it when you're right. I'll have Terrett tell him what he can and can't do during Conclave.

Thank you, I said. I didn't bother hiding my sarcasm. I also didn't need to point out that Teeg and Wyatt were both King Vampires because Lissa, their mother and grandmother respectively, was a Queen Vampire. I kept that to myself, because it would only aggravate Kooper more.

How are our guests doing?

Fine—keeping to themselves, mostly, although I think Jewl's Blevakians would like to have a few beers with Vik, David and me.

Right. I don't know that you can get a Blevakian drunk.

You don't know that we can't, either.

Good luck with that. I'll see you in a day and a half.

Right.

Travis

I learned two things. First, Jewl wanted dinner alone in her suite. She also wanted the two Blevakians put in the cabin across the hall from hers.

We made those changes for her quickly.

I wasn't surprised to hear that David invited the Blevakians to the galley for a drink after Jewl retired for the evening. If anybody could convince someone to have a drink, the dwarf could.

Did they accept David's invitation? I sent to Randl.

Yes.

You know not to let things get out of hand, I cautioned.

I know.

Good.

That didn't mean I wouldn't worry anyway, because I would. Trent had sent updated images to Mom and our dads. So far, we hadn't gotten a reply from any of them. I had no idea whether that was a good or bad thing.

I hoped they wouldn't be looking at us strangely when we saw them at Conclave. Sabrina often frowned and shook her head whenever she saw us.

Nothing else had changed—just a streak of our hair. You'd have thought we'd grown a second head or cloven hooves.

I sat in the Captain's chair on the bridge, considering those things when Trent walked through the door with a comp-vid in his hand.

"Message from Mom," he handed the comp-vid to me.

"Why didn't she send mindspeech?" I looked up at Trent.

"Read the message," he said.

I read the message. *I've contacted Bree*, Mom had written. *This is an anomaly and shouldn't have happened. I'm hoping Bree will know the reason why.*

Bree—*Breanne*. The Mighty Heart. She was also Mom's half-sister, but only a select few knew that.

Mom, we don't feel any different. It's just a streak of hair, I sent.

Honey, you're the child of a goddess and a Saa Thalarr. You shouldn't be affected by a suspension of time.

But we weren't suspended, I pointed out. *Neither were the mutant Ra'Ak.*

That may be the problem, but I don't know how that occurred. Suspending time generally allows for the person who's suspending time and perhaps one or two others. Even if the others are Ra'Ak, that shouldn't have been possible.

Randl doesn't call it suspending time, and I'll be honest, it wasn't the present time, anyway. I think it was time in the past, and he calls it split-time.

That's—unusual, she hesitated. *I'll tell Bree that, too.*

Did Trent tell you that we couldn't fold away during that time? If you can call it time, anyway.

He neglected to mention it, her sending was dry.

We were stuck there until Randl could get us out again.

Again, this shouldn't be happening to a child of the powerful, she said. *Remind me to have a talk with Randl when we see one another again.*

I will. You won't yell at him, will you?

No. At least I don't think so. He had my sons' lives in his hands, though, and that's something to consider.

Mom, it's not tragic. We made it out again, and I think we need to thank Zaria for part of that, at least.

Then I'll be asking Zaria questions the next time I see her, too.

It didn't make any difference how old Trent and I became; we'd always be Mom's babies in her eyes. Even though we now had a tiny brother and sister—you didn't mess with Mom's kids, no matter what.

She'd lost one of us to suicide, and it still haunted her. Trent and I —we hadn't known Torevik—Tory—very well. By the time we were born, he lived away from Le-Ath Veronis and kept to himself much of the time.

Teeg and Ry knew him much better, and they wouldn't talk about that loss to anyone.

He'd been Reah's first High Demon mate, and father to all her daughters, including Lexsi.

And then he'd died in terrible distress and under horrible conditions.

I shivered, alerting Trent to my dark thoughts.

"Don't think about it, bro," his hand dropped onto my shoulder. "We'll sort this out eventually."

Randl

"Mak," I handed a large bottle of Refizani Blue to the eldest Blevakian brother. "Jak," I gave him the extra bottle I held—it was standard Blevakian manners to serve the eldest male first. "Cheers," I lifted my smaller bottle and tapped it against theirs.

"Cheers," Jak grinned and lifted the bottle to drink.

"Damn, I'm impressed," David swore after watching Jak empty more than half the bottle.

Mak laughed, pounded his brother on the back with one hand, patted his head with another and lifted his bottle to his mouth with a third while resting the fourth hand on a knee.

"Totally efficient," Vik declared and lifted his bottle to salute the Blevakians before drinking.

"We tell everybody that, they just don't listen," Mak agreed.

"I'd listen," David declared. "Anybody who looks like a fucking mountain needs to be listened to."

"My thoughts exactly," I clinked my bottle with David's.

Mak and Jak looked at each other for a moment before bursting into laughter. I felt the tension drain out of Vik and he laughed, too.

Ice broken, David grinned at me and drank from his bottle.

Queen's Palace, Le-Ath Veronis

Lissa

"They think it's a battle scar, or something like it," I fumed. "Drake and Drew think so, too. I just can't wrap my head around what this could mean," I handed the comp-vid to Winkler, who lifted an eyebrow but wisely didn't say anything.

I could almost hear the Dallas drawl in the words he wasn't saying, however. That the boys were alive, they now had a white streak in their hair and nothing else had apparently changed.

"I think what bothers you the most may be that you can't explain where they were and how they were there," Winkler blew out a sigh.

He was right, but I was too far into my snit and wasn't prepared to let it go just yet.

What good did it do to be a member of the Mighty, albeit a junior member, when even I couldn't explain the shit going on around Randl?

"People may have said the same thing about you in the past." Breanne appeared in my study as if she belonged there.

"But," I pointed out.

"Your actions affected those around you—be honest," she added. Bree's dark hair was pulled back and fixed in an elaborate bun, but she was dressed in jeans and a cable-knit sweater. The boots on her feet told me she'd been someplace cold before dropping by for a visit.

"You called me, remember?" she said after I stood there, mutely gaping in her direction.

"What does the white streak mean?" I demanded, taking the comp-vid from Winkler and extending it toward her. She didn't take it; she already knew what it depicted.

"It means that someone thinks highly of your boys," Bree shrugged.

"What does that mean?" I asked.

"It means you're fortunate they have a white streak."

I opened my mouth to make a retort before examining her words more closely. "As opposed to—what?" I spoke slowly, reeling my anger back.

"Something far worse," Bree said and disappeared again.

~

Mountain Retreat

Brandl Gage

I was hoping to find a comp-vid in Randl's room that held fiction books. I was bored where I was; people were going in and out constantly, with little time to spare for me to have a conversation with any of them.

There were books in the library, that was true, but those were books made of paper and leather, and frankly, I was afraid to touch for fear I could damage them. A comp-vid novel would work fine for me.

That's when I found the coin in Randl's bedside drawer—the coin like the one I had from Vogeffa II, but this one was much brighter and less worn than the one I carried.

How he'd convinced Director Griff to allow him to keep the thing, as it was evidence, puzzled me. Lifting it to set it aside, it caused my hand to tingle. I meant to drop it immediately, but then the vision came.

I couldn't explain how I'd known it was Randl's vision engulfing me; I only knew that's what it was. My heart stopped when I saw the woman weeping. Then, a coin was flung on the bed beside her after she'd been abused by some filth.

Consciousness left me past that point, and I couldn't recall how long it lasted.

～

BlackWing X

Randl

The Blevakians weren't picky about their breakfast; Jewl was. I sent three different trays to her suite at the same time, so she could choose for herself.

At least there were no major complaints afterward.

While we'd drank together the night before, David ended up teaching Mak and Jak to high five and fist bump.

They were quite happy with their new knowledge, and I saw Jak fist-bumping David when they passed one another in the ship's passage between suites.

Randl? I received mindspeech from Trent, our Captain for the day.

What is it? I sent. I was on my way to the workout room to lift weights.

We have a message from your father. He says it's important that he talk to you right away when you get back.

Anything wrong? I asked.

He made it sound urgent.

Can you do without me for an hour or so?

Yes, but you can't—you don't have your energy back yet, do you?

I think I have enough for that, I replied. *I'll keep you posted.*

All right.

I folded space, my intention to work out forgotten.

Mountain Retreat, Campiaa

Randl

"Pap?" I cautiously opened the door to his suite. He sat on the side of his bed, his worn coin from my mother held gently in his fingers.

"I touched the coin you have in your drawer, while I was looking for a comp-vid I could read on," Pap said softly.

I made my way into the room and took the chair beside the bed so we could face one another. He studied the coin and didn't look up at me.

"What about it?" I asked. "I have to give it back to Kooper eventually, but I'm not done with it yet."

"I saw what you saw," Pap said, confusing me for a moment.

"Saw what?"

"Saw the woman, and the man or whoever he was, throwing the coin onto the bed."

"It's upsetting," I agreed.

Pap reached up to wipe tears away. "That was your mam," he said. "I'd recognize her anywhere, in any way."

I went cold at his admission. How could that be? Did someone rape her and then finish the insult by tossing a coin at her naked back while she wept?

"Are you sure?" I reached out to place my hand on Pap's shoulder.

He couldn't speak, he merely nodded.

"I don't know how, son," Pap's voice was broken and anguished when he regained control of his emotions, "but you find this bastard, and you teach him a lesson he'll never forget."

"Do you know who he is? All I see is a hand, and it isn't that of the Prophet," I said. "I'd recognize him anywhere."

"I'll lay odds that the Prophet knows where the coin came from."

Pap could be right—the Prophet could have a connection to either the man or to my mother, and that frightened me. However he came by it, the coin was the same and had, at one time, been in the possession of my mother.

"Don't worry, Pap," I said. "The Prophet is certainly in my crosshairs, as David would say. We'll find him, don't you fret."

"Find him. Make him pay." Pap's fingers closed tightly around his coin.

"I need to get back, Pap," I said, rising from the chair with a sigh. "Are you going to be all right until the ship docks?"

"I know you have important things to do, Son. I'll be fine, I just have to—come to terms with this."

"Then let me hug you before I go," I coaxed.

He rose to his feet and allowed me to embrace him for several seconds. "You know," he said, his eyes still misty as he pulled away, "Your mother, just before you were born, said something to me."

"What's that?" I asked.

"She said, *he's the light against my darkness.* She was rubbing her belly at the time, where you rested. You came three days later, and she died less than an eight-day after that."

"Why did I not hear this before?" I asked. I'd never seen it in him, either, so this was new to me.

"Because you were born blind, Son, and I thought talking about the light would only be cruel to you."

"Pap," I rested a hand on his shoulder. "I understand your reasoning. Thank you for telling me now."

"I'm sorry I waited," he said. "Go. Get back to your work. Things will turn out as they will."

"Yeah," I agreed. Things *would* turn out, and that worried me a great deal.

~

BlackWing X

Travis

Seven hours remained before we reached Campiaa, at our best speed. Randl appeared on the bridge after a brief visit with his father, gave me a nod and walked out the door.

I didn't miss his troubled expression, though. Whatever his father told him had made him worry.

As if we didn't have enough of that to go around already.

At least Jewl hadn't made any demands during Randl's absence—she trusted him more than she did the rest of us. Wyatt had stayed out of Jewl's way—I believe Randl convinced him to do so. Jewl was sharp—there was no doubt of that, and if she ever had revenge against Teeg San Gerxon on her mind, then Wyatt could become a target.

It was best she didn't know who Wyatt was.

The entire crew was involved in an elaborate dance around a well-known criminal, making her feel comfortable and protected, when under normal circumstances, she'd be a target for the BlackWing crews.

A necessary evil, Mom would call it. A deal made with a devil, so she wouldn't ally herself with a bigger devil—willingly or not.

I wondered about Adarr Gramm and Rale Linn. Had the Prophet taken them, yet? Wherever they were, I imagined they were surrounded by Sirenali bones. Before Cayetes was destroyed, he'd made more than enough money selling the bones of Sirenali he'd bred or cloned.

Any criminal who could afford those bones now hid behind a

macabre cloak of concealment, invisible to anyone powerful enough to find them otherwise.

That meant that we were back to searching for them the old-fashioned way, which took time and manpower, and with so many worlds available for space travel, it was all the more difficult to capture any of the bigger, criminally-inclined fish.

Cayetes had left a terrible legacy of crime in his wake, enabling them to hide themselves more successfully than ever. I imagined that V'ili, Cayetes' devoted Sirenali, had provided much of Cayetes' plans and ideas himself.

Zaria had done all the worlds a huge favor when she'd killed both.

"What are you thinking, bro?" Trent walked in to watch stars flash past the vid-screens on the bridge.

"That Cayetes' and V'ili's deaths opened the way for the Prophet to assert himself."

"You think Cayetes would have been able to destroy the Prophet if he'd operated during that time?"

I turned to look at my brother for a moment. "I can't answer that," I confessed. "What we know is that the Prophet wasn't on anybody's radar until after Cayetes died."

"But he was in business before Cayetes died," Trent pointed out. "Remember—some of the people ensnared by the Prophet were taken twenty-five to thirty-five years ago."

"He was working in the shadows," I mused. "I wonder how he felt when Cayetes died?"

"Did he even know of Cayetes?" Trent asked.

"Everybody knew about Cayetes," I huffed. "He'd have to live under a rock not to recognize that name."

"Or under a very heavy concealment shield," Trent responded.

"True. But did he provide the shield, or did somebody else? There's still the possibility that this is tied to the God Wars."

"I keep hearing that term. I hope it doesn't mean what I think it means."

"Funny, bro."

"I know I am, but what are you?"

"The Captain," I groused. "Go do paperwork or whatever."

Sabrina

I wanted to catch Randl alone, so we could have a private conversation. I wanted to know why my Falchani had a white streak, while Dori escaped wherever they'd been completely intact.

A small voice informed me that I hadn't been there and shouldn't be making these judgments, but a bigger part of me felt it wasn't fair, and that Dori received special treatment because she was more important to Randl than Travis or Trent.

I ignored some of my duties to go looking for Randl, because I wouldn't be satisfied until we sorted things out. I wanted to yell at Randl in all honesty, while he cowered and apologized.

He'd probably have that look on his face like he always did—the one that said he understood my thoughts on the matter, but they were dead wrong.

I wasn't wrong about this, and Travis and Trent wore the physical signs of it and would for the rest of their lives.

I hit the comm-locator beside the door into the galley, before asking it where Randl was on the ship. I was fuming and ready to give him an earful of my wrath.

"Randl is in his quarters," the ship's comp replied.

"Before you go marching off to his berth spitting venom, it's time we had a talk," a woman appeared beside me.

"Who the fuck are you?" I demanded before taking a step back.

She had wings. White wings, dusted with gold.

Zaria.

This was Zaria. A hand went to my chest, where the medallion she'd given me rested beneath my civilian ship's uniform.

The medallion had saved my life. Saved me from the Prophet and his minions. I still had nightmares about my capture.

"I, ah," I struggled to find words.

"I see you know who the fuck I am," she replied. "Come with me. It's time you learned a few things."

"What things are you," my speech was interrupted when she folded us into the galley. Cups of tea appeared before both of us, as if by magic.

Well, this was Zaria the enigma. Maybe it *was* magic.

"Power," she corrected me as her piercing blue eyes locked with mine. "Now, feel free to say to me what you planned to say to Randl."

"But," I began.

"Of course—there's always a *but*. What if I told you that Randl did what was necessary, to keep the four of them alive?"

"Travis and Trent," I pushed my anger to the fore.

"Have the least bit of evidence that they were where they were and did what they did. They had medallions to protect them. Dori didn't. I'm sorry that you think a white streak in Travis and Trent's hair is more important than Dori's life. I've always known you were a spoiled princess, but I hoped you'd grow out of it by now."

"You don't have the right to talk to me like this," I snapped at her.

"Want me to take back the medallion? Do you think you still deserve it?"

"I," my hand went to the medallion again—involuntarily.

"That's what I thought. You've been given many gifts, Sabrina Kend. Jealousy and entitlement do not become you."

"How the fuck do you know anything about me?" It was a stupid question, and flew out of my mouth before I could stop it.

"I know who you were in your previous life," Zaria shrugged. "You didn't make the best of decisions then, either."

"Like what?"

"Like committing treason, then killing yourself and murdering your child," Zaria said. "I know what your name was. I know all the names." She frowned at me. "Grow up, Sabrina Kend," she said. "Grow up before you lose those men who now sport a white streak in their hair."

That statement left me speechless for several seconds. "Could that happen?" My voice sounded weak.

"Yes. Consider your actions carefully from now on. You're an adult. Act like it. It's not all about you, you know."

She disappeared before I could form an apology and beg her to let me keep Travis and Trent.

I rose from my seat at the galley table and stalked toward the door. Even my own mother had never said those kinds of things to me.

And then I stopped dead still. Perhaps my mother *should* have said those things to me. I *was* a spoiled princess—my father had seen to it, with his vast wealth. Except for one brief episode of my life, when we'd been kidnapped and I'd helped many people survive by employing what I'd learned and inherited from my father, my life had been nothing but privileged.

That one brief episode is why you have a medallion, Zaria's mindspeech came to me. *Make sure you continue to deserve it.*

CHAPTER 17

BlackWing X, Campiaa Space Station
Travis

Kooper and Jett had brought Charla, and waited in a private area of the space station for us to disembark and join them.

Randl looked grim as we waited for the ship to be cleared so we could leave it. I had no idea whether he was worried still about his father, or the impending meeting between mother and daughter.

What Kooper planned to tell Jewl about the Prophet and the infection he was spreading was also an unknown. Kooper was keeping that information to himself, although I figured Randl knew what the Director intended.

I didn't ask and Randl hadn't volunteered.

What surprised me, however, was that Sabrina offered to bring me tea and a snack a few hours before we docked.

She acted—normal. Nice, even. Sabrina looked me in the eye instead of staring at the white streak, asked me how I was feeling and shocked the hell out of me by doing so.

Usually, our conversations were about her—what she was doing, how she was feeling, what someone else said to her.

She could be quite self-centered; I hadn't failed to notice that in the year we'd known one another. I considered asking her what precipitated the change, but like a much-needed rain, I was afraid to mention it lest it go away.

Trent must have noticed it, too; he went so far as to stand behind her while we waited for the inspection crew, and wrapped his arms around her. I didn't miss the closing of her eyes in bliss, either, when he did that.

"All clear," Nathan announced. My shoulders sagged in relief, while Jayna and Wyatt preceded Mak, Jak and Jewl toward the door.

Private VIP Suite, Campiaa Space Station
Kooper
The Blevakians were even bigger than I'd imagined when they stalked into the suite ahead of Jewl Yarro.

Charla, with two guards standing with her, jerked her head up when her mother entered the room.

"Charla?" Jewl asked, moving past her Blevakian guards.

"Mam?" Charla sounded lost.

I didn't know why that was, until Jewl was in front of Charla. She slapped her daughter hard across the face. "That's for the necklace," Jewl hissed.

Charla's guards stepped in front of Charla at that point—none of us had expected Jewl to strike her daughter.

"Go ahead and hide behind that riff-raff," Jewl threatened. "This isn't finished between us, you know."

"Ms. Yarro, we have an agreement," Randl appeared beside Jewl. "Strike your daughter again and I'll see that it's nullified."

"You have no authority," Jewl's voice was haughty.

"Try me," Randl snapped at her before disappearing.

"Where the hell did he go?" Jewl demanded. "I had no idea he was a warlock."

"He isn't," I approached Jewl, then. She recognized me right away.

"Kooper Griff," she said, her contempt for me in every syllable of my name. "What, then, is he, if not a warlock? A wizard?"

"No."

"Hmmph. No matter. We have an agreement. You put us up, we leave after Conclave is over."

At that moment, I considered letting Randl have his way with them when Conclave was over. "We also agreed for you to listen to what Jett and I have to say," I reminded her.

"Over dinner. Later. Take us to our rooms. I'm tired and I want a bath in a real bath, not something available on such a small ship." She waved her hand imperiously.

"Take them," I ordered her guards, indicating Jewl and Charla with a sweep of my hand. "If they need to be separated, see to it."

"Yes, Director." I watched as Jewl and Charla marched out of the suite. The Blevakian guards hung back for a moment.

"Give this to Randl," one of them handed David a note before he followed Charla out the door.

I was now determined to learn what the note said, no matter what.

"It's a comp-vid code," David handed the note to me when I requested it later.

"What does that mean? That they want to chat?" I frowned at David.

"Maybe. I don't know what Randl knows, so I can't say for sure."

"Nobody knows what Randl knows," I lamented.

"That's for damn sure," David agreed.

Randl

I knew Jewl was furious with her daughter over the necklace, but that was years ago, when Charla was barely into her teens and angry with her mother.

Jewl hadn't made up her mind whether she'd cooperate with Jett and Kooper—I'd known that since we'd greeted her on Avendor.

I'd hoped her decision would have solidified by now. Instead, she was more focused on her revenge against her daughter.

As fucked up as that was.

I'd folded space to the mountain retreat to check on Pap, only to find he was asleep in his suite after fretting about the images he'd seen for many hours.

I settled in the man cave instead, with a bottle of beer at my elbow, to stare out the window and think. That's where David and Vik found me roughly two hours later.

David dropped a scrap of paper on my lap. "Kooper's already seen it," he said. "He insisted."

I placed my hand on the scrap, and everything it meant enveloped my mind. Mak and Jak wanted to get away from Jewl.

They'd given me a personal comp-vid code, because they wanted to work for me.

In one sense, it was laughable. In another, there was nothing funny about it. I tucked that information into a corner of my brain, in case it became useful later.

"You have six hours before we have to show up at the Eclipse with Zanfield Staggs," Vik reminded me.

"Come with us," I said.

"But," he began.

"No, I'm serious. Come with us. We could use another hand in this, and I'd prefer it be yours."

"Fine. I'll have to clear it with Kooper," he shrugged.

"Then do it and be ready to go with the rest of us."

"Sabrina's coming as the snake charmer," Travis strode into the room. "Jayna and Susan—even though they know it's Bekzi—have uh, balked at the situation. Sabrina says she doesn't mind."

"Then make sure she's dressed appropriately," I sighed. "Vik here can walk beside her, in case Bekzi needs more support. You don't mind, do you?" I asked Vik.

"Not a bit," he grinned. *Poison doesn't affect me,* he added silently. He was High Demon, and I did know that about him. *Not that Bekzi would bite any of us, but just in case.*

I nodded at his words—spoken and silent.

Zanfield Staggs

I surprised Founder San Gerxon by showing up in his weight and exercise room both days I was his guest.

Did he think I stayed trim and fit by being slothful and decadent at all times? I was a credit to the ASD uniform I was now dressed in—in fact, I should probably pose for adverts on their comp-sites.

I moved my hair nubs about, then checked the mirror to see whether I looked better with a part in the hair or without one.

A part on the left side—yes. "Perfect," I said aloud and admired my image again. I looked more like a Director of the ASD than Kooper Griff did. There was no doubt I'd make quite a stir at the Eclipse when I and the others paraded through.

"Your entourage is waiting in the back garden, Master Staggs," Wyatt San Gerxon announced. I'd left the door open—I knew someone would be coming for me.

"Then I shall go."

The Founder's son didn't know whether to be mortified or amused as I motioned for him to follow me to the trans-vator.

Founder's Palace

Travis

Fuck me, Trent's mindspeech sounded in my head. He and I both stared as Zanfield Staggs, dressed in an ASD uniform identical to what Kooper would wear on formal occasions, stepped through the back door of Teeg's palace. Wyatt followed in his wake. If the outfit had a cape, I'm sure Zanfield would have made Wyatt carry it for him.

Gonna be a long night, David sent to all of us.

For now, Vik carried Bekzi's lion snake—Bekzi in that form was fourteen feet long and quite heavy. Sabrina stood with Vik, dressed in a slinky, leopard-print dress that hung to her ankles, with a long split up one side.

Vik was shirtless, with Bekzi draped across his shoulders. The man had worked out for a long time—he had plenty of muscle to carry a lion snake around.

Dori's ocelot stood beside Randl, who remained silent as Zanfield approached us. Randl was dressed in black leathers like a Falchani blademaster, and his blades were crossed over his back. I considered that he'd earned the leathers and the blades the hard way.

Not far away, the Sandswept Casino Hotel was already welcoming Conclave guests. It was anyone's guess as to when the Prophet would strike—Jett still had his people searching for the infected ones on Charla's list, but once he'd arrested the first few, the rest had disappeared like rabbits down a hole.

This had disaster written all over it, yet here we were, playing dress-up with an eccentric trillionaire.

Will this be worth it? I sent to Randl.

I think we need to follow the Prophet's people. These were hand-picked by him and stationed strategically, remember? Somehow, the logging industry is connected, although I have no idea how or why.

You're right. I just can't say I like the method of our surveillance.

I know. We won't have to baby-sit much, and can trade off whenever necessary.

Is David really going to drive Zanfield's vehicle?

He wanted to. The rest of us will be in a hover-van right behind the car.

A year ago, I'd never have predicted anything like this.

A year ago, we had no idea where we'd be at this moment.

We've had word—two of our targets have already checked into the casino hotel, Kooper sent. *No room numbers yet—I'll pass that information on when I have it.*

"It's even better in reality," Zanfield gushed as the Rolls-Royce Phantom pulled up behind us and idled a foot off the ground. The motor Nenzi and his brothers installed was so quiet I almost couldn't hear it.

The dark van designated for the rest of us pulled up behind the Rolls.

"Showtime," Trent whispered beside me, before we began to move toward the vehicles waiting to take us to the Eclipse.

P'loxett

Varok

"I thought he was going to wait and use these when we attacked certain worlds," Perill hissed at me as we walked along a narrow aisle in the catacombs.

Once, this vast, underground space had been a bomb shelter, with large parts of it dedicated to storage of supplies, equipment and emergency food rations.

It served as a different type of storage, now.

"He changed his mind," I told my brother.

Perill snorted his reply. Only in the past year had the Prophet changed his mind or failed in any endeavor. It had to do with an enemy that he hadn't named, yet. He'd attacked this enemy recently, and managed to kill his father and a former employer. Still, the Prophet had come no closer to the enemy himself.

He now planned to use what was in the catacombs to strike Campiaa, though, and that's why Perill and I were going through them, making sure all was in place. Perill stopped to adjust the position of a weapon before nodding to me and moving on.

Long ago, when P'loxett destroyed itself with nuclear warfare, the sick and dying were carried down to this place because there was no other safe place for them above ground.

They were shoved onto shelves where food and supplies had been removed for use. After a while, nobody thought to tend or remove them—even after their deaths.

The catacombs were filled with the dead. Someone had shielded the planet to keep the poison from escaping, and those things that would normally cause a body to decompose were also dead. This meant the bodies hadn't deteriorated much, even after four centuries had passed.

P'loxett was still a poisoned world—to those who hadn't been raised in the poison to begin with. When the Prophet found this place years ago, he'd designated it as a stronghold—few would be willing to assail us here, because it could destroy a living army set on its surface.

Lights in the catacombs only blinked on once you approached their section, and blinked off again once you left it. I imagined if all were illuminated at once, we'd see a virtual sea of the dead.

The Prophet would take all of them to Campiaa in four days, two days after Conclave began.

In the past year, we'd gathered and stockpiled the weapons we'd stolen from many ships, along with those the Prophet had taken away from others, most of whom held them illegally.

Why would someone report a weapon as stolen, when he shouldn't have it in the first place?

I found that humorous.

"Are Adarr Gramm and Rale Linn's forces in place?" Perill asked.

"The reports are positive," I replied. "The Prophet is quite pleased with his new criminals."

"What will he do with them once this is over?"

"No idea. You should be pleased, too—they have many ships between them. If we could have found that bitch, Jewl Yarro, we'd have even more."

"I want my own ship," Perill complained.

"We all want that," I said. "Bide your time. I think it will come soon."

"Once we take Campiaa, we can have our pick of vessels," Perill pointed out.

"We must wait for the Prophet to gift them to us," I reminded him.

"Hmmph." Perill had grown tired of waiting.

As had I. Regardless, I still valued my life and wished to keep it.

I stopped to fit dead hands more tightly about a laser rifle. It wouldn't do to have our dead troops losing their weapons—they would be sent in first, and, as our enemy had already seen, you can't kill what is already dead. Even if the dead were destroyed, the poison within them would still be released.

Campiaa and those attending Conclave would come to the Prophet's hand, and who could say what he'd do with them when all were under his thumb? Perill and I cared not; we only wished to fly among the stars, live wherever we wanted, have as much food as we wanted to eat and command those around us to bow to our will.

Eclipse Casino Hotel, Campiaa
  Randl

I doubt Zanfield had ever presented such a spectacle as he did now, stepping from the Rolls-Royce Phantom after David, dressed in a driver's uniform, opened the door for him.

Zanfield slid off the leather seats as if he were a king and his subjects waited to bask in his glory.

A hotel employee rushed to take the car to a safe place, while the rest of us climbed from our van and lined up behind Zanfield.

Dori hissed and growled nicely at the crowd as she reached Zanfield's side; thousands had come to watch Zanfield's arrival. Travis and Trent, dressed in their own ASD agent uniforms, followed him as he stepped toward the doors of the hotel, which were held wide open by fawning employees.

Bekzi's snake was wrapped around Sabrina's shoulders like a shawl, and I imagined he was keeping the bulk of his weight off her by employing power, because she walked along as if she bore nothing more than a cloak.

Vik, at her side, flexed and rippled his muscles at the crowd, and there were plenty of gasps from women and men.

I stalked behind them, gazing warily about me as any good Falchani warrior should. I heard the whispers, however, when I passed the close-pressing crowd.

He's blind.

It's a blind Falchani.

How does he know where to go?

I ignored them. I'd heard those things all my life, and they wouldn't upset me now. Unerringly, I followed Vik and Sabrina, as Zanfield Staggs' parade walked into the Eclipse. A concierge and a bevy of servants waited to take us to the top floor, where others would see to our every need.

Founder's Palace

Kooper

"It's on the fucking news-vids," I pointed at the screen in Teeg's library. Opal and Kell remained silent as we watched the debacle of Zanfield's arrival at the Eclipse. The field reporter was having a news-related orgasm as he described Zanfield's outlandish parade into the hotel lobby.

"It'll be forgotten by tomorrow, when we release the rainbow birds in the pergola for early registration," Wyatt said, attempting to soothe my anger.

"Don't play diplomat with me," I snapped. "I'm enjoying my fit, thank you."

Opal stifled a snicker. Zanfield had walked into the Eclipse as if he owned it, with some of my best agents on display for anyone to see and record on their comp-vids. After thinking about it, I considered that Zanfield could buy the Eclipse and barely use a fraction of a zero in his bank balance.

"They will be fine," Kell said, his deep voice a rumble. He seldom expressed his opinions—as an ancient vampire, he was used to keeping them to himself.

"Right." My tone was only half-conciliatory.

Randl

Travis and Trent offered to take the first shift with Zanfield, who wanted to play a table game he enjoyed. The rest of us had information from Kooper regarding the Prophet's replacements.

Seven had now checked in, with rooms close in proximity on the same floor. Nearly one hundred of them could stay on the same floor if they could arrange it.

If they all came, they could take up three full floors. I didn't think we'd be so lucky as to have them all so close together.

"You know," I said as Dori brushed out her hair in my suite after changing back to herself, "I should have paid closer attention at Charla's house."

"To what?" The brush stilled for a moment as she blinked at me.

"The people in the third-floor kitchen," I said.

"Why? You saw they had the infection. What else was there?"

"Because," I walked toward her, draped my arms around her shoulders and pulled her against me, "The Prophet's people aren't used to getting fresh food of any kind. Remember that they steal packaged foods when they go pirating? They seldom take anything that will spoil quickly, and they don't steal food often enough for it to be a staple of their diet."

"That explains why they were eating like pigs in the kitchen," Dori blew out a breath.

"Hey." I tipped up her chin before settling a kiss against her mouth.

A hand curled around the back of my neck and she deepened the kiss. I admit, I sucked and nibbled on her lower lip before her tongue met mine.

We have to check out the restaurants and buffets in the casino, I sent while Dori settled into multiple kisses and her nails dug into my flesh.

We'll find them there, won't we? Damn, I want your clothes off, she added.

Baby, I want the same, but we're on the clock, remember?

She pulled away from me then, her pupils large, skin flushed and her breathing uneven. "Randl Gage, when this is over, I want you flat on your back," she hissed.

"And I want exactly the same from you," I replied.

~

We found six of our seven quarry in a lower-level buffet, loading their plates with fresh fish, vegetables, salads and fruit, plus fresh-baked sweets and cold desserts.

I see what you mean, Dori's sending was dry.

Do you see this, Director Griff? I asked.

I see it. It makes an ironic sort of sense that we'd find them so easily. I'll have a few agents added to the kitchen crew of the buffets—they'll get the largest amount of food for their credits in those places, and unlimited servings of everything fresh that they don't see often.

They're not limited to the Eclipse, either, I reminded Kooper.

True. I'll have Jett supply some of his agents at other buffets. Keep your eyes and ears open—follow them to their suites if you can. We need their plans and we need them soon.

You don't have to remind us—we're aware that time is short.

"Do you remember the heavy perfume worn by Charla's replacement?" Dori linked her arm with mine and spoke softly as we watched six male replacements pile their plates high and eat voraciously.

"You said that," I nodded. "I couldn't smell it nearly as well as you could."

"They don't get luxuries like that, either," she pointed out. "They're still humanoid enough to want those things they can't normally get."

"Then we definitely have more places to look," I said. "I can place a tracking tag on these, here," I added. "It'll take the creation of a map to watch for them after I tag them, but I think I have solid plan, now."

Kooper, I sent, *I need a room at the Founder's Palace to place a spelled map.*

I can get you a small room in the library.

Good. Can you meet me there in a few?

I can be there in fifteen.

Thank you.

"Come on, sweetheart, let's head for the beach," I kissed Dori's forehead. *We can fold space from there since it's dark out, now.*

~

"I don't know how you did this, but I'm grateful," Kooper declared. Every casino—in miniature—with six small, bright dots moving about the Eclipse, was depicted in a floating, three-dimensional map inside the room Kooper obtained for us.

"I can have somebody watching this at all times," he added.

"That's the idea—to keep an eye on them and watch for a crowd of them to congregate together, or go someplace in the city where they shouldn't be," I said.

I rolled my shoulders—creating this map had been taxing, since I still wasn't at full strength.

"We may have another wrinkle to deal with, too," Kooper said.

"What's that?"

"The six worlds that house the six major logging industries are pushing for tourism in their own forests," Kooper replied. "It's weird, because parts of their forests are planetary parks set aside for tourism, and the loggers can't touch any part of that."

"What's weird about it? Most planets have places like that," Dori said.

"It's weird to me because the logging concerns have never attempted to get those sanctions lifted in any part of that. You'd think most businesses would want to work on their home world. That's why I think it's weird."

"I'll try to go by their displays sometime tomorrow, to see if I can get anything from the attendants," I said.

"I'd like a full report after you do."

"All right. I think I'm ready to hand the reins over to David and Vik for a while," I added. "This sort of drained me." I nodded to the images I'd created.

"Then go. Keep me updated, and I'll pass information to Jett."

"All right."

I folded Dori back to our bedroom in Zanfield's enormous suite. She almost had my shirt off while kissing me when her sister contacted her comp-vid.

Dori's parents had arrived and wanted to see us.

~

Nathan and Lavonna Anderson had been taken to the mountain retreat, so that's where I folded us after dressing more warmly.

Nathan was a vampire—one of the few who could walk in daylight. Lavonna was a shapeshifting lioness, which stood to reason, as both her daughters were large cats, too.

"Tell Daddy what you see," Cori said after initial introductions were made. Cori and Marco stood close by, waiting for Nathan to make a determination in my case.

"Celtic," I said. "Made vampire by Aedan Evans in the sixteenth century as Earth measures time. Would you like me to go on?"

"I don't normally tell anyone that much about me," Nathan snorted.

"You don't normally run into someone like me," I shrugged. "I hope I haven't offended you in any way. My blindness seems to offend Marco, for some reason, although his brother Sal didn't seem to mind it a bit when he taught me how to fight with blades."

None of us missed Marco's indrawn breath.

"Somebody say my name?" Salidar appeared wearing a wide grin.

"Ah. Now we can make the announcement," I said. "Mr. and Mrs. Anderson, you're going to be grandparents. Marco and Cori are pregnant."

"You dog," Sal rushed his brother and slapped him on the back. Lavonna Anderson was in tears as she hugged her daughter. Nathan waited for Lavonna to pull away before he hugged Cori.

"Family reunion," I said dryly to Dori. She laughed and kissed me.

~

"What can you tell me about this mess?" Nathan and I sat in the man cave having a drink together.

"Not much that I'm allowed to tell. I will say this, though. Cori will be granted leave the moment she tells the Director she's pregnant. You and your wife should leave before Conclave starts, and take Cori with you."

"You think a showdown is coming, don't you?" Nathan sipped his whiskey with a thoughtful expression on his face.

"Yes. I don't know what it is, or what damage it will end up doing."

"You'll keep Dorilou safe?"

"As safe as I can. I will give my life for her, if it comes to it."

"I wouldn't believe most people if they said that to me," Nathan said. "But I have a story to tell you."

"What's that?"

"You are favored by Zaria, who is favored by the Three. I have no problem with you courting my youngest. I think she'll want to marry you eventually, though. That's the kind of person she is."

"Good. I was worried about asking her," I breathed. "When I do, maybe she'll say yes."

Nathan laughed. For an old vampire, that was an unusual thing.

I saw Pap before Dori and I went back to the Eclipse. He was still troubled by the vision from the coin. He pretended not to be affected, but he couldn't hide it from me. I think he knew that and put up the façade anyway.

"I don't know about you, but that wore me out," Dori admitted when we arrived in our suite.

"We have to be awake again in less than six hours," I agreed.

"Sleep it is," Dori yawned.

"Yeah."

Fuck being a realist, I reminded myself.

CHAPTER 18

*E*clipse Hotel and Casino, Campiaa
    Randl

I have a message for you from Chief Markus, Travis sent the moment I wandered into the main room of Zanfield's suite, looking for tea or coffee to help me wake. Dori was still sleeping—I'd folded myself out of bed so I wouldn't wake her ocelot.

What's the message? I asked. Travis sat on a sofa next to a very tall, very wide window with an exceptional view of Campiaa Bay. We weren't talking aloud because Zanfield was buttering his toast at the breakfast bar across the massive room.

He says that the tourism table for Northon is giving away polished wooden balls as gifts.

Somebody let that through? Isn't that a violation of the rules? Let me guess, those were supplied by WildTree Industries, whose main offices are on Northon.

Yes. They've already given out quite a few, but I asked Kooper to have that shut down. They're giving out electronic postcards, now.

Where the hell did the wood come from to make those things? I asked. *Northon doesn't want their forests cut down—it's in their laws.*

We didn't ask. Chief Markus became suspicious, so he wants you to look at the people running the booth and display.

I'll go there after I'm cleaned up and dressed, I said.

Want me to come with you?

If you want.

Where is the supply of wooden balls now?

They removed them, but I have no idea where they are.

I'll try to find out. Something about this made my brain itch, and I wanted to get to the bottom of it.

"Tea's on the counter," Travis said aloud.

"Good. I need to wake up."

Zanfield was curious about what had passed between Travis and me—I could see it in him when I approached the breakfast bar and reached for a cup to fill with tea. A hotel employee had brought in a full breakfast, including drinks, and the tea and coffee was kept at the proper temperature in a warming pot.

"You have mindspeech," Zanfield crunched into his toast. It wasn't an accusation, merely a statement of fact.

"Yes." I wasn't going to lie to him. There was a stubborn, slightly narcissistic streak about Zanfield, but the man could keep secrets.

"Lucky you," Zanfield said after he chewed and swallowed.

"Hmmph." I added honey to my tea and stirred the dark liquid in a delicate cup. I'd prefer a mug, but that hadn't been supplied.

"Luck has nothing to do with it," Travis said as he joined me to refill his cup. The cups supplied were only a third of the size of a mug I preferred and would therefore need to be refilled several times.

"Are those real Falchani tattoos on your arms?" Zanfield turned to Travis.

"As real as you are." Travis poured tea and sipped.

"Yet you work for the ASD."

"Sure do."

"They allow tattoos?"

"In special cases. You haven't seen the one Randl has, yet."

"You have a tattoo?" Zanfield was very interested.

"On my back."

"Show me. Please."

I hadn't bothered to button the shirt I'd slipped on. I let it slide down my arms and turned so Zanfield could see the tattoo.

"Sun, moon and eye. There's an ancient story about that," Zanfield breathed.

"What ancient story?" Travis asked as I pulled my shirt up and turned around to reach my tea.

"About the god who could see everything, whether it was day, night, or hidden in the heart," Zanfield shrugged. "Is that why you asked for those images? To reflect that tale?"

"I didn't request it," I said. "It was given to me by the tattoo artist."

"Then he must be familiar with the tale. It's a lovely rendering of the idea," Zanfield said. "Where are you two going?"

I turned to Travis. Zanfield was far from stupid.

"Want to come?" I asked. "I can disguise you if you want."

"You think I want to hide this?" He trailed an airborne hand from chin to waist.

"I should know better," I agreed.

"Fucking right you should."

Less than an hour later, Zanfield, Travis and I folded to the Sandswept Casino. Travis and I were in our outfits from the night before as we trailed Zanfield Staggs. If we'd wanted to create a disturbance, this was certainly the way to go about it.

Half the people in the Sandswept whispered as Zanfield stalked past them; the other half were shocked speechless by his appearance.

Our destination was the ballroom where all the planetary tourism departments had their displays set up, and Travis had already warned Zanfield to be courteous and not make a dive toward Northon's booth first.

That meant he took his time, selecting this world or that as we traversed the ballroom. Bright displays drew his interest, like a bird who collected shiny things. He was offered brochures, comp-vid postcards and anything else the tourism departments had to give away.

They all wanted Zanfield to visit their worlds and spend plenty of money. I didn't tell them that Zanfield had grown tired of that, and only looked to gamble or for something outrageously different when he traveled at all.

At least Chief Markus was dressed as a civilian when he matched his steps beside mine.

We're slowly working our way toward Northon's display, I sent mindspeech to him. He couldn't reply, but his imperceptible nod let me know he heard and understood.

After a while, we followed Zanfield to Northon's booth. Two women and one man—employees of the planetary tourism department, gushed over Zanfield's visit to their booth.

I studied them before linking with Kooper, so he could see them, too.

Infected? Kooper asked right away.

The man is, and one of the women—the older one, I confirmed. *The young woman is from here—a temporary hire to help man the booth. I worry that she'll be infected before this is over, though. I can't see in them where the rest of the wooden spheres are located—they're too heavily infected. The young one doesn't know what happened to them, either.*

I'll arrange to offer her another job and pull her away from them. Can you add the other two to the map you built?

Already done.

Good. I'll have someone watching. I really need to see one of their wooden balls, I added. At that moment, the man reached beneath the table and set a wooden ball in front of Zanfield.

It was all I could do to slap a tight shield around it before Zanfield lifted the thing.

They were told not to give any more away, Kooper fumed.

I don't think that's our worst worry, here, I replied.

What's your worst worry? Kooper asked after a moment's consideration of my remark.

I can't say for sure, but the hair rose on my arms when he pulled that thing out. I shielded it before Zanfield touched it.

Good. We'll examine it later.

I should have known, however. Zanfield wasn't particularly interested in toys or collectibles. He had more than enough throughout his massive homes. He set the ball on the table and walked away.

The man snatched the ball and placed it beneath the table again.

When Chief Markus and I followed Zanfield, I *Pulled* the polished wooden ball to me with power, allowing it to drop directly into my pocket. It would stay safely shielded there until I could examine it and hand it to Kooper.

~

Kooper

"What do you mean, Jewl is asking for a massage therapist and a hairdresser?" I closed my eyes for a moment so I could reel my anger back.

Opal was the one to inform me of the latest request; any other lackey would have hesitated to approach me with that news.

She merely waited patiently, as she often did, dark eyes seldom blinking as I worked through my fury.

We'd attempted to explain to Jewl and Charla about the dangers the Prophet presented, and that Adarr Gramm and Rale Linn were likely in his clutches already, as Jewl couldn't get a message through to either one.

Charla, who'd been kidnapped and faced certain death at the Prophet's hands before a miraculous rescue, had listened carefully.

Jewl waved away our concerns, as if she thought herself immune to anything the Prophet might do. Now, she wanted to be treated like royalty instead of the criminal she was. It mattered not that the rest of us scrambled to solve the puzzle of the Prophet and those he'd infected.

What mattered was her comfort.

Charla, on the other hand, asked for meals, shampoo and food for Barkins. She also stayed in the suite on the opposite end from her mother, and didn't bother to attempt to talk after her mother slapped her in front of a crowd.

I didn't blame Charla for wanting to get away from the shrew; the woman was a vindictive murderer, among her many other crimes.

Again, I regretted the deal I'd made with her to bring her in. Jett was so furious with Jewl and her actions that his standard answer was a solid *no* to all her requests. She hadn't bargained for anything other than suitable accommodations, and he pointed that out as often as she asked.

Therefore, she came to me, hoping for better treatment, when she deserved nothing of the sort.

"Save us from criminal prima donnas," I said, employing one of Queen Lissa's phrases from Old Earth.

"Want Kell to place compulsion?" Opal wore a hopeful expression.

"For the duration of her stay here, yes," I waved a hand, giving my blessing to the idea.

"I'll have him word it specifically for that, then," Opal sounded satisfied as she turned away.

"Thank the gods," I mumbled and turned back to my work. Coordinating my agents with Jett's was a constant, moving beast, and that didn't include Zanfield Staggs and the agents at the Eclipse, all of whom were busy tagging the Prophet's replacements.

Randl

I taught Travis and Trent how to tag the replacements, so they'd appear on Kooper's map. They held the power to do it, so it was merely a simple instruction to make.

Bekzi watched and knew how immediately. He gave me a nod and a grin before going out to search for more. Jett's people had already identified most of them through their credit chips, so I was now using those as my guide while going through the list to place tags for the maps.

Somehow, I knew that many would come together at some arranged place when the time was right; that's why it was so important to place all of them on Kooper's map.

I still had the wooden ball from Northon Tourism, too, and hadn't bothered to study it yet. It lay on the desk beside my comp-vid, waiting for me to finish what I was working on.

"I thought I put that back," Zanfield stood over my shoulder, snooping into what I was working on.

"You did. I took it when they weren't looking."

"Can you tell me why?" I turned to look at him; he clutched a small cup of tea in long, agile fingers, while his purple-tipped yellow hair rose and fell, like a wheat field waving in the wind.

"Because the Prophet has had a hand in its making, and you can bet he's looking for a way to spread the disease he's already infected too many with, so they will obey his will. By the way, he likes to drown his prisoners in liquid concrete while his minions watch and cheer."

Zanfield went still, his fingers tightening on the cup he held. I could almost hear the increasingly rapid beat of his heart.

"Is—that true, or are you lying to keep me from knowing the truth?"

"It's true." I turned back to my task. "Right now, I'm trying to tag roughly two hundred of the Prophet's replacements—he has a way to make his people look exactly like other people, so he can take the real ones for his sacrifices while placing his minions in strategic jobs and locations to attack the rest of us."

"I thought we were looking for an assassin, perhaps, since the Conclave," Zanfield began. "This is the reason it was delayed last year, isn't it?"

"You're pretty sharp for a rich man," I said.

"He had a hand in destroying that ship before it reached Pyrik?"

"Yes. Several hands, actually."

"This bears thinking about." Zanfield turned to walk away. "Thank you for being honest," he tossed over his shoulder.

"No problem." I tagged two more from their credit chip information on my comp-vid.

We have three replacements meeting and talking with two criminals from Charla's list, Travis sent.

Track them. Don't let them get away, Kooper growled. He'd been included in the blanket mindspeech. *I want as much information as you can get,* he added.

On it, Travis replied.

Link with me, I told Travis. Immediately I saw what he was seeing.

We can't get close enough to hear anything, Trent said.

Hold on, I told him.

What? Trent began, until I could hear his audible sigh. He'd become an amplification device for the rest of us—I'd done it with power. We hadn't arrived in time to listen to the first part of the conversation, however, because all we heard before the five turned to walk away was *the Prophet's will be done.*

Fuck, Kooper swore as we watched the three replacements split up shortly after. Travis turned back to the two criminals—they were our only hope now of getting any information regarding the Prophet's will.

I'm in the map room, keeping an eye on them now, Kooper informed us after a moment. *I'll have Jett send two of his agents to apprehend them.*

Thank you, I said. *Make sure they're well-armed—the agents.*

I will. Travis, Trent, you don't need to be anywhere near the arrest—get back to the Eclipse, Kooper ordered.

Right away.

I cut off the connection with Travis and Trent with a sigh.

"Tell me what just happened." Zanfield's voice behind me made me jump—I'd forgotten he was there during the exchange.

Sandswept Casino

Sabrina

The rainbow birds were flying over the crowd of early registrants, all of whom were enthralled by the life-like, mechanical birds.

Somehow, Kooper had diverted the data received from the scanner each bird carried to a receiver in the Founder's palace library. So far, none with the infection had been detected, but the birds had been recorded on so many comp-vids it was staggering, and the information booth was inundated with requests for where the birds could be purchased.

"You could make a fortune off these and other flying creatures if you choose to manufacture," Wyatt said. He, Jayna and I sat at a bistro table in a nearby café, watching the crowd and the birds.

Jayna looked like herself; she'd dropped the disguise and wore civilian clothing to sit beside Wyatt, who would be recognized by many locals as the Founder's son. After Conclave was over, I imagined they'd announce their engagement.

I'd been allowed to leave the Eclipse to watch the initial response to the mechanical birds and to be close enough to deal with any difficulties arising from their use.

Truthfully, the others at the Eclipse had things well in hand and didn't need me—I was powerless to help in most instances, unless somebody needed to be shot with one of my special ranos pistols.

That wasn't likely to happen—at least not yet.

"This feels—surreal," I confessed to Wyatt.

"In what way?"

"Like impending madness," I said. "These people act so calm and happy, and here I sit, wondering whether we'll even survive the next few days."

"Politics, power and madness often go hand-in-hand," Wyatt replied. "We've seen some rough patches during my lifetime. You don't even want to know what Dad and Mom had to go through to put the Campiaan Alliance together."

"Everybody always says that your father built it by himself," I said.

"And they're wrong. My mother, Dormas, the reptanoids and the Starr brothers—the Starr brothers are Dad's warlocks—they all helped. If they hadn't been with him, he probably would have failed."

"Reptanoids?" I hadn't heard that term before.

"Bekzi is one of eight brothers. They were in the thick of it, too."

"You call them reptanoids because they're snake shapeshifters?"

"That's part of it, yes. Get Travis and Trent to explain it, sometime."

"All right."

"Hi, baby."

Queen Lissa arrived at our table, kissed Wyatt first, then Jayna and me.

"We were just talking about how the Alliance was formed, and who stood with Dad to make it happen," Wyatt said while standing and pulling out an extra chair for his grandmother.

"Hmmph," Lissa snorted.

"Gran's memories of that time aren't so fantastic," Wyatt grinned.

"That's an understatement," Lissa observed.

"Queen Lissa, I have something I'd like to ask you about," I said. Ever since Zaria had dressed me down and made me see the light, as so many people might say, I'd been puzzled and confused by something she'd said.

"What's that, honey?" Lissa asked.

"Well, Zaria came to see me a while back. She told me that she can see who everybody was before."

"That's—interesting," Lissa hesitated for a few seconds.

"Let's get Gran some tea," Wyatt tapped Jayna's shoulder. He understood that this needed to be a private conversation. "We'll be back in a few," he told Lissa, and he and Jayna walked away.

"She ah, told me who I was before. Not the name, just what I'd done. It's awful," I admitted. I'd been afraid to tell Travis and Trent, and frankly, I found it shameful, terrifying and embarrassing at the same time.

"How awful? Did something happen to you?" Lissa was now very interested.

"I may have—hurt someone else," I confessed.

"Who?"

"She said I committed treason, then killed myself and my baby," I said while tears filled my eyes. "I can't believe I would ever do something like that."

Lissa's face turned pale and she didn't speak for a very long time. "Every lifetime we are granted," she said eventually, "is a new beginning. A chance to start again. To make up for previous wrongs. To stand for what's right instead of what's convenient, or to allow our hatred to take us over. People let hate make their decisions for them every day, when they shouldn't."

"What can I do to make up for such terrible wrongs?" I begged.

"I think you've taken the first steps on that path. Keep moving forward, Sabrina Kend. You have the ability to save lives this time. Use it."

"But how?" I began.

And then I stopped. "The birds," I breathed.

"What?"

"The birds. I can buy a small manufacturing plant, build those mechanical birds, sell them in both Alliances and give the profits to benefit children everywhere. I hope you know some worthy charities, Queen Lissa, and which will be the best choices to receive those profits."

"I think I can put a list together," she said dryly. "At the top of that list will be the groups that work to find children sold into slavery, and to prevent it from happening to begin with."

"Good. That sounds wonderful."

"Sabrina?" Lissa said.

"What?"

"It's good to see you again."

I didn't understand what she truly meant for the longest time afterward.

❧

Eclipse Casino
   Randl

Lose this hand, I instructed Zanfield. Across the table at one of the biggest high-stakes games offered by the Eclipse, were the owners of WildTree Industries and Burche Industries, two of the Big Six logging concerns.

Zanfield's fingers hesitated for a moment before shoving a rather large pile of gaming tokens toward the center of the table. He was bursting to ask why, but he had no mindspeech.

Don't worry, we're reeling in the assholes across from you, I explained. A smile curled a corner of Zanfield's mouth as he took his hands away from his bet.

Zanfield lost the next two hands at my request. On the third hand, Zanfield was dealt the mother of all hands. I knew it was coming. *Only bet what you did before*, I told him.

The other two had substantial hands themselves, and rolled out a much bigger bet.

Stay with them, I instructed.

Zanfield met their bet.

They upped it again—and then twice more, neither of them dropping out. Zanfield's face could have been cut from stone; he gave no indication he was doing anything except losing money.

By that time, both his opponents had so much money on the table it was almost suicidal to drop out.

WildTree went all in, followed closely by Burche.

Zanfield followed suit, which meant there was a rather large fortune stacked on the table.

WildTree grinned as he revealed his game pieces. Burche's grin was wider as his hand beat WildTree's and elicited a groan from him.

Zanfield revealed his pieces, which beat both.

Almost a billion credits were won by Zanfield, who smiled at his opponents before asking the dealer to cash out.

I carried the credit chip he was given to the nearby cage, where the money would be transferred to Zanfield's account.

"Credit my account with my initial draw," Zanfield instructed. "Transfer the winnings to his credit chip," he pointed at me. "He's been an exceptional guard, today."

"Right away, Master Staggs."

I offered my left wrist—the one with my designated disguise issued by the ASD embedded in it. I could use the credits anytime I wanted, and be completely legitimate when I did so.

My right wrist held my official ID, and that was used for official ASD business.

I had no idea what to do with three hundred million credits, however, although some ideas did come shortly after.

"This is the most fun I've had in a while," Zanfield chuckled as we walked away from the cage. "Shall we have dinner, now?"

"You're the boss," I said. My smile was because Zanfield had just relieved two loggers of their money, and it made me happy in a perverse way.

~

Travis

Zanfield is going to the suite after dinner, Randl informed me.

Good, I replied. *Jett has the two criminals locked up and wants you to take a look.*

All right. I'll be there as soon as Zanfield is safely delivered to the room. Who's on guard?

David, Vik and Dori, I replied.

Good. That ought to be enough.

Trent, Sabrina and I are having dinner with Mom, I added.

Have a nice time.

Will do.

"Okay, baby, we're clear," I leaned down to give Sabrina a quick peck. "What are you hungry for?"

"What does your mom want?" she asked and smiled.

The new and improved Sabrina, Trent sent.

Damn straight.

~

Randl

"Where are you going?" Zanfield asked after I delivered him to the VIP suite we occupied. Dori, Vik and David stood inside the door, waiting to take custody of Zanfield so I could leave again.

"The CSD holding facility," I said.

His eyes lit up immediately. He wanted to go.

"If I take you," I warned, "You have to stay quiet and be disguised. We may be meeting minions of the Prophet, who don't need to see you at all."

"It's that dangerous?"

"It could be. I'm not taking chances with your life; I don't care what you say or think."

"Then disguise me," he held out his arms, as if he expected an elaborate production to commence.

"Done," I shrugged. "You could be any agent, now."

"I don't see a difference," he said, looking down at himself.

"Here." I pulled a hand mirror to me and held it up for him.

"I hate brown hair," he complained.

"Really?" I snatched the mirror away and sent it back to the bathroom. "If you want to come with me, you live with brown hair."

"I want my mommy," he teased.

"Oh, for cripes' sake," Dori sighed.

With Zanfield in tow, I transported the five of us to the holding facility.

Did you have to bring him? Kooper asked as Zanfield stayed close behind me at the facility. Dori, Vik and David trailed the trillionaire, keeping watch over his every move.

I have my reasons, I replied.

I hope they're good ones. I wouldn't normally allow anyone except agents and law enforcement in here.

I know.

"Come on, let's go see the prisoners," Kooper blew out a breath before leading the way toward the cells.

Travis

Mom chose the most exclusive restaurant at the Sandswept, and invited Wyatt and Jayna to dinner, too. Mom didn't come alone—Gavin sat on one side while Merrill took the other.

Those two old vampires were powerful enough to destroy anyone who came at her, if she didn't choose to do it herself.

Rigo is out snooping around, Mom sent as she studied her menu.

She'd named another ancient vampire, who, like Gavin and Merrill, was among her mated inner circle. Rigo, master of spies, was a member of the *Rith N'aeri,* The Order of the Nightflower, from Hraede.

He'd shortened his name from Rigovarnus I, a former king of Hraede.

He's snooping with Kell, am I right?

Kell was the one who, thousands of years ago, made the dying Rigo a vampire in the first place. Few knew that, however. The *Order of the Nightflower* was comprised of former Hraedan Kings, all of whom were vampires, now. They'd formed a spy network and were adept at creating undetectable poisons. They were quite useful when it came to planetary security.

Yep. Mom's reply was short.

Do you know what? I began.

It's better if you don't ask.

All right.

The waiter had arrived at our table, ready to take orders when the explosion happened.

"It's the holding facility," Mom half-shouted and pulled all of us out of the restaurant in a blink.

ounder's Palace, Campiaa
Randl

It happened in the oddest way—the explosion. The Prophet had made the two criminals into walking bombs, hoping someone would arrest them.

They were expendable to him, as he'd already made use of their particular talents. The odd part came when they were recognized first by Zanfield.

By all accounts, the holding facility was still on fire, and the occasional tongues of flame could be seen from the Founder's Palace. Kooper was now asking questions while fielding reports from Jett and the emergency crews surrounding the facility.

"I've made purchases from them—through an agent, of course," Zanfield held up a hand. "I like ancient coins. They deal in those things. All of mine have certificates of authenticity—I've had them thoroughly checked or I wouldn't buy," he snapped at Kooper, who was doing his best to intimidate Zanfield.

"He's not the enemy, Director," I said, my voice sounding weary, even to myself.

"Why would the Prophet choose those two—to act as explosives when you showed up?" Wyatt asked, attempting to draw Kooper's attention away from Zanfield.

"He's already tried that once—with Phorde Gaster," Travis reminded Kooper. "This is just another attempt on your life and Jett's life. You were both outside the cell when Zanfield named the two inside it."

"You're saying this was another trap?"

"I think the Prophet was hoping it would come to that," I said. "Look at it this way—you haven't found any other criminals on Charla's list, have you?"

"Not yet," Kooper grunted.

"The rest of them are waiting for their orders to come from the Prophet, I imagine. These two—they wanted to throw the ASD and CSD into turmoil, and with those that we couldn't save at the facility, it will certainly play to the Prophet's advantage."

"But dealers in ancient coins?" Zanfield frowned at me. "That doesn't make any sense."

"I wish I could have more time to study both," I sighed. "Maybe I could have seen something in them that would explain why they were used for this."

"Did you see anything at all?" Kooper asked.

"I saw fleeting images of Adarr Gramm and Rale Linn, so it's likely they've had dealings with those two. The spreading obsession wasn't completely overruling their minds, but it was close enough."

"Do you think they knew they were humanoid bombs?" Queen Lissa and two of her mates were nearby, listening to everything the rest of us discussed.

"I'm not sure they understood that, no. I saw no fear in either," I said.

"I'm concerned there may be more out there like them, set to detonate at inopportune times and in strategic places," Wyatt said.

"That's not a comforting thought," Kooper said. "Jett's trying to calm the city and his people at the same time. He'll have his hands full, so we have to pick up the slack and keep our eyes on the Prophet and his people."

"I think he was only hoping to target Jett and Kooper again," I pointed out. "Let's face it—if he bombs other places, the Conclave attendees will evacuate in droves."

"That makes sense," Merrill, one of Lissa's mates, agreed.

"You say you had Zanfield disguised?" Kooper turned to me.

"Yes—to anyone outside our group."

"The Prophet couldn't see who he actually was?"

"No, Director."

"Good. Staggs, I'd put you on the payroll if I thought you needed the money," Kooper blew out a breath. "From now on, if you see someone you recognize that isn't a gambler or a casino employee, let Randl know."

"I will, but only because I owe Randl for my life."

"Whatever it takes," Kooper said. "Everybody, back to your posts. Keep me informed if you see anything out of place."

"Does he bark like that all the time?" Zanfield asked when we set down inside his suite.

"Pretty much, but he has a tough job," David said. "You'd bark, too, if you had his responsibilities."

"I'm beginning to see that," Zanfield said. "Thank you for pulling us out of that facility," Zanfield told me. "All I remember is seeing the blast in front of my face, and then we were in the Founder's library."

"He pulled me and my crew out of an exploding ship," Dori said.

"Which ship?"

"Mine," she shrugged.

"You're a ship captain?"

"She is," I said. "As are Travis and Trent."

"Things only get stranger as we go along," Zanfield said. "Anyone want to share a bottle of Dark Royal whiskey with me?"

"I'll have some," David replied immediately.

Dark Royal deserved its name, I decided. I woke with a royal headache the following morning, and nursed it and a cup of tea while studying a live feed of the map I'd created for Kooper.

I was also reviewing the news-vids on the holding facility bombing, which was attributed to two criminal dissidents picked up the day before.

I'm sure the Prophet was crowing somewhere, although by all accounts, official and otherwise, he'd missed his two main targets.

"So." Zanfield pulled a chair beside my desk and settled there as if he were a King visiting his Prime Minister.

"And?" I asked, although I didn't interrupt my work.

"What say we look into what our coin dealers were doing before they exploded."

"How?"

"Ask the proprietors of the shop next to theirs, of course."

I lifted my head and stared out the window of Zanfield's suite for a moment. "Where is their shop? Does Jett know about it?"

"I doubt it. It's listed under different ownership."

"But you know about it because you're a customer."

"Yes."

"Let's go." I stood, attempted to work the kinks out of my shoulders and back, then turned to Zanfield. No evidence of a hangover, whatsoever.

"I hate you, by the way," I said.

"You don't mean that. It takes a while to get used to Dark Royal. Most people never get it."

"Because it's five thousand a bottle," I agreed. We'd emptied three the night before.

"You should try Mad King next—it's even more potent," he laughed.

"I'll take that under advisement. Where is this shop you speak of? Never mind, I can see it floating in your eyes."

"That's unnerv," he didn't finish because I folded him out of the suite.

~

"Master Staggs." The man bowed so low I thought he'd topple over when Zanfield walked into his shop. "What may we do for you today?"

The proprietor of the neighboring shop was also a coin dealer, I learned as I looked about me. The shop was quite discreet and hidden in an alley that housed other discreet businesses.

Jewelry shops, highly priced art and pottery, precious metal sculptures, gemstones—it was all here.

"Nang sent me a recent brochure of new acquisitions," Zanfield said. "I was hoping to ah, see them, only I learned that he may no longer be available to do so."

"Ah. So sad," the round-faced coin dealer agreed. "You will be pleased to know, however, that I took what he didn't buy from those vendors. I think you'll find these coins quite interesting. Very seldom on the market, too."

"Then of course I wish to see," Zanfield said. His tone implied that the dealer was wasting time in bringing them, in his estimation.

"Yes, yes. Just a moment, then." The dealer disappeared into the back of the store, only to reappear moments later with a sealed box and a security guard.

I blinked, because I now saw what the box contained and who the dealer received the coins from. He had no idea how Rale Linn came by a treasure of gold coins from Vogeffa II, but he wanted everything that Nang hadn't bought from Adarr Gramm.

The Prophet had both of them—in fact and not just in speculation.

That meant he had their entire empires, too, and Jett and Kooper had no idea who or what those resources were.

We were in big trouble.

Kooper, I sent, *Look at this*. The dealer opened the sealed box for Zanfield, and lying on black velvet were rows of gold coins from Vogeffa II. *The Prophet owns Adarr Gramm and Rale Linn, now*, I said. *These coins came from Linn, and the ones Nang had came from Gramm.*

How? Kooper sent, before he began to curse. *I'll get Jett. Have Zanfield buy that box of coins. We'll raid those shops later.*

All right. Zanfield, buy the box, I know what those are, I sent to him.

"I'll take the entire box," Zanfield said after studying the coins.

"Very good, sir. Your taste is impeccable, as always." The dealer slid a comp-vid in Zanfield's direction. Zanfield slid his own toward the dealer and the transaction was completed.

I'm sure there were more zeros tied to it than I may have dreamed any gold coins could bring.

Nevertheless, we walked out of the shop a short time later, the box in my hands as we searched for a hidden spot to fold space.

"What are these things anyway? I've never seen them before," Zanfield said as he and I ate sandwiches and stared at his purchase.

"Ancient coins from Vogeffa II," I said.

"You're joking. No wonder they cost so much. Those things are impossible to find—I've only read about them before, and nobody had images," he explained.

"You own some now," I pointed out.

We're raiding the shops, Kooper sent. *I'll let you know what we find.*

"ASD and CSD are raiding the shops," I said. "You may be the only one who got away with any of these." I jerked my head toward the open box.

"Even better," Zanfield laughed.

"Zanfield," I said.

"What?" He'd heard the seriousness in my tone.

"Do you have a way of protecting yourself?"

"What do you mean? Besides the numerous ASD agents around me?"

"Yes. Besides them."

"I have a laser pistol hidden in my trunk."

"Come with me," I said.

"Where?"

"To Travis and Trent's ship," I said. "I think you'll need something better than a laser pistol, and soon."

"This is genius," Zanfield breathed as the printing machine aboard BlackWing X set his new ranos pistol on the tray.

"A genius designed it," I agreed. "This pistol will only allow you to use it, and it fires a limited number of shots before it melts. Don't abuse your ownership or I'll melt it ahead of time, all right?"

"Yes, sir," Zanfield murmured as he lifted his new weapon. "I never thought I'd get to hold one," he breathed.

"Keep it hidden. Kooper finds out you have it and we're both dead, all right?"

"No worries, these lips are locked."

He'd picked up David's favorite phrase after drinking with the dwarf the night before.

"Right," I said.

"How soon?" Zanfield's voiced turned serious.

"Soon, I think. Don't let your guard down. Ever. If you see the dead approaching, fire at will."

"The—dead?"

"Know what a necromancer is?"

"Those are myths."

"Then the Prophet is a myth." I slapped Zanfield's shoulder. "Let's go back to the Eclipse. I feel a storm coming."

Founder's Palace

Kooper

"Do we or do we not release this information? Once it's released, it could precipitate the Prophet's attack," I said.

Jett, Teeg, Wyatt, Lissa and a few others, Ildevar Wyyld included, had met with me in Teeg's private study, after we'd raided two coin dealers and confiscated more than a billion in ancient coins from Vogeffa II. That was face value, not resale value.

"I remember these," Ildevar fingered one of the heavy, gold coins. "I recall Vogeffa II in its glory, too, before the polar ice caps melted and reduced the land mass above sea level to a large island. Everything worth anything is buried beneath the water, now."

"Is that where these came from?" I asked. Ildevar, long ago Founder of the Reth Alliance, nodded thoughtfully at my question.

"I believe so."

"Somebody knew where to look?" Lissa asked.

"I certainly hope so," Ildevar replied. "The other options are that the world was visited by treasure-hunting pirates, who would still have to know where to look, or someone, sometime in the past, bent time to go back to the former Vogeffa II."

"Treasure-hunting pirates," Teeg and I said in unison. "Those are the Prophet's people, you can bet on it. This is how he came by the coin spelled to pull Sabrina out of an ASD warehouse."

"You think he bought Gramm and Linn this way—by offering them this treasure in exchange for their cooperation, and then taking them in the less than courteous way he has of creating slaves to his will?" Ildevar asked.

"I think that's close enough," I agreed. "Randl says the same—that Rale and Linn belong to the Prophet now, and we have no idea what resources the Prophet can level in our direction as a result."

"You know they have a fleet of ships," Lissa huffed. "All hidden from the powerful with Sirenali bones, and holding legitimate-looking registration, no doubt."

"Plus tons of resources and many comfortable hideouts, criminal employees, paid-off politicians—the list could be endless," Wyatt said.

"I have six CSD ships in low orbit, and another fifteen Regular Campiaan Army ships in a higher orbit around the planet, in case things go wrong in a hurry," Jett said. "Only the CSD and RCA commanders are briefed as to what we could be facing, and all are equipped with poison gas and bomb gear if it's needed. I have other ships farther out, watching for unauthorized vessels approaching Campiaa."

"Then let's hope they're not transported in another way," I said. "I have some of Rylend's warlocks shielding the planet, but I'm concerned they're either already here or have a way to get past that."

"That's a scary thought," Lissa frowned.

"Well, it won't be the first time I've seen it happen, speaking from personal experience," I grumped.

"What do you mean by that?" Jett asked.

"Randl can slide right through my shields if he wants to. He's done it once already."

"You don't think for a minute that Randl," Lissa's feathers were ruffled and she was about to come after me—with words if not with claws.

"No, that's not what I'm saying," I held up a hand. "Face it, the Prophet has unusual talents—nobody can reanimate the dead, but he can. More and more, I believe that the Prophet, like Randl, may have roots in the mutants who inhabited Vogeffa II. The Prophet has shown a connection by his knowledge and possession of those ancient coins."

"You're saying a world that could turn out one mutant with powers we've never seen before could turn out a second one—or more?" Jett didn't sound pleased with my theory.

"I suppose that's possible, although their talents appear to be different for the most part," Merrill agreed after considering my words.

"Some of their talents may coincide," Lissa said. "I doubt he's called the Prophet for nothing."

"True enough. That's why I'm concerned about him getting past some very strong shields, no matter what," I said.

"I dislike the term mutant," Wyatt interjected. "It connotes a disability, an aberration or a penchant for evil. I don't consider Randl anything of the sort."

"Also true." I couldn't hold back a sigh. "Everything is as planned and ready as Jett and I can make it. Let's hope things go smoothly—in and out of the Conclave."

Eclipse Casino Hotel
   Randl

"Any gambling today, Master Staggs?" Vik saluted Zanfield with a rather large coffee mug. I wondered where he got it, until I saw the casino logo on one side.

"Damn, why didn't you buy us all a mug?" I complained and poured tea into the tiny porcelain things the hotel called cups.

"What, and make things easier for you? No way, dude." Vik stifled a snicker.

"The giant thwarts me at every turn," David grumbled as he climbed onto a chair at the breakfast bar. "I wanted a mug, too. He got the last one."

"Oh. Now I understand," I nodded.

Zanfield grinned and sipped his tea. He was having the best time, and it was because his employees always scraped and bowed, his so-called friends only wanted something from him, and nobody joked around with him.

Ever.

"No gambling today," Zanfield said eventually. "I'll be shadowing Master Gage instead."

"In or out of disguise?" Dori asked as she shuffled toward the bar, stopping only to give me a quick kiss on the cheek.

"Either way. Randl decides."

"Ooooh, Randl decides," David wiggled his fingers at me.

"I've been known to decide something now and then."

"I wouldn't mind watching the parade this morning," Sabrina looked a bit rumpled as she, Travis and Trent joined us at the bar.

"Parade?" Vik asked, turning toward me.

"New to me, too," I frowned at Vik. "When did this happen?"

"It's on everybody's comp-vid," Sabrina pulled hers from a pocket. She worked diligently to hide the pink spots on her cheeks—she'd spent the night with Travis and Trent. There was a happy glow about her, too, but I didn't want to point it out.

"I only checked mine for messages from Kooper and Headquarters," Vik was now looking at his device.

"It says many casinos went together to create this, in celebration of the start of Conclave," Sabrina read from her message.

"Ask the Eclipse management if they're a part of this," I rose from my chair. The hair on my arms was standing again, and I didn't feel good at all about this.

"Travis, Trent, get with Kooper. Find out which casinos went in on this parade," I barked. "When is it scheduled?"

"In about an hour," Zanfield held up his comp-vid to check.

"Fucking hells," I exploded before disappearing from the suite.

Founder's Palace

Kooper

"What do you mean, none of the casinos participated?" I shouted into a comp-vid.

"They were all thinking that it was the others, and they were excluded for some reason," Opal's answer was calm and measured as she reported her findings to me.

"How long has this message been going around?"

"Three days, I think, and it was sent out first to all those who'd arrived at the space port before we arrested Cleaster Leech. The Prophet had that information already. The rest—I can only assume that those whose comp-vid codes were gathered or set to receive information from the tourism departments were somehow compromised or hacked."

"My money is on those two who bear the infection from Northon," I growled. "Fucking hells. This is a disaster, and we have little more than half an hour to prepare for any of this."

"What if it's a ruse?" Opal asked.

"I hope it is, but what better way to get crowds of people gathered together, conveniently waiting for the Prophet's infected minions to appear and take them? Since this isn't an official event, and nobody on the planet seems to know about it except for a few criminals the Prophet has taken for his own, there's no way to cancel it. And, since the parade hasn't arrived in any location yet, we have no way to put up barriers to stop it, either."

"Put out a bulletin to all casinos, saying the parade isn't sanctioned and that everyone should stay away?" Opal asked.

"That'll just make them want to go more. Get a notice to all casino security, and tell them to do crowd control. Keep them away from the streets at all costs."

"There's already a huge crowd of people lining the streets," Opal said.

"I'll ask Jett to send in his RCA troops. Something needs to be done and fast," I said.

"They may not get here in time," Opal pointed out.

"Then they'll do damage control," I snapped. "Go. Now."

Randl

I stood inside the room set aside for my three-dimensional map of Campiaa. No, the dots indicating a tagged replacement or other infected individuals hadn't congregated together.

They didn't need to; not yet, anyway. For now, they were lined up obediently along the parade route, waiting to be used by the Prophet in some way.

Cleaster Leech was only the beginning of this plan. Deftly, the Prophet had salted his people onto Campiaa, and added the criminal element to his list of infected ones. No doubt they'd bring weapons when they arrived, if they hadn't done so already.

I considered that they could also have placed a cache of weapons somewhere, for the replacements to visit and take pistols or explosives away with them.

And then it hit me.

I'd never examined the wooden ball I'd gotten from Northon. Hastily, I pulled it to me with power, just as Kooper walked into the map room. Reaching out to the object with my mind, I began to study it.

The wooden ball was hollow, or at least it had started out that way. Other things about it teased my mind, but I didn't have time to dwell on them now.

"Is that?" Kooper began. I shoved a more powerful shield about the ball, cutting off its purpose.

"We're screwed," I whispered as I locked eyes with Kooper's.

"The CSD and RCA ships are under attack," Kooper's comp-vid squawked. "It looks like ships from Gramm's and Rale's fleets."

CHAPTER 20

*E*clipse Casino
Travis

"If you have any of those wooden balls that Northon gave out, I need to confiscate them now," I snapped after getting mindspeech from Randl.

"We don't," Dori shook her head.

"Nothing," Sabrina confirmed.

"None here; I look," Bekzi confirmed.

"Good. We need to get to the streets. Zanfield, Randl says for you to come with us. The casinos aren't any safer than the streets at this point, and at least we'll see the Prophet's army coming head-on. Weapons ready, everyone. We have no idea what's coming, and the CSD and RCA ships are fighting off an attack of their own. We won't get any help from them for whatever the Prophet has planned."

"Why are the casinos not safe?" Sabrina asked as I grabbed her hand to fold us away.

"Because those wooden balls now contain a powerful explosive, and you can bet the Prophet will pull that trigger soon."

~

Sandswept Casino

    Lissa

"How the hell are we supposed to pull those wooden balls away, when we can't even find them by *Looking*?" I asked, desperate for an answer. I'd folded out of one of many meetings held inside the Sandswept. Merrill and Gavin now stood with me outside the casino.

I'd felt something was wrong, and Kooper's mindspeech reached me after I'd left the Sandswept. Every polished wood sphere given out by Northon now contained explosives. "Half the people in the casino probably have them," I said. I wanted to scream, but that would get us nowhere.

"Pull the people out instead," Gavin suggested.

I looked at him as if he'd lost his mind, before realizing he was right. I just had to figure out how and where to send them.

"My ballroom at the palace," Teeg appeared beside me, Wyatt close behind. "We'll mist them out, but we have to do it now."

Quin, I sent, *you need to evacuate.*

Berel has already transported us to the mountain retreat. Is there some way we can help? she replied.

Have him take you to Teeg's palace ballroom. I figure you'll have plenty of crazy, frightened planetary leaders to calm.

I'll take care of it, Gran, Berel's voice came through clearly.

"Come on," Wyatt urged. "We don't know how much time we have."

The parade is starting, Kooper's grim voice filled my mind. *Either stay and fight or get out, but do it now.*

"Merrill, you and Gavin go help Kooper," I told them before turning to mist and following my son and grandson.

Founder's Palace

    Quin

Just as Wyatt, Teeg and Lissa dropped their loads of frightened, angry and bewildered planetary leaders inside Teeg's massive palace ballroom, the first of many, many explosions rang out in casinos nearby.

Then, the massive detonation of the Sandswept rocked the entire city, the sound of it sending shockwaves high into the mountains. It collapsed into a massive, burning heap, followed by the angry roar of fire and subsequent, booming explosions as chaos erupted on the north end of Campiaa Bay.

On the south end, where the Eclipse was located, the Prophet's parade was only starting. He had attacked, and Campiaa was now engaged in full-on war.

"They need your help, Quin," Dena's hand dropped on my shoulder. Drawing my visions back, I blinked to bring the new crowd around me into focus. Some were crying; some needed calming. A few needed medical attention. I went to those, first.

~

Kooper

At first, the waiting crowd paid little attention to the large booms coming from the other end of Campiaa Bay, until huge plumes of smoke obliterated the sky and the scent of burning reached them.

Then came the deadly march, and those who struggled to escape the tightly-packed crowd were shot at by an army of the dead.

"Shields," Merrill shouted as he raced past me as swiftly as only a vampire can. Gavin ran down the street on the opposite side, doing the same thing—attempting to shield the crowd from deadly laser blasts.

No matter what I did, people would die—had already died at the Prophet's hand. *Jett's ground troops are coming, but they won't be able to stop these*, Travis' mindspeech rattled in my head.

He and I knew that Jett's ground troops would only be more fodder for a massive army we couldn't kill because they were already dead. Tossing grenades would only make them explode, and what the explosion didn't kill of the gathered population, the resulting green mist would infect.

The Prophet had laid his plans so carefully, and I was angry.

Angry at myself, for not guessing any part of his plan.

I stood in the center of the street, watching the dead approach, their booted feet marching in unison, their weapons firing into the crowd regularly.

I could see where Merrill's and Gavin's shields had been placed; the laser blasts bounced off that part of the crowd.

If you use your power, you will violate the non-interference rules, a small voice reminded me.

I no longer cared. I was ready to let the Prophet know that someone was willing to sacrifice themselves to defeat him and his army of corpses.

"Kooper, let me handle this."

Randl's hand dropped onto my shoulder. I turned to look at him, knowing my eyes had turned reptilian. He didn't seem to be afraid, although most people would have been.

"What are you planning to do?" I snapped at him, my voice a half-hiss. The snake wanted out. The *powerful* snake, this time.

"Stay with me, and keep your shields up. We need you for the future, you know."

"Where are you going?" I demanded.

"We're going for a walk," Randl's voice was grim. "Down that way." He pointed at the approaching army.

"Right where I want to be," I agreed. "Let's go."

Travis

"What?" I frowned at Zanfield's words.

"Get behind them. Surely he has some live ones out there, too," Zanfield said.

"That makes weird sense," Trent agreed. "Send the dead ones first, and follow up with your live minions, to make sure things get done."

"I'm all for checking," Vik agreed. He, David, Dori, Jayna and

Sabrina stood with us in a blind alley, while we made plans to attack what we could of the Prophet's army.

Bekzi had left us moments earlier, saying he was going to walk with Kooper and Randl, wherever that was and whatever that meant.

Susan and Terrett had folded space to the Founder's Palace to beef up security there, because the palace now housed every planetary leader attending Conclave.

"Then let's go," I said. I still couldn't believe Randl had given Zanfield a ranos pistol, but then Randl was becoming a law unto himself.

Not that I wanted to argue with that, actually. "You know how to shoot that thing?" I asked Zanfield.

"I've been target shooting for a very long time." He sounded hurt that I'd ask.

"These are people—not targets. Get ready to shoot them instead." I slung a ranos rifle over a shoulder and folded my party to the back end of the parade.

I had no idea we'd be engaged in a firefight the moment we landed.

~

Varok

The Prophet heard and saw everything I did—with the power he held. When the small band of enemy troops hit the street behind us, I ordered my small, living army to fire at them. The Prophet immediately enhanced my small band by ordering his three hundred replacements from the logging industry to join forces with us.

We had enough weapons to arm them and soon enough, they stood beside us, firing at the ones who thought to take us down.

Farther north, the sound of continuous laser blasts drowned out the screams of the dying as the Prophet's dead troops killed residents and visitors alike.

I didn't mind, but the Prophet preferred to hear those things. "They have shields," Perill shouted beside me, pointing at the small band of attackers. "Our blasts aren't getting through."

"Then how are they firing at us?" I shouted back. Several of our troops were either dead or wounded, their bodies crumpled and bleeding on the street.

∾

Founder's Palace
Winkler

Once I had Lukas calmed down, he and I went to find Lissa. She hadn't needed to pull us out; I'd gotten Lukas away myself. The High Demon contingent also skipped themselves out; I found Reah, Lexsi and Kordevik talking with Lissa in a corner of Teeg's ballroom.

"Gran, Kory and I can help," Lexsi pleaded with Lissa. "You know burning is one of the few ways to destroy any of them."

That's when Amlis, Aurelius, Berel and Halimel joined our conversation.

"I think the High Demons would be an asset," Aurelius agreed. "Send them to Travis and Trent—I hear they're on the far end of this mess, trying to take out the living portion of the Prophet's troops."

"How do you know that?" Lissa asked. "I've been afraid to *Look* for them," she confessed.

"Opal and Kell," he shrugged. "They're nearby, trying to get people away from the slaughter. Travis and Trent are alive and doing what they can, but their numbers are small. They were doing well enough until the Prophet sent in three hundred more troops and many ancient war machines to shield his people and to fire back at Travis' group. They could use our help."

"Then I'll come with you," Lissa turned back to Lexsi. "Merrill and Gavin are out there in that mess, too."

"Tell them to keep their shields up and tight," Lexsi said. "Let's go."

∾

Travis

Steady, Trent sent when Mom, Lexsi and Kory landed behind us. I hadn't considered it—my mind was too numbed by the task at hand to recall that fire would work well enough against these.

A part of me worried that the destruction of this end of the Prophet's army would precipitate a mass explosion and release of gas on the front end, but we were screwed anyway, no matter what.

Hold off until I say, Randl's voice entered my mind. *I have to work this out, and there's little time to do that.*

I wanted to ask what he meant as I fired my weapon again. Somehow, the Prophet had made ancient tanks and other machines appear to protect his living minions from our shots and to fire at us with bigger blasts. The minions hid behind those things, which were shielded in some way, while they continued their barrage against us.

It had become a standoff of sorts, but with Lexsi and Kory's High Demons, they should nullify any power shields the Prophet built. Laser blasts fired by the enemy would also bounce off a High Demon's scales.

At least I hoped they would—I had no idea whether the Prophet had improved on the standard laser pistols and rifles his people used to fight us.

This could end well—or badly. There would be no in-between.

Kooper

They act like they can't see us, I sent to Randl. He, Bekzi and I continued our trek down the street, as if we were taking a Sunday stroll. Ahead of us, corpses continued to fire at hapless civilians, who were still struggling to get away.

They can't see us, Randl replied. *They won't know we're coming until we're there*, he added. He sounded distracted, as if his mind were working another problem while he shared mindspeech with me.

I turned my eyes back to the crowd. Many had fled into the waters of Campiaa Bay on the west side of the street, but those were being targeted by the shooters, too. There really wasn't a good way to escape this; the army stood between them and the side streets and alleyways on the opposite side.

Many casinos were still experiencing explosions, too, as if they were timed by the Prophet to keep the crowd on the east side from entering those structures. Dark smoke blew past us as the screams and cries continued. Most of the casinos had collapsed after multiple explosions, sending concrete and brick into side streets to block any escape route for the fleeing crowd.

They drive all to Teeg's palace, Bekzi informed me. *Prophet want him as final victim.*

Not going to happen, I growled back.

Overhead, a news drone flew past us, gathering images for a news crew somewhere. Briefly I considered bringing it down with power, before reconsidering.

This secret was out, and there was little purpose in calling it back. If any of us survived, we'd have to continue our hunt for the Prophet.

He hadn't bothered to show up for this shindig, as Winkler would say. He'd sent his minions, dead and alive, and they were doing a spectacular job all by themselves.

Travis

Mom, Randl says to wait until he sends a signal. I know you want to turn to mist and lop heads, but we ought to wait, I sent.

Mom frowned at my mindspeech, but she remained where she was, although she'd added her shields to Trent's and mine. If the living minions thought to get a shot past that, they ought to think again.

Vik and David had moved forward to flank Mom, though, and continued to fire their weapons at the enemy. Zanfield, on the other hand, had stopped firing and stood still, studying the machines the Prophet had dropped between us and his minions.

At least that's what I thought he was doing.

When he raised his weapon again, he wasn't pointing at the machines. He was pointing at the street. A single ranos shot destroyed the street beneath one wide, metal track, dropping the machine into the gap and leaving it teetering dangerously to one side.

"Holy hells," I shouted and aimed at the street just as Zanfield was doing.

In no time, we'd practically sunk eight of the war machines into the concrete, removing those barriers as protective covering for our enemies. Quickly, they scurried behind another row of machines; those turrets turned long, metal barrels toward us, preparing to fire.

"I got this one," David grinned and fired straight at the barrel. His ranos blast met the cannon blast from the ancient weapon, and we were nearly deafened by the subsequent explosion. The detonation rocked the street, creating wide splits in the concrete, which careened away in all directions from the damage we'd done to it already.

Get ready, Randl's voice sounded in my head. *Tell the High Demons to turn now.*

I did as he asked, never fully expecting the results I got from my command.

❧

Kooper

Randl let me see through his eyes, and what I saw was a swift journey I never thought I'd take.

Somehow, he'd connected a street in Campiaa to a street in Gungl on Vogeffa II.

A very particular street in Gungl, where I saw a cross-pattern of missing brick in a crumbling infrastructure.

What? I asked.

Randl didn't answer. Suddenly, the portion of the street in Gungl was now a part of the street in front of us—and the army of the dead was now so close I could leap and touch them.

Now, Randl's mental shout included Travis, Trent and anyone else he'd instructed to wait.

I didn't ask—I couldn't. The path to split-time had opened, and the corpse army marched right into it on our end.

Something else was happening on the other end, but I only heard the terrible roars of several High Demons before Randl shut the split-time gate behind us. We were now alone on a deserted world, where three suns bore down on us, nothing grew and hot sand threatened to melt the soles of our boots.

Shields, Bekzi instructed.

I heavily shielded my boots, then cooled the air inside my bubble of protection. The army of the dead continued their journey toward us, firing at us, now, instead of a fleeing crowd.

Randl had made us visible to them. Their shots pinged off our shield, as if they were made of metal instead of power. Whining, ricocheting blasts hit hot sand all around us, lifting fountains of hot grit high into the air.

This planet was very unstable, it appeared.

Where? I interrupted Randl's concentration.

The Great Desert on Tiralia, he replied.

That's when I noticed that the leaders of the corpse army were slowly sinking into the sand, which was swallowing them as if it were dying of thirst and dead bodies would quench it.

Travis

We had three High Demons instead of two. Vik had turned with Lexsi and Kory, and now he roared just as loudly as Kordevik as their flaming High Demons stalked the back end of the dead army.

Several minions had disappeared once the High Demons made their presence known; the rest, unimportant to the Prophet, I suppose, died when they came in contact with any part of the marching High Demons.

Once they reached the back edge of the dead army, Lexsi released her fire while Kory warned the rest of us to stay back.

I'd never seen Lexsi do this. Mom said she could, but I'd never seen it. She gathered fire from Kory and Vik, built it up, drained them of it, and then unleased it in a blast of volcano-hot fire at the dead.

"Get down," Mom shouted as a backdraft of fire bounced our way.

She jerked Zanfield down with the others and threw a shield up so we wouldn't get fried by what a powerful High Demon could do.

Somewhere, I hoped Opal, Kell, Merrill and Gavin were safe, as the Prophet's zombies went up like matchsticks in an inferno.

~

Founder's Palace

Wyatt

Dad, something's wrong, I sent. He and I followed Quin throughout the hastily set-up triage area, where she treated anything from sprains dealt by a rough landing in the palace ballroom to unsteady hearts, hyperventilation and other maladies.

Quin tended King Devarr's surrogate early on, easing her and making sure the baby was safe enough.

Still, I couldn't shake the feeling that somewhere within these walls, which should be shielded against most anything, something was very decidedly wrong.

I have that feeling too, but I can't tell what it is, Dad replied.

Gran? I sent.

Shields up, she shouted at me as half the ballroom exploded around us.

~

Great Desert, Tiralia

Kooper

Randl's eyes had turned silver when he gazed at me. I found myself falling through their depths. Not far away, the corpse army was slowly melting into the poisoned, heated sand of a world that had destroyed itself with chemical warfare.

I never thought to set foot on it—or survive if I did so.

"What now?" I heard my own words, but they sounded distant—as if someone else had uttered them.

The vision that came to me then made me drop to my knees.

Someone—or several someones among those rescued from the Sandswept, had carried trouble away with them.

They'd held onto the wooden balls—in pockets or comp-vid bags. I wanted to weep and curse at the same time—at their foolishness, and the ability of the Prophet to hide those infernal bombs from the powerful.

I caught the flash of wings, then.

White wings, glittering with gold, filled my mind before the vision was cut off.

"Stand up, Director," Randl commanded. He and Bekzi lifted me to my feet.

"Last of Prophet's dead drowns," Bekzi sighed.

"Please take me back," I begged.

"Of course, Director."

I found myself standing on the back lawn of the Founder's Palace with Bekzi. A hole large enough to fit a hover-bus gaped on one side, while smoke filtered into the air to join other smoke from still-burning casinos down the way.

"Where's Randl?" I asked, feeling dazed.

"He be back. Come. Go inside. Help Zaria."

I walked on unsteady legs toward the back entrance, while two guards opened the door to allow us inside.

Travis

David had several scrapes on his face from hitting the street when the fire blast came at us. Zanfield had rolled his ankle and twisted a knee in the same circumstances. I was surprised that one of the wealthiest men in either Alliance wasn't complaining.

Instead, he was blotting blood from David's face with a silk handkerchief he'd pulled from a pocket.

"I'm fine," David complained.

"I've had medical training," Zanfield snapped. "This needs to be looked at by someone better at it than I."

Mom, though, stood with her arms crossed, waiting for Kory, Lexsi and Vik to return. They'd become humanoid again, but Lexsi didn't want to be seen naked by the rest of our bunch, so she'd skipped away for some clothing.

Dressing afterward had taken a few minutes, so they were now walking back to us, Lexsi flanked on one side by her husband Kory and by Vik on the other.

Mom waited for them without saying anything. I couldn't read the look in her eye, however, and decided to wait with her, to see what was about to go down.

"Lexsi, honey, that was amazing," Mom said when the three High Demons reached us. "Kory, good job." Mom hugged Lexsi and Kory, while Vik hung back.

"Now." Mom sighed and allowed her shoulders to droop. Suddenly, she was wiping tears away.

"Baby, I thought I'd never see you again," she wept as she held her arms out to Vik.

"What the hell?" Trent now stood beside me as we watched Mom hugging Vik as if she knew him.

"It's your brother," Randl stepped up beside me. "Zaria and Quin— well, they saw to it."

"Tory?" Trent's eyes were huge as he turned toward me and mouthed our dead brother's name.

"You'll sort it out," Randl clapped both of us on the back. "I have to get to the Founder's Palace. There's something else I need to do, there."

~

Founder's Palace
Wyatt

Today, Zaria was a winged Larentii. Tall, blue, calm, efficient. She wasn't *Changing What Was* for all those who'd died.

She made her selections carefully.

I noticed she hadn't brought back the three who'd brought the wooden balls with them, or anyone from the Northon contingency. Several others she chose to leave where they lay, too.

Those bodies would be identified later, and word sent to the corresponding worlds. Dad was upstairs, talking with Jett and preparing to hold a news conference concerning the attack, intending to name it an act of war.

Soon enough, both Alliances would name the Prophet as their number one enemy, and offer a huge reward for information leading to his whereabouts.

He'd almost taken all of us down. The streets were still littered with thousands who'd died in the attack.

No casino was left standing. Many more had died in the blasts that took down those structures. As yet, there wasn't even an unofficial body count. Scores of Jett's agents had perished, too, in addition to many of Kooper's people, caught up in the attack.

Far above the planet, many ships on both sides were either crippled or destroyed. We waited for word on those, too, although the attacking ships had disappeared like smoke in the wind once the corpse army was defeated.

That didn't include the zombies that had exploded when fired upon—I had no idea whether any survivors were now infected with the Prophet's disease.

I have Charla, her guards and Jewl at the mountain retreat under guard, Opal informed me.

I didn't say what I wanted to say—that those four had been rescued, when so many others who were more deserving hadn't been saved.

Thank you, I sent. *I'll let Dad know.*

"Wyatt?" Quin and Zaria now stood beside me.

"Huh?" I turned quickly, startled by their sudden appearance.

"I'm finished. You can call in a forensics team—I suggest getting some from other worlds—you'll need them," Zaria sounded grim and weary.

"I will." I felt numb, as if the full impact of what happened hadn't settled in and wouldn't for a while.

"Wyatt?" Jayna appeared with Randl. She'd been with Travis at the other end of the bay. I could see she had a story to tell me, when we had time for ourselves again.

With all the trouble that now lay at our feet, I had no idea when that might be. Smoke blew in and out of the gaping hole in Dad's ballroom. Blood spattered walls around that hole. Burned and bloody corpses, whole and in pieces, were strewn across the floor as guards and servants pulled the living out of the ballroom toward private rooms in the palace.

"I've ah, asked for forensics teams from sixteen of the closest worlds," Kooper said when he joined our small group. "All medical teams are already on the street, recording images and preparing to identify and move the dead," he added.

"Director, I wish to add troops from Cloudsong to hunt this monster," King Devarr said when he approached us. "I have learned the value of strength in numbers," he added. "I do not want my child born into the same universe that holds such evil."

"Neither do I," Kooper said. "I will send recruiters soon. The pay is decent, and your people will receive the best of training."

~

Randl

He saw this, you know, I sent to Kooper. *Until the big explosion, that is.*
How? he asked.
The wooden spheres.
"Fuck."
"I feel the same," I said. "Will you walk with me, Director?"
"I did before. I can't argue with the outcome."
"Good. Shield yourself, it'll be cold where we're going." I transported us high up the mountain, not far from where Vik and I had gone to talk privately before.
Before.

Before so many terrible things happened. I should have expected what came, but I hadn't seen or guessed at much of it.

As the Prophet likely hadn't seen much of what I'd do in return. It was a real game of Irzu we played, with worlds as game pieces instead of colored stones.

"How high are we?" Kooper asked as I settled on the rock outcropping near the mountain's summit.

"High enough," I said, before drawing the wooden ball that I'd shielded heavily from a pocket. I didn't miss Kooper's intake of breath when he saw what I held.

"What?" he began.

"I'm going to remove the shield in a moment," I replied. "I'll have to split time again to use it, and I only have a small window to do that in. Place a strong shield about yourself, Director, and then another around me, in case this goes wrong."

Kooper stared at me in shock before closing his eyes and turning his face away. Finally, he nodded his acceptance. "I'll hope for the best," he whispered.

"Good." I waited for him to place both shields before I removed the one I held around the ball.

As I imagined, once the Prophet could sense it again, he sent power to make it explode.

I cast my energy to split time.

Who knew which of us would win this race?

'loxett
    V'dar

I'd been pacing and fuming at the destruction of my army, although the mounting numbers of the dead across Campiaa were rising beautifully. Soon, I'd take stock of how many survivors I could call to my will.

The release of a thick shield around one of my devices hit me like an arrow to my brain. Without thinking and purely on reflex, I sent power to it, to detonate it.

That brief moment hung in the air for a lifetime. I saw the blast, and then it changed. Morphed into something else.

An object cleaved the distance between the sphere and me. An image caused my mind to reel with the intensity of six suns.

He was on the other end.

Randl Gage.

My sworn enemy.

I ramped up the power to increase the blast.

It hung there, balanced on the head of the smallest and sharpest of pins.

How many angels can dance on the head of a pin? Whispered into my mind. It was a voice I didn't recognize—a female voice. Time had stopped—I had no idea how.

I see you. Randl's voice.

V'dar.

He had my name.

I spent more power, attempting to destroy this aberrant thorn in my heel.

Time resumed.

The wooden sphere hit me in the head before detonating. I was late erecting a shield. Pain blossomed and then darkness claimed me.

Founder's Palace, Campiaa

Queen Lissa

"I can't believe it," Teeg sighed.

"I wouldn't have recognized him, except for his Thifilathi," I said. "Lexsi knows. He asked her not to tell Reah."

"How?" Teeg, who would always be my son, Gavril, asked.

"Randl says Zaria and Quin did this miracle. I hadn't revisited those memories in years—they were just too painful," I admitted. "Now, when I look back on it, the circumstances are much different."

"He didn't die?"

"He was mortally wounded by his father," I sighed and tossed out a hand in confusion. "Zaria and Quin saved him."

"You still won't say his name, will you?"

"No. That name no longer exists for me." Torevik's father had gone mad at the end, and he'd committed terrible crimes as a result.

"What does Tory want to do?"

"He wants us to call him Vik. He likes his job with the ASD, so he'll keep it. He didn't ask for anything else."

"So family dinners are out of the question?"

"He didn't say that. I think we can sneak some in now and then. I haven't told Ry yet. That's where I'm going next, when we get some of this shit sorted."

"I have another press conference in a few," Teeg admitted. I could hear in his voice how much he loathed those things.

"Get Tybus to do it and come with me," I said. "Ry was hit the hardest by what happened to Tory in the past. I don't know how he'll take this."

"Dormas," Teeg said, knowing his ancient vampire assistant would hear him through several walls.

"Teeg?" Dormas poked his head in the door.

"Have Tybus handle the press conference. I have business with my mother."

"Of course." Dormas' head disappeared quickly.

"How's Randl?" Teeg asked.

"Still unconscious, although Quin and Karzac say he just doesn't want to wake up yet."

"So, no lasting damage?"

"I can't say that for certain. Word has it that he saw the Prophet clearly during that exchange, and may even know his name."

"Who gave you that information?"

"Kooper. Randl was connected with him during the entire ordeal, and Kooper is still trying to figure out exactly what happened."

"The Prophet still lives?"

"Kooper says yes, although he may have taken some damage in the exchange."

"Too bad. That would be too easy, I guess," Teeg sighed.

"Nothing has ever been easy where evil is concerned," I agreed.

"Wyatt and I have thirty-six memorials to planetary leaders to attend in the next few weeks," Teeg said.

"Have you looked at those? Closely?" I asked.

"What do you know that I don't?" he asked.

"That Zaria weeded out the ones that Jett and Kooper have suspected of criminal behavior," I said. "Zaria saw through them and didn't bring them back."

"Then we'll be watching who takes their place," Teeg drummed fingers on his desk.

"No need to continue on the same, rutted road," I nodded.

"You called?" Tybus folded into Teeg's office.

"Yeah. I need to go with Mom for a while," Teeg said. "Can you handle the press conference?"

"Of course." Tybus dipped his head to me and to Mom, before she folded us to Karathia to visit my brother Ry.

Mountain Retreat

Randl

"Wake up, sleepyhead." Dori placed a kiss on my forehead.

"That's a nice wake up call," I rumbled. "Seeing your pretty face hovering over mine."

"Pretty?"

"Gorgeous. Lovely. Beautiful."

"Nice," Dori grinned and leaned down to give me a proper kiss. "We can't stay here, though. Kooper gave orders to let him know the minute you woke."

"Great." I attempted to sit up in bed. "Kooper may have to wait. I have things to do, first."

"What things?"

"I thought I'd spend some time with my girl, then go steal her a ship."

"Oooh, keep talking, big boy. I like how your mind works."

Travis

"She hasn't stopped whining since she got here," Susan set a half-empty tray of food on the retreat's kitchen counter. "Kell's compulsion only lasted while she was kept at the hotel. That ended when they brought Jewl here. Even her guards no longer speak to her. They asked to be moved to an attic room, not far from Charla."

"Charla's been pretty quiet," I said.

"She watches the news-vids and cries now and then. The only

thing she's asked for are treats for Barkins and to see Randl. I told her he's not up for visitors, yet."

"Still no Randl?" Zanfield Staggs wandered into the kitchen. He'd refused to go home until he got to speak with Randl, too. As he'd rendered valuable service to the ASD, I'd let him stay with us at the retreat.

It actually appealed to the wealthy eccentric. Who knew?

"Not yet, but we're hoping soon," Susan said.

"What's the decision for the Conclave?" Zanfield asked.

"The members will be doing the meetings via vid-feeds from their homeworlds in three months," I said. "The word came in this morning. It's safer that way, at least until the Prophet is eliminated."

"We also have conspiracy weed-balls claiming that the CSD and ASD manufactured this whole thing," Zanfield offered.

"That happens every time," I grumbled.

"Hello, folks. Who wants to watch me commit a robbery?" Randl sailed into the kitchen with Dori close behind.

"Kooper wants to see you first," I pointed out.

"I know. I'm willfully disobeying him for the moment."

"Oh, I like this," Zanfield lit up with enthusiasm.

"Good. If you want to see this, come with me. If you want to report it to Kooper, then you stay here."

"Uh," I said.

"Bzzzzzz—wrong answer. Anyone else?" Randl sounded happy for some inexplicable reason.

Then it hit me—he'd gotten laid, then Dori filched breakfast for him.

"Come with me, rabble," Randl smiled and folded space. Susan and I were the only ones left in the kitchen.

"I'm not telling Kooper," she said and walked out.

~

Founder's Palace
    Kooper

"What do you mean, Jewl Yarro is in Lissa's dungeon?" I snapped at Winkler.

"I'm only the messenger," Winkler held up a hand to stop the impending rant. "Randl left her there, after telling the vampires to place as much compulsion as they liked to stop her whining."

"You found out about this after he left?"

"No," Winkler grinned. "I was there when she was tossed in her cell."

"You talked to Randl?"

"I suppose I did."

"What the fuck did he say?"

"He said that the deal with Jewl was between you, her and Jett. Neither he nor Lissa made a deal with Jewl. He says that he kidnapped her and handed her over to the palace guards, who were quite happy to incarcerate one of the Big Three."

"Oh, for the gods' sake," I mumbled and covered my face with both hands.

"He also says to tell you that he's taking over Jewl's holdings, including her fleet of ships. You should have transfers to this account soon," Winkler handed a comp-vid to me. "He says there should be enough there to rebuild Campiaa and compensate the families of those killed in the attack."

"What about her homes and other holdings?"

"I believe you'll receive messages when each and every one of them is razed to the ground. Without those and without compensation, her employees will leave and her empire will fall."

"Is Charla in the dungeon, too?"

"Nope. You may have to ask him about that. He says he'll contact you later."

"Great. I have an agent who's out doing who knows what," I growled as the comp-vid in my hand came to life.

An account balance in the billions began to appear, and then the numbers kept going higher.

"Randl, what are you doing?" I breathed. Winkler took the

opportunity to fold out of the library, where he'd found me to begin with.

"Hello, Director," the figures were replaced by Randl's image.

"Randl, I want to see you immediately," I snapped at him.

"That's great, but I'm busy right now," he said.

"Doing what?"

"Well, take a look. This was Jewl's flagship. It's mine, now. Actually, it's Dori's; I promised I'd get her a ship, even if I had to steal it."

Randl stood aside so I could see the new logo on Jewl's massive, dark-gray ship. It bore the black wings of the BlackWing Pirates, with the number XIII after it.

"What about the other ships?" I asked dryly.

"Sending them to the hidden space dock for the BlackWing fleet. You can conscript them or sell them, I don't care."

"How many?" I reeled in my anger.

"Twenty-four. This one was twenty-five, but I'm keeping it."

"I see that. I can declare you rogue, you know."

"I know. That's exactly what you need to do, Director."

"What the fuck for?" I exploded.

"Because the enemy of my enemy is my friend—at least temporarily. Put me on your most wanted list, Kooper. I'm counting on the Prophet to take that bait."

I wanted to count to keep my anger at bay, before deciding there weren't enough numbers or sufficient time to achieve that result.

"So—you're not coming in," I growled.

"Not right now. We can meet up later."

"I'm putting you on the most wanted list as of tonight, for aiding in the escape of a known criminal," I said.

"You won't be wrong—I have Charla and Barkins with me."

I considered that for a moment.

"Who else is with you?" My patience was now stretched far past its limit.

"I am. Hello," Zanfield's tilted head appeared in the frame as he waved at me.

"Zanfield," Randl turned his comp-vid so I'd see his face again.

"Dori, because she'll captain XIII, Chief Markus, Mak, Jak, Vik, David, Charla, Gerrett—Zaria brought him, actually, plus a few of Dori's old crew to act as navigator, helmsman and so forth."

"I trust I'll have dossiers on the crew plus a full report by tomorrow morning?"

"Of course."

"Well, aside from naming you one of the most wanted," I said, "There's only one other thing left to do."

"What's that?"

"I'm putting you in charge of the entire BlackWing fleet, Commander Gage," I said. "Your primary objective from now on is finding the Prophet and eliminating that threat. Smooth sailing, Commander. Kooper out."

The End

CHAPTER 22

List of Characters/Places Appearing in the BlackWing Pirates Series

(Characters from other series will be indicated by the series name for their first appearance. Those series will be listed in parenthesis after the names)

*A*dam Chessman: From Old Earth. Former chief of enforcers for the Vampire Council. Chosen to become a member of the Saa Thalarr. Mated to Kiarra. Also a member of the Al'Riyu. (Blood Destiny Series, Saa Thalarr Series)

Akrinn Lemm: Native of Jaledis, best friend of Fergue Bing. (BlackWing Pirates Series)

Amlis: Prince of New Fyris, a kingdom established on Harifa Edus after Siriaa's destruction. Father: King Tamblin of Fyris-deceased. Mother: Queen Omina of Fyris-deceased (First Ordinance Series)

Ardis: Avii Captain of the Guard for King Justis. Mated to Dena, Queen Quin's personal bodyguard. Daughter: Dara. (First Ordinance Series)

Ashe Evans: The Mighty Hand, or Strength. Owns SouthStar Groves on Avendor, which houses many. SouthStar is a haven, and those who reside there will never age because of the power wielded by Ashe. Mated to Kay and Breanne. (Legend of the Ir'Indicti Series)

Astralan Starr: Fifth-level Karathian warlock, one of four brothers who protect Teeg San Gerxon. Mated to Queen Reah. Member of the Nameless Ones—see Hierarchy of the Gods. (High Demon Series, BlackWing Pirates Series)

Aurelius: Vampire from Old Earth. Turned Gavin Montegue. Mated to Queen Reah. Member of the Saa Thalarr and Mil'Karha—see Hierarchy of the Gods. (High Demon Series)

Ba'Moru: Small vacation resort on Pyrik and home to Caille Morr.

Bargel: President of Pyrik. (BlackWing Pirates Series)

Barra Kend: Wife of Ruther Kend, mother of Sabrina Kend. (First Ordinance Series, BlackWing Pirates Series)

Bekzi: One of eight reptanoid brothers who are lion snake shapeshifters, although their births were manipulated by a criminal element to create assassins. Bekzi and his brothers had slightly slitted eyes, preventing them from passing as fully human, and therefore they were never forced into the role of assassins. Instead, they became well-versed in farming and the repair of mechanical things, providing maintenance and such to their criminal masters until they were freed by Reah and Teeg San Gerxon. Bekzi is mated to the Mighty Heart and to Zaria. Member of the Nameless Ones—see Hierarchy of the Gods. (High Demon Series)

Bel Erland Morphis: Crown Prince of Karathia. Fifth-level warlock and skilled at scrying and spells. Father: King Rylend of Karathia. Mother: Queen Reah of Kifirin. Mated to Queen Quin of the Avii. (High Demon Series, First Ordinance Series)

Bennall: A Campiaan Alliance world orbiting the same star as Kev'Ril.

Berel Charkisul: Son of Edden Charkisul. Mated to Queen Quin and serves as a liaison/ambassador for her after he was granted the blue wings of an Avii scholar by Zaria. (First Ordinance Series)

Bornelus: Non-Alliance world taken by the Prophet and guarded by mutant Ra'Ak.

Brandl Gage: Father of Randl Gage. Homeworld is Vogeffa II, until attack by Vardil Cayetes forced the population to relocate to New Fyris. Employed by Prince Amlis and later by Queen Lissa of Le-Ath Veronis and Queen Quin of the Avii (First Ordinance Series)

Breanne: The Mighty Heart, aka Love. (God Wars Series)

Bryan Riley: Vampire from Old Earth. Head of the News Conglomerate on Le-Ath Veronis. (Blood Destiny Series)

Caille Morr: Trail guide at a mountain resort on Pyrik—one of many hidden servants of the Prophet. (BlackWing Pirates Series)

Campiaa: Small planet and home to the Founder of the Campiaan Alliance.

Carek Prime: A non-Alliance world ruled by King Devarr, until it was destroyed by Vardil Cayetes. The population was subsequently moved to Cloudsong.

Caylon Black: Falchani warrior and the best Falchani blademaster ever produced on that world. Caylon Black trained Dragon, Crane and Salidar DeLuca. Member of the Saa Thalarr and the Mil'Karha—see Hierarchy of the Gods. (Blood Destiny Series)

Celestan Starr: Fifth-level Karathian warlock, one of four brothers who protect Teeg San Gerxon. Member of the Nameless Ones—see Hierarchy of the Gods. (High Demon Series, BlackWing Pirates Series)

Charla Dare: Wealthy Campiaan resident who has been working as a smuggler and committing other crimes quietly while passing as one of the planet's elite. (BlackWing Pirates Series)

Chloe: Naturalized Amterean Dwarf, originally from Old Earth. Owl shapeshifter. Mated to Morwin Quiffilis. Sister to David Hiboux. (Latter Day Demons Series)

Cleaster Leech: Campiaan space station employee who has been infected with the Prophet's spreading obsession. (BlackWing Pirates Series)

Cloudsong: A world recently accepted into the Campiaan Alliance and ruled by King Devarr. Has a spotty, checkered past, and was once rendered barren and useless by a rogue warlock who tapped the core. Restored by Zaria and others, to become home to all the refugees from Carek Prime.

Connegar: Larentii. Mated to Queen Lissa. (Blood Destiny Series)

Cord'ilus: An empty world, devoured by Ra'Ak long ago.

Cori Anderson-DeLuca: Panther shapeshifter and Co-Captain of BlackWing VIII with her husband, Marco DeLuca. Mother: Lavonna Anderson. Father: Nathan Anderson. Sister to Dori Anderson. (Legend of the Ir'Indicti Series, BlackWing Pirates Series)

Dara: Avii—daughter of Dena and Ardis. Named after Daragar of the Larentii. (First Ordinance Series)

Daragar: Larentii. Mated to Queen Quin of the Avii. (First Ordinance Series)

David Hiboux: Naturalized Amterean Dwarf, originally from Old Earth. Southern Boobook owl shapeshifter, who works as the ship's engineer for BlackWing X. (Latter Day Demons Series, BlackWing Pirates Series)

Dena: Avii bodyguard for Queen Quin. Formerly a yellow-winged castle servant. Now has multi-colored wings, like most Avii. (First Ordinance Series)

Devarr: King of Cloudsong. Husband to Hulce. (First Ordinance Series)

Derik: Prime Council of the Sirenali. (BlackWing Pirates Series)

Dori Anderson: Ocelot shapeshifter from Old Earth. Captain of BlackWing VII. Mother: Lavonna Anderson, a lioness shapeshifter. Father: Nathan Anderson, a vampire. One sister; Cori Anderson, a panther shapeshifter. (Legend of the Ir'Indicti Series, BlackWing Pirates Series)

Dormas: Ancient vampire who raised Gavril/Teeg after Kifirin removed him from Le-Ath Veronis. Taught Teeg woodworking, building and architecture. Now serves as Teeg's assistant in the Campiaan Alliance. (High Demon Series)

Drake Tatsuya: Falchani, serves as co-commander of Queen Lissa's army on Le-Ath Veronis. Father: Dragon Tatsuya. Mother:

Devin of the Saa Thalarr. Mated to Queen Lissa. Twin brother to Drew Tatsuya. One son: Travis Tatsuya. (Blood Destiny Series)

Drew Tatsuya: Falchani, serves as co-commander of Queen Lissa's army on Le-Ath Veronis. Father: Dragon Tatsuya. Mother: Devin of the Saa Thalarr. Mated to Queen Lissa. Twin brother to Drake Tatsuya. One son: Trent Tatsuya. (Blood Destiny Series)

Edden Charkisul: Former High President of Kondar, a large continent on Siriaa. Now serves as an Ambassador for the Avii, after he was given the blue wings of a scholar by Zaria. (First Ordinance Series)

Edward Pendley: From Old Earth of Elemaiyan ancestry. Now owns EastStar Groves, producing gishi fruit on Avendor. Mated to Queen Reah. Member of the En'Nurifi—see Hierarchy of the Gods. (Legend of the Ir'Indicti Series, High Demon Series)

Erland Morphis: Father of King Rylend of Karathia. Mated to Lissa, Queen of Le-Ath Veronis. Fifth-level warlock with strong spell-casting skills. Member of the Ba'Mirha—see Hierarchy of the Gods. (Blood Destiny Series)

Farisa: Avii guild master who has persecuted Quin in the past. (First Ordinance Series)

Fergue Bing: Former boyfriend of Sabrina, native of Jaledis. (BlackWing Pirates Series)

Flavio: Vampire from Old Earth; took over as Head of the Vampire Council when Wlodek vacated the position to join the Saa Thalarr. Now a high-ranking Council member in Queen Lissa's court on Le-Ath Veronis. Mated to Kyler. Auxiliary member of the Saa Thalarr. (Blood Destiny Series)

Flyer: Falchani warrior, member of the Saa Thalarr and member of the Nameless Ones—see Hierarchy of the Gods. (High Demon Series)

Fyris: Small continent on Siriaa, a planet destroyed by Vardil Cayetes. (First Ordinance Series)

Galaxsan Starr: Fifth-level Karathian warlock, one of four brothers who protect Teeg San Gerxon. Member of the Nameless

Ones—see Hierarchy of the Gods. (High Demon Series, BlackWing Pirates Series)

Gardevik Rath (deceased): Former High Demon Prime Minister to King Jaydevik Rath (deceased) of Kifirin. Mated to Queen Lissa. One son: Torevik Rath. (Blood Destiny Series)

Garwin Wyatt San Gerxon: Son of Teeg San Gerxon, Founder of the Campiaan Alliance. Goes by Wyatt most of the time, and acts as an ambassador for his father in Alliance dealings. Mother: Queen Reah of Kifirin. Grandmother: Queen Lissa of Le-Ath Veronis. (High Demon Series)

Gavin Montegue: Head of palace security for Queen Lissa. From Old Earth, he acted as the Vampire Council's chief assassin for centuries. Roman by birth, he served in the Roman army until his near-death in battle. Turned by Aurelius afterward. Mated to Queen Lissa. One son: Gavril Tybus Montegue, aka Teeg San Gerxon. Member of the Nameless Ones—see Hierarchy of the Gods. (Blood Destiny Series)

Gerrett: Sirenali, son of V'ili and Erithia Cordan, both Sirenali. Brother of Morrett and Terrett. V'ili had no idea that he fathered three sons with Erithia, and she held V'ili in such contempt that she only pretended to like him to get her way at times. Each time she bore V'ili's child, she sold that child into slavery at an early age, after removing his tongue so he could never place an obsession. (R-D Series)

Gord: Sabrina Kend's bodyguard, before she became an agent for the ASD. (BlackWing Pirates Series)

Gurnil: Blue-winged scholar and master librarian for the Avii. (First Ordinance Series)

Halimel: Vampire; former King of Hraede and member of the Order of the Night Flower on Hraede. Turned by Rigo. (Blood Destiny Series)

Haral Lebbon: Newly-elected president of Pyrik, after President Bargel's demise. (BlackWing Pirates Series)

***Hierarchy of the Gods:**
The One
The Three (aka The Mighty)
Wisdom (Charles Hoffman) Strength (Ashe Evans) Love (Breanne
Hayworth)
Ko'Ahmari
Ghi'Yisi
Al'Riyu
En'Nurifi
Ba'Mirha
Mil'Karha
Pan'Warha
Nameless Ones
Powers That Be

*members of the Hierarchy have strict rules of non-interference in the everyday happenings of mortals. Only the Three can completely override those rules, and they will only give permission for others to interfere when all the universes are in danger.

Hulce: Prince of Cloudsong, Chief of Sciences and husband to King Devarr of Cloudsong. (First Ordinance Series)

Ildevar Wyyld: Founder of the Reth Alliance. A Copper Ra'Ak, before the fall of the Copper Ra'Ak. Honest, trustworthy and of impeccable character. Member of the Ghi'Yisi—see Hierarchy of the Gods. (Blood Destiny Series)

Ilya Ironsmith: Powerful Fifth-level Karathian warlock, who has studied bladework and blade making extensively on Falchan. Before he was reborn as Ilya Ironsmith, he was Ilya Kuznetzov, a former Russian spy. (R-D Series and First Ordinance Series)

Jak: One of two Blevakian brothers who were hired by Jewl Yarro as bodyguards. (Blackwing Pirates Series)

James Draper: From Old Earth. Now works as the pilot for

BlackWing X. Mated to Nathan Cross, Navigator for BlackWing X. (R-D Series)

Jaydevik Rath (deceased): Former High Demon King of Kifirin. (Blood Destiny Series)

Jayna Dayle: ASD agent. Born on Vic'Law, a planet destroyed by Vardil Cayetes and his minions (First Ordinance Series)

Jerra: Avii daughter of King Justis and Queen Quin. (BlackWing Pirates Series)

Jett Riffler: Native Avendoran Fi'Gu, a dark-skinned race who tattoo the left sides of their bodies as a spiritual offering to their gods. Jett was named Director of the Campiaan Security Detail because of his bravery in the Campiaan Regular Army, where he rose to the highest position in its ranks. Jett is more than capable in his job, and is a good friend of Kooper's, as well as the Founders of both Alliances. (God Wars Series)

Jewl Yarro: One of the Big Three criminal kingpins since the demise of Vardil Cayetes. (BlackWing Pirates Series)

Jurris (deceased): Former red-winged King of the Avii, and half-brother to the current King, Justis. Father of Liron, who was named after the god before it was determined that the original Liron was a rogue god. (First Ordinance Series)

Justis: Red-winged King of the Avii. Formerly had black wings and served as his brother's (King Jurris) Commander of the Avii army. (First Ordinance Series)

Karzac Halivar: Physician originally from Refizan. He is more than fifteen thousand years old, served as a healer for the Saa Thalarr and is mated to Lissa, Devin and Grace. One son with Grace—Kevis Halivar. Member of the Ko'Ahmari—see Hierarchy of the Gods. (Blood Destiny Series)

Kay Zahn: Known as R'Kita, or *Changer* in the Elemaiyan language. Mated to Ashe Evans. Member of the Ba'Mirha—see Hierarchy of the Gods. (God Wars Series)

Kell (Kellik of Abenott): Former noble in the Hraedan Court; became vampire before his natural death occurred. He was responsible for turning Rigovarnus I, who formed the Order of the

Night Flower on Hraede. That order is comprised of former kings of Hraede, who have had their steady hand guiding the monarchy through millennia to ensure the safety and stability of that world. A master spy, Kell taught the order everything he knew, including a few things about the fine art of poison-making. Kell is mated to Opal. (First Ordinance Series)

Ke'Leru (skull) Pirates: A group overseen by the Prophet, to further his plans and desires. (BlackWing Pirates Series)

Kev'Ril: World destroyed long ago by nuclear warfare.

Kiarra: Strongest member of the Saa Thalarr. Father: Wisdom. Mated to Adam Chessman, Merrill Leopard and Pheligar of the Larentii. Also a member of the Ghi'Yisi—see Hierarchy of the Gods. (Blood Destiny Series, Saa Thalarr Series)

Kooper Griff: Director of the Alliance Security Detail (ASD). He is a lion snake shapeshifter, one of the few snakes that can blink. Their venom is deadly and so fast-acting that the use of an antidote must be immediate to save the victim's life. Member of the Ba'Mirha—see Hierarchy of the Gods. (God Wars Series)

Kordevik Weth: High Demon Crown Prince. Mated to Lexsi, Crown Princess of Kifirin. Father: Lord Nedevik Weth. Mother: Lady Verarok. (Latter Day Demons Series)

Lafe: aka Lafranza; Falchani Warrior and the ultimate tattoo artist. Mated to Quin. (First Ordinance Series)

Le-Ath Veronis: Reth Alliance world and home to most of its vampire population.

Len: Captain of the Furrow, a ship hauling food and supplies. (BlackWing Pirates Series)

Lenk: Captain of the Palace Guard on Cloudsong. (First Ordinance Series, BlackWing Pirates Series)

Lexsi: High Demon Crown Princess of Kifirin. Mother: Reah, Queen of Kifirin. Father: Torevik Rath. Grandmother: Queen Lissa. Grandfather: Gardevik Rath (deceased). (Latter Day Demons Series)

Liron: A rogue god who manufactured Quin to carry out his plan to keep the Avii and Fyris safe, in the event of his demise. Quin was rescued from Liron's clutches by Zaria. (First Ordinance Series)

Liron: Avii; son of Jurris (deceased), former King of the Avii. (First Ordinance Series)

Lissa: Vampire Queen of Le-Ath Veronis, also junior member of the Mighty. Father: Brenten Arden, aka Griffin, a former member of the Saa Thalarr. Mother: Harriet-deceased. See "Hierarchy of the gods." (Blood Destiny Series)

Lorvis Verll (deceased): Native of Jaledis and former best friend of Sabrina Kend. (BlackWing Pirates Series)

Lukas: New Grand Master of the werewolves of Harifa Edus. (BlackWing Pirates Series)

Mak: One of two Blevakian brothers who were hired by Jewl Yarro as bodyguards. (Blackwing Pirates Series)

Marco DeLuca: Werewolf from Old Earth. Co-Captain of BlackWing VIII with his wife, Cori Anderson-DeLuca. (Legend of the Ir'Indicti Series, BlackWing Pirates Series)

Markus: Chief of local ASD Department in Turbak, on Jaledis. (BlackWing Pirates Series)

Melton Timble: Native of Pyrik; Shella Karp's fiancé who killed her in a fit of jealousy. (BlackWing Pirates Series)

Merrill: From Old Earth. Roman by birth, was nearly killed in a battle. Turned by Wlodek, former Head of the Vampire Council on Earth. Merrill is a King Vampire, one who is not susceptible to any vampire's compulsion. Mated to Lissa and Kiarra. Member of the Saa Thalarr, and member of the Al'Riyu—see Hierarchy of the Gods. (Blood Destiny Series)

Morrett: Sirenali, son of V'ili and Erithia Cordan, both Sirenali. Brother of Terrett and Gerrett. V'ili had no idea that he fathered three sons with Erithia, and she held V'ili in such contempt that she only pretended to like him to get her way at times. Each time she bore V'ili's child, she sold that child into slavery at an early age, after removing his tongue so he could never place an obsession. (R-D Series)

Morwin: Often called Master Morwin, he works as a private tutor to the children of Kings, Queens and other important people. Amterean Dwarf by birth, who served twenty years in the

Amterean military before become a scholar and teacher. (Blood Destiny Series)

Nathan Cross: From Old Earth. Now works as the navigator for BlackWing X. Mated to James Draper, pilot for BlackWing X. (R-D Series)

Nenzi: One of eight reptanoid brothers who are lion snake shapeshifters, although their births were manipulated by a criminal element to create assassins. Nenzi and his brothers had slightly slitted eyes, preventing them from passing as fully human, and therefore they were never forced into the role of assassins. Instead, they became well-versed in farming and the repair of mechanical things, providing maintenance and such to their criminal masters until freed by Reah and Teeg San Gerxon. Nenzi is mated to Queen Reah. Member of the Nameless Ones—see Hierarchy of the Gods. (High Demon Series)

Northon: Homeworld of WildTree Industries.

Opal Tadewi: Opal is from Old Earth—a Native American shapeshifting velociraptor. She was a member of the Old Ones—a line of long-lived shapeshifters on Earth who held a place of honor among all shapeshifters. Opal has served in many capacities, including law enforcement. Member of the Ba'Mirha—see Hierarchy of the Gods.

Ordin: Green-winged Avii master healer. (First Ordinance Series)

O'Tunne: Presidential candidate on Pyrik, who lost the election to Lebbon. (BlackWing Pirates Series)

Perill: A highly-placed officer in the Prophet's army. Born on Pyrik, in the poisoned, abandoned city of Lee'Qee. Father: Vrak. Brother: Varok. (BlackWing Pirates Series)

Phorde Gaster: Imposter placed in WildTree Industries by the Prophet to carry out his plans. Now deceased. (BlackWing Pirates Series)

Phrinnis Tampirus: President of the Podl'Morphs, who can become anything animal, vegetable or mineral, according to their choice. Mated to Zaria. (First Ordinance Series)

P'loxett: A world destroyed by nuclear warfare; home base and hideout for the Prophet and his army.

Poll Endicutt: Small-time criminal from Campiaa, who is in love with his boss, Charla Dare. (BlackWing Pirates Series)

Quin: Queen of the Avii, a winged race from Siriaa, a planet destroyed by Vardil Cayetes. Began her life as a construct of the rogue god, Liron. Served as kitchen servant and page in Fyris, a small continent on Siriaa. (First Ordinance Series)

Rale Linn: One of the Big Three criminal kingpins to take over after Vardil Cayetes' death. (BlackWing Pirates Series)

Randl Gage: Blind clairvoyant born on Vogeffa II. Father: Brandl Gage. Mother is deceased. When Vogeffa II was attacked by Vardil Cayetes, most of the population was moved to New Fyris on Harifa Edus. Employed first by Prince Amlis, and later by the Alliance Security Detail (First Ordinance Series)

Reah: High Demon Queen of Kifirin. (High Demon Series)

Reemagar: Larentii. Mated to Queen Lissa. (Blood Destiny Series)

Refizan: Reth Alliance world; home planet of Karzac Halivar.

Renée Coffin: Queen Lissa's only female assistant, as female vampires are quite rare. Turned by Lissa herself, Renée has no knowledge of that and believes she was turned by Montrose, who acts as her sire and became her lover, once her five-year training period was over. (First Ordinance Series)

Revalus: Homeworld for the remnants of the Podl'Morphs and the Sirenali.

Rigo: aka Rigovarnus I of Hraede. An ancient vampire who was King of Hraede at one time. Founder of the Order of the Night Flower on Hraede. That order is comprised of former kings of Hraede —all of them made vampires at the end of their reign. The order has had a steady hand guiding the monarchy through millennia to ensure the safety and stability of that world. Rigo was made vampire by Kellik of Abenott, who taught the order everything he knew, including a few things about the fine art of poison-making. Mated to Queen Lissa, and serves as the director of Lissa's hidden spy network. Member of the Mil'Karha—see Hierarchy of the Gods. (Blood Destiny Series)

Rodrik: Heir and Bodyguard to Prince Amlis. Father: Rath-deceased. Wife: Beatris, one child (First Ordinance Series)

Ruther Kend: Owner of Kend industries. Married to Barra Kend, Father of Sabrina Kend. Kend Industries supplies the ASD and CSD with much of their weaponry and surveillance equipment. (First Ordinance Series)

Rylend Morphis: Fifth-level warlock and King of Karathia. Mother: Queen Lissa of Le-Ath Veronis. Father: Lord Erland Morphis. One son: Crown Prince Bel Erland Morphis. Siblings: Torevik Rath, Nissa Grey, Gavril Montegue (Teeg San Gerxon) Travis and Trent Tatsuya, Willow and Wayne Winkler. Mated to Queen Reah of Kifirin. (Blood Destiny Series)

Saa Thalarr: A term in the dead language of Neaboria, meaning *Hope and Vengeance*. It is a small race created and endowed with power specifically to destroy Ra'Ak and their spawn (Blood Destiny Series and Saa Thalarr Series)

Sabrina Kend: Genius daughter of Ruther Kend, owner of Kend Industries. Mother: Barra Kend. Kend Industries supplies the ASD and CSD with much of their weaponry and surveillance equipment. First mentioned in First Ordinance Series as an unnamed daughter of Ruther Kend. (BlackWing Pirates Series)

Salidar DeLuca: Werewolf shapeshifter. Taught the art of the blade by the Falchani blademaster Caylon Black. Mated to the Mighty Heart. (Legend of the Ir'Indicti Series)

Shella Karp: Native of Pyrik, works as one of President Lebbon's assistants. (BlackWing Pirates Series)

Stellan Starr: Fifth-level Karathian warlock, one of four brothers who protect Teeg San Gerxon. Mated to Breanne. Member of the Nameless Ones—see Hierarchy of the Gods. (High Demon Series, BlackWing Pirates Series)

Susan Plume: Hen shapeshifter (Buff Orpington). ASD agent who doubles as a cook for the crew of BlackWing X. (Latter Day Demons Series)

Teeg San Gerxon: Founder of the Campiaan Alliance. His given name at birth was Gavril Tybus Montegue. Mother: Queen Lissa of

Le-Ath Veronis. Father: Gavin Montegue, one of Lissa's mates. His nickname, Teeg, was given to him by his foster-father, Dormas. He took that name when he was separated from his parents by Kifirin (the god, not the planet), who exacted payment for a request made by a young Gavril. His last name, San Gerxon, was acquired when he was named heir to Arvil San Gerxon, a criminal kingpin who built the small planet of Campiaa into a non-Alliance gambling mecca. Teeg's siblings include: Rylend Morphis, Torevik Rath, Nissa Grey, Travis and Trent Tatsuya, and Willow and Wayne Winkler. Mated to Reah, Queen of Kifirin. (High Demon Series)

Terrett: Sirenali, son of V'ili and Erithia Cordan, both Sirenali. Brother of Morrett and Gerrett. V'ili had no idea that he fathered three sons with Erithia, and she held V'ili in such contempt that she only pretended to like him to get her way at times. Each time she bore V'ili's child, she sold that child into slavery at an early age, after removing his tongue so he could never place an obsession. (First Ordinance Series)

Tim'Bek II: An abandoned world taken by the Prophet.

Tiralia: World which destroyed itself with chemical warfare long ago. Still has a very poisonous atmosphere and none approach it. Only source of Tiralian crystal, a gem worth far more than any other.

Torevik Rath (Tory): See Vik Roth.

Travis Tetsuya: (Tatsuya): Son of Queen Lissa and Drake Tatsuya. Takes after his father, who is Falchani (God Wars Series, BlackWing Pirates Series)

Trent Tetsuya: (Tatsuya) Son of Queen Lissa and Drew Tatsuya. Like their fathers, Drake and Drew, Travis and Trent are twins (God Wars Series, BlackWing Pirates Series)

Turtle: Falchani warrior, member of the Saa Thalarr, member of the Nameless Ones—see Hierarchy of the Gods. (Blood Destiny Series)

Tybus: A very ancient vampire, born long before the destruction of Le-Ath Veronis by the Copper Ra'Ak millennia ago. Le-Ath Veronis lay dormant for eons before Lissa arrived to rebuild it. (God Wars Series)

Ula Karn: Native of Jaledis and former friend of Sabrina Kend. Having an affair with Fergue Bing behind Sabrina's back. (BlackWing Pirates Series)

Vardil Cayetes: A criminal kingpin responsible for too many deaths to count in and out of the Alliances. Killed by Zaria (First Ordinance Series)

Varok: A highly-placed officer in the Prophet's army. Born on Pyrik, in the poisoned city of Lee'Qee. Father: Vrak. Brother: Perill. (BlackWing Pirates Series)

V'dar: aka the Prophet. Born on Vogeffa II. Parents deceased. Has skills of a sorcerer and necromancer. Not much is known about him otherwise. (BlackWing Pirates Series)

Vik Roth: aka Torevik Rath. Brought back from death by Zaria, he now works under an assumed name for the ASD. High Demon son of Queen Lissa and Gardevik Rath. (Blood Destiny Series, High Demon Series, BlackWing Pirates Series)

V'ili: Sirenali Prince before the destruction of Sirena by the Larentii. Was rescued from that destruction by rogue gods, who commanded him to create chaos through the years in order to destroy the Mighty and the universes with them. (God Wars Series, First Ordinance Series)

Vogeffa II: A world which was nearly destroyed by climate change. All polar ice melted, leaving only one small continent for residents to live on. Drew a criminal element after a time, and became home to many who were considered mutants.

Vorina: Avii and wife of former Avii King Jurris. (First Ordinance Series)

Vrak: There are two, the original, conscripted by the Prophet, and an imposter placed by the Prophet to do his bidding and lead raiding parties to steal food and supplies from passing ships. (BlackWing Pirates Series)

Warlend Arden: Former King of Karathia. Abdicated in favor of his son, Wellend Arden. Now a member of the Avii race, through Zaria's efforts. Has red wings, denoting royalty of that race, along with retaining his warlock's skills. (First Ordinance Series)

Weldon Harper: Former Grand Master of the Werewolves on Old Earth. Member of the Saa Thalarr and of the Ba'Mirha—see Hierarchy of the Gods. (Blood Destiny Series)

Wellend Arden: Former King of Karathia. Attempt made on his life by his step-mother and her father, who wanted their natural grandson on the throne. Throne eventually taken by Wellend's half-brother, Wylend Arden. Father: Warlend Arden. Now a member of the Avii race, through Zaria's efforts. Has red wings, denoting royalty of that race, along with retaining his warlock skills. (First Ordinance Series)

Wib'burne: Homeworld of Zanfield Staggs.

Wimla: Avii and wife of former Avii King Jurris. Mother of young Liron. (First Ordinance Series)

Winkler: (William Wayne Winkler) werewolf and Former Dallas Packmaster on Old Earth. Mated to Queen Lissa, and serves as a Spawn Hunter for the Saa Thalarr. Member of the Ba'Mirha—see Hierarchy of the gods. (Blood Destiny Series)

Wisdom: One of the Mighty, aka Charles. (Blood Destiny Series, God Wars Series)

Wyatt: See Garwin Wyatt San Gerxon.

Wyyld: Home of the Reth Alliance Founder, Ildevar Wyyld.

Zanfield Staggs: Trillionaire from Felarku, Wib'burne. Loves to gamble and has a flair for the unusual or exotic. (BlackWing Pirates Series)

Zaria: Also known as Corinnelar the Vhanaraszh to the Larentii, and Corinne Watson on Old Earth. Zaria is a powerful enigma who holds the entire metal library, which contains information on everything in existence. Father: Wisdom. Mother: Unknown (R-D Series, First Ordinance Series, BlackWing Pirates Series)

www.ingramcontent.com/pod-product-compliance
Lightning Source LLC
Chambersburg PA
CBHW060938120726
47910CB00002B/386